The Pirate's Daughter

Margaret Cezair-Thompson

headline
review

*Also by Margaret Cezair-Thompson
and available from Headline Review*

The True History of Paradise

In memory of Louis Broman

Those innumerable groups of islands, keys and
sandbanks, known as the West-Indies . . . afforded a
sure retreat to desperadoes.
— *The Pirates Own Book*

Strangers, whether wrecked and clinging to a
raft or duly escorted with portmanteaus,
have always had a circumstantial fascination
for the virgin mind.
— GEORGE ELIOT, *Middlemarch*

Author's Note

Like many tropical adventures, this one begins with a sailor. Errol Flynn, the swashbuckling hero of Hollywood films, arrived in Jamaica in 1946 by accident when his schooner, the *Zaca*, washed ashore in a hurricane. Flynn, whose private life and public image were then in shambles, fell in love with the country and saw an opportunity to salvage himself. He bought Navy Island, an uninhabited islet off the north coast, and built a home there. This story is inspired in part by the years Flynn lived in Jamaica. As I looked more closely at this northeastern region of the island, certain facts piqued my interest – for example, that Captain Bligh of the infamous *Bounty* had visited Navy Island two centuries earlier. Also of interest was the fact that this quiet coastal region drew other luminaries around the same time that Flynn was there: Ian Fleming settled there in the 1940s and began writing the James Bond novels. Noël Coward lived nearby. As the title suggests, I also drew upon a childhood fascination with pirates and with the romantic adventure narratives of the eighteenth and nineteenth centuries, such as *Robinson Crusoe* and *Treasure Island*. There weren't any Jamaicans in those stories, and like the proverbial stone that the builder refused, their absence became the cornerstone of this story. While I make use of certain facts, this is a fictional work. All the characters, aside from Flynn, and most of the events related here are imagined, and while I've tried to render, as far as possible, an authentic sense of time and place, I have altered some facts for the purposes of storytelling.

Contents

Part Five

'He was surprised and pleased, supposing that now he would have a mistress to himself; but he was greatly mistaken and found that it was necessary to court her for his wife...' 317

Part Six

'I was persuaded to take passage to Jamaica...' 385

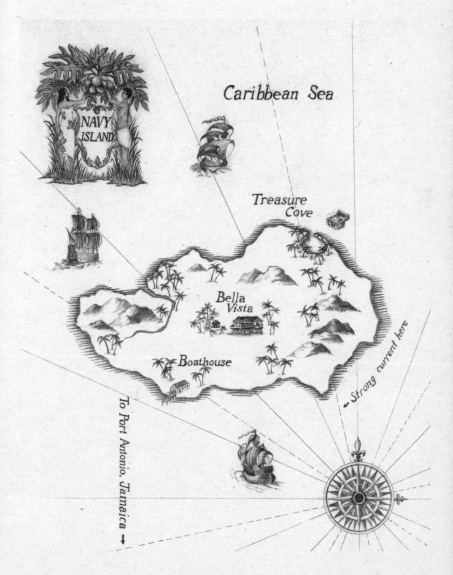

Caribbean Sea

NAVY ISLAND

Treasure Cove

Bella Vista

Boathouse

Strong current here

To Port Antonio, Jamaica →

Pages from May's book, circa 1961

Treasure Love
by May Josephine Flynn

Characters
Cayman Jack — a pirate
Lucetta Sharp — a lady who becomes
a pirate.
Sabine — their daughter who
becomes a ghost
Benito Diaz — a Spanish pirate
Captain Blight — a sea captain

These events occurred in
the West Indies

P.S. My step-father helped with
the spelling and eventually
bought me a dictionary for
which I am grateful.

I Sabine will tell you
how I came to be on this
desolate island.
My father was the infamous
pirate Cayman Jack. I never
knew my mother but heard
stories about her. She was a
pirate too. They abandoned me
and I grew up in the ~~streets~~
taverns of Port Royal which
was then one of the wickedest
cities in the world.
When I was twelve my father
returned from sea very ill
with a fever. I took care
of him and to reward me
for this good deed he
showed me a map where
treasure was buried.

Prologue

The Island that was Errol Flynn's

The stories my mother told me weren't the ones I wanted to hear, stories about the man she said was my father, stories that seemed to come not just from her but upon her, unguarded and effusive, or as we say in Jamaica, 'Mouth open, story fly out.'

I loved stories about the pirates who used to rove among these islands. True Accounts of Sea Robbers, Treasure Island *— these were the books I read over and over again until I knew whole passages by heart. And then at some point, with all those lofty phrases in my head, I began making up my own story. I called it* Treasure Cove.

That was also the name I'd given to a place here on the island, a cove where a coconut tree leaned out crookedly over the water. You could sit on the tree trunk and imagine it was a ship at anchor. A white bougainvillea grew on the slope above, and I used it as a landmark—

She can see it all from the veranda — the cove and the white bougainvillea that once served her so well. For a moment she sees herself too, a boyish-looking girl running across the lawn to the sea.

The lawn is overgrown now and nameless bushes have sprung up around the bougainvillea. Lizards have taken over the garden and the derelict tennis court. Even here on this upstairs veranda they no longer run away from her.

At twenty-six, May is a tall version of the girl she used to be. She still keeps her straight brown hair very short, and she has the same valiant curiosity she had at the age of ten. Gold hoop earrings and numerous bangles help to feminize her. She's become what people call 'a handsome woman.'

She's spent most of her life here on Navy Island, a place so small it's not on any map, not even maps of the West Indies. It's an islet really, about a mile off the coast of Jamaica ('a piece of Jamaica that drifted away,' she used to tell people).

Every day she sits at the wrought-iron table on this veranda, typing on an old manual Underwood. She's not sure why. She could say, like the hero of *Treasure Island*, that someone persuaded her: *My dear friend Nigel Fletcher, having asked me to write down the events that occurred here from beginning to end, keeping nothing back but the bearings of the island and that only because there is still treasure not yet lifted, I take up my pen* . . . She knows that she wants to do this now, not wait until things have become memories of things – nutmeg-smelling rooms, the rasping sea, how quiet it is on this veranda after a downpour.

Her father, the man who is said to be her father, bought the island when there was nothing on it but trees. People say he won it in a poker game, but her mother, Ida, remembers him paying cash, the money he made starring in *The Adventures of Don Juan* ('He had to take that money out of America quick-quick before the first wife found out about it; he wanted a house pink like the sunset,' Ida said). He built the house, pink with white jalousies and white railings, and named it Bella Vista. A good name, she's always thought. Bella Vista is a ruin now, a desecration; there's almost nothing that isn't broken or torn, but she can look out at the sea from every room of the house. From this veranda, she has the best view of all – the sudden descent to the whitewashed boathouse, then the turquoise water fluttering between the two shores.

Jamaica, or 'land,' as they say, is ten minutes away by taxi-boat. She can see the harbor town of Port Antonio across the water and, beyond its Anglican steeples and corrugated rooftops, the Blue Mountains. Sometimes she hears music from the town across the water, reggae pounding from the rum shops and passing cars. But it has been quiet of late because of the curfew and the soldiers and the fear: it is 1976, and Jamaica is in a State of Emergency.

Some soldiers paid her a visit.

She was out on the veranda and heard noises inside. There were two of them looking around the ransacked living room. One of them had sunglasses resting on top of his head. He was examining the photographs on the sideboard, picking them up one at a time: one of her mother, Ida, as a young girl on horseback, another of May by the swimming pool with the two dogs. Then something caught his attention. He called the other soldier over to look at it – a publicity photo of her father as Captain Blood. It seemed to amuse them.

The soldiers were surprised to find May there. 'We have to search the area,' the one with the sunglasses said. She wondered if they really had any authority to do so or whether, having heard about the place, they were simply curious, drawn to the relics of an extinct glamour.

When she walked down to the boathouse an hour or so later to get some kerosene oil for the lamp, she saw more soldiers on the pier. They were taking a break, drinking sodas and chatting. A song, something from childhood, bobbed around in her head:

Fan me, soldier-man, fan me, fan me . . .

She was eating an Otaheite apple that she'd picked on her way down the hill, and she remembered her mother telling her, *Don't eat in front of people unless you have enough to share.* These men were not enemies, she told herself, and the Otaheite apples were spoiling on the trees. So she called to them, saying they could help themselves to as many as they wanted. They glanced in her direction but didn't answer and went on talking and laughing among themselves.

When she got back home she found the soldier with the sunglasses sitting by the empty swimming pool. He had picked up a fallen umbrella and arranged the patio chairs around the table as though he were expecting company – her company. He asked for a glass of ice water. 'No electricity. No ice,' she told him.

His smile was obstinate. 'Why you stay in this mash-up place?' he asked.

Mash-up place. Maybe. But for the time being it is *her* mash-up place.

Across from her now, she can see the empty swimming pool, grimy with rotting flowers and leaves. Crabgrass is taking over the patio tiles. There used to be poolside parties, her mother, Ida, had told her, with calypso bands and limbo dancing. Her father got so drunk once that he drove his car into the pool. Marilyn Monroe danced here. And so much champagne spilled, May always thought that was why the tiles smelled yeasty.

Sometimes she dreams of her father walking ghostly in the dew. There are times lately when she has begun to feel like a ghost herself, when the bamboo creaking in the wind and the moths hitting the jalousies sound more real than her own footsteps.

Five thousand miles away in Switzerland, a graying man who is not her father sits in an opulent room, thwarted and quiet. A stack of papers lies on his desk beside an electric typewriter. On the shelves around him are photographs of himself with famous friends, some of them taken during what he calls his 'tropical years.'

He hopes for one thing: to hear from the young woman on the island, to get a letter saying that she is safe and well and thinks of him and even – here the hope dies, and, missing her, he feels again like a man grown small in the distance.

Sunset. Shadows approach the veranda. May gazes across the lawn and for the second time that day has a vision of herself as a child. She's climbing up from Treasure Cove, her clothes messy with wet sand, and she hears laughter coming from the house. Her mother, Ida, is on the veranda with party guests; her dark hair streams down her back, shining and beautiful, and she wears a red dress as bright as a hibiscus. She turns her head and sees May, the daughter so unlike her, and tosses her a smile.

The evening shadows widen on the veranda, and May can smell the night jasmine now. Mosquitoes will soon be after her. She wants to write as much as she can before dark.

Part One

Of his early life and motive for turning pirate we are as yet ignorant. He declared himself an Irishman by birth, but his real name and place of nativity was, he said, a secret he would never disclose. To the windward of Jamaica his ship ran afoul.

Treasure Cove

I

Shipwrecked

If her father had not been a justice of the peace, Ida might never have come to know the movie star.

On a sunny morning in 1946, Ida Joseph stood outside her house in Port Antonio, leaning against her father's car. She was glad to be thirteen because it meant the end of childhood and the beginning of womanly responsibilities like picking out her own shoes. Her shoes that day were white and went well, she thought, with her pink-and-white dress. It was good to be outside after three days of rain. Looking around, she saw no sign of the bad weather. The ground was dry. The early sun revealed a patch of mountainside and warmed the car behind her.

The street she lived on, Plumbago Road, was in the hilly part of the town, foothills of the Blue Mountains. From where she stood she could see the sea. Any minute now the ship would appear on the horizon. It was Saturday and that meant she would drive down to the harbor with her father.

Eli Joseph wasn't paid for his services as a justice of the peace. He earned a living operating a small taxi business. There were two taxis: a hired man drove the old gray Morris, and Mr Joseph drove the black Chrysler that Ida now leaned against. Most Saturdays she would go with him, first to the courthouse to see if anyone needed him to notarize documents. After that they made a few stops, maybe at the pharmacy or the Cricket Oval. Then they would drive to the harbor to pick up passengers.

When the United Fruit Company ships arrived, all the life of Port Antonio drew to the harbor. They were huge, sleek ships, part of the company's Great White Fleet, and they impressed Ida. Her father, who often went aboard, told her that above deck was 'luxury, pure luxury,' with air-conditioned lounges and spacious rooms for the American passengers. Below deck, the real business of the vessel took place: bananas – thousands of them, loaded into the refrigerated holds for the ship's return voyage to America. The loading of bananas always took place at night. During the daytime bustle of arriving and departing tourists, the banana workers were practically invisible. Instead, there would be cart men selling coconut water and souvenirs, straw weavers with jipijapa hats, calypso singers with maracas and guitars; the crazy man who called himself King George the Fifth would be there too, and taxi drivers would guide the passengers through the crowd.

'Ida!' she heard her mother calling from inside the house.

Ida turned to face the car window, where, after a quick approval of her reflection, she took in the beige seats of the Chrysler. It was a big car with room for four passengers in the back. One of the things she liked best about driving in the taxi was the way the foreigners smelled. She wasn't sure what it was exactly – it wasn't on them; it was around them and around their luggage as if they'd brought some of the foreign air with them.

It was unusual for a man like Eli Joseph – a white man and a Syrian – to drive a taxi. He was actually Lebanese, but in Jamaica they were all called Syrians: the Jews, Lebanese, Arabs, and actual Syrians who had come to Jamaica and made fortunes, all of them except Eli Joseph. A man of great ideas, he was often heard saying, 'If I could just raise enough capital.'

He was considered a 'character,' not so much by the people of Port Antonio as by his family in Kingston, the wealthy Joseph-Hanna clan who owned the beer and soda business. To the black people of Port Antonio, the fact that he was a Joseph, a white man, and a justice of the peace guaranteed him a certain amount of respect; that he played dominoes and drank rum with them earned him their affection.

'Ida! You don't hear me callin' an' callin'?'

Her mother, Esme, had come outside.

For a moment the mother and the daughter stood and eyed one another.

Esme was a stout black woman whose overweight body moved with surprising grace. She had small Chinese eyes and a saintly expression that concealed how strict a parent she was. Her daughter looked as if she belonged to a different race: fair-skinned with long black hair pulled back from her forehead with a tortoiseshell bandeau. Her dark eyebrows drew attention to large, expressive eyes. It was hard to describe her as anything but beautiful. But Esme, who did not want her to grow up vain and stupid, made little of her daughter's good looks.

'You out here idlin' while you father waitin' for the newspaper?'

Ida had forgotten that this was why she had come outside.

She picked up the *Daily Gleaner* and walked up the paved path between the gate and the trellised veranda. There was a row of conch shells on either side of the path. Her grandmother, who had put them there, said conch shells protected homes from natural disasters. They were pretty. The little garden was pretty too but crowded; her mother worked hard to contain the lush flowers in the small space — bird-of-paradise, heliconia, bougainvillea, and tree-orchids — vibrant things that clawed, latched, and climbed if they were not constantly pruned.

Inside, the house smelled of buttered toast. It was a shining, clean house with furniture that was too large for the rooms.

Her mother looked at her and frowned. 'Why you let out you hair? Go plait it,' she said and went into the kitchen.

Ida's father was drinking his coffee and listening to the radio. He took the newspaper from her, not seeming the least bit annoyed about having waited. He was a slender, unmuscular man, with deeply tanned skin that sometimes led people to think he was Indian. Like his daughter, he had large, dark eyes, and he had long eyelashes that might have made him look effeminate if he hadn't had such a wide, square jaw.

He was still wearing just his undershirt, and Ida could see the gold Virgin Mary pendant he always wore.

'Eh-eh, Ida. Look here,' he said, opening the paper. 'Errol Flynn is in Jamaica.'

She looked over his shoulder and saw a picture of a man with wavy hair and a sword. She read:

WORLD'S HANDSOMEST MAN IS HERE
Actor Errol Flynn Arrives in Jamaica Unexpectedly

'He's a big movie star,' her father explained.

Ida had seen only one movie, *Tarzan the Ape Man*, when someone had donated a projector to Father Reynold's school down the road.

Eli called to Esme back in the kitchen, 'You hear that, Esme? Errol Flynn in Jamaica!'

Flynn leaned against the railing of the hotel balcony, letting the sights and sounds of the tropical morning minister to him. The sun warmed his face and the green hills unrolled before him to a bright and tranquil sea.

He was almost forty and looked all right, he thought, in spite of the extra pounds around his waist. Yes, he looked all right but felt like a man who'd reached the end rather than the prime of his life. If only it worked like a sandglass – life, the accumulating years – now would be the time, he thought, to turn the whole thing upside down.

He'd made more than twenty films and was proud of only one, *Gentleman Jim*. His second marriage was doomed, just as his first had been. He had a son and two daughters he never saw; in fact, he had no idea where they were. And he'd been tried for rape! The statutory rape of two girls he swore he'd never even seen before they appeared in the courtroom. He'd been acquitted on all counts, but the long, highly publicized trial had dragged him through a stench that still lingered. How had he, Errol Leslie Thompson Flynn – son of the respected zoologist Professor Thompson Flynn – gotten himself so deep in the muck? He wouldn't have known what to do with himself if it hadn't been for the *Zaca*, his schooner. Its name was a Samoan word for 'peace.'

In an earlier century he would have been an explorer, he thought, like Magellan. Maybe a poet too. He'd always loved the sea, dreamed of a life at sea, and often felt nostalgic about his childhood on Tasmania's coast (darting in and out of the marine lab where his father had studied the platypus – an animal without a scrotum!).

A month after the trial, he'd set sail with his man Ramon, a first-class Mexican sailor, steering the *Zaca* through the Panama Canal, heading for Haiti.

At night watch he'd lain on his back on deck, looking at the stars, feeling like a weightless speck on the planet, or a kind of deviant Ulysses willing to sail anywhere but home. His house on Mulholland Drive was about as appealing to him as a pile of unread newspapers. Good Lord, anywhere but home.

One night during his watch the air grew unusually still. The next day the sky turned red like a puffy wound. The barometer fell. The radio signals went. Then the hurricane winds hit suddenly, unlike anything he'd ever seen or heard, ripping the storm sail. They'd put out the heavy anchors but even then the boat had skittered across the water. Then the galley put out, washing away all their supplies, their maps and passports.

There'd been hours when he hadn't been able to distinguish between the elements – black sky, black water. Strangely, the thought of death hadn't crossed his mind. Death wasn't action, and this was action: straining muscles and nerves. It had revived him. Yes, it had taken a hurricane to lift him out of his middle-aged slump.

The storm passed quickly, but for two days they'd drifted in a shark-filled sea with no radio, no supplies, and no idea where they were.

Then he saw a body of land in the distance, a hazy outline of mountains against the sky. They drifted toward it, almost running aground at a small desert island along the way. It was another hour before the current pushed them close enough for him to make out a harbor town nestled below the most serene mountains he'd ever seen.

As he got closer, he grew puzzled. He knew he'd never been to the place before, but there was something familiar about it, especially the stone fort at the edge of the water with its black cannons pointing to sea.

There were some boys sitting along the fort's wall watching the *Zaca* drift in.

'What is this country?' Flynn shouted across to them.

'Jamaica.'

He laughed. Jamaica!

'Onward to Jamaica and to victory!' had been his battle cry on the set of *Captain Blood*. His first leading role, it had made him a star. Of course, the whole thing had been filmed at the studio, not on location, but hadn't he defeated a Spanish fleet here – not once but twice – and saved the island? And won Olivia de Havilland's admiration to boot?

Some fishermen towed the boat in. They seemed unfriendly, and particularly suspicious of Ramon, whom they mistook to be Cuban. 'Cubana? Turtle? Tortuga?' they kept asking Ramon, who looked at them, baffled.

Flynn saw a sign that said, 'Welcome to Port Antonio.' A coastguard officer led them to a small wooden office that looked like an army barrack. Like the fishermen, he seemed agitated by Ramon's presence. Later Flynn learned that there'd been trouble with Cuban fishermen stealing sea turtles from Jamaican waters.

The coastguard officer telephoned his superior: 'I have a Cuban here, sir, and he's with an American named Earl Flint. What should I do, sir?'

Flynn found a scrap of paper and wrote out his correct name, and the man spelled it out over the phone. 'Awright, sir, yes.'

Flynn looked around. The boys who had been sitting on the seawall had gathered outside and were peeking in the doorway. No one seemed to know who he was. For a moment he had an odd feeling, like a man suddenly aware of himself dying, that something real and unfilmable was happening to him.

'Police car comin' to take you to Kingston,' the coastguard officer said.

Flynn asked if he and Ramon could have something to eat, and they were taken to a cart man selling food and soft drinks along the pier.

And it was there, out on the pier, that he was recognized by the Indian ladies selling bangles and khus-khus perfume. The usually demure sari-clad ladies became agitated. One of them ran down the pier shouting, 'Errol Flynn . . . oh, God!'

Soon there was a small crowd around him — tourists and Jamaicans, including the previously distrustful fishermen. The harbor's infirmary nurse appeared because in the commotion someone either fainted or fell. The coastguard officer was overwhelmed as the crowd started getting bigger. Finally the police Jeep arrived; Flynn and Ramon were given raisin buns and sodas and taken to Kingston.

The *Evening Star* reported:

FLYNN'S FANS FAINT
Women Fall Unconscious at Movie Star's Feet

It was not the sari-clad ladies who had fainted, and actually, the report was wrong: only one woman fainted, an English tourist buying straw baskets. She looked up when she heard the commotion and saw him – disheveled, unshaven, but unmistakably her matinee idol. ('Chu!' Esme said when Eli read this out loud, 'it was probably the heat why she fainted.' 'No man, is how the women go on when they see him,' Eli said.) After this report in the *Star*, fainting became epidemic among the young women of the island whenever they glimpsed Errol Flynn, or thought they had. Some pretended to faint so they could say they had seen him.

Ida and her father visited the harbor to look at Errol Flynn's wrecked boat.

'If his boat is here, he must come back for it sooner or later,' Eli said.

A policeman was guarding the *Zaca*. He seemed disgruntled, and Ida could see why. He'd enjoyed some fame after appearing in a newspaper picture guarding Flynn's damaged boat from onlookers. Now, a week later, people had lost interest in the wreck, and he had nothing to do but sit all day, waving away flies.

All the attention had turned to Kingston, where Flynn was being royally entertained and courted by the country's richest families. He stayed in their mansions. The British High Commissioner had a dinner in his honor. He had numerous invitations and met with all kinds of Jamaicans – radio-show hosts, the Jamaica Nurses Association. People sent him baskets of tropical fruit, rum, and native artwork. The admiration was not one-sided. Flynn told reporters, 'Jamaica's more beautiful than any woman I've ever known.'

A wealthy Jamaican named Aaron Levy invited him to stay at his beach hotel in Ocho Rios. As Flynn was being driven across the island to Levy's hotel, he was aware of a lightheartedness he hadn't felt in ages. Jamaica reminded him of the most enjoyable years of his life, the carefree, spirited years he'd spent in the South Seas before he'd become an actor. It occurred to him as he drove through the mountains, looking out on a landscape so rampantly green that the soil never showed, that he could be happy again. Here was everything he wanted: warm climate, wonderful food, deep-sea diving, sailing, peaceful countryside – and the people spoke English. He'd spend four or five months of the year here. It would restore him.

'This must be the Paradise written about in the Bible,' he said on a local radio show.

These words of appreciation delighted everyone and were quoted in local newspapers, living rooms, and tenement yards. 'Flynn Fever' broke out, as one newspaper put it. **FLYNN FANS FRACAS**, another headline stated, describing the disorder that broke out at a cinema during a showing of *Objective Burma* when members of the audience thought they saw Errol Flynn sitting among them. The article was written by the same reporter who had devised the erroneous headline **FLYNN'S FANS FAINT**. Another of his headlines, in fact his last on the subject, was:

FLYNN FAN FALLS DEAD

An elderly female died of an apparent heart attack as she walked out of the Cross Roads post office around 2 p.m. yesterday. Bystanders claim that they saw a vehicle with someone who looked like Errol Flynn going by. The Chief-of-Police issued a statement saying: 'There seems to be no relation between the two incidents.'

But there was still the problem of Flynn's passport having been lost at sea. Ramon, who had gone ahead to America, had experienced trouble getting back into the country without identification. The World's Handsomest Man actually had no proof that he was Errol Flynn. His wife in California sent him the only identification she could dig up, a copy of their marriage certificate. But since it was only a copy, he needed to have it notarized.

Aaron Levy remembered that his cousin, Eli Joseph, was a justice of the peace. Port Antonio was forty miles away, and Levy could easily have gotten someone closer to notarize the copy, but this way, he thought, Flynn would be able to see how the repairs were going on his boat, and Port Antonio would make a pleasant day trip for the movie star. 'Eli's a bit of a character,' Levy told Flynn, 'but he'll take good care of you an' show you 'round.'

Out on the hotel balcony now, Flynn looked at his watch. It was time to get ready. He looked forward to checking up on the *Zaca* and to once again seeing Port Antonio, the little town where he'd come ashore after the sea-storm.

2

Day Trip

Ida was vexed. She had picked out her best dress, certain she was going with her father, but her mother had shaken her head: 'You forget what day it is? You comin' with me.'

Yes, she had forgotten. On the first Saturday of each month she always went with her mother to see Oni, her grandmother, who lived way up in the Blue Mountains – up in the bush, as Ida thought of it.

Her father had tried to reassure her: the movie star would be in town all day. 'When you come back, I take you to see him. Or maybe I bring him 'round to the house later.'

'Errol Flynn comin' to this house?' Esme wanted to know.

'Maybe.'

Esme didn't think so. 'You father dreamin',' she told Ida.

Later Eli told his daughter in confidence, 'You mother not feelin' well enough to go up the mountain by herself.'

So why she don't stay home then if she not feelin' well? Ida thought.

She was outside now, leaning back against her father's car, as if stationing herself there would somehow help her cause. She hated going up the mountain even under ordinary circumstances; it was a long journey by bus and by foot.

'Ida,' she heard her mother calling from the house.

She spun around like a compass arrow and faced the harbor. A ship had come in and she was going to miss that too.

Her father was inside getting dressed in his white suit and Panama hat. She thought about her dress, white with red flowers and a red belt, spread out on the bed in her room. Well, she would wear it later. Her mother was inside getting ready too, packing a basket of things for Oni – talcum powder, batteries, Mills & Boon novels, things Oni couldn't get up on the mountain. *Why I have to go with her? If she wan' go bush, she can go by herself.*

'You ready?' Esme came out on the veranda, wearing the sensible, mannish shoes she always wore for such outings. She swept her eyes over her daughter approvingly, noting that Ida had remembered to carry a handkerchief.

Ida, watching her mother fold her own handkerchief and slide it under her brassiere strap, was immensely annoyed to see that their handkerchiefs were identical – white linen with tatting around the edges. *I'm not like her*, she thought.

'Go inside an' tell you father good-bye.'

Eli Joseph saw the displeasure on his daughter's face. It was unfortunate that she had to go with her mother, but there was nothing he could do about it.

No one was exactly sure what was wrong with Esme. For almost a year now she had complained about not feeling well. She was often tired and had stomachaches. Much worse, however, was the change in her personality: she had become quarrelsome.

'Mountain air do you good,' he said to his daughter.

They heard Esme calling. Ida looked as if she were about to cry.

'You have on you watch?' he asked; he had given her a silver watch that past Christmas. 'Come back by sundown, I take you to meet him. Go now, before you mother get vex.'

Their hankies were scented with cologne so that whenever the smell of the bus became unbearable they could cover their noses and sniff politely. No matter how crowded the bus was, Esme always managed to wedge herself and Ida into a seat. The size of Esme's hips made this quite a feat. People gave them bad looks, but Esme paid no mind.

Ida drew in her shoulders and huddled between her mother and another woman like an animal in an undersized cage. She didn't want anyone or anything to touch her. It was market day, so there were chickens on the bus and big smelly parcels and baskets underfoot. She could not believe she was on this stinking, overcrowded bus instead of in her father's clean Chrysler.

The bus dragged along Harbor Street, past the old trellised houses from centuries earlier, most of them dilapidated, some of them repainted bright pink or yellow like old ladies trying to look young. Large shady trees stood in the front gardens, mosses hanging from them like beards, creating a gray-green, cavernous loveliness. At the end of the street were the windswept cannons of Fort George and then the sea. Ida saw some tourists taking pictures.

This was the oldest part of town, built on a hilly peninsula that split the coast in two – on one side West Harbor and on the other East Harbor. She wondered what Errol Flynn would think of the place – the old Anglican church overlooking the sea, the market, smelling of dried thyme and fruit and noisy with market women. The bus drove by the old brick courthouse where wig-wearing English magistrates had once tried and condemned pirates; that was where the movie star would meet her father later that morning.

She imagined that Flynn would want to know the history of the town. Eli Joseph would be able to tell him. 'Lord Nelson,' her father would say, 'defended the colony here at Fort George.' And he'd go on to tell his favorite story – the history of the banana.

'You might not know this, but in America ripe bananas used to be a rarity. You couldn't buy them in the shops.' She'd heard him tell this to the tourists countless times. 'But that changed in 1871 when a Boston skipper named Lorenzo Dow Baker was sent here to pick up a cargo of coconuts. He saw the locals growing bananas, so on a whim, you know, just a whim, he decided to take back a few hundred stems of bananas too. He made such a profit on them in Boston that he kept coming back to Port Antonio for more. His shipping business grew and became the United Fruit Company. Yes, man, it started here! Ripe bananas! And tourism!'

Lorenzo Dow Baker had come up with the idea of bringing passengers to Port Antonio on the banana boats, and he had built the Somerset, Jamaica's first hotel. In recent years, though, fewer ships had been coming. Costa Rica had taken over the banana trade, and there were bigger hotels for the tourists now in Montego Bay and Kingston.

From postcards, Ida had an idea of what foreigners liked about Jamaica: waterfalls cascading to the sea, beautiful old buildings, and tropical flowers. These things filled her with pride. But half-naked children standing around the old clock tower did not seem a good way to show off the island. She had even seen a postcard showing an overcrowded country bus like the one she was on. She would hate to see herself in such a picture.

The bus began its climb into the rain-scented mountains, farther and farther away from Port Antonio. Ida looked at her watch. It was not quite ten o'clock. Her father was right; she would be back in plenty of time.

Her grandmother, Oni, lived about as high in the Blue Mountains as anyone could. Oni was a Maroon, a descendant of the African runaway slaves who had long ago hidden in these mountains. But Oni hadn't always lived up in the bush. She had once been married to a Chinese grocer and had lived on a large property she'd inherited from her parents near Port Antonio. But after her husband had left her for a Panama woman, she'd sold the land to the United Fruit Company ('for a whole heap a money,' Ida's father said) and gone to live in the old Maroon settlement up in these mountains.

The bus took them only halfway. Esme and Ida got out at a place known as Guava Ridge. There were no sidewalks, so when the occasional vehicle came by they had to step back close to the mountain edge so as not to get run over. Mountains and shadows of mountains surrounded them. A bit of corrugated tin roof could be spotted here and there in the leafy thickness.

It was there, in that green desolation, that they waited for Mr Brown and his donkey cart to come along and take them up the steep path to Oni. They never knew for certain when he would arrive.

Across the miles of undulating green, Ida could still make out the sea as a distant, vapory thing.

She imagined her father on his way to the courthouse by now. There were always people stopping to chat with him or ask a favor of him along the way. When she was with him people paid her compliments – 'How pretty you growin',

Miss Ida' – 'What a nice daughter you have there, Mr Joseph' – and so on. Even the poorest people who had no schooling would try to use their best English when they spoke to her: it made her feel important.

'Ida! Come out a de road! All day you actin' stupid,' Esme said.

'I not in the road. I'm on the side of the road!'

'You answerin' me back?'

'No, Mama,' she said quietly.

The odor given off by the damp tree trunks began to sicken her. Ida looked at her watch. An hour had passed as they stood there. She began to panic. It seemed as if she would be stranded up there in the bush with her mother.

'Lawd, it hot,' Esme murmured.

Ida saw her mother wipe perspiration from her neck

Though Ida could not have been more annoyed with Esme for dragging her up the mountain, she was also worried about her. Her mother was not all right, and this 'not feeling well' was part of something else, Ida thought, something bigger.

It seemed to Ida that it had started around the time the two strange women had come to the house.

She and her mother had returned from the mountain one Saturday and found them sitting on the veranda with Eli. They had been strangers to Ida, but her mother had known immediately who they were.

'Ida Delores,' she had said Ida's whole name, which she sometimes did when she was displeased, 'these are your sisters, Enid and Kay.'

Ida's first thought was that they seemed too old to be sisters of hers, and then she remembered something about her father having been married before to a Lebanese woman. But she'd thought that that wife was dead or in another country and anyway it had been a long time ago. The sisters, it turned out, were from Kingston. They wore a lot of gold jewelry and had bad yellowish complexions. One of them was plump and quiet; the other one wore glasses and was thin and talkative. They had wanted Eli to go back to Kingston with them, and the thin one with glasses said something unpleasant about Ida: 'She looks like she could be any white man's daughter.'

There had been a quarrel, loud and frightening, with Eli theatening to turn the dog on them if they didn't leave. The neighbors had come out of their houses to see what was wrong, and Ida had run across the street for Father Reynold, who had calmed everyone down.

After the sisters left, Father Reynold and Eli stayed up for hours playing dominoes and chatting. The two men had become friends long before Anthony Reynold had entered the priesthood, when he'd been an itinerant calypso singer known as King Tobago. That night Ida overheard Father Reynold telling her father: 'In God's eyes, Eli, you are Esme's husband, and that is more important than any marriage license.' He spoke in a slow, lilting way, partly because he was Trinidadian and partly because his full attention was on the dominoes in his hand.

'Esme want license,' Eli said. 'She don't like this common-law thing and I see her point. Is for Ida's sake.'

'When water throw 'way, it cyan pick up again. Wife number one not goin' divorce you, so what you goin' do?'

'If de bitch-dem come back, I kill dem.'

Until that day, Ida had not known that her father and

mother were unmarried and that her father had a wife who lived in Kingston.

After that, Ida began to understand certain things about her mother: why she often had such a severe, strained way about her in public, why some of the ladies in town talked down to her, and why there were places that Eli went without her. Esme, though she tried not to show it, was ashamed of being Eli Joseph's common-law wife. She was a Christian and the proud daughter of Mrs Oni Sen-Choy. After the disturbance on the veranda that the neighbors witnessed, Esme's shame had grown.

She saw her mother tucking the handkerchief back inside her blouse and heard her sigh tiredly.

'Maybe something happened to Mr Brown,' Ida said hopefully.

She was about to suggest that they return to Port Antonio on the next available bus or truck that came by. It was almost twelve o'clock. Just then Mr Brown's donkey cart arrived and the old man greeted them: 'Hello-good-mawnin'. How you feelin' today, Miss Esme?'

'Not so well, but I managin'.'

Esme always had 'a little something' for him, a cake or pudding, along with the shilling that she paid him for transportation, and while they rode in the cart she chatted with him about his health and family. They passed his cottage, where there were children and cooking pots scattered about the yard. The children stopped playing and stared as they went by. There was also a gray goat tethered to a tree, happily chewing something.

'What a nice goat you have there,' Esme told Mr Brown.

Ida could not believe how slowly they were moving. At

times it seemed as if they weren't moving at all. The path was so steep, the donkey kept stopping and the whole cart would slide back a little. She was glad to be far from the road, where no one would be able to see her bumping along in the back of a donkey cart. It was horrible at the age of thirteen to be transported like that, with her legs hanging off the edge and having to hold on to the jiggling sides of the cart.

The jangling of the silver bangles on her arm distracted her pleasantly for a moment and brought her father to mind. She could not wait for this ordeal to be over so she could be with him and the movie star.

As Eli had told his daughter, he had a lot planned for Errol Flynn and himself that day. Once the important business of notarizing the certificate was over, he took Flynn, whom he now felt entitled to call Errol, out for lunch at the Somerset and offered to drive him around the region. Eli didn't forget about Ida: 'My daughter wants to meet you,' he said, 'if you have time later . . .'

Errol sat in the front of the car, wearing all his usual accessories of disguise, sunglasses and the rest. No one expected a movie star to sit up front with the driver, and he'd found that by doing so he attracted less attention.

The more he saw of Port Antonio that day, the more he liked it. The banana industry was waning. The town was in decline, but because of that, it would offer him privacy. Also, the deep harbor was perfect for the *Zaca*. He decided to stay for a couple of days and look around at some available properties.

Eli had been thinking about venturing into real estate. So he told Flynn – Errol, 'I'm in the real estate business, you know. I can find you a good piece a land.'

The two men liked each other immediately. Errol found the black Chrysler extremely comfortable and thought Eli an agreeable, pleasant man to talk to. He appreciated Eli's generosity (Eli had paid for lunch and several rum cocktails). It seemed to Flynn that back in America people always wanted something from him. The kindness of Jamaicans made him feel almost humble.

As they drove around the region, stopping several times for rum-and-Cokes and spicy snacks, he found himself confiding in Eli: his second marriage was coming apart; his first wife was a financial strain. 'She won't stop till I'm in the poorhouse,' Errol said.

'I know, I know all about that,' Eli sympathized. 'That song, you know the one 'bout love an' marriage dem belong together like horse an' carriage – not true at all! Only woman I ever love is Esme an' she not me legal wife. The legal wife turned out to be a curse, I tell you.'

'A curse!' He liked the way Eli put it. 'I just don't think I was made for marriage. I'm forever drifting about and Nina's over there in a house I never really lived in.'

'A bad marriage is worse than a hanging.'

'You're absolutely right. It's like waiting to be hanged.'

Oni's wood-and-zinc-roof cottage had a fenced garden where she grew plants for bush-medicine. People for miles around knew her as Madda Oni, a bush-doctor and obeah woman; she could cure sicknesses, catch shadows, and predict the future.

'Hello, likkle mongoose,' Oni greeted Ida at the gate. She pinched her cheek vigorously. 'Wait! Are you a mongoose or a girl?'

It was a game they had played for as long as Ida could remember.

'A girl,' Ida said.

'A girl! Come, then. Me have some sweet-sweet asham for you.'

She was dark-skinned and muscular, with bowlegs which Ida always found fascinating to watch because they didn't seem to prevent her from walking fast. Her eyes were a lot lighter than her skin, and those jaguar eyes made her seem a bit frightening. Ida tried not to look at her grandmother's eyes. She stared instead at the raised moles on her neck that looked like ants.

'Come-come. Lunch ready. Miss Ida, you so vex this morning you no eat you breakfast. A true?' Oni didn't wait for an answer. She knew she was right. Then she turned to Esme: 'I t'ink you not comin' again. All morning I waitin' an' waitin'.'

'Mr Brown tek time comin'.'

'I tell him eleven o'clock.'

'Him slow like slow-self.'

'How you feelin'?'

'Not feelin' so well.'

Inside the cottage was a strange mixture of old plantation furnishings and greasy, painted-over things. On the bureau there was a cluttered assortment of bottles, tins, and jars, some of them filled with mysterious-looking liquids and dried bushes, and above that was a large tarnished mirror which Ida always found quite unsatisfactory.

The place smelled the way Ida imagined an African hut would smell, with drying leaves and straw baskets filled with yams and plantains. Now and then the outside smell of the chickens drifted into the cottage. She knew that her own mother must have grown up with these objects and smells, and the knowledge made her uneasy. There was nothing here that she wanted.

As Oni was serving out the callaloo soup, she suddenly looked at Esme and asked, 'How is Eli? Him all right?'

Esme didn't like the tone of her mother's question. 'Eli is fine.' It was clear to her that what Oni really meant was: *how are things between you and Eli?*

When Oni had learned of the incident with the Kingston sisters and the distress they'd caused Esme, she'd made one of her rare trips down the mountain to check on her. As she'd suspected, she'd found evidence of obeah: one of Esme's combs was missing, and there was an unusual, greasy substance on one of the windowsills – oil-a-fall-back. She had wanted to perform a shadow-catching ceremony, but Esme, a serious Methodist, had refused. Esme had no tolerance for her mother's African mumby-jumby. Bush-teas and bush-baths were all right; that was medicine. But the oils, potions, spells, and ceremonies of obeah were to her like blisters on her mother's soul. She wanted no part of it.

Oni continued as though she hadn't heard, 'You sure? Last night a bat come in de house. An' all day long me hand-middle itchin' me.'

Ida understood that when her grandmother spoke of bats she meant the big moths that were thought to be spirits of the dead. And when Oni's palms itched it was always a bad sign.

Esme's face tightened, but Ida couldn't tell if it was from fear or anger.

'Nothing wrong with Eli. Everybody is fine,' Esme said firmly.

By the time lunch ended, Esme had become agitated by Oni's talk of bats; she washed up the dishes with a kind of vigor that suggested she was eager to leave soon. Ida was glad. It was already after one o'clock.

But then the two women sat on the veranda for ages drinking pimento dram and chatting amiably. Esme even put her feet up. But Ida took comfort in the fact that her mother hadn't rolled her stockings down as she sometimes did when she was tired.

'Mama, remember you told Mr Brown to pick us up at two?'

'He don't mind waitin'.'

Oni said, 'Come sit with us, Miss Ida, have some pimento dram.'

'She too young,' Esme said firmly. Oni was always offering Ida things like rum punch and pimento dram. She was one of those older West Indians who believed that a drop or two of 'spirits' was fortifying.

Ida said, 'I goin' for a ride before we go.'

'Awright, don't ride too far,' her grandmother said. 'Mankind goin' blind.'

Mankind was Oni's horse. Before Ida had learned to walk, Oni had put her on the horse, and at six Ida was riding on her own. Esme had worried constantly that Ida would fall off. 'She too likkle,' she would say to Oni.

'She likkle but she not afraid,' Oni would point out. 'Chu, man, look how she sit up high. She understan' de horse.'

Ida pressed her cheek against the horse's face now, greeting him. She didn't like animals in general and was even uncomfortable around her father's dog, Rex. But horses were different. She rode across the river to an outcropping. The air felt cool, and there was a view of the coast. From these heights, the whole country, even the clouds, seemed to belong to her. Peppering all her thoughts and everything within view that day was the image of the movie star from the newspaper.

She wondered what her father and Errol Flynn were doing: driving around and laughing and telling stories about themselves. She was sure that Errol Flynn would like her father. Eli had been to many places and had a lot of stories to tell. 'My two brothers and I,' he'd say, 'when we were boys in Lebanon, we worked on the docks loading cloves onto the ships. We were so poor we used to suck the seeds people would throw out in the garbage. You can imagine that? We wanted bad-bad to go to Marseilles. That's where the spices were being shipped to. But we realized we'd never save enough for the passage, so one day we hid in the cloves.' From France his brothers had gone on to the West Indies, while Eli had stayed in Europe. Then he went to Venezuela, where he started a parrot-exporting business (it was in Venezuela that he'd met Anthony Reynold, otherwise known as King Tobago). When the parrot enterprise failed, he joined his brothers in Kingston but found the beer and soda business uninspiring, so he'd moved to the north coast, where he'd met Esme.

Often after a day of driving he'd take Ida to the Somerset for a sherbet. She'd sit by the hotel bar overlooking the swimming pool and listen to him talking to the tourists. He would speak knowledgeably about many places. 'You from Brighton? I know Brighton,' he'd say. Then at some point he'd begin describing the beautiful spots in Jamaica. 'I can arrange a tour for you,' he'd say, and he'd write, 'E. Joseph Transportation Co.' and the phone number on a slip of paper.

The Somerset. That was probably where her father would take her later. She imagined herself sitting at a poolside table with him and the movie star. She would talk to Errol Flynn, who would smile and say something very nice to her. The poor, dark image from the newspaper was all she had, and it had been grafted onto her young imagination. It would be a fine thing to meet him. That she would be one of the few people in Port Antonio to do so fit the regal idea she had of herself.

She rode back to Oni's. If her mother wasn't ready to leave yet, she must make her ready.

When she got back, she saw that Esme had rolled down her stockings and that both she and Oni were reading Mills & Boon novels. They didn't even look up at her.

Ida sat on the veranda steps and exhaled loudly.

'Patience,' her mother said without taking her eyes from the book. 'I jus' restin' me foot-bottom a while.'

Ida looked at her watch. It was after three. She had to do something.

'Madda Oni, you can tell me my future?' she asked.

Oni put down her book. 'I glad you ask. I was thinkin' to meself — "I wonder if the bat come here to tell Ida something." Wait here, I soon come.'

She went inside to get the calabash that she used for divination and for mediating between the spirits and the living.

The last time Oni had looked into Ida's future she'd seen her wearing a crown of diamonds. She'd also warned Ida about pirates. An enormous moth had arrived at Oni's cottage that time too, and Oni had said it was the spirit of her great-grandmother's sister, Ufuma, who had been captured by pirates during the old slavery days. The pirates were coming back and Ida had to be careful. *Wear silver, not gold. Gold will poison you.* Oni had given her a juju doll for protection and advised her to learn how to swim. Between the juju doll and poison-gold and pirates, Ida's mother had been so mad that day, she'd sworn she'd never go back up the mountain again.

As Ida had hoped, Esme stopped reading and looked at her watch. 'Is what o'clock? Eh-eh, Mr Brown must be waitin' all this time.'

Oni came back onto the veranda with the calabash. Esme told her, 'We don't have time for no future today.'

Oni protested, but Esme was adamant.

'Come, Ida,' Esme said, rolling her stockings back up and putting on the big country shoes. 'We need to reach home before dark.'

The two men sat talking in Eli's favorite rum shop. Errol Flynn was as drunk as a man could be without falling over. Eli was merely tipsy. No matter how much Eli drank, he never got fall-down drunk. He had a theory about it: the eighteen-karat gold Virgin Mary medallion absorbed the heat of the liquor, keeping his internal organs cool.

The rum shop, a one-room establishment with dark concrete walls and a corrugated zinc roof, stood alone in the mountains above Port Antonio. Through the open doorway Errol had a wide view of the town and the sea. There was only room for two small tables and a bar with unlit Christmas lights strung across it, but no bar stools. The cooking outside smelled wonderful to Errol: chopped-up pork, peppery and highly seasoned, and roasted breadfruit. He'd already had a plateful and was thinking about ordering some more.

They were the only two sitting there. Other men — banana

workers, truck drivers – came in, bought a pint of rum or a Red Stripe, and left again. Errol was grateful to Eli for bringing him here to this quiet, out-of-the-way place. What good instincts! Eli would be his man in Port Antonio. Earlier a small crowd had gathered at the courthouse and he'd been worried all day about people recognizing him, but in this little bar – or rum shop, as the Jamaicans called it – he couldn't tell whether or not people knew who he was. He had shaken hands with a few men and told them how beautiful he found their country. 'This man,' he'd told them, putting an arm around Eli, 'is my long-lost brother.'

He'd never had a brother, he told Eli, and had always longed for one.

The sun fell behind the mountains and the bar darkened.

'Imagine,' Eli said. 'You and me, we come to this place after years of traveling the world. After years of traveling. You. Me.' Here Eli stopped and placed a salt shaker and pepper shaker across from each other, then steadily drew them together in the center. 'We meet up here in this banana-tree town. Must be Destiny.'

Ida's heart was racing. She had managed to outwit her mother and get her moving along. But they had to hurry if she was going to have time to bathe, get dressed, and brush the country dust out of her hair.

As they passed by Mr Brown's house in the donkey cart, Esme suddenly realized she'd left something at her mother's cottage – a package of bush-tea Oni had given her for her stomach pains.

After some discussion and vacillation, Mr Brown sent one of his grandsons running up the mountain to get the package. Ida waited with her mother in Mr Brown's yard.

She waited and waited.

Sunset came. The goat she'd seen earlier lay on the ground of the slaughtering shed, its body split down the middle. Mr Brown's oldest son stood over it with a knife, removing its liver.

She knew it was too late to meet the movie star. She thought about her good dress laid out on the bed in her room.

Her mother was saying, 'Look like a nice fresh liver there, Mr Brown.'

'I can gi' you a piece fe tek home,' he said.

'If is no trouble, thank you. The meat in Port Antonio too tough.'

'Dem use too much science,' Mr Brown said, 'an' dem no care 'bout de animal.'

Something smooth was plucked from the dead goat's body and thrown into a basin with the other organs. One of the smaller children gasped, and the older children laughed.

'A true,' Esme agreed with Mr Brown. 'Everybody in such a hurry nowadays.'

I'm not like her, Ida thought. *I'm not like any of them.*

After Eli dropped Errol Flynn off at the Somerset that night, he found Ida alone and miserable on the veranda. Across the street, Father Reynold was setting up the projector to show one of Flynn's movies, *The Sea Hawk*, and Eli tried to use that to console her.

Ida didn't want to see the movie. Anybody could see a movie.

'But Ida,' Eli pleaded, 'he goin' stay in Port Antonio a few days. I convince him to stay.'

They heard Father Reynold shouting from across the road, 'You comin'?'

'So I can meet Errol Flynn tomorrow?' she asked her father.

Eli smoothed Ida's hair. 'Yes, man. Tomorrow. Come now.'

Father Reynold had hung sheets on the clothesline as a screen and set up four rows of chairs in the yard. There were people looking on from the road, leaning over the fence, just as there'd been a few months before when Father Reynold had first gotten the projector and had shown *Tarzan*. A cart man was selling sodas and peanuts.

While she waited for the movie to begin, Ida studied the poster of *The Sea Hawk* taped to the rectory door. Like the picture in the newspaper, this one showed Errol Flynn as a pirate brandishing a sword. A lock of wavy hair fell across his forehead, and he had a smile that revealed both rows of his teeth. It was a wolf-like yet handsome smile. The cleft in his chin held her attention. Father Reynold had a cleft in his chin too, though not quite as noticeable, and he had told Ida, 'God tickled me on my chin before I was born and left his fingerprint.' A mark of joyfulness, he'd said. The newspaper was right, she thought. Errol Flynn was the best-looking person she had ever seen.

The Sea Hawk began. The knob controlling the sound was broken, so the movie was five times louder than it needed to be. The people in the audience knew that Errol Flynn was there in Port Antonio. 'He love it here, man,' Eli had announced. 'He love Jamaicans. I helpin' him look for some property.'

A few months earlier, when *Tarzan* was being shown, the members of the audience had watched quietly. Now they smiled and joked and spoke in a casual way throughout the film, especially when the movie star was on the screen: 'I think I saw him down by his boat today,' somebody said. 'Him seem like a nice fellow.'

Afterward Ida heard her father and Father Reynold talking about the movies they'd seen in the cities where they'd lived. They spoke of Douglas Fairbanks and Gloria Swanson, and she heard again about the actress, Ida Lupino, after whom she had been named. *Ida Lupino, Ida Lupino*, the name sang inside her head now.

'Man,' Eli said to Father Reynold, 'what we need in Port Antonio is a cinema like they have in Kingston, with chandeliers. An upstairs and a downstairs—'

'Shilling seat an' sixpence seat,' Father Reynold proposed.

'Yes, man. We could even sell soda an' popcorn. If I could just raise enough capital . . .'

3

'They're Bangles, Mr Flynn'

Ida expected something to come from meeting Errol Flynn. She knew she was beautiful. How could she not know? All her life people had responded to her looks. They had either been generous – shopkeepers, for instance, giving her sweets and pretty things – or mean because they assumed she was spoiled. She had only one friend; most girls were jealous of her. Boys were afraid to talk to her. There was a photograph of her in the living room, taken when she was nine, and Ida always saw something in it that made an even deeper impression than the picture itself: the memory of her father standing beside the photographer while the picture was being taken, his eyes active with love and pride.

So with the confidence of an adored thirteen-year-old, she set out with her father that Sunday to meet Errol Flynn. Her hair was tied back with a white ribbon, and she wore the floral-patterned dress with the red belt. Having a waist had begun to be important to her; she frequently used her mother's tape measure to check that it was still twenty inches.

'What smell so? Is you smell so?' her father asked as soon as they got in the car.

Ida felt the blood rush to her face.

'Is Evening in Paris you have on?' Eli laughed, recognizing the perfume that he bought for Esme every Christmas.

They waited in the hotel lounge for about ten minutes before Errol Flynn came down. The hotel workers and a few guests had already gotten used to him; no one gaped. There were glances, though, and everything seemed to slow down around him.

He was larger than Ida had imagined. Looking down at his sandals, she spotted hairs on his toes.

He was shaking her father's hand energetically and laughing.

'This is my daughter, Ida,' Eli said.

She thought he must have just showered because his hair was damp and he smelled of nice soap.

'What pretty bracelets,' he said, touching the silver at her wrist.

'They're bangles, Mr Flynn.'

He was quiet for a moment as if surprised. 'Ah, bangles.'

Ida felt terrible. She had been rude.

He turned to Eli. 'Where can we get some good Jamaican food? I'm famished.'

His voice seemed to bounce back at him and was a bit too loud. Later Ida would learn that the loudness was an effort to overcome a hearing problem, a constant ringing in his ears.

Her body felt small to her as she walked out of the hotel beside him. They stood together waiting for her father to get the car, and he asked her about school.

'What's your best subject?' He spoke to no one but her now and his voice was softer.

She admitted that she didn't like school very much except for the poetry class and riding lessons.

'If I lived here,' he said, 'I'd do nothing but ride horses and write poetry.'

I don't write poetry, she wanted to say, I read it. She still hadn't looked at his face, but she was ready to tell him things: how she'd played Titania in *A Midsummer Night's Dream* and that she was preparing for a horse-jumping competition. But she said nothing and was relieved to see her father's car.

Flynn sat in front. At first Ida sat right behind his head, but then she slid across to the other end of the seat so she could get a better view of him. She saw him take something from his satchel. It was a fake nose that he attached to his face. Flynn saw the astonishment on Ida's face.

'I can hide behind this nose,' he said, winking at her.

Ida spent the rest of the day driving around with the two men.

Errol soon realized he didn't need the fake nose. He was beginning to understand the place: Port Antonio was not like Kingston. A lot of the country people didn't recognize him, and even when they did, they didn't hound him. He was amused when a market woman slapped his hand for 'feelin' up' the fruit in her basket; after that, he did the same to some other market women to tease them.

Ida watched him devour enormous quantities of food at roadside stands: jerk pork, curry goat, patties. 'I'm going to put on twenty pounds if I'm not careful,' he said to her in a confidential tone as though it were just between them. He patted his abdomen and drew it in at the same time. Ida thought he already looked twenty or thirty pounds heavier than the man she'd seen swinging on ropes in *The Sea Hawk*, but he was still handsome to her.

She tried to imagine what the country looked like to him and was quick to see what he saw, hear what he heard. 'There's music everywhere in this country,' he said, seeing an old man playing a kalimba, a thumb piano, out in his yard; and another time, as he looked up at the Blue Mountains, she heard him say, 'They look as if they might dissolve into the sky.'

'The way people speak here,' he said, 'it sounds a bit Irish.'

'A likkle a dis, a likkle a dat. Jamaicans proud a dem mixture,' Eli said.

They were sitting at a roadside place, a shack where the jerk pork was roasted on planks in front of them and sold by the pound with hard-dough bread.

'Ida speaks beautifully,' Flynn said, as if she wasn't there. He drained the rum punch from his glass; it was thick and tangy, the strong liquor deceptively hidden by the fruit juices.

'I get you another one,' Eli said.

'If you insist.' He smiled and turned to Ida. 'I bet you're a good singer.'

'She won a medal for reciting Wordsworth,' Eli said as he went to get more drinks.

'Shelley,' she corrected. ' "Ozymandias." ' She suddenly felt awkward and hoped she wouldn't be asked to recite it.

But Flynn was no longer paying attention to her. He was throwing scraps of food to a skinny brown dog that was hanging around, and talking playfully to the poor, neglected animal. The dog seemed more mesmerized by him than by the food.

Ida snatched up a yellow scotch-bonnet pepper and held it out to Flynn.

'Have you tried this?' she asked him.

'What is it?'

'A plum.'

He bit into it, and she saw him turn red. It was one of the hottest peppers in the world. He brought his hands to his throat as if he were choking.

'What happen?' Eli asked. He saw Ida's face and then realized what had happened – 'Ida. Shame on you.'

But she wasn't ashamed; she was curious. Flynn began to smile, and she could tell he was enjoying her prank. 'I think I've met an imp!' he said to her father.

They went to Blue Hole. Eli chose the best time to go, the end of the day when no one else was around. Here Ida noticed a complete change in Flynn. She had expected exuberance; this was one of the country's natural treasures, a two-hundred-foot-deep swimming hole formed from the crater of an ancient volcano and enclosed by tropical forest.

But Flynn's effervescence disappeared. He wasn't solemn, just quiet, like a man who had no one else with him. He stripped down to his bathing trunks and dived, a dive that was like a dive into himself, a recollection.

He swam and swam. Eli Joseph sat under a tree and waited. Ida pulled her dress up around her legs and sat on the bank with her feet in the water. The sun was going down. She saw his body disappear and resurface in the glimmering water, and she sat quietly as he floated near her with his eyes closed. He had forgotten her, and she didn't want to disturb him. For the moment it was interesting enough to look at him, but it was an interest she hoped would at some point be reciprocated.

The sky darkened, and the water lost its sheen and

became almost milky purple. The last light vanished from the tops of the trees. It grew cooler and the night frogs and crickets began their squeaking. He still swam. Eli Joseph, waiting on the banks, was restless, but he didn't complain. Ida shivered in the evening air. She felt mysteriously happy.

4

Baron Karl Von Ausberg Appears

No one could remember exactly when Baron Karl Von Ausberg had first arrived in Jamaica or when he had begun to be seen frequently with Errol Flynn. He collected and traded artifacts. Ida once saw a picture of him in the newspaper holding an Arawak pot that he'd discovered in the Blue Mountains. She also heard that he'd donated money to build a museum and that he was interested in the sunken city and treasures of Port Royal. He seemed to belong to that category of affluent foreigners who, on a short visit to the island, decide they have found the right place for themselves, and stay.

He was a large man, well over six feet, with a great blond head like a Viking, but he had an unimposing manner. He was fluent in several languages (Ida had heard him speaking Arabic with her father), he knew a lot about wine and jazz, and he had a great deal of money (from African diamond mines, some people said). Karl was unmarried, and, as Eli said with a touch of envy, he was 'a playboy like Flynn.'

Eli Joseph liked Karl: 'Is not every day you meet a baron. He's a nice fellow.'

Ida didn't think Karl was a nice fellow. She thought he was rude and self-absorbed.

The day she met him, he and Errol were taking turns diving off a boat. Errol had invited her to the beach, but since she didn't know how to swim she'd been left wading by herself in the shallow part. There was a river that fed into the sea, and when the two men had had enough of the saltwater, they took turns swinging from a vine and jumping into the deepest part of the river. Like boys they were, all day competing to see who was the better diver, the faster swimmer, who could perform the most daring stunts.

Karl was polite enough to Ida when they were introduced but seemed disinterested. There were other friends of his and Errol's on the beach, American women, with whom he was occupied.

'You're from Germany?' she asked him, trying to be mature and conversational.

'Austria.'

'Do you have a castle?' she asked and then realized how childish the question sounded. She didn't care one bit whether or not he had a castle.

'It was destroyed in the war,' he said and turned from her to talk with Errol and one of the American women.

Just then Errol grabbed her arm and pulled her toward the sea. 'Today you're going to learn to swim.'

She said, 'No, I don't want to,' and hung back, making it hard for him, but she relished the attention.

'I managin' him business,' Eli told people.

'Managin' him business, eh?' Esme responded.

Eli had appointed himself Flynn's social secretary, driver, guide, confidant, and real estate broker.

In between shooting *Cry Wolf* and *Escape Me Never* Flynn made frequent trips to Port Antonio. A year had passed since he'd first arrived, and, with Eli's help, he was still looking for the right beach property on which to build a house and marina. In the meantime, he bought some property inland where he intended to set up a horse ranch. He also bought the Somerset Hotel.

Eli made a good commission brokering the sale of the Somerset for Flynn. He sold the taxi company, had two new suits made, and set up an office in town with a sign that said, 'E. Joseph Properties.' 'Business treatin' you good,' people said to him. 'You lookin' well, Mr Joseph – must be Esme's good cookin'.' Now that he was properly established in the real estate business, Eli began looking into some property for himself right in the center of town, a site on which to build a movie theatre. He wasn't just saying 'if I could only raise the capital,' he was actually trying to. But whenever he wasn't pursuing his movie-theatre plan, he was busy, as he said, 'managin'' Flynn's affairs.

People sometimes called the house thinking they'd be able to reach Flynn.

'Hello, is Errol there?'

'Errol who?' Esme would ask, exasperated. 'Nobody by that name lives here.'

A group of not-very-good musicians calling themselves 'Flynn's Swamp Boys' began to hang around Flynn's hotel. Sometimes they stood outside the Josephs' gate, singing well-known or improvised calypsos. One day Esme threatened to turn the dog on them. 'G'way!' she shouted. 'You sing like ole rooster!'

'How come you father have to pay for everything?' she remarked to Ida. 'Big movie star like him no have plenty money?'

Esme still complained of 'not feeling well,' but her doctor hadn't been able to diagnose any specific disease. She took Andrews' Liver Salts for her stomachaches and Oni's bush-teas for everything else that ailed her. At first Ida thought her criticism of Flynn was just part of her habitual grumbling, but she too began to notice that it was always her father and never Flynn who paid for all the drinks and meals.

But Esme, in spite of her remarks, thought Flynn was charming, and she invited him to the house for dinner. Baron Von Ausberg was in Port Antonio, so he was also invited. Father Reynold came too. Esme did not make a big fuss as other women might have. It was like any other Sunday dinner: no special food or cleaning or decorating.

Errol and Karl seemed too large for the little house, especially Karl, who was by far the biggest man to ever come through the door. But anyone who sat down at Esme's table was immediately comfortable, and they were no exception. Karl enjoyed the food even more than Errol and said 'wonderful' about everything, which made Ida feel a little better toward him. They had roast pork, rice-an'-peas, plantain, callaloo, and for dessert Esme's special coconut-rum pie.

The men drank rum before, during, and after dinner and talked politics. Flynn was interested in the emerging Jamaican political parties and asked about them.

'Tweedledum and Tweedledee, one no different from the other,' was Father Reynold's opinion.

'Not true,' Eli argued. 'Let me explain. Norman Manley's party, the PNP, wants to see the whole region move forward independently of Britain. The other one, Busta's party, chu! They just a lot of loudmouth rascals.'

'No, man, they both want independence,' Father Reynold insisted.

'Why?' Flynn asked, and Ida noticed that the brown flecks in his eyes glinted when he was amused. It was often hard to tell whether or not he was joking. 'Independence isn't all it's cracked up to be. What's wrong with the way things are?'

'A lot of things,' Esme said firmly.

Everyone was quiet because it was rare for her to enter these conversations. 'For colored people in this country, for the women out there breakin' rock-stone.' She turned to Eli. 'I not so sure Manley has the strength of Busta. Busta is a lion of a man.'

'You cyan rush these things, Esme,' Eli said. 'Colored people not quite ready to rule this country by themselves.'

'Nonsense!' Esme replied. 'We should have taken over in 1865 during the Morant Bay rebellion.'

Eli looked at her, astonished. 'And then we would be poor like Haiti,' he said. 'No, man, we need to tek things slow.'

'What you think?' Father Reynold asked Karl.

Karl had excused himself from the table. He was sitting on the sofa smoking a cigar.

'All governments are annoying,' he said with a smile.

'Because you go digging up treasure in other people's countries,' Flynn joked.

'True,' he said and smiled again, a smile that was only for Errol, Ida thought, as though the rest of them weren't there. She went back to disliking the baron.

Father Reynold had brought his guitar, and Flynn asked him to play some folk songs. He sang 'Yellow Bird' so beautifully that everyone became quiet, and Ida remembered her father saying that before Father Reynold had become a priest his heart had been broken by a Venezuelan girl. When he played 'Matilda,' everyone joined in. Even Esme clapped her hands and sang.

As he was about to leave, Errol praised Esme's cooking and asked, 'Can you cook, Ida?'

'I fried the plantain,' she said,

Eli laughed because it was the only thing Ida knew how to cook and because he thought her adolescent flirtation with Flynn was charming.

One day Flynn said, 'She's the loveliest girl on the whole island, Eli.'

But Esme thought Ida was getting 'too familiar' with the movie star.

'You not a big woman. You mustn't call grown-ups by their first name. Call him Mr Flynn.'

'But he told me to call him Errol.'

'You acting too grown-up for you age.'

'I'm fourteen.'

'So?'

He arrived at their house once in a bright orange shirt with red birds on it. Ida told him the colors didn't suit him.

'Ida!' her mother and father shouted.

It was true; he looked best in dark, murky grays and greens. Flynn looked in the mirror and laughed. 'She's right.' He lifted her up and spun her around.

She felt embarrassed being spun around like a child and asked to be put down, but he didn't seem to hear her. Afterward she overheard him talking with her father out on the veranda.

'Look at that view. I'm telling you, Eli, this is the right place for me.'

'Yes, man.'

'But where exactly? We've seen a lot of properties but none of them have been quite right.'

'You will know is right when you see it. You play dominoes?'

'It's not just about the right piece of land. I have houses. I have land.'

'I know. Remember, I used to be a wandering man like you.'

'I don't look forward to dying any more than the next man—'

'Nobody. Nobody wants to leave this beautiful world.'

'—but when I do—'

'More?'

'Just a drop – thank you – when I take that last breath, the sea is what I want to be looking at. I'm not making any sense.'

'Yes, man, I understand.'

'It's not about dying either. I tell you – it's all the muck, the dirt that gets into people's minds and makes everything else seem dirty. I'm tired of my own dirt and everyone else's.'

'You have to take the bad with the good. That is the reality. You cyan bury you head in the sand.'

'I'm not. I'm not burying my head. I just want someplace where I can make a fresh start. You know what I mean, Eli?'

'Yes, man. Don't give up.'

He came and went over several months. Ida thought about him all the time. Everyone and everything else was a distraction to her. Her school report showed that she had failed every subject except English and Bible Knowledge.

Esme was furious. 'You got an F in mathematics! What? You forget how to count?'

'Come, Esme, ease up,' Eli said. 'She can read and write an' she knows the Bible.'

'She reads,' Esme conceded.

Literature was the one pleasure she and Ida shared. Their bookcases were crowded with novels: romance novels and a few classics like Jane Austen and the Brontës. They often spent time together, each quietly reading.

'Well, she goin' have to tek extra lessons to improve the arithmetic. No horse riding till you marks get better.'

At school Ida spent a lot of time talking about Errol with her friend Myrtle Tate. For Myrtle it was like an ongoing radio drama: 'We went riding Sunday . . . he said I was a *superb* rider . . . we went to the beach and he told me . . . maybe he will . . . I think he wants . . .'

Considering how much of the time Flynn was away, there wasn't really that much to tell. Yet Ida could talk for hours about him, often retelling the same thing so she could reap different experiences from it, a bit like throwing the same set of dice again and again.

Like Ida, Myrtle was a day student at the Pringle School for Girls, but unlike Ida, she was on a scholarship. Pringle was an expensive boarding school, mainly for white Jamaican and expatriate girls, the next-best thing to sending a daughter away to school in England. Although Myrtle was black, poor, and the daughter of a banana worker, she was not snubbed by the other girls. She was admired because she did brilliantly in her exams and was modest and affable.

She lived a mile away from Ida on Parrot Lane, a place of corrugated tin shacks and squatters' dwellings. Her family was not a squatter family; they owned a proper concrete house. Mr and Mrs Tate were Methodists like Esme, and they were strict parents. They had two children; Myrtle was the most promising. Larice, the older girl, was always in trouble: she stole money from her parents and sometimes disappeared for days.

Ida was as intrigued by stories about Larice as Myrtle was by stories about Errol. But then something happened to Larice that cast a shadow across the lives of everyone who knew her. She got pregnant and the boy — or man — ran away to Kingston. Larice was barely sixteen at the time; Ida and Myrtle, fourteen. This shadow stretched all the way to Ida's house, to her school, and over the whole town. Some of the teachers and students began to look at Myrtle suspiciously as if she were carrying a disease. Esme and the other Methodist churchwomen wavered: one day they would feel sorry for the family and another day they'd raise eyebrows and warn their own daughters, 'Look what happen to Myrtle's sister. You see how she bring belly into her house.'

Larice named her baby boy Derek. She began to work long hours loading bananas on the boats and started having sex for money with the men who worked on the boats. She began to look disheveled, to stink, and she could often be seen scratching herself indecently in public. Her clothes were stained and dirt-encrusted from the places she lay down. She rarely came home.

For Ida and Myrtle, Larice's life was a glimpse of hell — female hell. She was their opposite, a tarnished mirror they avoided because it was inconceivable that they would ever ruin their own lives that way.

The only bright feature was Derek, a fat, happy baby. Ida and Myrtle fought over who got to pick him up; they delighted in teaching him his first words. 'He has the best eyes,' Ida would often say because he had bright, eager eyes that always showed enthusiasm at the sight of her. 'This baby really likes me.'

～

Other girls had fantasies about movie stars; the difference for Ida was that her movie star was often right there in plain sight.

'Hullo, beauty!' he would say when he saw her, and he would not have to say more.

She tried not to stare at the freckles on his back and shoulders when they went to the beach. Her eyes were drawn guiltily to the dark hair around his navel. She wondered as she lay in her bed at night what it would be like to touch him there. Scenes from his movies (she'd now seen several of them) got mixed into her fantasies: he was a pirate or soldier and she was a woman in a tight bodice; the climax came with his unbuckling his belt. She felt that it would be wrong to let her eyes glide down below his navel, and for a while she was preoccupied with the effort of not doing so.

She was Roman Catholic like her father, but unlike him she went regularly to confession. She was careful to go only on Saturday mornings because that was when the visiting priest Father Simon would be there. Father Reynold would have recognized her voice.

'Bless me, Father, for I have sinned. It has been one week since my last confession and these are my sins: I thought about something I shouldn't think about, and I touched myself – where I shouldn't.'

'Say three Our Fathers, three Hail Marys, and the Apostle's Creed.'

Ida was grateful for the rather lengthy penance; it was not so arduous as to make her feel perverse but substantial enough to ease the burden of unutterable wrong. She wondered if it seemed suspicious to Father Simon that she confessed the same sins every week and she considered making up some new ones.

One morning after she confessed, she heard a long sigh.

'When did our Lord ever say you mustn't do these things, Ida?'

Father Reynold.

'You steal anyt'ing? You covet you neighbor's cow? Chu, man! Go love the Lord an' stop worry you'self.'

Love the lord an' stop worry you'self. But there was danger, wasn't there? Larice and other bad girls 'let' men do things to them. Had it started the same way for them, engrossed by desires that were easier to give in to than to deny?

She thought about Errol and took comfort in the fact that he had never pressed himself on her. He was not like that. But if she showed willingness? What would he do? This was where her imagination stopped. She knew she had to be careful but she wasn't exactly sure what that entailed. Her mother hadn't explained much – panties hid God's Wisdom, and if a girl revealed God's Wisdom to a man she could become pregnant. She didn't want to end up like Larice.

Some of the society people in Port Antonio began complaining about the prostitutes hanging around the Somerset, and they blamed Flynn. 'It used to be a nice place where you could go for dinner,' Ida heard a lady tell Eli. 'I wouldn't set foot there now with all that riffraff.'

One day Eli drove up to the house with Errol, Karl Von Ausberg, and a woman named Rosalie, known around town as a high-class prostitute. The three waited out in the car while Eli came in for something he'd forgotten.

'You know better than to bring that woman here,' Esme said.

'I jus' come back fe me wallet.'

'Wallet?' She held out her hand and he surrendered the wallet to her. She took out all the money. 'You not spending money on Flynn' street-gal.' She turned to Ida, who was staring out the window at the car. 'Come from the window! I wish Errol Flynn never set him foot in Jamaica.'

Ida wasn't jealous of Rosalie or the other prostitutes. She had absorbed her mother's social opinions and believed that those women were inferior to her. But the white women who came from abroad peeved her, and so did Karl. Karl had bought a maroon convertible, and he and Errol could be seen driving around in it with the stylish foreign women. They were all about the sun, these women, with their expensive sunglasses and scarves and tanning oil. Ida's father was impressed and she'd hear him bragging to his men friends about them, as though knowing about Errol's paramours somehow gave him playboy stature too: 'Yes, man, she's a model from Sweden,' or 'She's a contessa, you know, a lovely woman.' A model! A contessa! They made Ida feel invisible, these women who in succession visited Errol and seemed a vital part of his life.

5

A Deserted Island

Then it happened. After more than a year of traveling back and forth, Flynn found what he had been looking for, and it had been right there in front of him.

Ida was sitting with Errol and her father on the terrace of the Somerset Hotel. It was especially pleasant for her because she and her father had Errol to themselves for a change; Karl Von Ausberg wasn't there, and neither were the suntanned women.

The Somerset was on the peninsula between the twin harbors. Her father had once given pet names to the harbors – 'Business' and 'Pleasure.' On one side, they could see West Harbor ('Business'), where the heavy stems of green bananas were piled up against the walls. Some of the women-loaders slept on the dried banana trash along the wharf while others sat around talking. They were all waiting for night, when the loading would begin again. To Ida's left was the peaceful, sandy strip of East Harbor ('Pleasure'). A small sailboat was tied to the pier. The air and the water were calm except for a pelican swooping down unpredictably now and then.

'What about that place?' Errol asked, looking at the islet across from East Harbor. It was about a mile away from the terrace and of course had always been there, but he spoke as if it had just appeared.

'Navy Island?'

'Does anyone live there?'

'Not even duppy,' Eli said.

'Ghosts?'

'Nobody ever lived or died there,' Eli explained.

Actually, Ida had heard a story about a woman-duppy who was supposed to live on the island. But it was just something children said to frighten other children, so she didn't think it was a sensible thing for her to bring up.

'People used to sail over sometimes for picnics. Not so much anymore. I hear there's a nice beach,' Eli said.

They sailed over that afternoon.

As they drew up to the island, the whiteness dazzled them: the white sand and the clusters of white flowers hanging from the trees. Mounds of washed-up coral, bleached white by the sun, faced them like ancient totems. Behind the wall of sea-grapes and casuarinas, a small hill, thick with coconut palms, rose up behind the beach. She could make out bright-red Otaheites in the hilly forest.

'Reminds me of home,' Errol said, looking around.

'Home?' Eli asked.

'Tasmania.'

'All this time, I thinkin' you an Irishman,' Eli said.

'No, man,' Errol said, trying out a Jamaican accent. 'I born an' bred in Tasmania.'

'An island man.' Eli chuckled.

'So clean,' Errol said. 'I feel like we're the first ones to set foot here.'

They climbed over the big rocks that separated one cove from another, pushing aside the branches of prickly pear and sea-grapes. Now and then a seabird would fly out noisily from the trees as if to let them know they were trespassing.

Eli was wearing his good trousers and good shoes. 'You and Ida go on. I wait for you here,' he said, settling himself on a large piece of driftwood. 'Careful a snakes an' man-eatin' turtles.'

'We'll bring back buried treasure,' Errol shouted back, walking a little ahead of Ida. He seemed nervous or maybe just excited. She couldn't tell.

'The whole island is a treasure,' she said.

He looked back at her and smiled at that.

She wondered if she should tell him about Sabine, the ghost that people said inhabited the island. It might amuse him. Fishermen claimed they had seen her, and there was talk that she wasn't a ghost at all but an old, crazy white woman who lived there by herself.

'Do you hear that? Listen.' He placed his hand on her shoulder. 'Sounds like a river.'

They walked a bit more along the beach, then climbed over a pile of rocks, and there it was, pure and beautiful, flowing into the sea. 'My God,' he said. 'Let's follow it uphill to the source.'

He went ahead of her, turning to help her now and then, almost unconsciously. He was completely occupied by the new land around him.

'Look at that white bougainvillea,' he said pointing up at the cliff.

She was surprised at his knowing so many of the flowers. Spiny ferns covered the ground, and there were clusters of wild pink oleander popping up between the rocks. Ida wished they could explore the place on horseback. The island seemed made for riding trails, not too rocky or mountainous. But the thought was too heady — she and Errol handling the big, strong animals across the unknown terrain. She felt her face get hot and prickly.

'You know, when I left Tasmania,' he told her, 'I went to New Guinea. There was a copra plantation where I worked for a while, Laloki, a beautiful place. This reminds me of it.'

Laloki, Ida repeated in her head, liking the sound. 'You weren't an actor then?'

'No. I wanted to be a writer. Traveling round the world having adventures and writing about them. I wrote a couple of stories for the *Sydney Bulletin* while I was in New Guinea.'

They had not gone far up the hill when they came to a pool in the stream, sheltered by bamboo stalks so tall that some of them arched and met over the water. Bamboo River, she decided, would be the name of this spot. There were Otaheite apples here too. Some of them lay crushed on the ground, and the air smelled ripe.

He picked apples for them both.

'I grew up on Otaheites,' he said finishing one off in a few bites and flinging the core behind him. Then he took off his shirt and went into the water. It was fairly deep at the center, up to his shoulders.

Ida sat on the edge of the pool and dipped her feet in. The water was so clear she could see the stones at the bottom. It felt to her as if she had been there with him before, but she knew she hadn't, that it was what her grandmother would call 'till-when-again' — a déjà-vu. She looked at him and thought, *He'll buy this whole island. We'll ride here together.*

He came out, dried himself off with his shirt, and sat by her. The sun shone brokenly through the bamboo, warming the rocks. She had undone her ponytail and her hair fell around her. He looked at her.

'What hair!' he said.

It caught her by surprise, the way he looked at her. She looked down at the bottom of the river where an Otaheiti had fallen and stirred it with her foot.

'We should get back,' he said.

When they reached the bottom of the hill, he took her hand and walked beside her. It was not an amorous gesture, nor was it fatherly. He felt close to her at that moment and enjoyed holding her hand.

'Who named it Navy Island?' he asked. 'Do you know?'

Yes, she knew the history and she told it to him, or rather it seemed to tumble all by itself from her mouth. While she spoke, she thought only about his hand, and she worried about whether they would still be holding hands when her father came into view. But he let go of her when they had to climb back over the rocks.

In the distance she made out the figure of her father, looking expectantly in their direction. He waved at them.

'Such a small place, and so much history,' Errol said.

'There's a story too,' she said. 'Do you want to hear it?'

Eli watched them walking up the beach, his good-good friend Errol listening carefully to something Ida was telling him, and Ida, schoolgirlish and animated.

'The Otaheites are Captain Bligh's trees,' she told him.

'Bligh was here?' Errol asked her.

'Yes.'

'I seem to be following him everywhere.' He went on to explain: 'When I was in New Guinea, minding my own business, not a thought in my head about Hollywood, a film crew came there to make a picture about the *Bounty*, and they offered me my first acting job. That was how I started.' He was quiet for a while, remembering, and then asked, 'Was Bligh the first one here?'

'No,' she said. 'The island had a history before that.'

'Tell me. I know you're dying to.'

'Cattle stealers called boucaniers used to hide out here.'

'*Boucaniers?* Frenchmen?'

French, Dutch, English. Men who stole cattle, then roasted the meat on a grid of sticks called a *boucan*, she explained. They sold the meat to pirates. Some of them joined the pirates, and soon all those sea-robbers came to be called *boucaniers*, buccaneers. The English navy used them to attack the ships of their Spanish enemy. But once the enemy was defeated, the English betrayed the buccaneers. They hanged most of them and took over their hideout, using it as a place to repair ships, and that was why they called it Navy Island. But pirates still turned up over the years to raid the island. There was supposed to be gold here, buried treasure.

'Pirate treasure?' He smiled at her.

The sand was soft and deep, and as she walked unsteadily beside him she could see that he was charmed by her and her story. She imagined herself wearing sunglasses and a beautiful scarf around her head like the glamorous women she saw him with.

'What about Captain Bligh?' he asked.

That was later, she explained, when England went to war

with America. Food supplies to Jamaica were cut off and the plantation slaves were starving. The English sent Bligh to the South Seas to collect breadfruit and bring it here so it could be cultivated as food for the slaves. On the voyage his men mutinied; they took over the *Bounty* and set Bligh adrift with no food or water. But he survived. His little boat landed in Malaysia. Four years later he set out again, this time on the *Providence*, and finally reached Navy Island. He sent the breadfruit across to Jamaica to be planted while he stayed on Navy Island with his crew, resting and repairing his ship.

Along with the breadfruit, the crew had also brought some Otaheite apples with them from the South Seas. 'And that's where Sabine's story begins,' Ida said.

'You not tellin' him that ol' duppy story?' Eli said, walking up the beach to them.

'There are different stories about her,' Ida said.

Sabine sailed over to Navy Island with some other women and befriended the crew of HMS *Providence*. She fell in love with a sailor, and he gave her one of the apples. She spat out the seeds and that was how the Otaheite took root on the island.

When the *Providence* was leaving, she asked the sailor to take her with him. He told her he'd come back and that she should wait for him. The other women tried to persuade her to go back to land – Jamaica – with them, but she was afraid he'd return to Navy Island and not find her. She stayed and stayed. She lived alone on the island eating wild fruit and the meat of wild boars. At night people saw fires burning on the island and knew Sabine was still there.

'Now, when fishermen sail by they sometimes see a ghost with long white hair in the forest.'

'I see.' Errol said. 'Why is it uninhabited? I mean – aside from Sabine?'

'The British navy stopped using it long ago, and no one bothered about it after that.'

'Until now,' Errol said.

6

A Gift and a Mother's Concern

Errol bought Navy Island and began building Bella Vista. It was 1947. In between shooting *Rocky Mountain* and *The Adventures of Don Juan*, he flew back and forth in a single-engine Navion to check on the progress of the house.

Ida rarely saw him. Her mother had grown more ill and needed bed rest, so it had been decided that Ida should board at the Pringle School.

One day she got a letter from Errol. He'd heard that she didn't like being away from home. In the letter he told her that he'd also gone to boarding school for a few years: 'I fooled my parents into believing I was homesick so they would send me cakes and all my favorite foods, but I was actually having a marvelous time. It was great to have so many pals around. Enjoy your time with friends, Ida. Have fun. The time will pass quickly.'

The movie star's letter would have impressed the girls in her class, but Ida didn't show it to anyone, not even Myrtle. It was too important to her. She kept it hidden, slept with it under her pillow, and reread it so often that it seemed like many letters.

She was almost fifteen and getting a lot of attention from boys. She was pleased by the attention but not impressed with the boys. An English boy, the brother of one of her classmates, often came to the school to see her. 'She's pretty, but she's colored,' Ida overheard his sister say to him. Ida was one of only a handful of colored students there. 'I don't care,' he answered. Ida agreed to go for a walk with him. A few days later she learned that he had spread a rumor about her, saying she'd let him kiss her and touch her breasts.

After that she came to the conclusion that she despised all boys — with one exception, her friend Clive Goodman.

Clive was the son of Esme's hairdresser. The Goodmans were not prosperous; they lived in three rooms above the hairdressing salon. Clive was a scholarship student at St. Augustine's, the boys' school near the Pringle School. He was an outstanding student and the first colored captain of his school's cricket team. He was also a fantastic runner. Once when Ida left her favorite pair of shoes at school, he ran the ten miles there and back to bring them to her.

'You don't have to thank me,' he told Ida breathlessly, and she noticed he was growing a mustache and that his shirt was neatly tucked into his pants even after all that exertion. 'I really like running,' he said.

'Surprise for you at home,' Eli said one day when he picked Ida up from boarding school.

For weeks there had been an atmosphere of secrecy in the Josephs' house. The surprise was in the backyard. It was a present from Errol — a mare.

'From Mexico,' her father said. 'Her name is Pearl.'

'Horse eat plenty,' Esme droned, looking out from the kitchen doorway.

Ida couldn't speak: a horse! She was white and somewhat dainty, reminding Ida of horses in nursery-rhyme picture books — *rings on her fingers and bells on her toes, she shall have music wherever she goes.*

'She small but swift,' Eli said

That night they had a party and invited everybody on Plumbago Road. There was the new horse to celebrate and something else: Eli had raised the capital to start building the Palace Theatre; that was what he'd decided to name the cinema.

Father Reynold brought over some Lord Invader calypso records. Esme felt well enough to make a big pot of curry chicken, and while everyone was eating, Eli talked about his plans for the Palace Theatre (chandeliers, red-cushioned seats), and then he told the story of how Errol had sent the horse from Mexico: 'Flynn bringing horses from Mexico to start a ranch here.'

'On Navy Island?' someone asked.

'No, man, right here a-land. He buy that big property out by Fairy Hill. Goin' breed horse an' cattle. He tell me as soon as he see Pearl him think — yes, man, that is the horse for Ida.'

Ida felt her face grow warm.

'But then there was the quarantine,' Father Reynold filled in. He too had been in on the secret.

'I never hear 'bout horse quarantine before,' Mr Cousins said. He was their next-door neighbor and he was also the new owner of Eli's taxi company.

'Yes, man. Horse quarantine is a serious business,' Father Reynold said. 'Nobody want race horse-dem fe drop dead.' He put a record on the gramophone, a popular song everyone knew about the Yankees and the young girls in Trinidad. They all sang as they danced.

Ida drifted in and out of the party sounds. She was remembering a scene in *Captain Blood* where the governor's daughter goes riding with the hero, Peter Blood. The details of the scene had impressed her: the windswept palm trees, the horses, Errol's body bearing down on the horse, his hands on the reins . . .

'Turn up the music,' somebody shouted. 'Is a fete we havin' or Sunday school?'

'Play "Rum an' Coca-Cola" again!'

Ida slid back into the remembered movie scene and saw herself, not Olivia de Havilland, showing Peter Blood the beautiful spots on the island.

'But from the day Pearl reach Jamaica,' Eli continued the saga of Pearl, 'she stop eatin'! Father Reynold go with me one night to see her. She was lookin' almos' like a skeleton. No true? Father Reynold talk to her in Spanish — "*Que bonita potranca? Tienes hambre?*" An' the horse look him straight in him eye.

'Yes, man.' Eli went on, 'I begin to see wha' wrong: the horse no understand Jamaica people language! So we go every night fe talk to the horse in Spanish. An' slow-slow, we start teach her some English words.'

'No wonder you come home smellin' a rum.' Esme said, 'Is Father Reynold you out with every night.'

'We looking 'bout Ida horse,' Eli said.

'Educatin' the horse,' Father Reynold confirmed.

'Yes, man. Is a bi-lingo animal now,' Eli ended the story. 'That remind me. You ever hear the joke about the man who had two sides: Jamaican in front and French behind . . .'

Esme realized the conversation had taken an indecent turn, so she began gathering up the dishes and asked Ida to help.

As usual, Father Reynold was the last to leave. Ida's bedroom had a window onto the veranda, and she lay in bed listening to him and her father take their own sweet time getting from chair to door, from door to gate, speculating about things near and far: Would the West Indies cricket team win that year? Would the day soon come when tourists would arrive by plane rather than by boat?

For the rest of her life, she would remember their voices as part of her childhood nights, along with the night crickets calling and the canna lilies flapping softly against the wall.

She had Errol's creased letter under her pillow, and as her mind folded into sleep, she had a vision of herself riding with him like the governor's daughter in the movie, pointing out interesting things on Navy Island. He cared about her; he'd given her a horse.

She rode Pearl whenever she came home from boarding school. There would be three of them: Myrtle behind her on the saddle and Clive running alongside on the banks of the Rio Grande. She thought of Errol on those rides and how he liked to go rafting there. The people who lived along the Rio Grande had gotten used to him and his pranks. She'd heard that he liked to startle the women as they washed clothes in the river by diving off the raft and suddenly emerging in front of them stark naked.

Ida also rode at the Equestrian Club. It was an establishment mainly for whites and expatriates. Although there was no written rule saying Jamaicans couldn't go there, few did. The gate displayed a PRIVATE PROPERTY sign, and a white wall hid the magnificent grounds and sea view. There had been a spice plantation there once, and the smell of nutmeg hung in the air. While she was riding, Eli would have a few drinks in the clubhouse with the polo-playing set. He didn't much enjoy being there, being a dominoes man, but thought it might be useful for his real estate business.

Ida saw boys and girls her own age there. They were white and ignored her. She never saw anyone darker than herself there; even the stable boys were light-skinned, as were the uniformed waiters inside the clubhouse. Ida didn't dwell on the prejudice; she just wanted to be with Pearl and perfect her jumps, but she was aware of the color bar.

So when Esme said she was going with her to the club one day, Ida was surprised. Not because she thought anyone would give her any trouble, but because Esme had never really taken much interest in Ida's riding, and because it just wasn't her kind of place. Esme had her own social regimen: church, market, dressmaker, hairdresser, and occasionally tea with her church friends. Ida couldn't imagine her in the clubhouse with the bridge-playing ladies.

'I want to see you jump,' she said, putting on a favorite white hat and her 'road gloves,' as she called them.

Eli drove them, and as they passed Reach Falls, Eli reminded Esme about the picnics they used to have there together before Ida was born.

'Ida you should-a see you mother in her bath-suit. What a figure!'

'Chu! Stop!' Esme could not help smiling.

They drove through the gate, down the club's long driveway, and Ida found herself looking at it all through her mother's eyes. It was like a well-tended cemetery, a landscape meant to subdue rather than stir. A row of coconut trees guarded the vast front lawn and there was a bed of roses in the center of the lawn. A flagpole bearing the Union Jack stood in front of the blue-and-white clubhouse whose jalousie doors were open to the breeze.

When they walked in, the chatter turned crisp, then stopped altogether. The only sound was the swooshing around of the ceiling fan.

'So much breeze,' Esme said, 'you could catch cold in here.'

'My wife, Esme,' Eli said to the club manager and loud enough for everyone to hear. That was how he always introduced her, even though they were not legally married.

There was a look of shock on some faces, impolite stares from others, then a tense return to their conversations. *Like they never saw a dark-skinned person before*, Ida thought. She was impressed by her mother's composure, and she remembered that as far as Esme was concerned there were only two kinds of people in the world: those with 'broughtupsy' and those without. Ida thought her mother looked as good as any of the women there in spite of her deteriorating health. Her skin was flawless, and her quiet Chinese eyes made her face quite striking. Most of all, Ida noticed, she was impeccably dressed in a blue linen dress and comfortable navy-blue shoes – not seeming at all 'dressed up,' which one might expect of a woman going to such an elite club for the first time. She felt proud of her mother.

Eli was popular with the waiters, especially one named Devon with whom he often talked politics. Devon approached Esme. 'Miss Joseph, ma'am,' he said, 'can I offer you some lemonade or tea?'

'No, thank you. I will just go out and watch Ida. They must have a bench or something outside where I can sit down?'

'Hot outside, Esme. You will get tired.'

'I have my umbrella for shade an' a book if I get tired watchin' her. I'm awright.'

Eli left because he had some business in town. Esme sat all morning in the shade of a lignum vitae tree. She watched Ida for a while and then grew absorbed in her novel. Ida noticed that at some point she had put her book away and was watching her again. She thought her mother might be ready to leave, and she rode over to her.

Earlier a waiter had brought out a folding table with a drink and a plate of little sandwiches for Esme. She hadn't touched the sandwiches.

'Coocoomba,' she said, pronouncing 'cucumber' the Jamaican way and waving her hand in scorn. Ida knew her mother would enjoy describing these pitiful sandwiches to her friends later.

Esme patted the empty space on the bench beside her. 'Come sit with me, darling.'

Affectionate words were rare for Esme and they always had a magnetic effect on Ida. She was immediately at her side.

'Aunt Carmen is coming from New York to stay for a while and help out.'

'You going back to the hospital?'

'No, I don't think so.' She stopped for a moment. 'You're almost a grown woman.'

'Yes, Mama,' Ida murmured politely. She knew there was something else.

Esme took a deep breath. 'Sometimes I wonder how a woman's life can mash-up so easy. I believe what the Bible says, but it seems to me like we get enough punishment already for Eve's stupidness. Look Myrtle's sister, her baby no have no father. All the same,' she sighed thoughtfully, 'no father is better than a bad father. I praying you will marry a good man.'

'I'm going to marry Errol.' She blurted it out and was immediately sorry.

'Stop this nonsense!' Esme said.

'Why you call it nonsense?' Ida asked.

'He is a movie star! Lawd help me, you livin' in a dream-world. Dr Hastings's son, Victor, he likes you so much, an' he goin' be a doctor like his father. An' look at Clive – anybody can see him have a big future. You're a lovely girl, and you can choose from the very best in the country. Doctor, lawyer, an' if Jamaica ever get independence, you could even be a government minister's wife one day. You don't see that?'

No, Ida didn't see. She said nothing. She knew that if she persisted in arguing, her mother would ridicule her and her hopes.

Her eyes rested on a group of English boys and girls passing by as they made their way to the polo field. They were laughing and talking among themselves and did not seem to notice her or her mother.

'I'm going for another ride,' she said.

'Go on, then.' Esme sounded defeated.

Ida felt bad for her then, but she felt bad for herself too. Her eyes welled up. The tears blurred everything in front of her, and she rode and jumped recklessly as if she didn't care whether or not she fell, but Pearl knew where she was going and got her safely over the bars.

7

'Commander' Nigel Fletcher

Ida was home for Easter and went with her father to pick up Errol in Oracabessa, a coastal town about an hour's drive from Port Antonio. Errol had been spending a few days there with some English friends.

'How very nice to meet you,' Nigel Fletcher said to Ida, and his voice and handshake felt truly welcoming to her. His wife, Denise, however, seemed standoffish.

Nigel was a tall Englishman with the alert stance of a hunting dog. Ida thought there was something un-English about his style, with his colorful shirt and the fragrant brilliantine in his hair. He was handsome in a long-faced, aristocratic sort of way. The bridge of his nose was remarkable, starting between his brows and flush with his forehead, reminding Ida of a face on a Roman coin.

Ida hadn't seen Errol in almost a year. She was a little nervous about what he would think of her new hairstyle; she'd cut her waist-length hair to a more fashionable shoulder-length style.

'You're all grown up – and look at your hair.' He hugged her tightly and stroked her hair.

Ida smelled liquor and, beneath that, his own smell, a smell that reminded her of soil around uprooted plants except that because it was his smell it was nicer than that. He stood back to get a better look at her, then turned to his friends.

'Isn't she ravishing? Doesn't she remind you of Liz Taylor?'

'I was going to say Claudette Colbert,' Nigel said.

'Who, by the way, is coming to visit us next week,' his wife said. 'You'll miss her, Errol. We'll have Noël over to make a foursome.'

'Noël? Replace me?'

'Not sure he'll quite fit in your knickers,' she said, and they all laughed.

'I should think not! But Noël's a good sport.'

Ida knew they were talking about the writer Noël Coward, who lived not far from there along the coast. They started chatting about other friends they all had in common until Nigel remembered that Eli and Ida were still standing. 'I beg your pardon. Do sit down. Mr Joseph, what can I get you? We're having Cuba libres, otherwise known as rum-an'-cola. Will that do?' He turned to Ida. 'And what about you, young lady?' Ida accepted a Coca-Cola.

She thought Nigel was staring at her oddly and then realized that he looked at everyone that way. One of his eyes seemed not to work as well as the other; it seemed inward-looking. Later her father described it as a 'wandering eye,' but Ida mistakenly heard this as 'wondering eye' and always thought of it that way.

She'd already heard quite a bit about Nigel Fletcher. He'd had a top post in the British Secret Service. On a postwar assignment he had come to Jamaica for a conference and had liked it so much that he'd retired, though he was only in his midthirties, and built a house there. He was known up and down the coast for his hobbies: flying his small plane and deep-sea fishing. He enjoyed lassoing sharks and then releasing them. The Jamaicans in the district called him 'Commander,' maybe because of his British war background. Ida thought the title suited him.

But she thought his house was odd. It was hardly more than a cabin, a squat wood-and-tile thing with windows set so high that it was hard to see out except through the open doorway. There was no indoor plumbing and so a bathtub had been placed under a coconut tree in the back garden. The best part of the house, as far as she could tell, was the flagstone patio outside, shaded by casuarinas, with a view of the surrounding cliffs and sea.

She was disturbed by the paintings and photographs of snakes around the house. She had a phobia about reptiles and couldn't even bear the sight of small garden lizards. One large photograph showed Nigel with a boa constrictor coiled around his arm. She prayed there was no pet snake around.

A new bottle of rum was opened and passed around the table at lunch. The meal was very Jamaican, thanks to their cook, Beryl: black-crab soup, plantain, bread pudding with guavas. Ida ate heartily; so did the men, but Denise, who said Jamaican food didn't agree with her, had a ham sandwich. Ida got the feeling Denise wasn't fond of Jamaica.

After lunch Nigel served coffee with a lot of ceremony, explaining, among other things, how the beans had been roasted, ground, and then percolated twice. It had never occurred to Ida that a cup of coffee could be a topic of conversation. He passed around some of the coffee beans and talked about their distinctive color.

This got Eli and Errol rhapsodizing about the complexions of Jamaican women (and Ida noticed more rum being poured). Errol said something about 'Chinese mixed with Black.'

'We call that Jamaica Royal,' Eli told him.

'Jamaica Royal!' Errol repeated. 'What a marvelous country!' He broke into a song that sounded familiar to Ida, about a brown-skin girl and her baby, but he was tipsy and he got the words wrong.

> *Daddy's gone away*
> *On a big white ship*
> *An' if he won't come back*
> *Then sell the damn baby*

'That's awful!' Denise said but laughed too. She had short blond hair and almost translucent blue eyes, and she wore a close-fitting top that showed off bountiful breasts; the rest of her body was long, narrow, and shapeless. Ida gathered that Nigel and Denise had recently gotten married, though they'd been friends for many years.

Eli went out of the room for a moment, and Ida felt as if she'd been left by herself in a foreign country.

Denise reached over to Errol with her foot and began rubbing his leg playfully. Her eyes fell teasingly on her husband, who showed no reaction. Errol was leaving for the States the next day and Denise asked him, 'Can't I please please please go to California with you?'

'We're still on our honeymoon,' Nigel pretended to chide.

Errol looked over at Ida and said, 'Ida's quite a horse-woman. I've nicknamed her Ida-Rider.'

Denise shot a puzzled glance at Ida, trying to ascertain whether she was worthy of such attention.

'And she's grown astonishingly pretty while I've been gone,' Errol continued.

'A nymph,' Nigel said, wagging his finger at Errol. 'Be careful.' This caused a new burst of laughter.

Ida got up and went over to look at some books on a shelf.

'Now look what you've done!' Denise tossed a cushion at her husband.

Facing the bookshelf, Ida blinked away hot tears. She thought the Fletchers were the most detestable people she'd ever met, and of the two of them, Denise was the most hideous.

'Bella Vista will be finished in March,' she heard Errol say, 'and then I'll be here for good.'

'I can't wait,' Denise said. 'I suppose it's a real house with bathrooms and a proper stove.'

'Denise doesn't appreciate the rustic charm of Oracabessa,' Nigel explained.

'Has Nigel told you he wants to live here all year-round and write books?'

Errol said, 'That's what I plan to do at Bella Vista.'

'What? Write? You?' Denise seemed surprised.

'Why shouldn't we write?' Nigel asked. 'Noël writes.'

'He also reads,' she sneered.

Eli came back in and said they should probably leave if Errol wanted to get to Navy Island before dark. While Errol went to get his bags, Eli complimented the Fletchers on the wonderful view from the patio. There was not much else about the house that one could praise.

Ida had taken a book off the shelf and was pretending to be absorbed in it — a leather-bound volume of Conrad's stories, inscribed 'To my darling Nigel with love, Denise.'

Nigel came over to her and, assuming Ida knew nothing about literature, began to tell her who Conrad was; he described him as an adventure writer and asked her if she liked books.

'I've read *The Secret Sharer* but not these,' Ida said somewhat haughtily, fed up with the Fletchers and their sense of their own superiority. The truth was she'd only seen *The Secret Sharer* in a schoolbook anthology.

'Take it,' he said.

Ida looked at him, surprised.

'Oh, go on. Denise knows it's too highbrow for me.'

Eli had a camera with him and wanted to take pictures of everyone. He took several, and then Nigel offered to take some that included Eli. So they all posed, smiling and laughing, as though they were the closest of friends.

Eli wanted one of Errol and Ida.

Errol leaned in toward Ida and put his arm around her; it was like poses she'd seen of couples on honeymoons. He kissed her cheek, a kiss that was meant to be small but turned out big, drunk, and messy, with his lips sliding across her mouth and down to her chin. They were all laughing and joking, so no one seemed to notice except her. Errol didn't even seem to notice.

When they got in the car, Denise leaned into the window where Errol sat, giving him an eyeful of her bosom.

'Naughty boy, what are you looking at?' she crooned.

'Can't a cat look at a queen?' he flirted with her.

''Bye. Come again,' Denise said to Eli, 'and bring your little Jamaican girl too.'

Jamaican girl.

On the way back to Port Antonio, the words of songs came to Ida, beginning with the one Errol had sung earlier: 'Brown-skin Gal' then 'Matilda', about the girl who stole her man's money and went to Venezuela. Jamaican girls, it seemed to her, had no luck. When they were bad, they ran away; when they were good, men ran from them. What sort of Jamaican girl was she going to be?

As a child she had been intrigued by a newspaper clipping that her father kept: 'Miss Jamaica 1938, cutting a ribbon at the opening of the Glasgow Exhibition, Scotland.' A Jamaican girl. Did her father know this Miss Jamaica? He said he kept the picture because she was pretty and had come second in the Miss World contest, and because Glasgow was such a beautiful city. The beauty queen's name was not printed, and Ida could hardly distinguish her features; she saw only that she was dark-haired and fair-skinned – a bit like Ida herself. Hundreds of balloons were being released over Glasgow, and Miss Jamaica 1938 had had the honor of cutting the ribbon that released them. Ida had become preoccupied with her for a while and with the Scottish city which she hoped to one day visit; she'd even given the beauty queen a name – Joan – and Joan had become her imaginary friend.

Once she'd asked her father what had become of Miss Jamaica 1938. 'Oh, she married an Englishman and lives abroad now,' he'd said. Ida had been glad to hear that. For a Jamaican girl, she hadn't ended up badly.

Ida had looked forward to seeing Errol but the Fletchers had ruined it, making her feel sullen and uninteresting. She felt like that too when Errol was with Baron Von Ausberg and his other friends. She tried to imagine where she would fit in as a grown woman – in the Jamaica of people like the Fletchers or in that less glamorous world sketched by her mother, the one where she might marry a Jamaican like Clive or some other promising young Jamaican man. But wasn't it her life and up to her to choose? For some reason she remembered her grandmother Oni asking her playfully, 'Are you a mongoose or a girl?' Ida felt there was a lesson in the riddle, but since she always answered 'girl', she wasn't sure what the lesson was.

While the two men talked up front, she listened, watching the back of Errol's head and enjoying his voice. She heard her father telling Errol about the movie theatre. The land had been bought and the building was about to proceed, but Errol still hadn't contributed any of the money he'd promised toward the venture. Eli's brothers, who had invested in it, had begun to nag Eli about the movie star's share.

'Most of my money's still tied up in this new house,' Errol said.

'I know, man. Don't worry. I lookin' after the business side till you ready.'

'It's a marvelous idea, Eli. I'm one hundred percent behind you. If you can just wait till the house is finished—'

'Yes, man.'

Then they talked about the Fletchers. This was Denise's second marriage; she had been married before to an English lord who had died, and she had a three-year-old son, Martin, from that marriage. Errol talked about his own marriages and divorces and the children that he hardly ever saw.

'When I see you and Ida together, I know I'm missing a lot,' he said.

'A child is a wonderful thing,' Eli agreed.

'I've had a bad run,' he began to say, 'but I'm feeling hopeful, Eli. Very hopeful. Maybe there's a good husband somewhere inside me. I can't go on drifting like this.'

'It took me a while an' I mek plenty mistakes too in my time. But it come out awright in the end.'

'Well, let's hope it'll turn out all right for me too.'

He was building a house here; he wanted to get married and have children. Suddenly Ida leaned forward, pulled his head back, and planted a kiss on his cheek.

'Hey!' he cried out. 'What are you up to, Ida-Rider?'

There was a sharp turn in the road ahead of them. A girl was standing there waiting for the bus. It all happened fast. A truck, speeding around the corner, threw her across the road and then headed straight toward their car. Eli swerved out of the way just in time. Their car went off the side of the road into the bushes, but it didn't turn over or hit anything; they weren't hurt.

People came running down the mountainside to see what had happened.

'Mek way, mek way,' Eli said with authority, and the small crowd parted to let them through.

'It's Myrtle's sister!' Ida said.

Her head was at a strange angle to her body like a broken doll. The rest of her was strangely intact. Was it really Larice? Ida noticed that she was not as dirty or unkempt as usual; she wore a clean skirt and satiny blouse and even carried a handbag as if she were going somewhere important. Errol knelt over her and felt her pulse. He shook his head.

'The son of a bitch never even stop,' Eli said.

Errol led Ida out of the crowd. They leaned against the

car, waiting for Eli, who had taken it upon himself to organize the crowd and delegate duties. The sun was low in the sky. Shadows and spots of light played across the road.

'You knew her?' Flynn asked quietly.

'She's my friend's sister. She has a baby boy named Derek.'

'Are you cold?' He saw that she was clutching herself around the shoulders. 'I've got a jacket in my bag.'

'No, it's all right.'

The sun had drawn back behind the trees, and the day sagged around them.

The police arrived and Eli talked to them for a while and then returned to the car. Ida didn't want to leave Larice lying there. She thought about Myrtle and Mrs Tate and the baby Derek.

'Nothing more we can do,' Eli said gently.

As they drove they talked about how narrowly they had escaped the accident. Flynn tried to cheer them up by telling them about some of his other narrow escapes: from boats, planes, film sets, and the bedroom windows of married women.

It wasn't until they had dropped him off at the Somerset that Eli realized his camera was missing. 'Dem scavengers-dem,' he hissed, 'Dem woulda steal clothes from the dead girl if I wasn't there. I don't know what dis island comin' to.'

What dis island coming to. It was the kind of remark no one was supposed to take seriously. But Ida did that day. The offhand phrase added another layer of gloom to an already disturbing day that had included the Fletchers' haughty airs and the awful ending of Larice's life.

That night before she fell asleep, she thought about Errol.

She couldn't remember exactly what he had said or done in the wake of Larice's death, but she began to feel an anchoring peace as she recalled them sitting quietly together, not hiding their distress from one another and not minding as the day grew darker around them.

8

A Marriage and a Death

Errol returned three months later, newly married. His house on Navy Island was finished, and he and his American wife, Paulette, planned to spend as much time as possible there while maintaining the cattle ranch just outside Port Antonio. The day Errol brought his new wife to Plumbago Road, the Josephs were having a party to celebrate Eli's birthday.

Ida greeted Errol coolly. He noticed and so did his wife. She glanced at her husband and raised her eyebrows with amusement as if to say, 'Now, what's all this about?' Flynn was facing new accusations of statutory rape, and Paulette was taking the whole thing in her stride: the bad jokes, the bad press.

Esme wasn't well. She spent the whole time sitting on the sofa. Paulette sat nearby and attended to her, getting up now and then to bring her a drink of water or something to eat.

'A real lady,' Eli said later, 'and pretty. Remind me of Grace Kelly.'

'Him find a good, sensible woman finally,' Esme agreed. 'She wants to learn how to cook Jamaican food. I goin' write up some recipes for her.'

Paulette was unlike any of the women Ida had seen with Errol. To begin with, she was a grown-up, and she was courteous and unpretentious. There was nothing tawdry or stupid about her, nothing to dislike. Ida was miserable.

She did not want to speak to anyone about Errol's marriage, especially her mother. Esme was the only one who knew how high Ida's hopes had been, and now Ida was deeply humiliated at having had those hopes. The world had not collapsed, and Ida resented that – that nothing and no one was adversely affected by the marriage except her. She went around in angry silence, barely answering 'yes' or 'no' to her mother's questions.

One day Esme said to her, 'I don't feel well enough to go church by myself. Come with me.'

Ida could think of no way of excusing herself. She was not so self-involved as to have lost sight of her mother's illness. Esme was able to eat fewer and fewer things and subsisted mainly on clear soups. She rarely left the house.

After the service they stood outside the church waiting for Eli to pick them up. Ida noticed how loosely the dress hung on her mother, and that her face was quite thin under her hat. There were purplish shadows under her eyes, yet Ida saw more clearly than ever the beautiful face that had attracted her father.

'I don't like to see you actin' so stupid over that man,' Esme said quietly and not without sympathy. 'But you can learn something from the disappointment. In time—'

Esme stopped, and Ida thought she was going to say, 'In time you will forget him' – forget *him?* But her mother didn't say anything else.

~

When Esme's sister, Carmen, arrived from New York her visit brought a welcome, distracting change. To Ida she seemed very American and her suitcases had that interesting smell all foreigners seemed to have. Ida hadn't seen her for many years, and she was struck by how different the two sisters looked: Esme was dark; Carmen was fair. Esme had short, kinky hair; Carmen had long, straight hair like her Chinese father.

For Ida, it was like having a sister of her own in the house. Aunt Carmen shared her room, and when Ida was home from boarding school they stayed up late in bed looking at the fashions in *McCall's* and listening to the Perry Como records Carmen had brought with her. It was Aunt Carmen who taught Ida to protect her complexion by never going out without a hat and a pair of gloves. Ida thought at first, since Carmen was a nurse, that this sun protection was for a medical reason, but she learned otherwise: 'Why would you want to darken this pretty-pretty skin?' Carmen made her rub lime juice on her knees and elbows to bleach the dark spots.

She was a fast-moving, efficient person. Ida never saw her hands idle. She also smoked more cigarettes than Ida thought humanly possible. She had made a good living as a hospital nurse in New York, then had gone into private nursing; now she had come to nurse her sister, who had developed diabetes along with her other mysterious, debilitating illness.

Carmen accompanied Esme to Kingston, where she was admitted to the university hospital. When they returned a week later Esme was helped into her bed, and she never left it again. The doctor had 'opened her up,' as Aunt Carmen explained later, and found a terminal cancer.

Eli refused to believe it. He talked with Esme about how

the Palace Theatre would soon be finished; there would be a grand opening and she would be well enough to attend and wear the sapphire necklace he had recently bought her. He convinced himself that Esme would improve using the teas and medicines Oni provided. 'They don't know anything, these doctors. Chu! Every single one of them says something different.'

Ida wanted to be hopeful too, but one day the Methodist pastor came and spent an hour alone at Esme's bedside. After the pastor left, Esme asked for Ida.

Eli ushered Ida into the room. Then he joined Aunt Carmen on the veranda so Esme could talk privately with her daughter.

Ida began to cry as soon as she sat down beside her mother on the bed.

'Don't cry, darling. I'm going back to my Maker.'

'No.'

'Yes. Soon.'

But for almost a month she lay there, growing thinner, her face becoming another face, skull-like. In the meantime, Eli talked about the grand opening of the Palace Theatre (the building was almost finished) and the beautiful gown Esme's dressmaker would make her for the occasion. Carmen and Ida would exchange glances as he prattled on crazily.

Oni hitched her horse, Mankind, to a cart and came down from the mountains to stay for a while. She had bush-teas to ease Esme's pain but realized there was nothing more she could do for her. She turned her attention to Eli, giving him ganja tea for his nerves. 'Him *draumatize*,' she said to Carmen and Ida.

'But what we can do? He won't listen, not even to Esme,' Carmen said.

Oni said, 'Catch 'im when 'im collapse.'

Oni was also concerned about Ida. 'You need tonic,' she said and made her drink a putrid mixture of molasses and Irish moss. She stayed for a week, which nearly drove Carmen crazy. Oni called Carmen's cigarettes 'ashes' and told her that if she had to smoke something, ganja would be better for her health. 'Why she don't go back a-bush?' Carmen complained.

But Ida liked having Oni there. One sunny afternoon Ida saw her grandmother sitting in the backyard staring at the mountains. Ida had never seen her looking so sad or tired. When she saw Ida, she smiled. 'So, now, are you a mongoose or a girl?' she asked, pulling her close. The fabric of Oni's dress was thin and soft with age, and she smelled like many trees.

'Mongoose,' Ida tried.

'Mongoose! Then you ha fe come back a-mountain with me,' Oni teased.

The day that Oni was leaving to go back up the mountain, Ida shook the bangles on her arm: 'Look – silver. No gold. The pirates can't hurt me.'

Oni slipped one of the bangles off Ida's wrist to examine it more closely. 'Sometimes bird ha fe learn how fe swim.'

A little later, sitting in the cart and saying her good-byes, she told Ida, 'Tell Mr Flynn good-evening. I sorry to miss him but I don't want moonlight catch me a-road.'

'He's not here. He's in America.'

'Him not in America,' Oni said, 'an' you just a girl, not a big woman.'

About an hour later, Errol and his wife arrived unexpectedly at the house with flowers for Esme. They had returned to the island that morning.

Paulette was noticeably pregnant. She sat in Esme's room, talking with her, and Errol waited in the living room.

'Get Mr Flynn something cool to drink,' Esme told Ida.

He didn't see her at first when she came into the room with the lemonade. He had his chin in his hands and was looking down at the floor. As soon as he saw her, he recovered and smiled. 'How are you doing, Ida-Rider?' he asked.

'I'm fine.'

He made small talk with her but still seemed uneasy. She wondered for a moment if it was her mother's illness that perturbed him, but she didn't think that was it. *He should be happier now with a new baby coming,* Ida thought.

Paulette invited Ida to come over to the ranch the next day to go riding. 'I'm not doing much riding in my state,' she gestured toward her growing belly, 'and Errol doesn't like to ride alone.'

'That's very kind,' Esme said. 'It will be a nice change for her.'

As Ida watched the couple leave, she wondered if they were truly happy together. She could think of no reason for them not to be. And yet something didn't seem right. They were not what she would describe as mismatched, but they weren't well-matched either.

When Ida visited the Flynns the next day she found Karl Von Ausberg there. It upset her to learn that the two men had already gone riding together before her arrival. 'But I'll take a little jaunt with you in a minute,' Errol promised her. He said she could try out the new horse, Gentleman Jim.

'Go easy on him,' he told her. 'None of your circus tricks, now.'

The men stood by the stable doors talking while Ida rode around the corral. She heard Errol talking excitedly about a map he'd gotten and wondered if he was going on a sailing trip.

She rode around and around waiting for Errol. Now and then he looked up and smiled at her, then went back to his animated conversation with Karl. Karl didn't pay her any attention at all.

She began to feel restless. *None of your circus tricks*, he'd told her.

She galloped a short distance away and then turned around to see if Errol was looking. She saw him glance at her, and she took off as fast as she could, jumping the garden wall.

'Ida!' she heard him call out. Soon she heard him following on his own horse.

'What are you doing?' He jumped down and took the reins from her. 'He's not a jumper. You could have broken your neck. And the horse's neck too.'

She dismounted and looked up at him. In the past he had always been amused at her pranks, and amusement was what she expected to see now in his face. But there was something else, involuntary, unchecked. He seemed to know how she felt about him and to find her, with all her precocious desire, appealing. Then his expression changed to something muddled, almost panicky.

'What's the matter with you, Ida?'

That wasn't the response she'd wanted. It had gone all wrong.

'Is it your mother?' He had relapsed into his fatherly feeling for her.

She said, 'I don't know,' and then 'Yes,' and then she felt

dreadful because she hadn't been thinking at all about her mother. She started to cry.

He hugged her awkwardly, then said, 'Let's go back. Paulette will know what to do.'

Paulette offered her a cup of tea but she said no, thank you. She wanted to go home. So they called a taxi for her.

As she was about to leave, she saw Errol chatting with Karl. The map that Errol was so excited about was spread out on a table in front of them, and neither of them noticed that she was leaving. Ida had glanced at the map earlier; it was different from other maps she'd seen, prettier, with illustrations of ships and people.

'Men and their little toys,' Paulette said to her in a conspiratorial tone. 'He got it last week and can't think about anything else.'

'Is he sailing somewhere?' Ida thought it might be a nautical thing.

'No. It's a very old map, beautiful but utterly useless.' Paulette smiled as if she and Ida shared a joke at the men's expense.

Ida didn't want to go to school the next day. 'I want to stay home with Mama,' she told her father.

There was a charity lunch at the Somerset Hotel that day, and Eli had tickets. Ida suggested that he take Aunt Carmen. 'Don't worry. I can take care of Mama.'

Ida tried to feed Esme some strained callaloo soup, but she would only take a spoonful. Afterward Ida sat in a large armchair across from her mother, feeling no need to talk, content just to be there. They stayed like that all through the afternoon, and then suddenly Esme's voice rose from the bed: 'What you want for you next birthday?'

The question surprised Ida. After a while she said, 'A trip to Glasgow.'

Esme said, 'Hhmm. You must ask you father. You must ask him for what you want.'

The sun had set, leaving its glow along the windowsill but darkening the rest of the room. Ida wondered if she should turn on the lamp.

Esme cried out, 'Wha' mek so fe me, mek so fe you, bamba yay!'

Ida drew back into the shadow of the armchair. Her mother sounded crazy, her words half reprimand, half lament.

In a while, Esme spoke like herself again, calmly: 'He doesn't always remember things—'

Ida knew she was speaking about Eli.

Esme continued, 'That is why I worried about money. Why I saved. Carmen keepin' it in the bank in New York for you. A thousand dollars. In New York, you hear.'

That evening she died.

9

Seduction

Parties. There were many of them, though since she'd had the baby, Paulette didn't like staying up late. Errol couldn't remember when last he and his wife had slept together. Was he just incapable, he wondered, of making a wife — any wife — happy? It was like a curse: conjugal disaster. And again tonight, Paulette had gone to the baby's room. He knew she'd stay there for the rest of the party and right through the night. He didn't care anymore. *Let her go*, he thought. She'd want a divorce soon, like the others. But he wouldn't give up Navy Island. She could go find her own piece of paradise. For once, he had really tried: he had been faithful; he had shared this beautiful home, Bella Vista, with her; and there was the baby girl, Tara. He'd gone into this marriage with so much hope. Paulette had fallen in love with Jamaica just as he had. She'd learned to cook like a Jamaican, even speak like a Jamaican, and she seemed perfectly happy to spend the rest of her life here. She was gracious; everyone loved her — Americans, Jamaicans. When there were guests she seemed more relaxed, cooked a lot, organized day trips, even laughed at his jokes. So they had lots of guests and parties. Then she complained: it was his fault that they never had any privacy between his movies, her movies, and the constant entertaining.

Now, upstairs in the child's room, as if he didn't exist . . .

Maybe he had gone a bit far tonight in his tomfoolery – driving the car into the swimming pool. No one had been hurt, luckily, and it had given the locals something to talk about and write up in the newspaper.

He had left the party and driven down to the boathouse to pick up their friend, Truman Capote, an interesting but irritating little fellow, allergic to everything, even sand. He had to be carried across the beach into the saltwater pool like some sort of invalid (he'd never risk the open sea). Why he kept visiting was a mystery since he didn't like sailing, swimming, or the tropical heat and had to be rushed to the hospital every time he got bitten by a mosquito. And exactly which one of them he was in love with – Errol or Paulette – was hard to tell.

So there was Truman in the car, with his big white hat and those ridiculous canvas shoes he insisted on wearing even in the water. Maybe it was the shoes that had finally done it.

'Hang on, Tru!' Errol had shouted as he'd cut across the lawn and headed straight for the pool. The deep end. It was a first-class rescue effort.

The party was more or less over after that, with the Cadillac still in the pool and Truman taken to his bed, pale and vomiting. Only Nigel and Denise had stayed on, and so had Eli Joseph, who had brought Ida with him to the party.

Errol could tell that this was her first grown-up party. How old was she now – sixteen? She was slightly overdressed in a long evening gown and a sapphire necklace, but he thought she looked lovely, and he made sure to tell her so. Her dress was cut low in front and back. Such beautiful skin color she had; he'd wondered for a moment, looking at her, how he would describe the exact shade – café au lait was too dark, and anyway, it was cliché ... All this was before he'd driven the car into the pool, when he was only half-drunk. He had danced with her to some slow, romantic song, something Andy Williams had made into a hit. She'd scolded him for having drunk too much rum punch and had seemed pleasantly confused when he'd placed his hand against her bare back.

'Your hair looks nice pinned up like this. How long's it going to take to bring it all back down?' he whispered in her ear.

The band started a new song, and he was about to dance with her again when Nigel cut in.

At the end of the party, she fell asleep on one of the lounge chairs. Later her father carried her inside to the sofa.

Nigel and Denise went up to one of the guest rooms, and Karl, who had been upstairs helping with Truman, came down to say good-night. Only Eli stayed up the whole night chatting and drinking with Errol. They talked about the possibility of growing coffee on Navy Island, about the movie Errol wanted to film in Jamaica, and, as in the early days of their friendship, they talked about women.

'Paulette's always angry with me. I can't do anything right.'

'Is how women are right after they have baby. Chu, man, give her time, she soon mellow.'

'I don't know, Eli. I think the flame is out.'

'It will light up again, wait an' see. I tell you, I really miss Esme.' Eli mourned for her all the time, but especially when he went to the Palace Theatre. On opening night, the proudest night of his life, she had not been there to sit in the 'royal box' with him and Ida. His oldest brother had come for the occasion and had called Ida 'a lovely girl.' Neither of his brothers had ever met Esme. 'You finally make it happen, eh, man?' his brother had said, looking around the lobby with its murals of Rudolf Valentino and Mary Pickford. How impressed Esme would have been in her own quiet way (when he'd first met her and told her of the things he wanted to do — own a fleet of buses — a taxi company — she'd said with a certain firmness that had become familiar to him, 'I believe you can do anything you put your mind to, Eli'). Yes, he missed her, even her grumbling. She had been gone now for almost a year.

'I know,' Errol said to console him. But he didn't know. He had never missed anyone. He decided he was like his mother, who had been shockingly unfaithful to his father. He remembered looking for her once when he was a boy and finding her down at the beach with one of her boyfriends. He'd run back home and found his father in his study writing one of his tracts on the platypus or something.

The two men stayed up until morning. Errol felt no need for sleep. The 'dip' in the pool had refreshed him.

Ida heard men's voices when she woke up. She saw her father and Errol on the patio and realized she'd fallen asleep sometime after the car had gone into the pool.

It had happened so fast. She'd seen Errol's head pop up in the water, and then her father and everyone had rushed over to the edge of the pool. Errol had gone back down and pulled out the other man who'd been in the car with him. He looked as though he'd drowned. Someone tried to revive him with brandy and he threw up. The car tipped back and forth for a bit, then sank. A white hat floated on the water, and Ida heard someone say Errol had gone too far this time. For some reason, what caught her attention in all this was Nigel Fletcher; he was the only one not hurrying around trying to be helpful. He sat calmly watching the whole thing. *That is an interesting man*, she thought, but she still wasn't sure she liked him.

'Good morning, beauty.' Errol placed a tired arm around her waist as she came out to the patio. 'Did you sleep well?'

She could see the car at the bottom of the pool.

Her father smiled at her; his eyelids were drooping, unable to fight off sleep. A minute later he was snoring.

'We're the only ones awake on this whole island,' Errol said to her.

'Let's go for a ride,' she suggested. Then, looking down at her party dress and feeling a bit self-conscious, she asked, 'Is there anything I can borrow? I don't think I can manage in this.'

'You probably could,' he said, teasing her, but he got her some of Paulette's riding things.

He let her go ahead of him. They took a favorite path where the bamboo stalks were tall and formed an archway. She could tell he was admiring her. It felt wonderful to perform in front of him, and she raced ahead a bit to make him chase after her. But he didn't. She turned around and watched him ride slowly toward her.

He was tired of chasing and being chased. He just wanted to fill his eyes with her. If he went slowly enough maybe the path would never end and neither would the picture of her, young and welcoming. Her horse seemed impatient, ready for a good run, but that was too bad. He was in no hurry. Ida's eyes were on him – beautiful eyes, large and swimming with a kind of hopefulness he'd seen before. What was he remembering? What did a girl with silky black hair riding a horse in the early morning remind him of?

He caught up with her and they rode together without words. He knew exactly where they were going, where they both wanted to go.

By the river, tender as a kitten, she kissed his forehead, then his cheek. He found her lips and her sweet tongue, oh Lord, her body was delicate and taut like a harp. He was afraid of breaking her.

She felt a crushing pain and was aware of him on top of her, groaning as though he were in pain too. She shut her eyes and listened to the sound of the river. After a while, he rolled off her and onto his back. He looked happy, and he pulled her close to his damp chest. The world continued dreaming.

That morning was the first time Karl Von Ausberg really noticed Ida.

He had become a regular house guest at Bella Vista, partly because he'd become interested in some shipwrecks about an hour's boat ride from Navy Island; they were believed to be Columbus's last two ships, the *Capitana* and *Santiago*. Errol and Paulette were fond of Karl. He had been a generous, loyal friend to them during various crises like Errol's statutory rape trials. Errol relied on his friendship more and more; so did Paulette; and he came and went from Bella Vista more or less like a member of the family.

So the morning after the party, when no one could find Errol and Ida, Karl offered to go look for them.

He saw Ida first, lying by the river. Her hair was out and the sun was shining on her. She looked almost unreal to him, like someone from an ancient myth, and for a few moments he just stood staring at her.

'Will you join us?' Errol's voice rang out from the river.

Ida sprang up. She drew up and hugged her knees in an attempt to cover herself. Her clothes were not at hand. Karl was somewhat amused. She was no longer a dryad, just a mortified schoolgirl.

'No, thanks,' Karl said. 'I've already had my exercise.'

Errol came out of the water, not at all embarrassed by his nakedness, and his nonchalance confused Ida. He was making no effort to hide the fact that they were lovers, and she wondered what that meant. Would everyone find out now?

'Breakfast is ready,' Karl said. 'I'll see you — both — back at the house.'

There was a huge breakfast waiting — plantain, herring, bacon, eggs, johnnycakes, pawpaw, mangos, bananas, and fresh guava nectar. Errol ate hungrily. She was too nervous to have anything but a slice of toast.

We went for a swim. So refreshing, the river water. That was the story they told.

Paulette had taken the baby girl with her to Kingston for the day. Ida was relieved. Errol suggested to Eli that he let Ida spend the day there and go rafting with them.

'You want to stay an' enjoy you'self a little longer, then?'

She couldn't look at her father or even speak. She just nodded.

Karl had finished breakfast and was sitting on the sofa across from them. She saw him looking at her, not in an unpleasant way, but it made her feel unpleasant.

They did not go rafting with the others. Errol took Ida upstairs to one of the guest bedrooms. She noticed a box of cigars and a bottle of aftershave cologne, the same kind her father used, on the dresser and wondered whom they belonged to. He led her over to the bed and began to undress her. She was intrigued by the unfamiliar bedroom but also worried about Paulette coming back home and about what would happen or change now.

He didn't seem to notice her nervousness. He was absorbed in the happy surprise of his own rejuvenation. She felt a little disappointed. It seemed to her that he should not be so lighthearted; the situation was grave – wasn't it? But his enthusiasm and sheer sense of fun gradually began to affect her.

'Good girl, good girl, sweet little poppet,' she heard him whisper. He studied her face with a sort of mischievous intensity as if daring her to enjoy him. She had entrusted him with so much – nakedness, virginity – but had held something back, her capacity for pleasure, and he sensed it. He let her know, in so many ways, that he was willing to do anything, risk anything – even looking ridiculous – to please her. At some point the whole new strangeness of having sex with him passed: this man who was her lover was still Errol. She did trust him. She did.

They stayed in bed all morning. He seemed happier than she'd ever seen him. He said and did hilarious things – made puppets of the different parts of his body, spoke in funny voices, teased her. She grew playful and teasing too, told him that he was full of poppycock, and he burst out laughing.

Around noon they began to get hungry. Errol realized his wife would soon be back. His mood changed. 'My marriage is pointless,' he said, 'and it makes everything else seem pointless too.'

Ida nuzzled against him the way she would nuzzle against a horse, and he seemed grateful and smoothed her hair. She closed her eyes, suddenly tired.

When she woke up, Errol wasn't there. She saw Baron Karl Von Ausberg in the room, standing in front of the mirror with his back to her.

He heard her stirring. 'You fell asleep,' he said as though answering a question. She thought of screaming out for Errol. But then Karl went over to the bathroom door and knocked and Errol came out, wearing a bathrobe. She heard them talking quietly but didn't hear the words. 'We'll be down in a minute,' Errol said, and Karl left.

She felt ill and confused. How long had she slept, and how long had Karl been there? Maybe this was Karl's room.

'Come,' Errol said. 'I'll show you the view.' He handed her his shirt to put on and they went onto the covered terrace. He said nothing to her about Karl and so she told herself his presence hadn't meant anything; it was probably his room they were borrowing, that was all. She was at a loss as to what was or was not an impropriety in the world of lovers. She was happy to be out on the veranda with Errol, and it felt wonderful to wear his shirt; it smelled like him

They were quiet for a while looking beyond the sloping lawns and white bougainvillea at the glistening cove. She imagined Errol and her in the future, having coffee here in the early morning, beginning their day with such a view.

He suddenly said, 'I thought this place would save me.'

She knew he was talking about Jamaica, and Navy Island in particular. She also knew he spoke sincerely. Still, she couldn't help thinking how much he seemed like Errol Flynn the actor speaking lines in a film. He couldn't help it, the theatrical tone, but at that moment it made him seem distant.

'I thought I'd be able to do better. But I'm not doing better. I'm a wreck.' He laughed suddenly and sat down on a large rattan chair. 'An expensive wreck.'

Still looking out at the sea, as if entranced by what he saw, he said to her, 'I don't want you to change. I don't want this place to change.'

She wished he would look at her. To be there and alluring like the view, like the sea in the quiet of the morning, she could try to do that if it was what he wanted, but she wanted to be with him wherever he happened to be, not just here in this tiny Shangri-la.

She moved closer to him, and he patted her head. 'Let's get dressed,' he said with forced cheerfulness.

Paulette returned while Ida and Flynn were eating lunch by the pool. 'Where's everyone?' she asked.

'Gone rafting. How was Port Antonio?' He began playing with the baby girl.

'She's all tired out,' Paulette said, taking her from him and going inside.

Ida felt uncomfortable, and for the first time in her life, she disliked herself. It was impossible for her to dislike Paulette.

On the boat later, taking her back home, Errol grew affectionate again and pulled her onto his lap. 'My dear girl,' he said, 'you're saving my life!' He told her he was going to shoot a film in Jamaica that would show the beautiful marine life of the island. It would be about a sea expedition. The first part had already been shot in California along the Pacific coast. He wanted her to be in it. 'But you'll have to learn how to swim, Ida-Rider.'

In Port Antonio he stopped the taxi outside a jewelry store. 'Wait here,' he told the driver and Ida. He came back about fifteen minutes later.

'For you,' he said, presenting her with a small jewelry box. Inside was a gold charm bracelet with a miniature sailboat.

She kissed him lightly on the lips, but he drew her close, kissing her hard and long, surprising her. He was too large to sit comfortably on the back seat of the small taxi, and the energy of his caress, which was more like an eruption, rocked the whole vehicle.

That night Ida dreamed of her mother and grandmother. She and her mother approached Oni's house up on the mountain. Oni came out to the gate and asked Ida, 'Are you a girl or a mongoose?'

An obeah-man found a baby mongoose in the grass. He took the little mongoose home and, since he had no children, he used his obeah to turn the mongoose into a child, a little girl. He loved the girl like a daughter and protected her from everything that could sting, bite, or poison her. When she grew up, he decided to look for the very best husband for her, and that meant the strongest, because he knew he was getting old and would soon die, and he wanted to make sure she was always protected.

So he spoke to the Sun: 'You are the strongest, please marry my daughter.'

But the Sun, though he would have liked to marry the beautiful girl, replied, 'I am not the strongest. The Cloud is stronger than I am because it can cover me.'

So the obeah-man went and spoke to the Cloud: 'You are the strongest. Will you marry my daughter?'

The Cloud also declined and said, 'The Wind is stronger than I am because it can blow me across the sky.'

Then the obeah-man went to the Wind: 'Wind, you are the strongest. Will you take my daughter as your bride?'

But the Wind also had to refuse. 'Ask the Mountain,' the Wind said. 'The Mountain is stronger than I am because as hard as I might blow, I will never be able to move it.'

The obeah-man went to the mountain. He was sure this was the strongest one of all. He called to the great Mountain, 'You are the strongest in the whole world. Will you marry my daughter?'

To the obeah-man's surprise the Mountain answered, 'I am not the strongest. The Mongoose is stronger than I am because he can dig a hole in me.'

So the obeah-man took his daughter to the little Mongoose who lived in a hole inside the mountain. He knocked — rat-a-tat — on the mountain side. The mongoose stuck his head out.

'You are the strongest of the strong,' the obeah-man said. 'Here is my beautiful daughter.'

But the Mongoose, who fell in love with her right away, shook his head sadly and said, 'She will never be able to fit in this hole with me.'

So the obeah-man turned the girl back into a mongoose, and after that the boy and girl mongoose lived happily together in the hole in the mountain.

'But I don't want to live in a hole,' Ida said in the dream, pulling away from her mother and Oni.

Three days went by and Ida didn't hear from Errol. Finally she telephoned Bella Vista. Karl answered. Errol, he said, had gone to California and wouldn't be back for a month. Paulette and the baby had gone too.

'Is there anything I can do for you, Ida?'

His words were courteous but sounded hurtful to her.

'No, thank you,' she said just as courteously, and then she

slammed down the phone like the temperamental women she'd seen in movies. But it was too loud and dramatic a gesture for her small house.

10

Catastrophe at Sea

August came. School would soon begin again for Ida. It was to be her last year of high school and she had important exams ahead, but all she could think about was Errol. He had been in California for five weeks, and she hadn't heard from him.

She threw herself into any superficial thing that seemed connected to sharing a life with him. She taught herself to cook, or rather tried to, following the recipes her mother had written out so neatly (there had been some idea once of her writing a Jamaican cookbook); it was a torment for her father who had to eat the oversalted, undercooked meals. She tidied and decorated rooms in the house with the thought of Errol visiting her there.

When Errol returned, she went to meet him at his private airfield. He had asked Karl to bring her there. Paulette and Tara had stayed in America.

'Ida-Rider!' He picked her up and swung her around as easily as he had when she was a girl of thirteen. She saw his eyes laughing and warm as he looked at her, and she almost cried with relief.

'Did you hear? Paulette and I have separated,' he murmured to her. He gave her no time to respond to this news. In a completely different, exuberant tone he asked her, 'Are you ready to be in the movies?'

The very next day his crew arrived to begin shooting the Jamaican sequences of his sailing expedition film.

At first he planned to have Ida play one of the native dancers, but because of her light skin she didn't fit in with the others. He decided to create a scene for her at Blue Hole: she would be the girl that Errol discovered swimming alone in the lagoon. There was no time for her to learn how to swim, so they had to shoot most of her scene in the shallow end of his swimming pool. To get that distinctive turquoise color of the lagoon, Flynn put green dye in the pool. It dyed Ida's skin, and she couldn't wash it off, not even by scrubbing. She tried one of Oni's bush-baths and that didn't work. Eventually she had to bathe in turpentine.

He was on a tight budget. The cameramen had been hired for four weeks only, so the filming went on day and night.

His parents joined him. His father, a zoologist, was part of the crew and was helping to identify much of the marine life. Errol said his mother was there for the sole purpose of driving him crazy. Between the heavy shooting and his parents being there, Ida didn't have a chance to be alone with Errol except for one afternoon when he made love to her unexpectedly and quickly.

Eli had a lawyer draw up a contract — a 'dramatic agreement' — whereby Flynn, as producer, was to pay Ida a hundred dollars for her role in the film. It seemed an incredible amount of money to her. Flynn was a bit taken aback at being presented with the contract; none of the other Jamaicans appearing in the film had contracts. He bantered with Eli, and then finally signed it with an amused expression on his face.

Another Jamaican was to play a significant role in the film. His name was Orville Brown, but everyone called him Brasso because of the coppery sheen of his skin. He was a muscular man, very proud of his physique. His face was more interesting than handsome, with a high, wide forehead and narrow, almost pointed chin. He was well known along the north coast as a tourist guide, driver, and gigolo. Errol's mother described Brasso as 'a Bantu-of-all-trades.' He liked going around shirtless, wearing only tight cut-off jeans, and he was happy to pose for photographs, especially with female tourists.

Karl was the one who had originally picked up Brasso. Brasso had hung around him for about a month, offering himself as errand boy, guide, drinking partner, whatever suited Karl. When Karl didn't need him anymore, he drifted over to Flynn, who paid him now and then to take friends rafting on the Rio Grande.

When the shooting started, Brasso went around Port Antonio bragging about how Flynn was making him a movie star and paying him a lot of money. He had big plans to move to Hollywood (Mrs Goodman, Clive's mother, told Ida, 'I hope he reach there fe true because him bottom get too big for this place'). He played himself in the film, poised handsomely on a raft going downriver. He also had a technical job as Flynn's 'wildlife assistant.'

There were live crocodiles in the film.

Errol, with the help of his father and Brasso, captured the crocodiles at Black River in the southern part of the island.

He had their jaws sewn together with wire and they were kept chained at one end of the yacht. He planned to shoot scenes where he would fight the creatures, Tarzan-like, underwater.

Ida thought this was odd since the animals were not saltwater creatures. But no one asked for her opinion. She told herself it was a movie so anything was possible. However, as she had a terrible fear of all reptiles, she stayed as far as possible from the crocodiles.

She was not having a good time on the set; in fact, most of the time she felt miserable. There were too many people; she hardly got to speak to Errol. She didn't know what was going on most of the time with people moving around heavy equipment, and she kept worrying about tripping on the cords and cables.

She tried to gain an appreciation for the underwater life that Flynn was filming. It wasn't easy; apart from not being able to swim, she'd never been comfortable on boats. She wished he'd written a horse-riding scene for her.

His father, Professor Flynn, was very nice to her and willing to share his knowledge of marine biology. He offered to take her snorkeling. 'We can do it in the shallow water.'

'No.' She was afraid of snorkeling. She agreed, however, to take a glass-bottomed boat out to the reef with him.

He told her the Latin names of the fish and crustaceans while the boatman supplied the local names. She had never imagined anything like the world she saw under there. The colors amazed her – pink, orange, the purest white. It looked like the world of a fairy tale, the fragile fortresses of coral, the translucent sea fans waving, sea anemones and sea lilies (nymphs that some lusty sea god had changed into flowers).

'They're animals, not flowers, and they sting,' Professor Flynn told her. Bright-colored fish darted under them. She began to see why Errol loved diving.

Something bat-like with large wings leapt close to the boat, startling her. 'A stingray,' they said, and at that moment she remembered Oni saying, 'Sometimes bird ha fe learn how fe swim.'

When they got back, she helped to label the coral and crustacea that the divers brought up though she privately felt that they shouldn't disturb so much of the sea floor; the weightless bits of coral seemed to her like spirits. She told Errol this. He smiled, and she felt interesting to him.

One morning she got sick after drinking a glass of orange juice. Then she began throwing up almost every morning.

She asked Myrtle to go with her to Kingston. All the doctors in Port Antonio had known her since childhood and she couldn't bear having any of them confirm what she suspected. She and Myrtle gave the excuse that they were going to a museum in Kingston for a school project. On the way back, Myrtle asked gently, 'Will he marry you?'

She knew what Myrtle was thinking and she was shocked. 'Of course!' She was not like Larice or girls like that. She was the daughter of one of Port Antonio's most important men, and soon she would be known as the exceptionally lovely Jamaican girl whom Errol Flynn had fallen in love with.

'When you goin' tell him?' Myrtle asked.

'He's busy. There're all these people around. I have to wait.'

She didn't tell Myrtle that she was afraid — of what he would think, of what everyone would think. She knew from all the times she'd spent with Oni that there were bush-teas that would end the pregnancy. But it would hurt; she couldn't bear the thought.

When she returned to the set the next day, she saw Errol bustling about giving orders to everyone, and she knew it would be a while before she got to talk to him. In a way she was glad; she could guard the secret in her belly from everyone else's reactions for a while longer.

Nigel and Denise Fletcher joined them on board and brought a lot of liquor. But no one was in much of a party mood. It was the final week of filming, and the crocodiles were not looking well. They wouldn't eat; they were dehydrated and being kept in the hot sun for too many hours of the day. Errol couldn't get them to move or even swish their tails from side to side. He was getting anxious. The underwater battle with the crocodiles was to be the climax of the movie.

He and his father fought over them.

'*Crocodylus acutus*,' his father said. 'They're freshwater creatures, for God's sake. They've been on this island since the days of the dinosaurs and look what you're doing to them!'

One of the crocodiles got so weak that it was taken back to Black River to die.

'What's gotten into him?' Errol asked one day when his father suddenly left the breakfast table in the middle of a conversation.

His father overheard and shouted back, 'What's gotten into *you*?' and walked on purposefully to his temporary marine lab below deck.

Ida was at the breakfast table. She saw Errol raise his eyebrows and shrug.

His mother lit a cigarette: 'It's the crocs he's upset about.'

'Why? He's a scientist. He cuts up animals,' Errol protested.

'After he's anesthetized them.' She studied her son for a moment and then added, 'He's remembering those ducks you tortured.'

'You tortured ducks?' Nigel asked.

Ida was sitting beside Nigel. She could smell his lavender hair pomade and his aftershave lotion through the cigarette smoke. She admired the care he took with his appearance even here on the *Zaca*, with his parted hair and ironed shirts; it seemed to her like a form of politeness.

'It was an experiment,' Flynn said, shrugging it off. Then he seemed amused by the memory and went on, 'Actually, I did it to impress the old man.'

'He was impressed all right,' his mother drawled.

'Do tell,' Nigel said.

'Does it have anything to do with duck à l'orange?' Karl asked.

'You're always thinking about your stomach,' Denise remarked.

'You're always thinking about sex.' Karl's tone was courteous, as usual.

'Which is both lucky and unlucky for me,' Nigel quickly threw in, smiling at his wife.

Denise beamed like a dog that had just brought back a stick; she loved the attention.

'So tell us about these ducks you tormented,' Nigel said.

'Or marinated,' Karl added.

Ida felt certain that she didn't want to hear this story, but before she could excuse herself, Errol began, 'Well, we had a lot of ducks around the yard—'

'Qu-aa-ack!' Mrs Flynn interjected and someone laughed.

'—and I discovered,' Flynn continued, 'that if you fed a duck some fatty pork it would excrete it right away. You could see the whole digestive process from beak to rectum.'

'Charming,' Nigel said.

Errol continued, 'So I came up with the idea of tying a long string — about ten feet — to the piece of pork fat and holding one end of the string while the duck ate and excreted the fat at the other end. Then I fed it to the next duck . . .'

Everyone except Ida was smoking. The pungent vapors settling around the listeners seemed to hold them together in a trance.

'. . . so finally I'd made a live necklace of ducks, joined beak to bum.'

No one said anything for a few moments. Errol poured more vodka into his Bloody Mary during the appalled silence.

'You naughty boy.' Denise's voice rose. 'Playing with ducky bottoms!'

The rest of the group began to recover.

'A fascinating tale,' Karl said.

'I call it playing foul.' Nigel chuckled at his own joke.

'Are you all right?' Karl suddenly asked Ida.

She was trying not to be sick. The boat seemed to rock unsteadily under her. 'Have a peppermint,' Errol's mother said, handing her a wrapped sweet. Ida tried to catch Errol's eye as if that would somehow steady or reassure her, but he was busy chatting with the others.

A few days later, it came time to shoot the scene Ida had been dreading. She was supposed to spot the crocodiles in the water swimming dangerously toward the 'Captain,' and she was to shout out and alert him.

She kept remembering the river scene in *Tarzan*: Maureen

O'Sullivan screaming as the hippos overturned a raft and the white hunters shot at the animals. Did they really shoot them or just pretend to? She had asked her father but now she couldn't recall his answer. In this scene, Errol planned to wrestle the crocodiles, then kill them with a dagger.

But he wondered how on earth he was going to make the sickly animals move, much less put up a ferocious-looking fight. He had given them glucose injections, but that hadn't helped. Digitalis had seemed to have the reverse effect and the animals had grown even more lethargic. The cameramen were leaving in three days, and Errol was becoming desperate. The memory of his childhood experiment with the ducks kept coming back to him; he didn't want to disgust anyone, especially his father, and he didn't want to seem cruel. On the other hand, what did it matter since he was going to kill the crocs in the scene anyway? He came up with the idea of injecting ammonia into their rectums. If that didn't wake them up, he thought, nothing would.

He got into the water. Ida was on the boat, trying to keep a safe distance from the animals. The crocodiles were injected just before being heaved overboard. They went crazy. One went after the underwater cameraman. The other never left the boat; it turned around and lunged at Brasso, whose job it had been to push it overboard. In its frenzy, it managed to snap apart its jaw wires. Ida heard Brasso screaming, and she saw Nigel trying to lasso the creature.

She ran and tripped. The charm bracelet Errol had given her snagged on something. The boat heaved to one side and suddenly she found herself, attached to a swinging pole, falling overboard.

She beat at the water for a few moments, then went under. Eyes wide open, she fought her way to the surface again.

Someone grabbed her and swam with her, holding her in the crook of his arm. Several other arms pulled her onto the boat and laid her flat on the deck.

She opened her eyes and saw Nigel Fletcher above her. 'I never rescued a nymph before.'

11

Karl Intrudes

An ambulance came to take Brasso and the cameraman to the hospital. Ida heard someone say Brasso was 'a bloody mess' from the waist down. 'Crocodile bit off half his ass and God knows what else.' The cameraman had only minor wounds on his arm, but his camera had been wrecked, and Errol was worried that some of the underwater footage might have been destroyed.

A maternal-looking Indian doctor examined Ida a few hours later back at Bella Vista. She realized Ida was pregnant and didn't want to prescribe a tranquilizer. 'Just try to rest, dear.'

She could tell Ida was worried about the baby, so she put the stethoscope to Ida's belly and let her listen. It was the first time she had really considered the life going on inside her, hidden and lovely like the things she'd seen under the glass-bottomed boat.

There was a flicker of sympathy in the doctor's eyes for this young mother-to-be. But she was a country doctor and had seen pregnant girls even younger than Ida. 'The baby is fine,' she said, smiling.

Ida slept a bit, and when she woke up Karl was there.

'You're expecting a child?' His German-accented syllables sounded like the sliding of heavy rocks. It was more of a statement than a question. 'Does Errol know?'

He sat down on the bed beside her. 'Does he know?' he asked again.

What was he doing there? She turned her face to the wall. 'Would it be easier for you if I told him?'

Ida turned such a look of fury on him that he instinctively drew back. She hated him for implying that he was closer to Errol than she was. But it was true. She burst into tears.

He held her and stroked her hair. The unexpected gentleness caused her to cry even more. She was grateful to have someone hold her. But then his being there, he and not Errol, bothered her. She became repelled by the peculiar warmth of Karl's body and the harsh crispness of his shirt collar. Composing herself, she became aware of him looking at her in a direct, disconcerting way, like a thief of hopes.

'How old are you?' he asked.

'Sixteen. Almost seventeen.'

'When is your birthday?'

She thought it an odd question. 'October eleventh.'

He frowned. 'And you are – how many months pregnant?'

'I don't know.'

There was a quiet knock on the door. Karl said, 'Come in.'

It was Nigel. He tried not to look surprised at finding Karl in the room with her.

'Thought I'd check on the patient,' he said.

'I'm going to take Ida home,' Karl said.

'Actually, I thought I'd escort her.'

They began a polite argument about which one of them

should see her home. Ida could tell they didn't like one another.

'Where's Errol?' she asked.

'He went to Dunn's River,' Nigel said, 'to shoot the waterfall scene with Denise.' He noticed her disappointment and added, 'He asked me to check on you.'

Ida didn't like the idea of Errol spending time with Denise Fletcher. She had seen the glances between the two of them. Being Oni's granddaughter, Ida had been thinking about various bush-teas that would give her rival a bellyache and have her running to the toilet for days. But she remembered that obeah was actually against the law.

'I'm not ready to go back to Port Antonio,' she said. 'I want to wait here for Errol.'

Later, from the upstairs terrace, she could see the lawns of Bella Vista sloping down to the water. Smoke was rising from the servants' quarters, where someone was cooking, and down at the tennis court Karl and Errol had just finished playing a game. She was feeling a bit better. When Errol had come back home from shooting at Dunn's River, he had been like his old self, worried about her, calling her Ida-Rider and hugging her. He'd had a nice chat with her father on the telephone ('Ida's fine, just a bit shaken up. She can spend the night here with the rest of the crew. Denise and Nigel are here too and send their love').

She looked out over the grounds and imagined herself living there one day with Errol. It seemed not just a possibility but a certainty now that she was pregnant. He and Paulette were already living in separate homes.

The men finished their game and sat on the bench talking. She couldn't hear anything but from the looks on their faces she believed they were talking about her pregnancy. It bothered her that Karl was telling Errol. But there was nothing she could do. She was tired so she went inside and lay down.

Hours later she woke up in the dark bedroom, not knowing what time of day it was. She heard music downstairs and a lot of people talking – an impromptu party going on in the living room.

She heard a splash and went out to the terrace. Errol was in the pool swimming laps. He stopped and looked up at her standing on the well-lit terrace, and then he continued vigorously swimming.

She was startled when Karl came up from behind and stood close to her. Did he think because she had cried on his shoulder that they were now close friends? Errol came out of the pool and looked up at them. She was about to go down to him but Karl's arms caught her. She was confused.

'Don't go to him just now,' Karl said. 'He's not in a good mood.'

Karl waved to Errol – a reassuring gesture – and Errol seemed to relax and waved back. Something she didn't understand passed between the two men.

She pulled away from Karl. She was tired of all the people in this house. It was time for her to go home.

Ida knew she would soon have to tell her father. But first, and more important, she needed to speak to Errol. She knew he would be leaving for London in a week, so she went to see him. As the boat headed toward the island she remembered the first time they had gone there together almost three years earlier and had discovered the bamboo-sheltered river. And years later they had returned to that very spot as if it had been a promise they'd made each other. Now here was his child in her, a little warm being, not an error but an answer to the steady, prayerful desire she'd had since she'd first met him.

She would tell him she was pregnant, and he would marry her.

He was sitting by the pool, drinking. He smiled when he saw her; it was a sincere, spontaneous smile, and it encouraged her.

'Hullo, beauty.'

She went over and sat on his knee. He smelled of rum. She saw a checkbook and some papers on the table and also a bottle of pills.

'Are you sick?'

'I am.'

'With what?'

He slapped his chest and rolled his eyes dramatically. 'Heartache.'

'I can cure that.'

He brought her hand to his lips and kissed the fingertips. She let her fingers stay, tracing the outline of his mouth. He closed his eyes, and she knew she was arousing him.

'I'm going to have a baby.'

'At the tender age of seventeen,' he said with false lightheartedness.

She didn't understand his tone or like it.

'What's wrong, Errol?'

'It's called depression, my dear.'

'The pills—'

'—are supposed to help. Actually, if I take enough of them they might put me out of my misery forever. Do I want to die? Only if I can't live.'

'You won't be miserable with me.'

He pulled her close and she smelled the special odor of his skin.

'Dear – Ida.'

He looked down at her hand and played with the silver bangles, then laid his own hand softly on her belly. They sat quietly like that. Then the silence was broken by the phone ringing.

The maid came out and said, 'Mrs Flynn on the phone,' and she gave Ida a sharp, curious glance before she went back in.

While he talked on the phone inside the living room, Ida looked at the sheaf of papers on the table. It looked like a contract of some sort, and she saw that he had been balancing his checkbook.

He came back out and invited her to join him in the pool, but she said no.

'Don't go swimming right now.' She heard the pleading in her own voice and realized she was close to tears. 'I want to talk.'

He seemed slightly put off and sat on the chair across from her. He poured himself some more rum.

The sympathy that had been there a few minutes earlier had been broken. His wife had called. What Ida had heard of their conversation had sounded calm and ordinary. Ida knew that Paulette was back in Jamaica and was now living on the ranch near Port Antonio.

'How's Paulette?'

'She's well. A little angry with me, but that's typical. She's given up trying to change me. She's still trying to decide whether she can put up with me as I am or if she'd be better off on her own.'

It wasn't what Ida wanted to hear.

He went on, 'No one's ever tried as hard as Paulette. I'll drink to that.'

He saw how upset she looked, and he put the glass down on the table and came over to her. He cupped her face in his hands. She loved his hands.

'Ida,' he said softly, 'there's a better way. Go home to your father. Marry a fine Jamaican lad with mango trees in his garden and be happy.'

She threw her arms around his neck.

He began stroking her hair, which was loose and falling all around her; he lifted it to his face, breathing it in.

'If I could, I would escape with you to the South Seas. That's what you remind me of – Laloki, the best time of my life. Look, Ida, I'm not a good husband or a good boyfriend. I'm not even that good an actor.'

She heard only what she wanted to hear. Escape. With her. She knew his health and happiness would return if he were with her. She wanted to convince him of that, and she thought she knew how.

She found his lips and kissed him sweetly while her hands felt out his body. He lifted her onto him and lay back against the tiles. It was as if she touched raw nerves, what she set off in him with her hands. And it was because she loved him, loved even the flabbiness, the soft brown hair of his underarms, the lines and creases and perspiring, sticky flesh of the middle-aged man he had become.

Afterward they fell asleep on the cool tiles.

'My God, what time is it?' he asked, waking. Then he saw her and smiled.

For a moment he was convinced that a resurrection had occurred; the young Errol Flynn had risen from the pointlessly aging body. She saw it in him too, this renewal, in his easy smile and slow, contented inhalations. She realized that he had looked at other women this way before, and that for him good sex was merely a reflection of himself. He was vain, and he loved her less than she loved him. She knew this but she still wanted him.

The next day Ida slept late, long after her father had gone to work. A loud knocking out at the gate woke her. Someone looking for a day's work, she thought. The knocking grew more persistent. 'I comin', I comin'.'

She put on an old dressing gown and went out. It was Karl.

'Good morning, Ida.' He studied her and her dressing gown, and then he remembered to smile. He held out a brown envelope.

'Errol had to leave for London last night. He asked me to give you this.'

'I thought he was going next week.'

Karl paused a moment, then said, 'There was something urgent.' He continued looking at her in a pleasant way, as if he expected further conversation or even to be invited in. What did this man want from her? she wondered. There was something unnerving about his closeness to Errol. The morning sunlight brought out the blondness of his thick but well-barbered hair, and she noticed how large his chest was in the spotless white shirt. He was too clean, like a brand-new man-doll.

'Let me know if I can do anything. I'll be at Bella Vista for a few days.' He seemed to consider smiling but just nodded instead.

As soon as she got inside, she opened the letter:

Dear Ida,

You and your father are among my dearest friends. I hope there will never be any misunderstanding between us, and I trust that what you and I have shared was given freely without the expectation of anything in return. Business, as usual, calls me away, and I will probably be gone for some time. I wish you much happiness.

Your friend, Errol

Ida read the whole thing quickly, and then she read it in parts slowly, repeatedly, trying to extract what was true from what was false. These were his words, his handwriting, but someone else's intentions. The sense of finality was a sham.

Nonsense. She crumpled it into a ball and threw it away. It had no meaning, no meaning whatsoever. He would be back and she would be as irresistible as she had been yesterday. Hadn't Oni once seen a crown of diamonds on her head and said she'd have a child, a daughter who would swim as fast as a bolt of lightning? And hadn't she predicted once that she, Ida, would marry a tall, important foreigner?

'So what we celebratin'?' Eli asked as he and Father Reynold came to the dinner table. Ida had set champagne glasses on the table, and she had managed to make a roast beef, using her mother's old recipe. To Eli's relief, it actually looked and smelled edible.

When they were all seated, she lifted her glass of champagne and turned to her father with a nervous smile. 'You're going to be the grandfather of Errol Flynn's child.'

He seemed not to hear at first. After a while he said, 'Godfather?'

Father Reynold and Ida exchanged a quick glance. Then Father Reynold spoke up: 'Ida havin' baby for Errol Flynn.'

'Wait a minute – let me get this straight. You and Flynn havin' baby together?'

She nodded.

Eli put his head in his hands.

'No. Listen, Papa—'

'I never see what happenin' right in front of me.'

'Eli. Don't blame you'self.' Father Reynold said.

'We're getting married.'

'He tell you so?'

'We haven't had a chance to talk about it yet.'

Eli looked at Father Reynold, who looked down into his glass of champagne. Ida went over to her father and put her arms around his neck.

'Papa, it will be all right.'

'So you love him and he loves you? That's what you saying?' He looked at her hopefully.

'Him will get a divorce quick an' marry Ida,' Father Reynold offered. 'Flynn know all 'bout divorce already. Ida will be wife – number what? Number four.'

Ida fell asleep that night to the familiar sounds of her father and Father Reynold drinking and chatting about the new turn in events, delighting in their own inebriated philosophy.

'Who woulda think it, eh? For all the ups and downs of my life, I never thought I would be Errol Flynn's father-in-law one day. But me no like how him give Ida baby before dem married. That not right.'

'But look here. Is pot callin' kettle black? You never marry Esme.'

'True. But this is different. Ida is me daughter.'

'No worry, man, him will get divorce an' marry her.'

'You is one hell of a Cat'olic priest, you know! Talkin' 'bout divorce. I mean, drinkin' rum is one t'ing, but divorce, don't that is a capital sin?'

'These things are not for us to decide. Is for God-one-Himself to decide. But let me tell you how I see it . . .'

But Eli couldn't help worrying. Ida was so young, and he was sure Flynn was backing out. As Ida's father, he felt he had to do something. He knew Flynn's friend, Karl, was around because he had seen him lunching at the Somerset. He sought him out and asked how he could get in touch with Flynn over a real estate matter. Karl gave him Flynn's hotel number in London but called Flynn first to prepare him.

The days became weeks, then months, and Eli Joseph could not reach Flynn by phone. He left messages, but Flynn never called back. Eli's heart hardened toward his former friend but he tried not to show his concern to Ida, who was growing closer and closer to delivery. Finally he went to see a barrister in Kingston to find out whether Flynn could be held legally responsible. What he didn't know was that Flynn's lawyer had already been in touch with another barrister in those chambers, trying to find out about the Jamaican laws governing age of consent, paternity claims, and so on. The young barrister entrusted with the Josephs' case was sympathetic but informed him that there was no legal action to be taken.

Ida was concerned too; she hadn't heard from Errol, only from Karl, who told her there had been delays with the film and that Errol had been hospitalized because of an injury to his arm. Both were true. Ida herself had read about his injury in the newspaper.

She learned to wait.

She would sometimes go to her father's movie theatre early in the morning and ask Gideon, the projectionist, to show one of Errol's films. Gideon seemed not to find anything out of the ordinary about Ida's growing belly or her desire to see Errol Flynn's movies repeatedly. He had worked at the Palace since it had opened and was a bit of a character around town. A dark-skinned, soft-spoken gentleman, he was always well dressed in a hat, suit, and bow tie, and he spoke with an impeccable British accent that he'd picked up as a soldier in World War I. It was a comfort to Ida to know Gideon was there, dependable and discreet the way she imagined butlers to be in grand homes. He would set up the movie and leave her alone.

Sitting with her hands on her large belly, she spoke softly to the baby: *This is your father; hear his voice; know him.* There was a kind of magnificence in knowing Errol so intimately. She would envision herself at those moments as his true wife and eternal companion.

But she couldn't deny how lonely she was. She had also noticed how strained her father looked and guessed that it had to do with her pregnancy. A week before the child was due she summoned all her courage and spoke to him: 'Papa, remember how much you loved Mama? I'm not saying it won't work out for me and Errol. But if for some reason it doesn't, it won't be the end of the world for me or for my baby.'

He grimaced and his face darkened to an unnatural color as if he were straining.

'What, Papa?'

'You mother wanted more for you.'

She looked at him. His graying hair lay across his head in untidy streaks. His face sagged.

She rallied: 'I'm not going to disappoint you.'

A few days later her daughter, May Josephine Flynn, was born.

Part Two

With a savage smile, he repeated his assurances that I had nothing to fear. But there was something truly terrifying about the man. Nearly six feet in height, of swarthy complexion, his eyes were large and penetrating, and the look he gave me was one of pure evil. He was chief among these pirates, he said, and if I would be reconciled to my situation and subservient to his will, he would protect me. But Providence interposed to save me from the hands of this villain!

My rescuer was no angel but rather another devil of the high seas — Cayman Jack! The man who would make a pirate of me!

Treasure Cove

12

'I'm Writing to You Because . . .'

Ida watched as eighteen-month-old May tottered over to the hedge and tried to grasp a hibiscus flower that was almost within reach. She fell on her bottom, sat for a moment, then stood up and tried again. The bright sunlight and humidity put a varnish on everything in sight: the blue woodwork of the veranda where Ida sat, the grass where May played barefoot; even the small black ants that crawled over May's discarded bonnet seemed to be dark, shiny globules of heat. May rebelled against every attempt to protect her head from the sun and against the wearing of shoes. So she went about uncovered and unshod like the street children.

Ida continued to watch the small being who had supplanted her old life with an entirely new one. There were moments, like those rare occasions when she woke up before May, when she'd briefly recall some girlhood dream, and then she'd feel horribly cut off. But she told herself that she would catch up with them all again one day.

The child's cry suddenly disturbed her thoughts. A wasp had frightened May, but she recovered all on her own and watched it hovering over a bush.

She waddled over to Ida. 'Ma-ma, Ma-ma.'

Ida picked her up and held her sturdy, warm, energetic body close. The little body continued to twist and turn and reach for things as if her mother were only a large rock in her way. She opened her tiny palm against the stucco wall, and Ida remembered doing that herself as a child, fascinated with the sandy texture, remembered it so clearly that she could hear her own mother calling out to her, 'Don't pick-pick the wall.'

She looked at her watch. It was a little past four, the time Eli was expected back home from Kingston.

'Grandpa coming soon,' she told May, 'and he's bringing you a present.' She was beginning to worry. Eli was taking pills for high blood pressure. 'He seems to be under a lot of strain,' the doctor had told Ida.

A few weeks after May was born, Eli Joseph had visited Flynn. It was right after Ida had signed May's birth certificate. She had chosen Josephine as a middle name in recognition of her father's name. But she had insisted on giving May Errol's surname, and this had upset Eli.

Ida might never have known about her father's visit to Errol if her old friend Clive Goodman hadn't told her. Clive, who sometimes helped his father in the taxi-boat business, had taken Eli out to Navy Island that day. 'I goin' talk to him, man to man.' Eli had muttered this more to himself than to Clive.

Clive had felt protective toward Ida's father that day and hadn't wanted to let him out of his sight, so he had sat on a bench out by the tennis court waiting for him. From there he could make out the two men, Eli and Errol, sitting across from one another on the poolside terrace.

Errol, who had been drinking, smiled, almost by reflex, at the sight of his old friend. Eli managed to smile back. After tense but polite greetings and the pouring of drinks, the two men became strangely silent. They drank; they looked everywhere but at each other and smoked cigarettes, each wanting desperately to relapse upon the old friendship. After a while Eli couldn't bear the strain of not speaking.

'She's my daughter, Errol.'

'Yes, but she's not exactly a little girl anymore, you know.' Errol remembered once seeing Karl's arms around her, and he imagined there might be some young Port Antonio fellow in the picture too.

Eli knew of Errol's separation from Paulette: 'You can get divorced now and marry her.'

'You and I both know that's not the solution for Ida.'

Eli had no idea what Errol meant. He suspected there wasn't any meaning in the words and that Errol was saying anything that came into his head except the right thing.

They were silent again. Eli watched his cigarette end burning against the ashtray and began to wonder what he could possibly accomplish here. Errol wanted the meeting to be over.

'This is getting rather uncomfortable for us, don't you think?' Errol said.

'For us? What about Ida and her baby?'

Errol lit another cigarette. Merciful heaven! Ida with a baby! He had to do something. How many paternity suits had he already had to fight in court? Maybe he should consider a vasectomy. It was supposed to be painless but that was hard to believe. Suppose it made him impotent? And how could a vasectomy help him now? It was like owing money: the debt didn't automatically disappear when you stopped spending. It was a royal mess. He looked at Eli and thought, *These people are tough and will do all right in the end; they're not under the sort of pressure I'm under.*

'Hasn't it dawned on you,' he said to Eli, 'why Ida hasn't come here herself, crying and accusing? Go ask her. She knows I'm not responsible.'

'You're a disgrace,' Eli said.

After that meeting, Eli had said only one more thing to Ida about Errol, with as much kindness as he could muster: 'He jus' not good enough for you.' For several days after that, Eli had shut himself in his room, appearing only to eat and bathe. That had been followed by a few weeks of stifled anger, and when that phase ended, he had seemed to become a sad, tired old man.

Out on the veranda, Ida looked at her watch. Six o'clock. And Eli still hadn't come back from Kingston, where he'd gone to take care of some bank business. The evening sun vanished behind the mountains, and the sky turned to dullish silver. May, full from her supper, nestled peacefully against her mother on the veranda rocker. Darkness came gently, and it was only the persistent whistling of crickets that made Ida conscious of its being night.

Where was her father? Ida remembered that his supper of beef stew was still waiting on the stove and realized that she herself had not eaten.

Had he stopped for a drink of rum along the way? Across the road the rectory lights were off. Maybe he had run into Father Reynold and they had gone out for a meal and a drink. The possibilities bounced around in her mind, but there was a churning sense of something gone wrong. She thought about how unusually lighthearted he had seemed for the last few days. Why that should worry her she could not say.

She carried May in to bed, put away the food for the next day, and fixed herself a small plate of crackers and cheese. Then she turned off all the lights and went to bed.

Just before she fell asleep — that was the time she allowed herself to think about Errol. Two years had gone by since she'd seen him. Everyone believed that she had put the affair behind her. She had not. A mistake had been made. There had been fear on his part, naivety on hers, and yes, pain, but they were both in pain. This was how she saw the still unfolding, rectifiable course of events. And anyway, it came down to this: she was nineteen and couldn't imagine being with anyone else.

Someone knocked at the door very early the next morning. It was Father Reynold with bad news. Eli had suffered a stroke while driving back from Kingston and had gone off the road.

They drove in the old blue church van, the baby, Ida, and Father Reynold, and got to the hospital that afternoon.

At first it seemed like there was someone else lying there asleep. Ida had never seen her father looking so helpless. One side of his face drooped grotesquely. He looked trapped and defeated.

'He has some difficulty speaking now,' said the doctor, a young Jamaican man with warm eyes. 'But that will improve. He's a lucky man, considering the accident and all.'

'But he cyan walk or feed himself,' said a female voice.

Ida turned and realized that the blur of faces she had seen on entering the room belonged to her two half-sisters, Enid and Kay. She had not seen them since that horrible day when she was twelve years old. They had kept in touch with Eli, though, letting him know, just a short while after Esme had died, that their mother had also died ('Esme haul her up,' Mrs Goodman, the hairdresser, had said). They still wore a lot of gold jewelry just as Ida remembered.

The doctor said, 'With proper therapy, he could regain use of his right arm and leg. He seems to be quite a fighter.'

The half-sisters hummed and sighed in agreement. 'True-true. Papa was always a fighter. He don't let anything stop him.'

Ida silenced them with a look. What did they know about her father?

But they behaved surprisingly well toward her, complimenting her on the beautiful child in her arms and showing a readiness to dote on May. Ida, remembering that they were spinsters with no children of their own, softened a bit toward them, especially as they even invited her and the baby to stay with them while Eli recovered.

She thanked them but declined. She had left home in a hurry, carrying only a change of clothes for the baby. Besides, the doctor felt Mr Joseph would be home by the following week.

Back in Port Antonio, Ida began arranging things for her father's convalescence. She bought a walking stick to help him move around, and she was about to buy a daybed for the veranda when Father Reynold decided to have a frank talk with her about Eli's financial situation.

Her father was broke.

The bad news from his Kingston banker had probably brought on his stroke. After months of anxiety, he'd thought he had found a way out of his troubles. Money had come to him from his late brother's will. What he had not realized was that his debt to the bank was larger than the amount of his inheritance. Eli would have to sell the movie theatre.

'You mean we don't have anything?' She had never, in her whole life, had to consider such a thing.

'You have this house. It belongs to you and your aunt Carmen.'

'That's all?' She was thinking of her child, of food, shoes, doctor's visits.

Father Reynold was moved. He looked at her sitting up straight, dark-eyed and serious. When had that child of dazzling prettiness become this mature figure of grace?

'No worry you'self,' he said. 'We will take care of Eli together. I can pay for the new bed.'

But Eli had another stroke the night before he was to leave the hospital. Ida was about to go to him when she discovered that May had a fever and rash.

The doctor made a house call and said, 'She has measles,' and prescribed St Joseph's aspirin. But May's fever got worse. Ida sent a boy up the mountain with a message to Oni, who quickly sent back a bush-bath and a note saying, 'No aspirin.'

Two weeks went by, and then she received a letter from her half-sisters telling her that 'Mr Joseph' would remain in Kingston under their care. There was more: it had been necessary for them to take charge of his business affairs, and the movie theatre was being sold.

'They can't do that. We have to go for him,' Ida said.

'We cyan just bruk down the door an' tek him,' Father Reynold reasoned.

'Why not? They keeping him prisoner.'

'You need a barrister, Ida, to do this thing properly.'

But she needed money for that; she needed money for everything. Her own savings were almost gone and she could not bring herself to ask Father Reynold for more help. It had also dawned on her that her father would never be able to work again. She would have to find a way to make money. But would he even come back? Was it legally possible for those wretches to keep him? Was there anything she could do to prevent the selling of the movie theatre? What about the other Joseph-Hannas, her father's other brother, for instance? Or her rich cousin Aaron Levy, who lived close by? She was shocked at her own ignorance of these things, and her pride kept her from speaking to the sisters or to others in her father's family.

'I have to make plans. I have to make decisions,' she told herself.

She didn't want to ask Oni. Oni had land but not cash. Then it came to her: she would ask Errol for help.

He was said to be living on his yacht off the coast of Spain. The only way she could reach him was through Karl, who was often at Navy Island, or – and this would be humbling – Paulette, from whom Errol had parted on good terms.

She remembered that Paulette had sent a present when May had been born, a hand-knit sweater. Ida tasted the salt of shame thinking about it now. Her eyes welled up, and later that day she told Father Reynold, 'I'm sorry if I hurt her. I wasn't thinking about anybody but myself.'

'Accept your weakness and God's abundant strength,' he told her.

The phone call was simpler than she'd imagined. Paulette was gracious and seemed concerned about Mr Joseph's illness. When Ida put down the phone she thought about the word her mother had often used – 'broughtupsy.' Class. Paulette had it.

Ida wrote to Errol. There were many versions of the

letter, some of them describing how May had grown, others expressing concern for his well-being and falsely presenting a happy picture of her life. Finally, worn out by her repeated efforts, she simply wrote:

> Dear Errol,
> My father is ill and we are short of money. I'm writing to you because you said that you would help us if we ever needed you.
> With love, Ida

A few weeks later Ida received a call from the local bank. It seemed that Errol had come through: five hundred dollars, which was about three hundred Jamaican pounds, had been wired to her.

13

Eli Joseph's Journey

Eli was still in Kingston. He'd been there for over three months. One Sunday the Joseph sisters, Enid and Kay, went to church as usual after giving him his breakfast. There had been some delay that morning because he had insisted on being dressed in trousers and jacket, as opposed to lying around in pajamas. He'd expressed a desire to go with them, but after they had taken pains dressing him, he'd changed his mind.

He lay on the sofa now, listening to their heels clacking hurriedly on the cement path outside, then the car going down the road. After fifteen minutes or so, he reached for the wooden crutch that he had been using since he'd left the hospital. Pulling himself up slowly, he wondered for the hundredth time why they had bought him one and not two crutches. Those blasted women, his offspring, were so mean, and they could afford it with all the money their mother had left them. Damn them to hell.

He stopped to lean against a table and made his way to the armoire where his daughters had put his wallet. 'Blasted two-face bitch-dem!' The drawer was locked. Enid and Kay distrusted their maid. Wallet or no wallet, he had to leave the house.

'I still have one good foot an' one good hand,' he told himself. He limped to the parlor and with a trembling hand reached for the cupboard door where his hat, steeped in the scent of mothballs, awaited him. He put it on and sighed.

He felt something in his jacket pocket. To his delight, there were a few loose pound notes. It was not enough for the train, but he could take the bus to Port Antonio.

As he stepped out into the warm morning air, he swayed weakly and rested with his full weight upon the crutch. There was a bus stop at the corner of the avenue. If he could make it there, the bus would take him to Constant Spring market, where he could catch the country bus.

It took him a long time, but he finally reached the corner and saw a bus approaching.

There was a boy sitting on the curb by the bus stop.

'Boy! Come help me,' Eli barked.

It was a command that did not promise any gratuity, but it was met by the obedience he expected. The boy came over to him.

'I wan' go Constant Spring,' Eli said.

He leaned on the thin but surprisingly sturdy child, who was about ten, Eli guessed, and who had probably not eaten in a while. Paying the bus driver two fares, he ordered the boy, now in a more grandfatherly tone, to help him over to a seat.

He was on his way home.

The boy, Eli noted, had an alert, intelligent face. He was a black boy with bare, dusty feet and a stomach caved in with hunger. He reminded the older man of himself as a boy.

The boy returned his gaze, sensing a question or command. But Eli Joseph was no longer seeing the boy. He saw himself swaying in the back of a milk cart in Marseilles with his two brothers and with nothing but the clothes he had worn on the ship from Lebanon. He had smelled of cloves because on the ship he had slept against sacks filled with the spice. He remembered his hunger that first day in Marseilles and how tempted he had been to steal a bottle of milk. He could still taste that first meal, a cold pastry filled with cheese, a delicate thing about the size of his palm that he had found near a café; how the salty crumbs and buttery wholeness of that pastry had restored him.

At Constant Spring the rain and thunder came. He and the boy sat under the corrugated iron roof of the market waiting for the Port Antonio bus, the rain coming down hard like knives in front of them. He took some change from his pocket.

'Here, boy, go buy you'self a bun.'

To his surprise the boy brought back a bun and soda for him too. After that he was not surprised at the boy's staying with him until the bus came, and when it did come and the boy helped him in and got him seated, Eli wondered if he intended to stay with him all the way to Port Antonio. But the boy's movements had become more hurried and he appeared eager to go, as if a sudden awareness of his own kindness had befuddled him.

'Wait, I have something for you.' Eli felt inside his pocket and took out a pound. The boy looked amazed, and he hesitated.

'Come on, boy, come tek it. I was young like you one time.'

The bus driver released the brakes. The boy took the money and said, 'T'ank you, sa.'

'G'wan now,' said Eli, waving him away.

He slept for most of the ride, waking now and then as the

bus lurched to a stop. He dreamed he was on a bicycle in Caracas with a basket filled with fabric swatches. He had worked for a while at a tailor's establishment, and it had been his job to go to the food-canning companies on paydays to show the fabric swatches and measure the men for cheap suits. That was how he had earned the capital for his parrot-export business.

He woke hearing the driver announce Port Antonio. A smile broke from him as he thought about the shock Enid and Kay would get when they discovered his escape. Someone helped him up, but he lurched, then fell back onto the seat. He had no feeling in his feet, and he felt a combustible force rising from his neck to his forehead. He panicked. He had come so far and still had not reached home.

The whole busload of passengers seemed to be helping him descend to the street.

'Easy, now.'

'Dis' way.'

'Hol' him good.'

A taxi driver waiting idly by the bus station recognized him. 'Mr Joseph?' he said incredulously and then uttered an oath. 'It look like a duppy come off a de bus,' he said later, describing the scene and Mr Joseph's decrepit appearance. But it was nothing compared to the scene he witnessed when he brought Mr Joseph home to Plumbago Road. Ida opened the door, gave a shout, and ran out to her father, and her father stood in the street and cried.

14

Ensnared

The Palace Theatre was sold. Ida went there with May one morning before it closed. She woke Gideon, who lived in a room at the back of the theatre, and asked him to show *They Died with Their Boots On*.

May ran up and down the familiar aisles and climbed over the seats, her pattering feet and squeals tangential to her mother's absorption in the movie. The pattering came closer as she came back to check on her mother. Ida lifted her onto her lap and May clung to her neck as they both watched. It had been a while since Ida had seen the film; it was her favorite, and the parting scene between General Custer and his wife always made her cry.

Janice, the ticket-seller, was there when they came out. Ida remembered that she had been working there since the theatre had first opened.

'Oh, my, look at May. How old she is now?' Janice asked. 'Two.'

'What! An' so big a'ready?'

Ida asked if she'd found another job. They would all be out of work soon: Gideon, Janice, and the other ticket-seller,

Sweetie. 'I goin' work at the pharmacy an' Gideon get some work at the hotel. But Sweetie still don't find anything.' They had all accepted the change ungrudgingly, even Gideon, for whom the Palace was literally home.

Outside she bought a pineapple snow cone for May, and they continued walking down the street. It was Friday, payday for many people in the town. The shops and outdoor stalls were busy. The flower-seller sat under a shady tree with a bucket of colorful bouquets — orchids, roses. A bale of pink satin behind a shop window caught Ida's eye. She had money in her pocket from Flynn, and she wanted things. Stockings. Nice new underwear in pretty colors. It had depressed her, wearing yellowing underthings and having holes at the tops of her stockings. But today she didn't need to pass by the shops feeling sorry for herself. Pretty things. New things. She could go in and handle them knowing they could be hers. A new blouse. Pretty little things for May.

It was a blessing to have her father home. He enjoyed sitting on his old wicker chair on the veranda looking out at the comings and goings of the street and keeping an eye on May as she played in the garden. He always managed to pull something out of his pocket for her — sweets, peanuts, or a penny to buy an ice-cream cake. Every evening he sat there chatting with Father Reynold, who never failed to visit.

The money from the sale of the Palace had paid his debts. But Ida knew she would have to get a job soon and find someone to look after Eli and May. There was also her horse, Pearl, to think about.

She hadn't ridden Pearl since she'd been pregnant, and her visits to the stables had become less and less frequent. A family in Montego Bay offered to buy Pearl for a hundred pounds. And Ida agreed.

She paid one last visit to Pearl, bringing the horse's favorite treat, coconut cakes. May came too, demanded most of the cake, and had to be watched carefully as she was bent on tugging the horse's tail. The horse responded with her usual gentleness as Ida stroked and nuzzled her, and Ida mourned not only the loss of the horse but also the loss of her former intense feeling for the animal. May occupied her fully now.

There was a pink rosebush near the stable; she picked a flower from it and took it home. It was a sentimental gesture, but she needed something to remember Pearl by. The rose would be fragrant for a few days, and then she would press it inside the photograph album where there were pictures of her with Pearl. It took more determination than she'd imagined, getting around to pressing that flower before its petals turned crisp and crumbled. But one night after she had finally gotten May to sleep, she sat up exhausted with the thick album and the fading rose.

The Flamingo Hotel in Ocho Rios hired her as a receptionist. It was almost fifty miles from the house, so she used some of the money Errol had sent to buy a secondhand car. She also had some new clothes made for herself and May, bought much-needed underthings, shoes, and a tricycle for May. There were ninety pounds left from the bank wire. Ida calculated that at three pounds a week for household expenses, five shillings for petrol – then there was the girl who would be coming to help in the house for ten shillings a week – the money would be finished in about five or six months. But by then she would be earning paychecks.

She was proud of herself for getting a job at such a nice hotel, and she knew it was the combination of being good-looking and well spoken that had earned her a place at the front desk.

The girl, Shirlene, who came to live in the house and care for May and Eli was from the poor fishing village of Manchioneal and was the oldest of eight children. Ida put a bed and an old dressing table in the pantry for her, and she could tell, from the dreamy smile passing over the girl's face, that it was the first time she'd ever had a room to herself. Shirlene bathed, fed, and generally watched over both her charges. She was a good cook, much to Eli's relief, and Ida was impressed with her cleaning; the only problem she could find with the girl was that she seemed vacant, like her mind was always elsewhere. Still, she did all that was asked of her.

Ida had been working at the hotel for several months when one of the guests asked her to go out with him. It was not the first time; other guests had flirted with her and a few had asked her out. She always refused with a shy smile that she had perfected just for that purpose and reminded them that she was a 'widow' with a small child and no time for going out. Besides, there were rules at the Flamingo about workers going out with guests.

So she declined as usual, but the gentleman was persistent.

His name was Courtney Hart. She could tell he had been attracted to her from the minute he'd first seen her. It was a good feeling to dress nicely every day for work and look attractive. She wished Errol could see her now. Hart sent presents to her house: flowers for her and chocolates for May. He didn't say much; he smiled gently as he passed the front desk, sometimes lingering there to chat with her as he waited for his messages or key.

'He likes you,' the other receptionist who worked alongside her said. 'Go with him. Chu! The other girls do it. Nobody will know.'

Hart left the island, then returned about a month later and this time called her at home to invite her out.

The day he called, Ida had been thinking about Errol. He was back on Navy Island. She had seen a picture of him in the newspaper with Princess Margaret and Lord Snowden, who were visiting Port Antonio. The photograph showed two couples around a restaurant table: the princess and her husband, Errol and a new girlfriend, Sofia, a Spanish actress.

Errol had put on some weight, especially around his face, and he seemed sloppily dressed compared to the others, wearing a tropical print shirt and a ridiculous straw hat. Ida was a bit embarrassed for him. He looked like the fat chief of some tribe posing with his foreign visitors. She looked at the woman, Sofia, sitting so close to him, inhaling him. Ida would have given anything to be in her place. It seemed an aberration to feel the weight of his memory bearing down on her like that, knowing she was utterly absent from his thoughts.

She agreed to meet Courtney Hart that evening, not in Ocho Rios but at the Somerset.

'G'wan, go enjoy you'self,' her father said. 'Me an' Shirlene will tek good care of May.'

Ida thought Shirlene seemed a bit grudging. She knew the girl liked to walk into town on a Saturday evening; well, she would give her some extra time for herself the following week.

She felt many eyes on her as she walked into the hotel restaurant with Courtney Hart, and the sense of her own radiance made her tremble slightly. She wore a red blouse, a color that went well with her dark hair, and a black gipsy-like skirt with red embroidered flowers. There were silver hoops in her ears and silver bangles on her arm.

The band was playing 'Yellow Bird' and some couples

were dancing. Scenes like this felt so familiar to her from movies that she failed to realize this was the first time she'd ever been out on a date with a man. The rum cocktail tasted like a sweet drink for children; she finished it quickly and he ordered her another. She got tipsy and had to make an effort to listen to what he was telling her. Her dinner of steak and baked potato had no taste, and there was a green vegetable she'd never seen before in her life, covered in yellow sauce. It was tasteless too, but she politely ate everything.

When Hart touched her hand, it startled her. He placed a small box in front of her.

'Go ahead, open it,' he said. Inside was a pair of gold earrings. 'Solid gold. Try them.'

'I'm sorry—' she began.

He looked disappointed. She found it hard to say 'because my mother told me it was wrong to take jewelry from a man you hardly know' or 'I was warned by my grandmother, an obeah-woman, never to wear gold.'

She said, 'I'm sorry, I can't.'

'For me, please.'

It seemed a little thing to do for him. She put them on, slipping the thin hooks through her pierced lobes.

'Gold suits you. You should have lots of gold,' his voice floated over to her. 'Let's dance.'

She was glad to; it was a relief to get up. He was taller than Errol. The top of her head didn't quite reach his shoulder. She felt they were too close, and she pulled back. 'Relax,' he said. His lips were against her ear and he was softly telling her that he had 'something nice' waiting upstairs. She was confused. Wasn't he staying at the Flamingo anymore? He lifted her chin and brought his lips down to hers. She turned her head away and felt his mustache brush her cheek.

She pressed her face against his chest to prevent him from kissing her again and he took this as a sign of affection and held her tighter. Her heart beat fast, and she thought how exhausting the evening had become.

When the song ended, they went back to the table but didn't sit down. He paid the bill. Would he take her home now? She had never been so affected by alcohol before and tried to calculate how much she'd drunk: two of those rum drinks, a bit of wine. She concentrated on trying not to look as drunk as she felt. Her bones felt heavy as they walked out the restaurant and past the hotel bar, where she saw Rosalie, the prostitute who used to hang around with Errol, sitting with a white man.

Ida almost tripped as Hart led her into an elevator. He grinned at her with every part of his face except his mouth. 'You're so pretty,' he said. 'Wait till you see what I've got for us upstairs.'

Inside there was a basket of fruit and a bottle of champagne. In an adjoining room a king-sized bed was turned down for the night.

He kissed her neck. His lips were moist, his mustache abrasive. 'Relax,' he said. On the sofa he leaned over, took off one of her shoes, and rubbed her foot. This felt silly to her.

'You're so pretty,' he said again.

'I've had a very nice time, but it's getting late. I have to go.' She got to her feet, picked up the shoe he'd taken off, and dragged her handbag off the sofa all in one sweep.

He caught her arm.

'You're kidding, aren't you?' He was still smiling, but in a different way now. 'You like playing games?' he said, pulling her to the bedroom. 'Did you play like this with Flynn?'

Her body went stiff, but he didn't seem to notice. He

kissed her on the mouth and pulled her down onto the bed with him.

'I'll treat you a whole lot better than he did.'

She scrambled off the bed. 'I'd like to go home,' she said.

He hit her and pushed her onto the bed again. Grabbing her hair, he wrenched her head back and pressed his mouth down on hers. She was afraid that her neck might break.

He pulled at her blouse, tearing it, and began whispering things, horrible things like a cruel, teasing boy. She felt his hot hand around her neck, pinning her down, and was afraid. What if something happened to her and May never saw her again?

She found a voice and tried to calm him. 'I'll stay. I want to.'

She wasn't sure he heard her, but it no longer mattered. She closed her eyes and let him believe whatever he wanted to as he found his way into her.

She lay as quietly as possible, not in her own bed but in May's little one in the room they shared. She didn't want to disturb the child's perfect sleep. May's lips were parted, making her look like the statue of a surprised cherub, and her limbs were thrown out in complete rest. The peacefulness of the child's body permeated the whole room.

Ida looked up at the ceiling and relived the trail of misjudgment that had brought her to this night of humiliation. She saw her mother's worried face. She closed her eyes and imagined herself floating away from her painful body, once again riding Pearl in the fresh, cool air.

She did not go to work the next day. 'What happen to you face?' her father asked, seeing the bruise under her eye. 'I ran into something at work,' she said with a finality that allowed for no further questions, and she tried not to look at his worried expression.

She left the hotel and gave the excuse that she wanted a job closer to home. It was partly true; the long drive back and forth and many hours away from May had been less than ideal. She began making enquiries in town every day but found nothing that would suit her; she had no secretarial skills and there were no vacancies for shop assistants. Her last paycheck from the hotel took some time to come and in the meantime she was overdrawn at the bank.

Still, she was happy to be at home with May; they had missed each other.

'Mama stay home?'

'Yes. It's a Mama-day!'

May squealed and begged her mother to pick her up and swing her 'round and 'round. Ida thought, *Nothing else matters as long as I have her.*

But it was taking a long time for the bruise on her face to heal.

'Try some cocoa fat,' her father said. 'That's what you mother used to put on scars.'

May laughed. She thought 'cocoa fat' sounded very funny, and she kept saying it over and over again: 'Co-co-fat! Co-co-fat!'

Nothing had ever marred Ida's face before. The bruise looked strange to her, like something cancerous, growing worse, not better.

She put on a hat, driving gloves, and a pair of sunglasses that were big enough to hide the bruise and drove with May to Robinson's Pharmacy in Annotto Bay. She didn't want the Port Antonio pharmacist knowing her business. Mr

Robinson looked at the bruise and sold her two ounces of cocoa fat. It looked white and soothing. She was to rub a little of it on the bruise twice a day. 'And watch where you goin' from now on. No more walkin' into doors.' Handing her the salve, he winked at her.

It was not a kindly wink; it was a leer. Ida's heart beat quickly as she paid the cashier. Did all men now think they had permission to make advances? She held May's hand tightly as she left the store.

May saw the sea outside the car window as they drove back along the coast. 'Sea. Sea. Sea,' she chanted.

Ida pulled over to the side of the road under some casuarinas. She would let May play in the water a bit. It wasn't a proper beach, just a thin strip of pebbly sand. But the water was clear and shallow.

Rolling her pants up to her knees, she waded in with May. May was ecstatic, jumping up and down naked.

'I want to swim,' she said.

May hadn't learned to swim yet, but Ida held her in the water and let her kick her feet. The child was a fish; she had no fear of the water. Errol's child, she was. How could he bear not knowing her?

Her thoughts wandered on to Errol's friend, Karl Von Ausberg. He had called shortly after May was born: How was everything? he'd asked. Did she have a boy or girl? He had even sent a present for May, a recording of nursery rhymes that they played on the gramophone almost daily.

May suddenly put her head under the water and came back up spurting water happily. Ida smiled. She herself had never cared much for the water. There were beaches she thought were pretty, and she had been fascinated as a child with the ships coming and going at the harbor, but the sea had never given her any peace. Right now the blue expanse was especially oppressive to her. The sky seemed ominously empty; the usual seabirds were not around. But she stayed a while and let May splash her and drag her farther in, and by the time they left her own clothes were soaking wet.

Ida finally got a job with the telephone company as a night-shift operator. It didn't pay enough to cover her bills, so she took a second job in the afternoons doing manicures at Mrs Goodman's salon. May woke her up early every morning, delighted to have her mother there to play with, so Ida, arriving home at four every morning, got almost no sleep.

'There's a scientist from England visiting the college,' Myrtle said to her one day. 'You should meet him.'

Ida had just picked up Myrtle and her nephew, Derek, who was now almost six years old. She'd invited them to the house for lunch.

'Why?' Ida asked. 'You think I lookin' a boyfriend?'

'A husband would be good for you.'

Ida laughed. She thought this was funny advice coming from Myrtle, who had never sought any romance in her own life. She had done very well for herself, graduating from the Teacher Training College and now doing advanced training so she could 'teach people how to teach,' as she put it. She had had a matronly figure even at the age of eleven, and still did. She wore huge glasses and never attempted to straighten out her short, kinky hair, which she pulled back into a neat little puff. Nor did she seem to mind the growth of facial hair that looked a bit like sideburns.

'He's a nice man,' Myrtle continued.

'So you marry him, then. I don't want to marry anybody. I sick to death of men.'

'Not every woman needs a man,' Myrtle said slowly. 'But you do.' She looked compassionately at her friend to see her response. Ida's face was unreadable; her eyes were fixed on the road.

'Ida?' she asked softly. 'You still think about Flynn?'

Ida bit her bottom lip; it was an expression Myrtle knew well. She was sorry she had spoken.

When they got to Ida's house they saw Clive Goodman in the garden giving May a piggyback ride while Eli watched from the veranda, smiling.

'Good afternoon, ladies,' Clive said.

Ida noticed that he wore his usual greased-up mechanic's pants but that he had put on a clean shirt. He wore running shoes (he still ran several miles a day for exercise) and he had a sprightly, athletic body, but his receding hairline made him look almost middle-aged.

'Mama!' May shrieked. 'Giddy-up, giddy-up.' She kicked her heels against Clive's back.

'All right, one more time.' He turned to Ida. 'I just come 'round to drop off some pumpkin and cho-cho. We have whole heap at the yard.'

'Thank you. Shirlene can make soup tomorrow.'

He continued standing there despite May's urging and shouting for a ride.

'Mr Joseph lookin' well,' he said.

'Yes, he seems to be doing better—' She decided not to say more and instead looked over at her father. What she didn't go on to say was that he was running out of medicine and Ida did not know how she would pay for more. She saw Clive staring at her as if he knew there was something more. May pummeled him with hands and feet. 'I want giddy-up!'

Derek said, 'I can give you a ride, May.'

'No! I want Clive! I want Clive to giddy-up me!'

'You doing awright?' Ida asked Clive. 'Mr Wallace treating you well?'

Mr Wallace owned a garage where Clive worked as a mechanic. 'Yeah. I doin' awright.' It had been a great disappointment for him after high school not to have won the islandwide scholarship to study engineering abroad. Still, he had hopes of trying for the scholarship again or saving enough over a few years to pay his own tuition.

'Would you like to have lunch with us?' Ida felt a strange formality and stiffness in her words.

'No, thanks.' His eyes were shy and gentle. 'I helpin' my father out with the boat today.'

It was a strange mixed-up world, Ida felt, which gave her an edge of superiority in Clive's eyes. Here she was, the daughter of a Joseph-Hanna, inviting a car mechanic to her table. No other person in her clan would have done that: they were white and rich. But what was she? A shell tossed every which way. It was almost laughable: one day heiress to a movie theatre, the next day practically destitute.

'You sure?' she asked him more warmly. 'We have enough.'

'No, thanks – another time.'

'I wa-aa-ant giddy-up!' May yelled.

Clive galloped up and down the lawn with her.

Myrtle was already on the veranda chatting with Eli. Ida looked inside the two bags that Clive had brought; they were filled with pumpkins, cho-cho, a breadfruit, and Otaheite apples. 'Enough to feed us for the whole week,' she muttered.

It was the country way. Only Kingston people starved. In the countryside, most people had something growing in the yard that they could share. Ida, calculating what was left after she paid Shirlene's weekly wages, realized there was just enough for some rice, condensed milk, and a bit of salt pork to cook in the soup. She was truly grateful to Clive. *We're living like poor people*, she thought. *I have to do something about this.*

But where was Shirlene? She had called her twice to come get the bags from the veranda. Was she even in the house? Recently Ida had found her on a little stool by the fence talking with the neighbor's maid or just sitting out there reading magazines. Yet when Ida reprimanded her, the girl was always polite and apologetic. Well, everybody needs a rest now and then, Ida told herself.

'Yes, Miss Joseph.' The girl appeared on the veranda.

'Take these bags inside, please. And you can set the table for dinner.' Ida wrinkled her nose after Shirlene left and shook her head. 'She wearin' my perfume and thinks I don't notice.'

'Be careful she not takin' anything else,' Myrtle warned.

After lunch Eli went into his room to lie down. Ida and Myrtle sat on the veranda talking and watching the children play. Ida looked at Derek. When had he lost his baby cheeks? she wondered. When had he stopped being a chubby baby and become a boy? He was so careful with May. He watched her attempting something acrobatic along the edge of the driveway and caught her as she was about to lose her balance.

'He's a good boy,' she said to Myrtle.

'Yes, I'm sending him for music lessons. I asked him what he wanted for his birthday and he said he wanted to learn to play the guitar.'

Ida watched him thoughtfully and recalled seeing him alone drumming on a piece of pipe or tapping two sticks on a garbage can while the other children whooped around in the dust. She thought about Clive Goodman's disappointment over the scholarship and was suddenly concerned about what would happen to Derek. Would Myrtle be able to do enough for him?

And while Ida was silently thinking these things, Myrtle glanced at her and noticed the dark circles under her eyes and the thinness of her face. She had too many troubles.

'Ida,' she said kindly, 'have you considered going to Flynn?' She spoke haltingly and was surprised that Ida didn't interrupt. 'I mean, taking May with you and going to him? She's such a pretty baby an' looks just like him, his heart must melt.'

Ida took a deep breath and there was pain in her face.

'I keep having the same bad dream: I'm at Bella Vista. Errol is holding May and there's a crowd of people around. They're pushing me away. I'm screaming for Errol to give May back to me. But everybody's saying, "Lock her up, she's a madwoman."'

'Oh, but—'

'Then I wake up and thank God that May is still here. The dream is finished but it's still close. I don't want to stir things up, Myrtle. Somehow or other I might lose her. I keep telling myself, just wait. One day it might all work out.'

'But your life is too hard.'

Ida looked out into the garden, and Myrtle followed her gaze to where May and Derek crouched over the standpipe.

They let a minute go by before calling out: 'Turn off the pipe. You goin' catch cold.'

'Only dawg suppose to drink pipe-water.'

'I have to do better than this. I have to manage things better,' Ida told herself as she prepared to leave the house for work the next morning.

There was only a little butter left in the butter dish.

They needed new lightbulbs not only for the kitchen but for the bathroom now too. Her father had exactly one week's supply of pills left, and the gas was running low in her car. It was still only the first week of the month and she had almost no cash left to carry them through to the next paycheck.

Every day the same thought crossed her mind: 'I must sit down and think things through.' But when was there time to think or plan? It just grew worse. Every month her bank account was overdrawn. She owed the doctor, the pharmacist, and the gas station.

She remembered one day when she'd taken May out for ice cream, she had seen that prostitute Rosalie who usually hung around the Somerset, buying ice cream for her two youngest children. Ida often saw the children, who were older than May, on their way to and from school. At the ice-cream shop, Rosalie had not seemed like a degraded woman – not even with her tight dress and the makeup so thick that her face was like a mask. She had seemed like a mother whose children were happy to have her there. Ida interrupted her own thoughts. Why was she thinking about that? What was she imagining for herself?

That afternoon she wrote to Aunt Carmen in New York asking her to send the money Esme had saved for her. She was afraid her own bank would devour most of it to pay off what she'd overdrawn, so she had it wired to Myrtle, who passed it on to her as one thousand dollars in US bills, a fortune.

She used two hundred to pay off her bills, and she hid the rest in an old biscuit tin where she kept things like old zippers, buttons, and unused scraps of cloth. The letter from Errol that she'd read again and again as a teenager was also there. She kept the tin on the top shelf of a huge armoire. The extra money was there if she ran out again, but she hoped she wouldn't. She remembered her mother's lessons in frugality: she sewed some dresses for May; she got Shirlene to make several meals from one pound of salt pork. She herself ate only one meal a day – the hearty lunch Mrs Goodman provided at work every afternoon. She had a deeper appreciation than ever for the way her mother had saved that one thousand dollars, and she was determined not to squander it.

Maybe Myrtle was right. Maybe she needed a husband.

She agreed to meet Myrtle's friend, the visiting scientist, for tea at the guesthouse where he was staying. She agreed only on the condition that Myrtle would be there too.

His name was Cecil Palmer, and he was an animated, red-haired man whose khaki shorts revealed pale knees. He was studying Jamaican tree ferns, and he told amusing stories about his work and travels. He seemed to take a mischievous delight in catching Myrtle off guard, teasing her and making her laugh. A nice man, Ida thought, but not for me.

Cecil left them for a moment as he went up to his room for a raincoat. There were a few moments of silence between the two women. Myrtle looked pleased with herself and the surroundings. The guesthouse was at the top of a hill, and there was a wonderful view of Port Antonio and the twin harbors.

Ida was unable to share the pleasure. She knew Cecil was the reason Myrtle was so happy, though Myrtle herself didn't seem to realize that, and she was suddenly angry at not being free, like Myrtle, to enjoy herself. For the first time she blamed Errol. Like a hawk, an old, sick hawk, he had swooped down and caught her, nourished himself, and then dropped her, not caring in the least where she fell. She wanted to hurt and astonish him.

'Ida?'

'Sorry?' She hadn't heard what Myrtle had been telling her.

'He likes you,' she repeated.

'No, you big dunce. He likes you.'

Things would work out for Myrtle. Perhaps they would for her too.

15

Shoes for May

Ida had been working both at the telephone company and Mrs Goodman's for nearly six months, and things seemed to be getting harder, not easier. She was sitting at the table one night adding up the month's bills when there was a knock on the door. It was Clive Goodman and he was carrying an old brown suitcase.

'You going away?'

He nodded. 'Florida. Boat leaving tonight.'

'Tonight?' She sat down on the veranda chair. Clive sat down across from her.

'I just wanted to come 'round an' say good-bye. May gone to bed?'

'Yes, she just fell asleep. Why you going?'

'Well, you know – I not mekin' enough workin' for Mr Wallace.'

'What you goin' do in Florida?'

'Farm labor.' He sighed heavily. 'I can mek a whole heap a money. Is through the government.'

'I know.' She had heard of the Farm Labor Program.

'I have a two-year contract, an' I get room and board so I can save up plenty.'

Ida thought about her own need for money and of women she'd heard of who had gone to America to work, not on farms but as domestic servants. She felt she could never do that.

'I hear the work is hard-hard like punishment over there.'

'So they say. But I want to have my own business, you know, and I don't see no other way.'

'What about university?'

'That goin' tek too long. I'm a good mechanic.'

He smiled, showing a chipped tooth she had never noticed before. It was somehow attractive.

She was afraid for him. He was strong, but his nature was essentially gentle. She'd heard stories of West Indian men dying over there at the hands of vicious, prejudiced white men. It was not like Jamaica. There were laws there that kept black people from going wherever they wanted; she had heard of a case where a Jamaican man had died because the white hospital wouldn't admit him. Clive seemed to read her thoughts.

'If it don't kill me, I come back rich.'

'An' is really tonight you leavin'?'

'Yes, tonight.' He stood up and picked up the suitcase. 'Tek care a you'self an' the baby. An' I hope to see Mr Joseph still looking well when I come back.'

She stared at the suitcase. It was much too small. She thought how hard it must be, deciding what to take and what to leave.

'Well, I better go now.'

Her eyes wandered back to him.

'I'm glad you came to see me. I pray you'll keep well.'

'You too——' He was never sure what to call her. He wanted to call her 'Ida' because they had been friends as schoolchildren, but 'Miss Ida' came instinctively to his lips because she was a lady of a higher class. So he stopped short and turned away.

He walked out the gate without looking back. Night had invaded the little street and all its yards. She watched him go. There was quickness, almost a glide, in his step as though migration to an unknown land were a relief compared to the awkwardness of sitting on her veranda. Yet they were friends. He got to the end of the street and disappeared from view. The darkness was impenetrable now; they were expecting heavy rain. She stayed out for a few moments breathing in the night air.

The next day May would not stop crying. Ida was getting dressed for work and heard her. She saw Shirlene, agitated, on her knees trying to put shoes on May's feet.

'She won't let me put on her shoes, ma'am. Every day, same t'ing. Yesterday she tek the shoes an' t'row dem cross de room.'

Ida saw what the problem was. The shoes were too tight. She snatched May up to her.

'You don't see the shoes too small?' she shouted at Shirlene. 'And anyway, why she not wearin' her sandals?'

'The sandals tear-up an' t'row way long time, ma'am.'

'Well, she mus' have other shoes in her room.'

No, she did not. Ida remembered now that the other shoes had been donated to the church jumble sale because they no longer fit May. The child had no more shoes.

'Hush, sweetheart.' She gently rubbed and kissed the little toes. 'Mama will buy you new shoes.' She turned to Shirlene, who stood watching them with thinly veiled exasperation. *That girl is getting facety and out of order*, Ida thought.

'She don't need shoes today. She can go barefoot.'

'Yes, Shirlene,' May took on the authority in her mother's voice, 'I can go boyfoot today.'

Ida suppressed a smile. The last thing May cared about was shoes. If she were allowed to, she would be running up and down the streets and gullies with the little half-naked, barefoot boys.

'But she will catch worms in her foot-bottom,' Shirlene drawled.

'Rubbish. The worse that can happen is maca juk her. She jus' out here on the grass. She not goin' street or market.'

She kissed May, who ran out onto the veranda, stopping in her tracks suddenly to watch a lizard.

Ida did not have money that month to buy shoes. Not unless she took it from the tin.

She thought about Clive on his way to Florida. Life was certainly hard here on this island. No one starved in the countryside but people needed more than food. Could she wait a whole month to get May shoes or would she have to take more money out of the hidden savings?

She stopped by the post office to collect the mail. Across the street she saw the betting shop and the usual crowd of unemployed men with their racing papers. For the first time in her life, she considered gambling. She had five shillings in her handbag that she could place on the favorite. If she won, it would mean five pounds. But if she lost the five shillings, there would be no money for milk or bread, not to mention the sixpence ice-cream cone May was treated to every Sunday after church. How that child loved ice cream. The image of her daughter's concentrated pleasure and the fact that she had never disappointed her when it came to this special treat put the thought of betting completely out of her mind. The five shillings could not be risked.

The postmistress handed her the usual mail: Eli's *Daily Mirror* from London, which his brother continued to pay for, several letters from the bank, and something that made her heart beat faster – a thin brown envelope from Spain addressed to her.

She waited till she was back in her car before opening it. It was from him. She could barely read it because of the pounding in her chest: 'Dear Ida, There's no need to thank me,' it began, and she realized that it was a reply to the letter she had sent thanking him for the money.

She started again:

Dear Ida,

There's no need to thank me. I'm not sure what to do with such gratitude. No woman ever thanked me before for anything. I'm sorry not to have been in touch with you. There is never enough peace for me to think much less write. So now it feels good to put pen to paper. I know your father despises me, and maybe that's the reason I haven't written. But I won't make excuses. I no longer have the energy or the sobriety to separate the truth from the muddle of lies. But I can say, most truthfully, that I never meant to cause you any trouble.

With fond memories, Errol

Instead of eating lunch with Mrs Goodman and the others, Ida went for a walk down by the harbor.

It was a bright, breezy day. There was the familiar smell of the briny air mixed with the odor of bananas, the ones that hadn't made it onto the boats and had ripened on the wharf. The usual loaders were there, women sleeping and half sleeping against barrels before the night's tallying began. It was quiet. All she heard was the haphazard creaking of wood and the water lapping against the planks.

Across the road from the harbor, a tree-cutter was eating his lunch, with the sawed-off branches and the massive tree-saw beside him. She saw him watching her. Maybe he was wondering what a pretty woman in a pleated sky-blue skirt was doing there all by herself. She was conscious of the poetry of it all and wished she had the ability to write something that would capture what was in and around her: the eyeless, surging sea, the tree-cutter's stare, the blue skirt, and the strain of her unfulfilled hopes. In his letter, Errol hinted at a muddle of lies. Let that be his portion, then. She had her child.

Nigel Fletcher paid an unexpected visit with his little boy, Ian. He had just recently heard about Eli Joseph's stroke. 'I thought I'd pop over and see how my old friend's doing,' he told Ida.

Since she had last seen him, Nigel had become the author of two successful spy novels ('Denise thinks they're dreadful,' he told her dryly). He spent half the year in Jamaica, where he did his writing, and the other half of his time in Europe. Denise spent very little time in Jamaica, though she often sent one or both of her sons for holidays with their father.

Ian was clinging to his father's knee and watching May with that deep curiosity children have when they meet others their age. May sat on the veranda floor playing with her teddy bear, 'Lassie.' She glanced now and then at the little boy and his father.

There was a rumor that Ian was not Nigel's son but Errol's. Ida had also heard that Karl Von Ausberg might be the boy's father. Looking at the child, Ida dismissed both notions right away. This dark-eyed, solemn boy looked nothing like Errol or Karl, and Nigel had a genuine fatherly affection for the child.

Nigel visited for about an hour, and as he was leaving he had a few private words with Ida. He had heard about Eli losing the movie theatre and could sense that they were having a difficult time. He wanted her to know that she could call him if she needed help. While he spoke, his eyes remained steadily on May.

'Does Flynn ever come by?' he asked.

'No.' She tried to answer without expressing any particular emotion.

'Pity,' he said. 'Look, you will call me if you need anything?'

Ian had been completely absorbed in May's play-world. Nigel noticed this and made Ida promise to bring May with her to Oracabessa soon. 'They play well together,' he said and turned to May: 'I think Ian likes playing with you.'

May nodded and said, 'We played-ed.'

'Played,' Ida corrected. 'Yes,' she told Nigel. 'We'll visit soon.' But privately she thought there was something sullen and disturbing about the little boy.

Nigel's visit bothered her. She couldn't stand being pitied, especially by Errol's friend. She looked at her father, who lay on the chaise longue with his eyes closed. He had enjoyed listening to Nigel's World War II stories, but the visit had exhausted him.

He opened his eyes and saw her sitting there.

'What you thinking 'bout?' he asked.

'Nothing.'

Eli blinked slowly, watching her.

She was gazing at the house across the road where a family of eight people lived. They had a smaller house than the Josephs', with no telephone, no car, not even a bicycle. Yet they seemed happy enough. Ida wondered: Would she worry less if she wanted less, if she could 'small-up' herself, as Jamaicans said?

She asked her father, 'Why do people like the Fletchers have everything? You think it's because they're white?'

'You think Nigel Fletcher has everything?'

Ida didn't answer.

'He don't have squat. Nigel Fletcher lives in his books. I read one the other day. Donkey piss. Don't misunderstand me. I like the man. But he not better than you or me.'

He stopped for a moment. then added, 'You shake him hand, you no shake him heart.'

She knew exactly what he meant. Who could tell what was hidden in Nigel's heart? He flew planes in rough weather and hunted sharks. His spy novels seemed to be just another way of thrashing about.

Eli spoke again: 'You can still do great things, Ida. God don't finish paintin' you picture.'

'I know,' she said, more to console him than herself. 'Things will get better.'

But things got worse.

A few nights later Ida was working the night shift at the telephone company and feeling very unsettled. She telephoned home around nine o'clock. Shirlene had put May to bed and her father was listening to the radio. Nothing was out of order. She wondered if it was the conversation she'd had with May the night before that was bothering her.

They had been talking about Nigel's visit and May had asked, 'Is Ian my friend?'

'Yes, I think you and Ian will be good-good friends.' Ida realized how lonely the child was, playing so much by herself. She would remedy that. Maybe they would drive to Oracabessa on Sunday and visit the Fletchers.

'Is Ian's daddy your friend?'

'Yes.'

'Where's my daddy?'

The question shot her like an arrow. There were several answers she could give, none of them easy.

It had been some time since she had shown May her father's picture or pointed out his face in a movie. She realized that the face and its meaning had vanished from the child's memory; there was just a hollow where May sensed a father should be. The least difficult thing to say would be 'Your father is dead,' but how could she lie to her daughter? The truth was slippery. Ida, whose life had been blessed, even defined, by her own father's love, felt the void even more deeply than the child did.

If only she could point to a place on a map and call it 'Father.'

These were her thoughts as she sat in front of the quiet switchboard. There were rarely any long-distance calls on her shift. She would sit for hours with the knobs and switches before her, feeling completely unnecessary. She usually read or did some sewing, but that night she found it hard to concentrate.

By one a.m., she was fretful. She could not help calling even though she knew it meant waking Shirlene and possibly everyone else in the house. But the phone rang without an answer.

With three more hours left on her shift, she couldn't stand it any longer; she called the rectory and woke Father Reynold. Yes, he agreed it was strange that no one was answering the phone. He would go over and take a look.

He called back about fifteen minutes later and told her that Shirlene was gone and something was wrong with May; Ida was to meet him at the hospital.

Ida arrived a few minutes after he did. The hospital was eerily empty. A nurse, who appeared to be running everything, came over to Ida: 'I think her appendix is ruptured. The surgeon is on his way.'

'Where is she?'

'Come, see if you can calm her down while they prepare her for surgery.'

May held out her thin arms to her mother and sobbed, 'I cried-ed a long time, but nobody comed!'

The door opened and the surgeon walked over to the bed. He smiled reassuringly at May while he examined her. 'It isn't ruptured, but we need to operate right away.'

While Ida waited, Father Reynold explained how he had seen the light on in May's room from outside. He had gone in to find her on the ground curled up and crying, and the bedroom lamp knocked over beside her.

'Shirlene?'

He shook his head. 'I don't see no sign of her. I woke up Eli and told him I tekin' May to the hospital.' He put his hand to his forehead, suddenly remembering the old man. 'He must be sick with worry. Let me call somebody to go stay with him.'

May spent a week in hospital, and Ida stayed with her. She remembered May complaining about a tummyache that afternoon, and she remembered how the worry had been nagging at her all during her shift. She had been so certain that something was wrong. And the child had been alone there on the floor. She might have died.

It was apparently not the first time Shirlene had left during the night to be with her boyfriend. Frightened after hearing what had happened to May, Shirlene had returned to Plumbago Road only to collect her few belongings and leave Port Antonio for good.

Ida stopped working and stayed home to look after May and her father. She didn't want to leave her child with a stranger again.

The problem of shoes arose again.

She hated having to do it, but she had promised to take May to the shoe shop, so she took down the tin where she had hidden her money. The old torn-out zippers were there, and the buttons and scraps of cloth; Errol's two letters were there too, as useless as the old zippers. The money was gone.

Ida sank down into the kitchen chair with the open tin on her lap. She barely noticed when May came into the room.

'Come, Mama.'

'Come?'

'To the shop.'

Ida said nothing. She pulled May close.

'We goin' buy shoes?' May asked.

'No. Not today, darling.'

May looked at her mother.

'Why you sad?'

'Shirlene stole Mama's money.' Then she heard herself, in her complete despondency, worrying out loud: 'What we goin' do?'

'Go boyfoot,' May said.

16

Ida's Decision: The Niagara

The *Niagara*, a banana boat, was sailing from Port Antonio to Boston, making a stop in New York on the way. For twenty American dollars, Ida purchased a third-class passenger ticket.

She gave what was left from her last paycheck to Myrtle's mother, Miss Gloria, to take care of May and Eli, and she promised to send more once she was settled in New York. She kept five dollars for herself.

She visited Oni before she left, taking May with her. The old horse, Mankind, had died and had been replaced by an unfriendly mule. 'Don't go near that mule, she will kick you,' Oni warned May several times that afternoon.

Ida looked out at the view of Port Antonio. 'Look,' she pointed to May, 'over there is the Rio Grande where your father went rafting, and that's where Mama used to ride her horse.'

It was the first time she had brought May up the mountain. Oni had seen May only once before. When May was six months old, Oni had visited them at Plumbago Road. 'This one is a real African, a Yoruba pickney,' she had said without sarcasm, staring at the pale, blue-eyed baby. Ida and her father had laughed about it later: Oni was going either mad or blind.

Now Ida had come to say good-bye and also to hear what cautionary words Oni might offer.

'No worry you'self,' Oni said, almost dismissively. 'I tell you already, you have the Lord o' Stars up on you head-top an' Shango down at you foot-bottom.'

'How long before I come back?'

'Before long.'

Ida wondered what that meant. She hoped not to be gone for more than a year.

'Before long you come back with diamonds and a silk frock. Let me read May's future?'

'No,' Ida said, and her face was full of grief as she watched May chasing birds. 'She doesn't know I'm going.'

'Hush, now. I mek up some bush-tea for you. It will calm you nerves. Plenty woman leave dem pickney nowadays to look work abroad.'

Ida had considered leaving May up there on the mountain with Oni, but Oni was so isolated; there were no doctors, no post office or telephones.

She had been shocked when Aunt Carmen had said no to her bringing May with her to New York. That had been her initial plan. Her cousin, Linette, had two small children and lived in Aunt Carmen's house. Why not May? She had written a pleading letter. Aunt Carmen had written back:

Linette is moving to Harlem with her boyfriend and she is pregnant again. The whole lot of them are finally leaving my house, thank God. I've had enough. I'm too old to have children around. There is nobody here to take care of May while you are at work. I know this is hard for you, but please have some consideration for my age.

Ida realized that Linette had drained Aunt Carmen of patience. Ida had been hearing news of Linette's antics all her life. Aunt Carmen had admitted once that the girl was 'a little touched in the head.' That seemed to be the case when Linette shaved her head and took to the street begging, holding up a sign saying she was raising money to go back to China. She had become obsessed with their grandfather, Tan Sen-Choy.

There is room for you to stay now that Linette is leaving, but I intend to keep an orderly, quiet house. Aunt Carmen's message had been clear.

There was no choice but to leave May in the yard with Myrtle's mother, where the little boy Derek lived. The Tates seemed to be good, hardworking people, and there were other children there for May to play with. Myrtle was still rooming at the college but she would visit on weekends and check on May. Once Ida got a job in New York she would be able to send enough money to feed and clothe May well. Eventually, if things turned out well, she would get her own place in New York and send for her.

On a cloudy evening, Ida stood with May in the dirt yard on Parrot Lane. This would be home for May and Eli.

Ida watched Miss Gloria help her father up the steps of the house while Derek followed, struggling with Eli's suitcase. They had already installed her father's favorite veranda chair so he would be able to sit out in the fresh air. It broke her heart to watch him walking with such difficulty now and to see him leaning heavily on a woman he barely knew. Now and then he turned around and, seeing her still there, smiled.

May held her teddy bear, 'Lassie,' in one hand and tugged at her other hand, which her mother held tightly. She wanted to go play with Derek and explore the new yard, a level clearing, without toys or trees. Ida had explained to her that she, May, and her grandfather would be staying with Derek's family for a while because Mama had to go away. She had been surprised by May's calm response. 'OK. We'll wait for you,' she'd said. Ida thought she was just too young to understand. Or was she? There had been a change in her. She was still a happy, energetic child, but more pensive; she pondered over things where before she had merely reacted.

Thunder came, threatening a downpour. It would take some time for Miss Gloria to get her father settled in his room, and Ida's taxi was waiting at the gate.

'Derek,' she called, and he came running over.

Quickly she gathered May up, kissed her, and set her down in front of Derek.

'Look after her till I come back.'

Derek's usually playful eyes were serious. 'Yes, ma'am.' He took May's hand.

' 'Bye, Mama,' May said.

No, Ida thought, *she doesn't understand*. She saw the face of a trusting child who expected her to return in a few hours.

'Say good-bye to Miss Gloria and my father for me,' she said as she turned away.

Ida was relieved that Father Reynold had been unable to see her off at the boat; she didn't want another good-bye. All week long there had been those sympathetic looks and mournful words meant to soothe her. It was as if the whole town of Port Antonio knew she was leaving to find work in New York, and every face seemed to say, 'What a shame, poor girl.'

She wore her mother's sapphire necklace hidden beneath her blouse and as usual, she had her silver bangles. In her handbag she carried the rosary Father Reynold had given her after her first communion, a photograph of May, and the directions to Aunt Carmen's house in New York. The five-dollar note was tucked inside her shoe. With these few belongings, she went down into the steel belly of the ship, which was already rife with human odors. Unusual sounds, human and machine, leapt out at her. She was almost blind with sadness over May.

She walked down several flights of metal stairs to the third-class berths, where, for an extra ten dollars paid by Father Reynold, she would share a space with three other women. She had her father's old brown leather suitcase, a source of pride to her because he had bought it in London in better times and it had remained in excellent condition.

Her berthmates were already there. A hefty, dark-skinned woman lay across the bottom bunk sucking a peppermint. Her eyes shifted slowly to Ida, and she seemed taken aback for a moment, seeing someone so light-skinned and well dressed, but the surprise instantly hardened into feigned indifference. The other two seemed to take their cue from her – initial surprise at Ida and then withdrawal. There was no word of greeting from any of them.

Ida placed her suitcase on the floor next to the other women's luggage and looked at the woman sitting on the upper bunk with her legs hanging down, with whom she would be sharing a bunk. She looked part Indian, and Ida guessed she was about her own age. The woman wore her 'good' dress, white flat-heeled shoes, and a white hat that covered her whole head. A churchgoing woman, Ida decided. She held a balled-up handkerchief in both hands.

They were all dark-skinned, and, by their dress and demeanor, of a lower class than Ida. The heavyset woman had the look of someone from the city – Kingston or Montego Bay; she wore gaudy gold-plated jewelry and her hair had been recently pressed with a hot comb. The other two with their subdued, timid manner were clearly from country villages.

'Look here, Miss Whitey-White, mind how you fling you bag down on me shoe!' The big woman spoke without bothering to look at Ida.

Ida pushed her suitcase away from the woman's wide, misshapen shoes.

'My name is Ida Joseph and for your information, I'm not white.'

The big woman stared at her for a moment.

'Ku yah!' she exclaimed, then laughed.

Ida left the room with the woman's mocking laughter behind her. She found a porthole and looked out at the harbor, busy with the departing passengers. She remained there at the porthole, people jostling back and forth past her, even as the ship sounded its horn, lifted anchor, and began pulling out to sea.

It was night. The United Fruit Company's lighters sailed alongside, each of them carrying four or five men. They were bare-chested and shouted out a work song as they heaved the heavy stems of bananas into the hold. She was glad they were there. The ship glided farther out to sea and away from the lighters. The men were no longer distinct figures, just part of the shimmering darkness of the harbor. She felt surprisingly unafraid as the island disappeared from sight. It was not so unbearable. She was the descendant of staunch voyagers from Africa, China, Europe, and Lebanon; they had all survived their partings. So would she.

Part Three

On this day August 28th in the year of our Lord 1764, I was forced aboard the sloop Maribella. I shall now proceed to furnish you with details of my misfortunes as they occurred with no exaggeration.

Treasure Cove

17

A New Country and
an Unlikely Courtship

September 30, 1954

Dear Papa,

I'm finally here in Cambria Heights, Queens, New York. Aunt Carmen has a big two-story house. She rents the upstairs to a man who works in the city, and Aunt Carmen and I live downstairs. It makes me happy to see the pictures of all of us in her living room. So many things here remind me of home. Aunt Carmen keeps her necklaces coiled like snakes on top of the dresser just like Mama used to.

I had a hard time finding my way here even though Aunt Carmen gave me directions. She didn't tell me that the train was *under* the street. She told me to get on the IRT train and I thought it was a word, pronounced 'ert,' you know, like hurt, and so I kept asking people directions to the 'ert' train. Everybody looked at me like I was mad. Then I spent a long time on one train before I realized I was going in the completely wrong direction, uptown not downtown.

Everyone expects you to know these things. Anyway, two more trains and a bus ride brought me to Cambria Heights.

There are no fences between the houses. The yards are tiny and there are no verandas, but I suppose that's because of the cold. Aunt Carmen says it will start getting cold soon. She's going to lend me a coat until I have enough money to buy one. So don't worry about me catching pneumonia.

I got a job today at a restaurant called Bernie's Steak House. I greet people at the door and take them to their seats. I also supervise the waitresses. Thirty dollars a week and free lunch! Aunt Carmen was amazed that I found a job so fast. She says Bernie's Steak House is no fenky-fenky place; it has a very good reputation. I offered to give her part of my pay as you suggested, but she says not to worry and that I can help her out around the house.

She doesn't seem in the best of health — smoking more than usual and coughing up a storm. Frankly, I don't think retirement suits her. It has made her fat and a bit miserable. Can you imagine Aunt Carmen fat! I almost didn't recognize her.

Please give my baby girl a kiss and a hug every day from me. Show her my picture and let her kiss it if it makes her feel better. How is she doing, Papa? Remind Miss Gloria and Derek that she likes to sleep with Lassie and that she can suck her thumb if she wants to. I don't care what the doctor says; it's her thumb and not hurting anybody. Remember you promised to teach her how to count to twenty and to sing that Lebanese song about the seashells. I miss you both so much. I'm sending a letter for May. Please read it to her. Say 'Hello' to Father Reynold when you see him.

Your loving daughter, Ida

September 30, 1954

Dear May,

I will bring you something special from New York. Eat all your food so you will grow strong. Say your prayers every night. Look after Grandpa. And remember how much I love you. You are my darling little girl. I will write again very soon.

Love, Mama

December 15, 1954

Dear Father Reynold,

Thank you for your letter. I cried with joy reading it. You are such a good friend.

My first job lasted less than two weeks, and frankly I'm glad to be gone from that place. The owner must have thought I was white when he hired me. I didn't even notice that only white people ate at the restaurant, after all most people in America are white (even the garbage-collectors!). But the head cook kept telling me terrible things about the Barbadian men who work in the kitchen. How I was to be careful around them because of what black men will do to white women and that kind of thing. So I told him that he was damn prejudice and that as a matter of fact I was colored too. He must have talked to the owner because the next day I was asked to leave.

One of the waitresses at Bernie's said to me, 'You could pass for white, so why do you want to lower yourself?' I began to wonder how she knew so much about it, and whether she was really Portuguese like she said. I told her I can't pretend to be something I'm not and that my mother was a colored lady.

I'm relieved to hear you rented the house. Please give Miss Gloria the money for May and Papa and if there's anything left over save it for me. I want to send for May as soon as I'm settled in my own place.

You asked me about the Empire State Building. I suppose it's still there, but I wouldn't know. Except for the day I arrived I haven't been outside Queens. To tell the truth, it's all too big for me, the roads, the buildings, and never mind the subway – I hope to avoid that if I can. But my cousin Linette says she is taking me to a dance club in Manhattan, so I'll look for your Empire State Building.

Thank you for taking May out for ice cream. I dream she's in the bed sleeping with me and I can feel her warm little body. Then I wake up and feel like hell. I didn't know what brokenhearted meant till now. Pray for me, Father, and don't drink too much rum.

Love, Ida

February 25, 1955

Dear Myrtle,

I'm sending this letter with a pair of shoes for May and some pants for Derek. Let me know what size shoes he wears because I know a store on 34th Street where I can get good-quality shoes cheap. There is a darling old Trinidadian man named Hubert who works the elevator there and he shows me the 50 per cent off racks.

How is your dear Cecil? Please say hello to him for me.

I feel so fortunate to have this new job. I owe it to crazy Linette and her boyfriend. Linette took me to a club in

Harlem where her boyfriend plays the trumpet. My dear, she doesn't think of herself as Chinese anymore; she calls herself a mulatto. I almost didn't go with them because I didn't have anything nice to wear. Linette lent me a dress; she's petite, and the dress was so tight I could hardly walk in it much less dance. Anyway, I went and I have to admit it felt good to finally put on nice stockings and shoes and feel pretty.

I had a wonderful time in Harlem. It wasn't just the good music and dancing, it was seeing all those different kinds of colored people all around me. Handsome colored people, from light-skinned like me to coal-black and nobody worrying about it. There were white people too and everybody was getting on just like in Jamaica.

I went to church in Harlem with Linette the next day and talk about music and hand-clapping! She introduced me to a doctor who has just opened a practice there, and he offered me a job.

Traveling from Queens to Harlem was too hard so I have moved in with Linette though Aunt Carmen told me not to. She thinks Linette will ruin my life. It's true my cousin has made some mistakes but she's not a bad person. I share a room with the children. They are very sweet and I don't mind. I look after them on nights when Linette and Gene go to the clubs. I'm not too sure about Gene. I don't like the way he speaks to Linette. He doesn't help her at all with money.

Dr Thomas is a real gentleman and I've learned a lot about running a doctor's office. I'm putting a little money aside every week to buy an airplane ticket for May.

I miss my daughter so much. What feels worse though is when I realize I'm not missing her. That must sound terrible, but it's true. Sometimes I feel just like other girls my age — making plans to go out to the movies, spending money on nice clothes for myself, and the hours go by without me thinking about May. I couldn't forgive myself if those hours turned into days, then weeks. I've met some women here who haven't seen their children for years. I'm not judging them. But I don't want that to happen to me. I'm going to be with my little girl soon.

Let me know if I can send you or Miss Gloria anything. There is a Woolworth's around the corner that sells everything under the sun from instant mashed potatoes to nighties cheap-cheap.

Your good friend, Ida

P.S. Please assure Papa that winter is not treating me so badly. I'm keeping warm.

August 20, 1955

Dear Myrtle,

I'm wiring you one hundred dollars along with the usual thirty for Miss Gloria. I'm worried that it will end up in Linette's hands if I don't get it to you now.

I need to look for another place to live although I feel terrible leaving these poor children.

Gene is a drug addict and Linette takes drugs too. I had to pay the whole rent last month and have been buying food for the children. I almost wish I could take them with me; they are no trouble. The oldest one, Merle, is twelve and when she comes home from school she looks after the two little ones.

Before I go, let me tell you something surprising that happened. I went back to the jazz club on 125th Street. Not with Linette but with Dr Thomas and some of his friends. Guess who I saw there? Errol's friend, Baron Karl Von Whatever.

My dear, he came over to the table as if he was some good old friend and gave me his phone number. He has an apartment here in New York. He asked me where I was living but I said I was about to move (which is true). I don't want him calling me, and I have no intention of calling him. I was glad that I was wearing my auntie's nice fur coat so he couldn't look down his nose at me.

How is Papa doing? I heard he had a bad cold. Is it better? If not, could you please arrange for the doctor to see him and let me know how much it costs? I will repay you. I don't want it to turn into pneumonia. Give my little girl a special hug from her mama when you see her.

Love, Ida

November 12, 1955

Dear Myrtle,

I'm glad that I have you to confide in, just like the old days at school. I can't tell Papa or Father Reynold these things, they would worry too much.

Last week we were put out on the street. Linette used all the rent money I gave her to buy drugs and clothes for Gene. She was so desperate to hold on to him. But he left her anyway for some other woman. I thought Linette was going to kill herself. She was in such a state. I had to take the two youngest ones with me to work because I was afraid to leave them with her. We came back home and Merle, the oldest, was out on the steps crying. She said, 'Mama broke the windows.' I went up and saw she had taken a hammer and broken every window in the place saying they were devil eyes staring at her. The landlord came with the police. What with the broken windows and unpaid rent, we were forced out the next day. The police sent Linette to a psychiatric hospital.

I have the children. All I could do was gather up our things and get on the train back to Queens. But Aunt Carmen is threatening to send them to foster homes. I don't think she really will, but she is too old now to bear Linette's burdens.

Here is the worst part. I lost my job with Dr Thomas because of all this trouble. He didn't like the children coming to work with me, and then I had to miss some days. He said that when things settle down for me I should give him a call again. But he already has another receptionist.

So here I am with these sad children who are not mine and no job. Don't tell anybody. I will find something soon and things will get better.

Aunt Carmen says I need to get a profession like nursing. But that takes too long. And how will I earn money if I'm studying? But I might take a night course that will help me get a job as a florist. The course is only six weeks. Pray to God to show me the way. This is a hard country.

Love, Ida

March 2, 1956

Dear Derek,

I heard you just had a birthday and so I am sending a little present, a book about famous musicians. Your auntie says that you are quite a good musician yourself. Thank you for looking after May. I heard you came to her rescue the other day when some children were teasing her. I love you for doing that and God bless you. She is so little, please hug her when she is sad and don't let her go in the street with the older children. Enjoy your birthday present.

Best wishes, Auntie Ida

June 3, 1956

Dear Papa,

I will write a longer letter soon, but I just wanted to let you know I'm well.

I was unemployed for quite a while and helping out with Linette's children while she was in hospital. But I have a new job now as an assistant to an old lady in Manhattan. I live in her apartment six days a week, but go home to Aunt Carmen on Saturdays. By the way, the father of Linette's oldest child has taken her and her two sisters to live with him and his wife. I am so relieved and happy for them. He is a good man and his wife is an angel. Aunt Carmen has terrible arthritis. She still smokes a lot and coughs a lot. She thinks that eating raw garlic every day will prevent heart attack. Does madness run in Mama's side of the family?

Love, Ida

December 12, 1956

Dear Myrtle,

So much has happened since I last wrote you. Thank you for the pictures. It's good to know May has loving people around her like you and Father Reynold. She has grown so tall and no longer has a baby face. Why isn't she smiling in any of the pictures?

A Barbadian woman I know told me about an agency that sends women out as nurse's aides. She said it was like being a companion to old people who lived alone, not really being a nurse. After six months you get certified and then you earn twice as much. I imagined it would be things like reading books to an old lady, driving her to doctor's appointments and doing grocery shopping – the kind of things I used to do for Papa – easy and even pleasant since I like the idea of helping people. And eventually five dollars an hour! So I went to the agency.

They sent me to an old lady on the East Side of Manhattan in a building that looked like a castle. The entrance was all marble, my dear. This was a live-in job. I was to stay with her for six nights a week.

She was eighty-three with arthritis, and she had a rash all over her body and her scalp. She needed help moving from room to room and couldn't bathe herself. The agency sent a supervisor on the first day to show me the proper way to get her in and out of the bath and where to put the garbage. That was the extent of my nurse's aide training!

This old woman, Miss Potts, was so distrustful of me. 'Are you really from Jamaica?' she kept asking. 'You look white.' Then she told me the agency had sent her a Puerto Rican last time and she didn't want any more Puerto Ricans in her house. Prejudiced! I assured her I was not Puerto Rican and my good English convinced her.

By day number two I realized I was not working as an aide but as a maid! I had to do everything from wiping her bottom to cleaning the floor, which always needed to be mopped because she was incontinent. I began to think she pee-peed on the floor just to annoy me. Finally I told her that I was used to having maids in Jamaica and never treated them the way she did. She didn't believe me of course. She didn't believe anything I told her about myself. One day I just couldn't take any more and I told her I didn't like being shouted at, that my name was *Ida*, not *Girl*, and I was not a dog to be given her leftover food. After that she behaved a bit better. I think she was afraid I would leave her and the agency would send a Puerto Rican.

But she was a real tightfisted witch. Here she was with an eight-room apartment all to herself (she had a niece in New Jersey who she complained never visited her – no wonder!), thousands in the bank (she told me), and she ate tongue for dinner every day. I wouldn't eat one bit of it! She wouldn't even let me boil it with any seasoning, not even salt. And she wouldn't let me cook my own food because she said it smelled up the place. Like the boiled tongue didn't. She had the butcher shop deliver it every week. I began to tip the delivery boy with my own money because I felt so bad at the few cents she would tell me to give him.

The only time I got out of the house was in the mornings and evenings to walk her little dog that looked like a bald cat. Mind you, he was a sweet, good-natured dog, but he smelled bad and she wouldn't let me bathe him in case he caught cold. I had to put a sweater on him before I took him outside. I liked walking Prince because I got to sit on a bench by the river with some other West Indian ladies. Some of them brought out their old people in wheelchairs.

At first they didn't know I was West Indian. But one day I decided to talk to them and after that it was all right. They said, 'You look white but you lick salt jus' like us.' The half hour I spent with them every morning was like a tonic. They worked hard-hard, but the way they talked you would think they owned the world. They were proud as peacocks about the money they earned and all the things they could buy for themselves and their families back home. I was amazed at how they stood up to all the insults they got. Maybe it was because they had each other to laugh and joke with.

Miss Potts watched television all day. But you think she would ever let me sit down for a minute and watch something? If I looked like I wasn't doing anything, she found something for me to do. One day she asked me to clean the metal hangers in her closet. You ever hear such a thing?

Myrtle, it's getting quite late, so I will continue this letter tomorrow.

I stayed with Miss Potts for four months. I stayed with the bad smells, bad food, and all the nastiness she could force on me because I was making one hundred and fifty dollars a week. I should really have been earning more because the woman had me up all hours of the night, and it was really twenty-four hours a day I was working. But I said to myself, 'Bide you time, by the end of summer you have enough saved up to take typing lessons and send for May.'

One evening I was sitting by the river. For once I had some time alone, without the dog. I told Miss Potts I left something out on the bench and had to go back for it. I felt if I didn't have a little time by myself I would go mad.

I sat on the bench staring at the water. It was a few days after I got those pictures of May in her school uniform. I couldn't believe she was almost six. I started to think crazy things like maybe she was better off without me. I thought about drowning myself in the river. How could I have left my baby? I was another person, not the same Ida Joseph. And when I say that I mean I actually felt like somebody else was inside my skin.

Right then I decided I had to go. God forgive me for leaving an old woman by herself, but I felt she would be better off with someone else.

I couldn't face Aunt Carmen without a job, so I stayed with a friend in Brooklyn. But my money started to run out. I didn't want to draw on my savings, and I couldn't imagine cleaning up after anyone again. I searched the newspaper listings and inquired in shops and restaurants but I couldn't find work.

I don't know what it was that made me think of Baron Von Ausberg. He had been nice to ask about May and send a present after she was born. I thought maybe he could help me get a job. I still had his card, so I called him.

He was surprised to hear from me and invited me to come over the next evening. I felt strange and almost didn't go, but I reminded myself that I wasn't asking for charity. I wanted a job.

There were some beautiful old-time pictures of palm trees in the entrance of his apartment. For some reason that made me feel better. But further inside, the place wasn't very warm or welcoming, at least not to a woman. It was a manly place, spotless though. He took me into his study, where there were many books on the shelves and a fireplace. I could tell that this was where he spent most of his time.

One thing that made me uncomfortable was a photograph I saw there of him and Errol together on the *Zaca*. I pretended not to notice it. He offered me some sherry, and I took some. For courage. Then I came right out and told him I was looking for a job.

He looked at me strangely, as if he wasn't sure I was

telling the truth, and he asked me what kind of job. I told him I had experience as a telephone operator and a receptionist and that I was willing to learn typing. Suddenly he said, 'You don't look well,' which made me feel horrible. And then he asked me if I'd like to go out for dinner.

We went to an Italian restaurant around the corner. I ate some veal that he recommended. It tasted better than anything I'd eaten in a long time. We hardly talked. For some reason I felt unattractive and disappointing to him. I began to think he was annoyed by my coming to him, or maybe he was just bored. I was very glad when the meal was over.

I didn't hear from him for about two weeks. Then he telephoned to say he had a friend at the Museum of Natural History who could give me a job there. By that time I was fed up and thinking about coming back to Jamaica, and I told him so.

'You want to go back now, defeated?'

'I've saved five hundred dollars. I'm not defeated.'

'Stay and save five thousand.'

'Money isn't everything.'

'No. It isn't.'

He said if I changed my mind I should let him know. I didn't like the thought of being 'defeated.' So I stayed and took the job.

I'm glad you enjoy reading these letters, Myrtle. This one could fill up a whole book.

I worked in the gift shop at the museum. It paid less than I earned being a nurse's aide, but it was definitely more dignified.

Karl came in one afternoon and took me around the museum on my lunch break. He showed me some African masks. I thought they were ugly as sin but I didn't say so. He told me about the things he collected — ancient pottery, 'artifacts' he called them. I can understand people collecting art, but collecting broken old pots seems strange to me. He came again and we ate sandwiches out on the museum steps, huge sandwiches which he brought with him. I could barely hold the thing in my hands much less eat it all. But I actually enjoyed his company. I thought maybe I had misjudged him. He seemed different from the way he'd been in Jamaica, more relaxed. He invited me to walk with him in Central Park to see the autumn leaves. Some of the leaves had turned bright red and orange. It's funny I've lived here through two autumns but never noticed how pretty a season it is. The colors look almost tropical.

He told me he was about to go on an excavation in a few months. I decided to ask him about his work, mainly because I didn't feel I had anything interesting to tell him about myself. He laughed in a nice way when I asked him if he was a 'treasure hunter.' He said he was only interested in other people's treasures, people like the ancient Phoenicians. 'Didn't they write on papyrus?' I asked. I was excited to have actually remembered something from high school. 'Yes,' he said, 'and they used it for sails.' He kept looking at me to see if I was really interested. I wasn't, but he'd been nice so I pretended to be. He told me he was especially interested in shipwrecks, like the ones offshore Jamaica. Then we began talking about Jamaica. I wondered if he'd say something about Errol. All I hear about him is what I come across in the newspapers and magazines. But he didn't mention him. He talked about how much he loved Port Antonio, and that made me feel very good.

There was something else about him. This will sound

funny. The way he smelled reminded me of home. I think he uses the same cologne as my father.

Karl invited me to a dinner party he was having. I was nervous about going. I knew he had rich and important friends.

I spent days looking for a dress and was about to buy some fabric to make one for myself when I found something really nice at B. Altman. Even on sale, it was more than I could really afford, but good quality. It will last for years. I went to the hairdresser and had my hair put up. I had mentioned to Karl that I might cut it short, and he said, 'That would be cruel.' It was the first time I ever heard him say anything remotely funny.

It was hard to tell if he was falling in love with me or just being very kind. Sometimes I wondered if he was queer because he just didn't seem interested in me in that way, you know. But then I remembered seeing him with women in Jamaica.

Was I falling in love with him? No. I was curious about him though, and I have to admit that the thought crossed my mind, that here was a man who had the means to look after me and my daughter.

That evening during the dinner party I began to genuinely admire him. He asked me to come early to see his collection. There were a lot of truly ugly things, Myrtle, let me tell you, like a carved stool from Africa shaped like a Pygmy! He said it was about four hundred years old and invited me to sit on it. I said no, thank you. I really didn't want to sit on the little man-stool.

But I saw one nice thing — a silver jar that would make a nice vase for some roses. I told him that, and he said it was Aztec and something *urinary*. I was a little embarrassed but asked anyway, 'You mean like those things in men's bathrooms?' He looked at me strangely so I said, 'Urinals.' You can imagine how I felt when I realized he'd said *funerary*! But he smiled and said that ancient urinals were interesting too.

It was a dinner party for sixteen people around a big, long table. Thank God for Miss Willoughby's deportment classes. Remember how she made us set the table for a five-course meal and showed us how to hold the wine glass at the 'stem' not the 'flower'? I thought Karl would be watching me to see if I used the right knife and fork and that kind of thing, but he wasn't. His friends were very courteous too.

Doesn't this remind you of when we were in school and I used to tell you all my secrets about Errol in *every single detail?*

After the others left, he put on a Billie Holiday record and sat next to me on the sofa. I thought he might try to kiss me and I wasn't sure I was ready for that, so I just kept talking about what a nice apartment he had and how wonderful the view was of the park. He told me that I should have an apartment in the city, and I wasn't quite sure what he was suggesting. He was holding my hand and sitting very close. I started to worry. Did he think because Errol had made love to me that he could too?

I wanted to set him straight. I'd heard of rich men who rented apartments for their girlfriends so they could have sex with them whenever they wanted. I didn't want that. I was interested in marriage, nothing else, so I told him, 'I'm saving up to get my own place so I can send for May.'

He said, 'She's better off where she is.' It was so cold and abrupt, the way he said it. I didn't know what to say. One minute he was holding my hand and looking like he wanted to kiss me and the next minute he was being really horrible.

'Have you ever thought about having children?' I asked.

He said he wasn't 'the least bit interested in children,' that they seemed to be a lot of trouble. Maybe he saw how appalled I was because he went on to explain: 'I don't have any interests to share with children. I mean, they can't appreciate a good cigar or a good wine. I suppose that's why I've always been a bachelor.'

All right, then, I thought; be that way till you drop dead.

We listened to the record until it ended but had nothing else to say to each other. He didn't get in touch with me for a few days and I thought we'd come to a dead end over the subject of children. I was a little sad. It wasn't so much that I missed him; I missed the attention he'd been giving me.

But then he called again and took me to the ballet. *Swan Lake*. It was fabulous. I don't think I've been so thrilled since I was a child.

I wanted to do something for *him* for a change. I couldn't think of anything I could give him as a present, and then I realized that what Karl loves more than anything else is *food*. So I took him to a West Indian restaurant in Brooklyn. He was very happy eating curry goat and drinking Jamaican beer. It was there that he brought up Errol. He'd seen him recently. I asked if he saw him often, and he said no, that they mostly spoke together on the phone. He stopped as if he wasn't sure he should say more, and then he confided that it was Errol's girlfriend who made him uncomfortable. 'She's a child, just fifteen or sixteen years old,' he said.

I couldn't help saying to him, 'And you're not the least bit interested in children, are you?'

He smiled and said, 'Touché.'

Just before I got into the taxi that night, he bent down to kiss me. But I wouldn't let him.

'Don't confuse me,' I told him, and I got in the taxi and left it at that.

I didn't see or speak to him for a few weeks. Then he called. He said he was going to South America soon and wanted to see me. We went to Estelle's. Aunt Carmen was very excited for me and said it's one of the most expensive restaurants in New York. She lent me her fur coat and pearl necklace. I have to say, I looked damned good.

I've honestly never seen anyone eat as much as Karl. He started with a big bowl of oysters and then had about five courses after that. No lie. He drinks practically a whole bottle of wine by himself at dinner and then he has dessert wine or brandy at the end. But I've never seen him the slightest bit drunk. He said he was glad I'd decided not to go back to Jamaica because he had been enjoying my company. 'You've been very kind,' I said.

'If I've been kind, it's because I adore you.'

That surprised me. I really didn't expect him to come right out and say that. I thought for a moment that he might be teasing me, but he looked very serious.

'I'm twice your age, but not an old man yet. At least I hope you don't think of me as old.'

I smiled and shook my head. *He wants to seduce me,* I thought, and I waited to hear what he would say next.

'I live alone, but I'm not a monk. There've been women. Women I don't care very much about, you understand, and who don't really care about me. I find that sort of thing – not very interesting.'

I could see that he had more to say.

'I know what you've been through – with Errol. It's been very hard, I'm sure—'

I put my hand up to stop him. The mention of Errol

made me feel hopeless — like I'd been branded as a certain kind of woman, one that men could just use and leave behind.

I knew what I wanted to say to him, but I was shaking and felt I might cry, so I waited until I could speak clearly. The pearl necklace felt hot on my skin. What was the use of all this preening and prettification when it all came down to one thing?

'Karl. You've been very, very nice, but I can't be any man's mistress again.'

'I'm asking you to marry me,' he said.

So there I was, the biggest, happiest fool on earth, surprised out of my wits because I was about to become a baroness.

Your friend, Ida

P.S. You see how life is strange? Madda Oni predicted this!

February 8, 1957

Dear Papa,

We signed the marriage certificate last week and had a quiet dinner afterward with Aunt Carmen and a friend of Karl's. I am officially Baroness Von Ausberg, Papa, but you can go on calling me Ida! We're going on our honeymoon next week. I have no idea where. Karl says it's a surprise! I think it must be somewhere warm like Mexico because he bought me a bathing suit.

I wanted to send for you and May right away but we will be traveling shortly to South America and after that, Karl says we might be moving to Jamaica for good! He says this is the last excavation he's going to do because he's getting too old for it and plans to let other people do the digging for him from now on.

I sent a box of new clothes and toys for May and some bedroom slippers for you. Did you get them? I'm taking Spanish lessons because Karl says that will be useful when we travel.

Papa, I pray that I will see you and May soon.

Love, Ida

March 1, 1957

Dear May,

I can't believe what a big girl you are and that you can write so well now. Did you really write it all by yourself? Such big words! Mama is going to South America for a while. I will send some nice presents for you from there. Can you find Venezuela and Peru on the map? Ask Grandpa to show you. I miss you very much, darling.

Love, Mama

May 30, 1957

Dear Myrtle,

I'm so happy about your engagement to Cecil. What took you both so long? I'm hoping we can be there for the wedding. It's hard to believe that I haven't seen my May for nearly three years.

We left Peru and are now in Venezuela. My Spanish has gotten quite good. I hardly ever speak English now except with Karl. He's leaving tomorrow for British Guiana – taking a boat down the Amazon River into the jungle! I'm worried as there has been some fighting there. Before we return to New York (God knows when that will be!) we're taking a little holiday on the beach in Brazil. I pray we will be in Jamaica by Christmas at the very latest. Karl, who is so thoughtful in every other way, just doesn't understand how much I want to see May. He tells me this is my chance to see the world, and although I'm longing to see May, part of me feels that too. I like traveling and staying in these grand hotels and all the royal treatment that comes with being a baroness! Who wouldn't?

Speaking of traveling – it's nice that you're going to England to meet Cecil's family. Karl has no family. He doesn't talk about Austria. His parents and sister died in the war. I've seen photographs of them and of his best friend, Max, who also died. Someone told me that Karl was a hero in the Resistance and helped people escape from Hitler. But he won't talk about it.

He says we will have a house in Jamaica, but he doesn't know exactly when or whether it will be on the north coast or in Kingston. I asked him if I could go down by myself, but he wants us to go together. I've discovered that he's a little bit jealous.

Let me tell you something that happened.

It was before we left New York. I answered the phone one day. It was Errol. He didn't recognize my voice. I can't tell you how much that hurt me, Myrtle.

Later I asked Karl about the phone call. He got upset and wanted to know if I was still in love with Errol. I told him I wasn't, but it's not true. I can't help it. Errol is the only one I ever wanted. If he wanted me to be with him, even now, I wouldn't be able to say no.

I have to stop. Karl just came back. I will write again soon. Congratulations again.

Love, Ida

~

It had been raining that morning when Errol called, a light, steady rain that could be seen through the large windows of the study. There was an entire wall of bookshelves, a desk, and a daybed with a green velvet cover where Karl liked to lie down and listen to music.

Ida was looking for books to take with her on the trip to South America. She had already chosen an old illustrated copy of *Persuasion* and was looking for the volume of stories by de Maupassant which Karl had recommended. 'You'll have a lot of time to read,' he'd said. She wondered how many of these books Karl had read, and when he had read them. Had he brought some of them from Austria?

The phone rang and she recognized the voice: 'Hullo. Is Karl there?'

After so much time – his voice was just the same and it was as if he were right there in front of her.

'Hold on. I'll get him.'

She kept her face to the bookshelves while Karl was on the phone. What she could hear of the conversation sounded pleasant. There was just a hint of impatience in Karl's tone. She could tell they had spoken recently; each seemed to know what the other had been doing and would be doing next.

After the phone call, Karl lingered at the desk. She could hear him handling papers, opening and closing a drawer, and she felt that he was waiting for her to speak.

'Was that Errol?' she asked.

'Yes. Did you have a chat with him?'

'No. He didn't even know it was me. Does he know we're married?'

'I told him.' He opened another drawer, put something in, and took some time closing it. 'This damp weather makes these drawers so stiff.'

Ida sank down on the daybed and looked out the window. 'Tell me—' he began.

She fixed her eyes on the rain outside.

'—are you still in love with him?'

The question should have surprised her, but it didn't. She had been expecting it for some time. In fact, having discovered how possessive he was, she had prepared an answer.

'No.' She looked at him with warmth that was not insincere, even if it was driven by sympathy, not passion. 'I'm in love with my husband.'

He got up and was beside her, kissing her with a kind of savage gratitude. It caught her off guard. Before this, his lovemaking had been cautious and unimposing.

It was Sunday, the servants were gone, and the apartment seemed more cavernous than ever in the dim, sunless morning. There was no one to intrude on this sudden indiscreet pleasure, no one to spy them in disordered half nakedness among the velvet cushions and fallen books.

Afterward, in the silence, she felt his heart beating fast against her. It had stopped raining, and sunlight washed over them like a prolonged wave. They lay with limbs flung out upon each other, exhausted, a bit bewildered, and peaceful, as if a great battle had been fought and won.

One afternoon in Venezuela, two letters arrived for the baroness, forwarded from her New York address. One was from Father Reynold and the other was from Clive

Goodman, who was back in Jamaica. The message was more or less the same in both. Could she come home? Her daughter needed her.

Part Four

After taking view of my condition, which was very gloomy, I began to suspect that I had been left on this desolate island to perish . . .

Treasure Cove

18

Castaway

Miss Gloria's yard hadn't changed much in four years except that it was more unkempt. The rainy seasons had muddied the walls. Some shingles had fallen from the roof, and they lay around like scabs. There were two shacks behind the main house; one housed a family of tenants and the other hid the latrine and shower. Nothing grew in the yard; it was a dirt clearing, exposed to hours of baking sun or to flood-rains that turned it into a pit of mud. The only shade was on the small covered veranda. Eli Joseph often sat there in his undershirt and loose trousers, watching his granddaughter play with the children who, unlike her, were as black as the yard.

The children played quietly, shooting marbles and rolling old tires. They had learned how to be invisible, camouflaged by the dirt and the bits and pieces around the yard; none of them wanted to be singled out – 'Derek, sweep de yard' – 'Is who leave de water running? Who dutty-up de bat'room?'

There was a wood crate, big enough for two children to sit inside, and it had become a favorite place for May. Inspired by *Robinson Crusoe*, which her grandfather had read to her, she made the crate into her ship, raft, and lookout. A hungry brown dog turned up now and then in the yard. May tried to befriend the creature and get him inside the crate with her, but there was not enough goodwill around to stop him from continually straying. Here, for four years without her mother and with no relations other than her aging grandfather, May grew like a strange plant.

On this particular day, she was the only one outside. The other children were at school, and her grandfather was inside getting dressed to go down to the harbor. Ida was supposed to arrive that afternoon.

'Chile won't come in an' tek her bath,' Miss Gloria complained to Miss Walker, her elderly tenant.

'But look how much time the mother say she comin' an' she no reach,' Miss Walker said in May's defense.

For four years there had been promises – 'You mama comin' from New York,' or 'you mama sendin' for you.' Miss Walker's grandsons would tease May: 'White witch, white witch, you mama not comin'!'

May threw stones at them. She aimed well, and they learned to run fast from her.

She was seven now, and the question of whether or not her mother was coming had ceased to be important to her. What interested her that day was the novelty of having the whole yard to herself. She wandered over to the circle of rocks where the garbage had been burned the day before. She picked through the ashes, looking for anything interesting that might have survived the blaze, and lifted out a charred biscuit tin.

'No dirty-up you hand-dem! Come inside an' bathe,' Miss Gloria yelled from the kitchen.

Through the latticework May saw Miss Gloria at the

stove. Miss Gloria, who moved her overweight body as little as possible, was a slovenly housekeeper but a very good cook, and she made wonderful hearty lunches for her boarders: fried fish, stew peas, dumplings, breadfruit, and sometimes rice-an'-peas.

As soon as May stepped inside the kitchen, she was disappointed. Miss Gloria was not cooking; she was heating up the hot-comb to straighten Miss Walker's hair.

'G'wan go tek off you dutty clothes,' Miss Gloria told May, dabbing grease around Miss Walker's hairline.

May walked past them to her bedroom. May shared a bed with a timid girl her age named Ula. Ula's father was said to be from a wealthy Indian family. He never visited her. Her mother, like May's, worked in America. The bedroom was small and airless with an accumulation of dusty magazines, old newspapers, and sagging cardboard boxes. There was just enough space between the bed and dresser to kneel down for nightly prayers. The frosted-glass windows were kept closed, except for a bit at the top. There was a door between the girls' room and Mr Joseph's, and there were many nights when May woke up and wandered into his room.

May could see him in there now, fully dressed, lying across the bed. He had been sleeping a lot recently.

The house was dark and smelled of perspiration. The sitting room was the tidiest part of the house and it was used only when guests like Myrtle's English fiancé, Cecil, visited. Clear plastic covered the sofa and there was a little vase of artificial flowers on the coffee table. The children were not allowed in there, but May liked to look at the things in the glass cabinet: bric-a-brac and framed photographs, one of them a picture of her mother and Aunt Myrtle in school uniforms standing among a row of girls.

Even the kitchen with its open latticework seemed hot and airless. When it rained the corrugated zinc roof was deafening, but May, who was always ready to eat, liked it better than any other room in the house. It seemed cheerful with its sea-blue walls and calendar pictures. There were always plenty of ripe bananas in a basket near the stove.

May passed through the kitchen, stopping for a banana, and then went back outside.

'But see me dyin' trials,' Miss Gloria exclaimed, pressing another section of Miss Walker's hair.

'She gone outside again,' Miss Walker droned.

May stood by the gate, eating the banana. The novelty of having the yard to herself had worn off. She wanted the other children to come home.

There was only one other brick house on Parrot Lane. It was across the road from Miss Gloria's and like hers it housed tenants. A prostitute named Doris Pewsy ('Miss Pewsy' she made the children call her) lived there, and occasionally sailors came to the house. There were always two or three transient young men living there too, who sat around and did nothing except smoke cigarettes and wait for night. Then they would dress up in colorful shirts and tight pants and swagger down the street into town. Sometimes these men called to the children to run to the shop for cigarettes. They were intrigued by May, whom they believed to be white. They spoke to her differently than they did to the others, in a soft, cajoling tone, and tried to touch her hand or her soft hair. Although they said nice things to her, she was a little afraid of them.

The rest of Parrot Lane consisted of vacant bushy lots and squatters' dwellings – makeshift shacks of wood and corrugated zinc. It was not an especially ugly or oppressive place. The sea, which could be partly viewed from Miss Gloria's veranda, brought cool breezes. Behind Miss Gloria's house, the tropical forest flourished for miles and rose up to meet the Blue Mountains. No, it was not a bad place, but it was strangely quiet, even with the sounds of the children, the domino games on the veranda, and fierce sheets of rain. None of these sounds seemed to penetrate the languor.

The children were fairly content except when Mr Tate was at home. He worked at nights on the banana boats, spent most of the day at home, and drank a lot. Mealtimes were tense and miserable when he joined them at the table. He would become violent if his food wasn't cooked exactly as he liked it, if the orange juice was too sour, or if one of the children spilled something. He suspected everyone of being an idler and would threaten the children: 'I goin' lace you behind!' He had a switch he had cut from a tamarind tree, which he used to beat them. The only person he did not berate was Mr Joseph, with whom he played dominoes.

He beat May when he learned she had been diving in the harbor with boys. Girls weren't supposed to dive for pennies, and what was worse, she did this half naked. She didn't wail like the other children when she was beaten and this made him even more furious.

Myrtle was upset when she visited and saw the marks on May's arms and legs from the beating, and she spoke harshly to her father. Mr Tate was in awe of his accomplished daughter, and besides, he did not want to lose the twenty US dollars a month that Ida sent for May's and Mr Joseph's room and board. He didn't beat May again, but kept threatening to, coming after her with mad red eyes: 'One day I goin' teach you.' But he beat Derek constantly for having a 'smart mouth' and for 'idlin'.' These beatings upset everyone in the yard and up and down Parrot Lane; even Miss Gloria, who never contradicted her husband, would moan, 'But him is a good-good boy.'

They were all good-good children: quiet, stoic little hearts. May never fussed, except at bathtime. The indoor bathroom depressed her. There was a layer of sticky grime along the edges of the linoleum, and the airless room smelled bad. Miss Gloria used to bathe May and Ula together when they were very little. The tub was high, and the girls were too small to see over the edge. Miss Gloria scrubbed every inch of their bodies with a rough washrag and a bar of Lifebuoy soap while she complained about her aching back and aching legs. Every now and then one of the two girls would begin to cry, setting off the other. For some reason this caused Miss Gloria to scrub even more vigorously. The crying would get louder, soapy water would sting their eyes, Miss Gloria would lose patience, and their soapy limbs would flail around as they tried to reach for the sides of the tub.

On Sundays, when the whole yard attended church, Miss Gloria dressed May in the nice clothes her mother sent from America. May disliked these foreign clothes; they made her stand out even more than she already did. She would not have worn them at all if it hadn't been for her grandfather. He was delighted by anything that brought Ida to mind: 'What a pretty frock you mother send you, eh?'

May loved her Grandpa Joseph. They had been left together, and he was the only one in the dusty house who breathed love into her daily. She was gentle around him, sensing his frailty. Sometimes when he sat with his eyes closed for a long time, she checked to see that he was still breathing. She had learned that people could die with their eyes open, and so sometimes when he sat staring ahead, hardly blinking, his effeminate dark lashes even more pronounced in his sunken face, she would touch him lightly. He spoke to her constantly of her mother, and of her grandmother Esme, and of things that had happened long before she was born, even going back as far as his own childhood in Lebanon. She liked to sit under the tree with him while he sang Arabic and French songs to her. To May, he was family, past, even memory itself.

Watching her, he sometimes felt waves of curiosity: she was the thinnest of the children in spite of the great amount of food she ate. She was dressed as shabbily as her black playmates and spoke like them, but she looked like an English girl. Though her skin was tanned like his, she did not have the dark Middle Eastern eyes or glossy black hair of the Joseph family. Her eyes, which had been blue at birth, were now a dark, mottled green; her baby curls had straightened, and her hair was the brownish-blond of whiskey. She looked like her father.

May never asked her grandpa about her father. Once or twice she had brought up the subject and had been worried by the look on his face.

But other people – neighbors, schoolchildren, shopkeepers, and even strangers – told her things: 'You see Navy Island over there? That's where you father lives.'

She often looked out at the little island – concerned, wondering.

'You father is a white man.'

'Him have a big house wid swimmin' pool an' t'ing.'

'You t'ink you special because you father is a white man?'

Derek told her, 'No pay dem no mind.'

She used to wish that Father Reynold was her father. He

took her out for ice cream, and he had bought her a plastic sword. But he told her priests were not allowed to have children.

'Am I an albino?' she asked Derek one day.

'Who call you that?'

'Those boys down by Mr Chang's shop.'

'You not an albino. What else dem say?'

'White witch, dem call me.' She paused as if deciding whether or not to say more. They had also said things about her mother and the man who lived on Navy Island.

The next time she was sent to the shop, Derek went with her. The scrappy boys were lurking in front of the shop. Derek told them, 'No trouble her.' They left her alone for a few weeks, then started taunting her again: 'White witch! You white like duppy!'

Derek was known around town as her special guardian, and no one dared to harass her when she was with him. They were often seen together, May sitting on the handlebar of his bicycle as he rode through town, and people said Derek was the only one who could get her to behave decently; they'd heard the stories of her stoning other children, using bad language, and so on. 'She growin' up wild,' they said.

'You mother coming,' he had said to her just before her sixth birthday. 'She comin' for your birthday party, and then, you know what? She goin' tek you back to America.'

'You goin' come with us?'

'No, I'm a big boy now. I can tek care a meself.'

'I can tek care a meself too.'

'No, you can't,' he said, and then, seeing that she was about to get mad, he tickled her and made her laugh.

Ida didn't arrive for that birthday, and no one gave May or Derek a reason, but Myrtle made a birthday cake with yellow icing because that was May's favorite color. That night, after the birthday celebration, May woke up from a dream that her mother had died, and, frightened, she went into her grandfather's room.

'No worry you'self,' Eli said. 'She goin' come back soon.' He had become weak, and as if to make up for it, he gripped her hand too tightly. 'No mind. No mind,' he said, and after a while his grip loosened and he fell back asleep.

Then a year later a death did occur that shocked everyone in the yard. Myrtle and Cecil died in a car crash while visiting Cecil's parents in England.

Miss Gloria collapsed. How could the Lord take this pickney who was so good? She went into her room and stayed there. Mr Tate took it so badly, the children felt sorry for him. For weeks he spoke to no one and would not even go to work. One day his boss came to the house and had a talk with him, and after that he went back to work. But his wife could no longer be depended on to serve meals, wash his clothes, or collect money from the tenants. So he began to quarrel and drink even more than before, and there was peace only when he left the yard, which he did for days at a time.

Myrtle had promised May and Derek that they would live with her after her marriage. The night they heard about her death, the two children sat in the yard inside the crate and watched people coming and going with food, bush-tea, and condolences. Light glowed from the house windows, and they heard Miss Gloria crying.

'What we goin' do, Derek?' May asked.

'Look like we have to stay here now.' Derek looked down at the black dirt.

'We could go Cuba,' May said, 'and hide in the mountains.'

Her grandfather listened to Radio Rebelde, the broadcasting station of the men who were hiding and fighting in the Sierra Maestro. He told her they were good, brave men and that if he were younger he'd try to help them. Cuba was just an hour and a half by boat.

'We can't go Cuba,' Derek said. 'We have to stay here.'

Things got worse in the yard. Father Reynold found a woman to come in and help because one day he noticed that Eli's bed sheets were soiled. Derek and the two girls took turns preparing rudimentary meals – cornmeal porridge, fried plantain. May learned to wash her own school uniform. Mr Tate brooded more than ever; he seemed to hate the sight of the children, especially May, doing his wife's chores.

'Miss Gloria will mend and be herself again,' Father Reynold tried to assure them. He came by as often as possible to check on them and to bring groceries, but he too seemed disheartened. He was no longer young himself; his hair had turned gray, his once attractive face looked drawn, and he suffered from arthritis.

May hated going back to the yard after school, but there were few other places she could go. Except for Derek and shy Ula, she had no friends. So she sought company among adults. Miss Morrison, the town librarian, was nice to her. There were two wide, low shelves of children's classics at the library. May couldn't read most of the words, but she became familiar with the titles. Sometimes Miss Morrison would leave her desk and read to her. After the library closed, she'd walk down the street to see Clive Goodman.

Goodman's Gas, Repair, and Transport, across from East Harbor, was a one-room office with a mechanic's shed at the back and two Texaco gas pumps in front. Clive had returned after two years in America and had set himself up in the gas-station business, incorporating his father's ferrying business and Mr Cousins' taxis. Along with the ferrying back and forth to Navy Island, he arranged rafting trips on the Rio Grande and sightseeing day trips for tourists. Though Clive was primarily a car mechanic, he could repair anything. So there was everything from refrigerators to sewing machines in his shed. It was a busy place, and Clive was there all hours of the day and night.

He didn't mind having May there while he fixed things. He enjoyed telling her stories about her mother, especially the one about him running all the way between St Margaret's Bay and Port Antonio to bring her a pair of shoes.

'She had mirth,' he said, remembering the word from the Bible. 'And she was pretty-pretty. But it was that joy inside her that made her different.' Then he felt awkward, realizing he spoke about her in the past tense as though she were dead. 'She's a sweet woman an' she's my friend,' he told May.

One afternoon as May left the library she saw some boys across the street. These were boys who never lost an opportunity to bother her, so she was suspicious that day when they acted as though they hadn't noticed her. She stayed on her side of the road and walked quickly to Clive's repair shop.

'Father Reynold is a priest so I can't live with him,' she told Clive as he lay under a car with only his legs visible. 'Why can't I live with you?'

Clive stopped knocking under the car and emerged. She always wondered how come he never seemed to get his mustache dirty under there.

'Where all this come from?' He wiped the grease from his hands and noticed how thin she was. 'Miss Gloria treatin' you awright?'

She looked out at Navy Island. She could make out a roof beyond the treetops.

'Is true my father lives over there?'

Clive wondered how much she knew. The child badly needed a parent, father or mother, it didn't matter. Why didn't Ida come back? He had heard that she had married a wealthy man who would be able to support her and her child.

'Is true?' she asked again.

He thought about it for a while. A father, he reasoned, was someone who behaved like a father; that man on Navy Island who had made Ida pregnant was no father to May.

'I'm not the one to ask,' he finally said.

It was true, then, that the man who lived across the water was her father.

'Is he white?' she continued.

'Yes.' Then to change the subject he asked, 'When last you see Madda Oni?'

She turned around and looked in the direction of the mountains. Now and then Oni sent someone down to Miss Gloria's yard with fruit and coconut cakes for May. 'She don't come down no more.'

The fact that Oni lived in those high mountains made her seem especially powerful, even omniscient, to May.

'Oni isn't white.' It sounded almost like a question or something she was pondering.

'Oni? No man, she's a Maroon.' He went on to explain to her, 'The first Maroons were African slaves who escaped to the mountains.'

'So she black like you?' She had only a vague recollection of the day her mother had taken her to see Oni.

'Even blacker. Pure African.' He looked at her. There was a big stain on her uniform where an iron had scorched it, and she had holes in both shoes. If not for her whiteness, she would have looked like a poor street urchin. She certainly talked like one.

He remembered the day when she had been diving off the pier with the other children and a white American couple had noticed her. They had been alarmed, thinking she was the lost child of some tourists. Derek had told them repeatedly, 'She belongs to the yard,' but they'd kept asking, 'Where are her parents?' May had been mystified, wondering why the strangers had so much interest in her and her parents. 'Where are your parents, little girl?' She couldn't say. Finally Derek had run down the street for Clive, who'd come and explained that the child was not lost, that she did indeed belong there (and May had finally spoken up because the couple had still been skeptical; she had said, echoing Derek and Clive, 'I *belong* . . .' *Be-long*, one syllable fell, the other one soared, a plunge and a leap of faith). Afterward Clive had told her that if she ever got lost or anyone asked her about her family, she should say she was Eli Joseph's granddaughter.

Clive watched now as she squatted in the dirt unselfconsciously, her uniform skirt hitched up over her thin legs. She was still looking at the mountains. His heart went out to her.

'You want me to take you there?'

'To Navy Island?' She brightened.

Clive sighed. 'To the mountains to see Oni.'

'Oh.'

'Why you wan' go Navy Island? Nothing for you over there.'

That wasn't true, she wanted to say; there was the island itself. She hardly ever saw anyone coming or going from there. She imagined sailing over and building a shelter for herself among the trees like Robinson Crusoe.

'You ever see him?' she asked.

Clive became exasperated: 'Chu! Go home. You need to eat lunch, look how mawga you getting.'

As he watched her walk away, he thought that he should write to Ida.

He called to May, 'You can come back an' visit another time, awright?'

She took the long way back that day, passing a churchyard where some schoolgirls were playing a ring-game and singing: '*A shine-eye gal is a trouble to a man, A shine-eye gal is a trouble to a man . . .*' They were intent on their game and didn't seem to notice her going by. There was a spot by the water she especially liked, she and the white-plumed egret that she often saw there. It was a rock-strewn bit of beach sheltered thickly by trees. Small mangoes fell from one of the trees. May would eat the fallen mangoes and watch the bird standing in the shallows. Her grandpa, who knew a lot about birds, told her that these white egrets nested on the islets off Port Antonio. She had seen this one flying back and forth from Navy Island. For weeks she had been observing its growing interest in the mango seeds she discarded. It would turn its head but remain stationary by the water's edge. She wondered if the bird would come to trust her.

As she walked along, balancing on the piled up rocks that served as a seawall, some of the boys she had seen earlier appeared in her way.

She reached for a big stone to throw at them, but the boys were fast. They grabbed her and threw a coarse cloth bag over her head. She felt herself being dragged over rocks and through thick, scratchy bushes. One of her shoes fell off.

Then they stopped and pushed her to the ground. She felt a wall behind her and heard a man's voice: 'She clean?'

'Clean-clean. Look.' They uncovered her face, and she saw a man with a shaved head and a lot of bumps on his face.

She knew where she was, inside the broken-down walls of the Folly estate – a mansion whose roof and walls had collapsed long ago. She had always been afraid of the place, which was full of scorpions and long-tailed lizards. She wasn't that far from the road but she couldn't see it because of the bushes and trees. Ahead in the distance, though, she could see Oni's mountains.

The boys were dividing money among themselves. She realized the strange man had paid them to bring her there. Once they got the money, the boys left, except the two who were standing right by her. The man came closer, and he told them, 'Cover up her head.'

They're taking away the mountains, she thought. The shout that came from her was unlike any sound she'd ever made. It stunned them. She ran and heard the boys behind her, chasing her. Her sock got caught on the barbed-wire fence, trapping her as she climbed through to the main road. She felt a searing pain in her foot as she pulled herself free. The boys were close behind.

She ran not toward Miss Gloria's yard but through the center of town toward Clive's shop. The boys were shouting excitedly, running after her as if it were a game. She turned the street corner and slammed into a group of market women. A basket of tomatoes turned over.

A woman grabbed May's arm and yelled, 'Warang wid you? Look how you mash-up me tomato-dem.'

The boys tore around the corner, then stopped suddenly as if they had come to a wall.

The woman who was holding May also managed to grab one of the boys. 'Why you runnin' down de pickney? You tryin' fe man-hangle her?'

The other boy tried to slip away, but one of the women caught him.

The tomato-seller sized up the situation and turned her attention from May to the boys. 'Is oonu cause dis! Look 'pon me tomato-dem how dem spile!'

The other women joined in the cussing: 'You run down de chile an' mash-up de place.'

'Wait! Don't is Mr Joseph' granddawta dis?'

'Mr Joseph who did own Palace Teer-ta?'

'Same one.'

One of them asked May, 'Dem try fe fingle you?'

'Is a shame! She jus' a baby!'

'Is jus' romp we was rompin' wid her,' one of the boys said meekly.

The tomato-seller boxed him. 'Rompin'? You t'ink you ole enough fe bounce poom-poom?'

The women laughed loudly and coarsely.

From the center of this commotion, May glanced around her. These were large women. She took in the breadth and rotundity of their bodies, bodies so close to her own that she thought they might crush her without anyone noticing. The layers of fabric which they wore – head-ties, kerchiefs, aprons, pouches, and big pleated skirts – seemed to add to their imperviousness. But she gradually understood, listening to their jabs, rebukes, and crude laughter, that these women, who resembled mountains, were on her side.

'Wait! Is blood dat? Look de chile foot a bleed.'

'You cut her foot? You wretch! Call de police! Police!'

May looked down. Was that her blood? It made her ill to look at it. Out of the corner of her eye she saw Mrs Goodman crossing the street from her hairdressing salon to see what was going on. The last thing May heard before she fainted was Mrs Goodman shouting for someone to call Clive.

The boys got away while everyone was attending to May. The police came later, and May told them about the strange man at the ruins. She heard Mrs Goodman saying in a low voice to the others that there had been other instances like this, of men who believed that virgins could cure them of 'vee dee.' May guessed that 'vee dee' was a disease. She wasn't so sure about the word 'virgin' but she had seen her grandfather's medallion of the Virgin Mary and also statues and pictures of Mary, so she thought it might be another way of saying 'white girl.'

Clive took her to the doctor, who stitched up the wound on her foot. By the time she got home it was past suppertime, and her grandfather had gone to bed. He had been worried so she went in to let him know she was home and safe. He smiled gratefully, patted her hand, and drifted back to sleep.

Everyone in the yard made a fuss of May that evening. Her supper was warmed up and she was allowed to sit in Miss Gloria's chair at the end of the table. Miss Gloria even gave one of the Walker boys some money to buy some ice cream, not just for May but for all the children.

Mr Tate sat silently at the other end of the table. He poured himself a glass of white rum. Then, while everyone was eating ice cream and trying to find nice things to say to May, he said loudly, 'Is her fault.'

Everybody grew quiet.

'She traipsin' aroun' half naked. Ula, go bring me de switch.'

Ula did not want to; she stayed where she was, looking down into her bowl.

'I say bring me de switch or I get it meself an' lace you behind wid it.'

Ula did as she was told. Miss Gloria said quietly, 'Sampson—' and then she was quiet.

Derek left the room.

Mr Tate was so drunk, he had trouble getting up from his chair. He wobbled to the other end of the table, where May sat with her hands together on her lap.

Derek came back inside with his cricket bat. 'Leave her alone,' he told Mr Tate.

'What you say?'

Derek raised the bat, making his meaning clear.

Mr Tate cursed everyone in the room for a full, drunken minute, then left.

Later that night May sat in Derek's room watching him pack an old brown suitcase.

'Is his house,' Derek explained, 'an' he goin' come back. Next time somebody goin' dead or end up in jail.'

'Where you goin' go?'

'I don't know. Maybe Kingston.' He wouldn't look at her. He went on packing as he spoke. 'I promise you mother I would tek care a you. But I cyan tek care a you no more. Is time she come back.'

She stared through the open window; there were fireflies outside and their unpredictable illuminations made her feel worse than ever.

'I goin' ask Father Reynold to write her a letter an' tell her she mus' come back,' Derek went on.

'Suppose she won't come?' May asked.

Derek sighed. He continued packing but without fervor. He folded a pair of pants and placed them in the suitcase.

May decided she would go away too, not to Kingston, which seemed almost as far away to her as New York, but to Navy Island. 'Is all right,' she assured Derek. 'Go. I can tek care a meself.'

'You cyan tek care a you'self,' he said wearily, and he stopped packing. 'Look what happen today. You think I can let something like that happen to you again?'

He sat down beside her and told himself, *As soon as her mother comes back, I will fly like a bird from here.*

Mr Tate returned but did not trouble either of them again. Derek still longed to leave the yard. He asked Father Reynold to write a letter to Ida.

19

Errol Flynn Wakes up from a Bad Dream

There was a drought and heat wave on the island. Even in Port Antonio, which was known for plentiful rain, there was not a drop for almost a month. At night the temperature didn't fall below a hundred degrees, and there were flies everywhere because of the bananas rotting along the wharf. The banana workers couldn't work properly in such heat. No one could. Bus drivers abandoned their buses in the middle of their routes, the post office closed early, electric power failed, and water began to be rationed and turned off periodically except in the hotels.

The secretary at Goodman's Gas, Repair, and Transport got a call from Mr Errol Flynn. The refrigerator had broken down over on Navy Island. Mr Flynn needed to have it fixed and also wanted several large bags of ice sent over.

Clive was happy to do the job himself; it had been a long time since he'd sailed out to Navy Island and maybe there would be some breeze out on the water. As he pulled up to the pier and began unloading the bags of ice, May appeared from behind a stack of boxes. He remembered seeing her around the garage earlier, chatting with his secretary.

'Gal, you mad?'

The triumphant look on her face reminded him of Ida.

'Awright. I hope you satisfied now that you reach Navy Island.'

He finished unloading the ice and his bag of tools. 'Sun hot,' he said more to himself than to her. He used a small towel to wipe the sweat from his neck and then realized she was probably hot and thirsty. He broke off some of the ice he'd brought over for Flynn. 'Here. Now I want you to stay on the boat till I get back.'

She sucked on the ice and nodded vigorously. Clive shook his head and muttered to himself as he walked down the pier.

That morning Errol Flynn woke up from a horrible dream. His first wife lay decomposed beside him. He had been buried alive in the coffin beside her. He had thrashed about, then woken and realized he was in his own bed with Brenda, his extremely alive, though now sleeping, sixteen-year-old girlfriend. She was one of those people who could sleep through anything.

If only his first wife really were dead, he thought. He didn't need a psychoanalyst to interpret the dream. Vera would never release him, not until she had leeched every penny from him and was dancing on his pauper's grave. What day was it? Saturday, June 16, 1957 – the middle of the month, the middle of the year. He had sent the alimony check and wouldn't send another penny till September, no matter what tricks Vera or her lawyer got up to. *She can't reach me or my dough here*, he thought, and was glad that every time he'd gotten a paycheck in recent years he'd sunk the money into his Jamaican estate.

He looked at the clock. It was a little after ten and his

head was pounding. Today he would try not to have a drink until lunchtime. Not that he was worried about being an alcoholic. It was just that the morning cocktails stopped him from getting any work done. In the morning, while Brenda slept, was the best time for writing, and he wanted to finish his screenplay about the Cuban rebels by the end of the month.

He raised himself up on his elbows. His breath stank; it was a good thing Brenda woke up hours after he did so he could shower, brush his teeth, shave. Not that she would mind a bit of bad breath; she was crazy about him. The affair had begun a year and a half ago when she had just turned fifteen, and he knew that at first it had been a sort of father thing. Her own father had died when she was young. As usual, everyone was disgusted with him – at his age living with a teenaged girl. But he'd been more faithful to her than he had been to any other woman. Brenda's mother liked him; she even traveled with them sometimes.

He enjoyed looking at Brenda's face while she slept. She looked so peaceful. What a face she had! Her father had been Norwegian and she had remarkable Scandinavian features.

His eyes swept over her uncovered nakedness, her delicate limbs and girlish breasts. Her short, boyishly cropped hair was so blond it looked almost white. The hair at her crotch was fair like that too, and unusually sparse so that her genitalia looked pronounced and childlike. It had excited him beyond belief the first time he'd seen her naked. And it aroused him now.

Brenda went right back to sleep after they made love. He showered and then went out to the balcony, wearing his towel.

There was the sea, his first great love. Here in Jamaica, he could feel the real core of himself. He supposed that 'soul' might be another word for it. But that had such an airy sound. He had felt just like this as a child in Tasmania when he'd get up earlier than everyone and run down to the sea, and later in the rivers of New Guinea, sun pouring down on him and wild, bright-plumed birds staring at him from the trees. What was that poem he'd learned in school, something about old men having no country? The poet, if he remembered rightly, wanted to change into a golden bird and find immortality. He wasn't sure about the bird part, but sailing, sailing anywhere, did feel a bit like immortality. Sailing, diving, and his beloved Navy Island.

Everywhere else he just dragged his dead weight around. But at Bella Vista, and especially out there below the blue surface where he went diving alone, all the debris and decrepitude fell away. The tropical lushness, both on land and in the sea, never failed to appeal to his curiosity. And Brenda made life bearable; her young acceptance of him despite his flaws was refreshing. Maybe he would finally find happiness here with her. He might marry Brenda and live happily ever after, maybe even have a kid with her. Why not? The alternative was loneliness and then death.

There was a sudden burning pain just below his ribs. What was that? The solar plexus – sun, heat, flame-within, soul – there was that word, 'soul,' again. His doctor had said to take it easy, quit smoking, lay off the drinking. Was his heart failing or was it just his damned liver acting up? These doctors never gave you a straight answer. In a year and a half he'd be fifty. He wasn't ready.

He noticed the sun high in the sky. It was almost noon. He might as well go down and pour himself a rum-and-Coke; it was too late now to get much work done. He'd take a swim in the pool, have lunch with Brenda, and go diving later.

Clive had just put the ice in the gardener's pickup truck when he saw May walking toward him. 'Didn't I tell you to stay down by the boat?'

'I 'fraid to stay by myself. Let me come with you, please.'

'Awright, but behave you'self.'

They drove up a gravel road, winding through the forest, where she spotted Otaheite apples among the coconut trees. Bright flowers snaked among the vines. She had expected just trees and sand. It was startlingly beautiful; she might have been in a dream about heaven if Clive had not been bumping along in the truck with her, and if not for the news of Cuba's fighting on the truck's radio. The Cuban president had sent a battalion up into the Sierra Maestro. Clive was talking to the driver about whether the rebels would win this battle or be captured. 'They fightin' hard,' Clive said and she knew he meant the rebels. At the top of the hill, they turned a corner and went through pink gates where the name 'Bella Vista' was wrought in gold letters. The house was pink too and huge, with so many windows and terraces that it looked to her like a hotel. It stood at the highest point of the island and when she got out of the truck, she could see the sea all around her.

Clive placed May at the bottom of some garden steps under a big, shady almond tree. He stroked his mustache, which she knew he did whenever he was considering something. She hoped he would change his mind and let her go inside the house with him. 'Stay here an' don't move till I come back,' he said and went around to the back of the house.

She looked up at the wide stone steps and wondered what

they led to. Then she heard splashing. She had never seen a swimming pool except in magazines, and she'd always longed to see one, maybe even swim in one. Clive was busy. She was sure she had time to go up the steps, look quickly, and come back before he was finished.

There were many steps to climb. By the time she reached the top, the splashing had stopped. No one was in the pool, but she could see a wet trail leading from the pool's edge to the house doors.

The swimming pool dazzled her. She walked over to the edge and gazed down. Ribbons of sunlight wavered across the bottom. She knelt down and put her hand in the water.

'Hullo?'

The voice startled her but she did not pull out her hand.

'You'll fall in if you're not careful.'

She saw a man standing wet in the doorway with a towel around his waist and a drink in his hand.

He saw a child who looked white but who wore a loose, faded old dress like the kind the servants' children wore. He noticed, however, that she had on a good pair of leather sandals. Where on earth had she come from?

'Who are you?' His voice rang out.

'May,' she said, standing up, and then she remembered to say, 'I'm Eli Joseph's granddaughter.'

She heard the crackle of ice as he lifted the glass to his lips. He studied her for a few more seconds.

'Well, come in, then,' he said and stood aside so she could go in.

Inside, the floor tiles were larger than any she'd ever seen and she believed that if she were to touch them they would feel cool against her palms. Some of them were wet from the man's feet. Her eyes swept around and she took in everything quickly: the dark, polished railing of the stairway, a bar with high stools, and a huge brown leather couch where she sat down, a little embarrassed at how unsteadily she sank into it. The walls were white and bumpy, and there was an enormous painting of a black horse on the wall.

He studied her as he made himself another drink. His hands were shaking. The child's resemblance to him was astounding.

'Where did you come from?' he asked.

'Port Antonio.' He was not so white, she thought. She had seen whiter people. His tummy was big, almost like a pregnant woman's, and she thought his chest looked a bit womanly too. He was almost as dark as her Lebanese grandfather except for his very white feet. Was this the rich, handsome movie star everyone talked about who might be her father? Maybe not. She decided to question him.

'Where you come from?' she asked.

His eyebrows lifted in surprise, and he thought for a moment before answering her.

'Tasmania,' he said.

She had never heard of it.

'It's an island far from here,' he explained.

'Are you my father?'

He took a sip, put his drink down, and then walked over to the couch.

His weight threw her off balance when he sat beside her, and she almost toppled onto him. He was too close for her to look at without straining her neck, so she looked at her own feet.

He touched her hair. 'And you just appear, like Peter Pan,' he murmured.

She looked at him, not understanding.

'Come,' he said, 'I want to show you something.'

He led the way down a flight of stairs, and as he walked ahead, he readjusted the towel around his waist. She saw the line of pale skin above his buttocks where his tan ended, and it embarrassed her a little, like the times she'd seen her grandfather sitting with his pants open.

'Errol?' a woman called from above.

'I'm down here with a little girl,' he called up.

'What little girl?' she shouted back but he didn't answer.

They reached a cool, dark room. 'This is where I work when it's too hot or raining,' he explained. 'Usually I work out by the pool.' He spoke fast. 'I'm writing a screenplay. A movie. Do you like movies?'

She wondered if that was why he had brought her down there, to show her a movie. She began to worry about getting back before Clive noticed she was gone.

The room was messy, with open drawers and cupboard doors and with untidy piles of books and papers everywhere. There was a daybed with a bamboo-print bedspread and matching cushions, and high above the bed, a shelf filled with shells, pieces of coral, and other sea things. A baby turtle shell caught her attention.

'What do you want to show me?' she asked.

Clive wiped off his hands and appraised his own work. There was a new, tight belt now around the freezer fan and he could hear the machinery humming pleasantly. When it came to well-paying customers like Mr Flynn, it was always best to do the job himself and make sure it was done well.

He went outside for May.

She wasn't where he'd left her, and he'd half expected that. In her own quiet way, she was as willful as her mother.

Different from Ida, though; May hid things better. You could always tell when Ida was up to something. He suddenly pictured her bright, dark eyes and expressive face.

'May?' he called not too loudly as he walked around a hedge of bougainvillea. He saw the gardener planting something.

'You see a little girl round here?'

'No. No pickney 'round here. Check down the bottom.' He pointed down to the servants' shacks.

He lifted her onto his lap. She felt strange but not unhappy being held like that; it was a fatherly gesture that she had seen before but never known.

'Look,' he said, showing her a map that he had unrolled on his desk. It was not like the maps her grandfather had shown her in his atlas. This one had pictures of ships and people drawn on it. There was strange writing that looked like English but seemed misspelled, like 'Eaft' instead of 'East.'

'It's old,' she said, disappointed.

'It's *very* old – and very valuable.'

He spoke quickly and she didn't catch everything: 'Australia,' he said, 'used to be called New Holland back then . . . and Otaheite is now Tahiti. Here's Tasmania—' She began to slip from his lap, and he caught her. She was skinny, he noticed. Her dress was too big for her and exposed a bony, tanned shoulder. 'This is Captain Bligh's map. He brought breadfruit trees to Jamaica. Do you like breadfruit?'

She began to wriggle and slip off his lap again, so he helped her down and then stood up. She wondered what would happen next. The towel around his waist was big, with red-and-white stripes; she had never seen such a big towel, and now she saw that his legs were not flabby like the rest of him but muscular like in pictures she'd seen of athletes. She felt it was impolite to be looking at a grown-up man's legs so closely. Her eyes fell instead on some strange, dirty-looking coins on his desk.

Clive knocked at the front door and a minute later, a young blonde woman in a two-piece bathing suit opened it.

'Yes?'

'I beggin' you pardon, ma'am. Is Mr Flynn home?' He told her he'd come to fix the refrigerator and to bring the ice and the little girl who was with him was lost. He wondered if by any chance she was in the house.

'Come in. I'll go find him.' She saw how distressed he was. 'Don't worry. I'm sure Errol can help you.'

May heard people talking and walking around upstairs. She wanted to see the swimming pool again and not just be down there in that room with him. 'I want to go,' she said.

There was so much he wanted to tell her. *How thin she is*, he thought.

'Let me show you something quite special,' he said and lifted her once again onto his lap.

The door opened. May saw a woman who looked startled to find her there.

'Errol?' She frowned, looking first at May then at the map unrolled on the desk. 'There's a man upstairs who says he's lost a little girl. Is this her?'

'Probably.'

'But she's white.'

May said, 'My great-grandmother is a Maroon.'

Errol smiled at that.

'Come along.' He took her hand and led her into the living room.

Relief spread across Clive's face. Then he noticed Flynn undressed, wearing just a towel, holding May's hand.

'It's Clive Goodman, isn't it?' Errol said cheerfully. 'May came by and introduced herself. I hope you weren't too worried about her.'

The voice threw Clive off balance; it was so movie-like that for a moment it seemed to come from somewhere else. But he shook himself free of the spell. May was his only concern.

'I told her to wait out in the garden,' Clive answered stiffly. He added, 'Sorry, Mr Flynn.'

'It's quite all right. We were having a little geography lesson.' He looked down at May, smiling. Then he turned to Clive again. 'I remember you. You used to come over on the boat with your father when you were just a boy.'

'I own the garage at East Harbor now. I brought you some ice and fixed the refrigerator.'

'Yes, yes. Thank you.'

No one said anything for a moment. Then the woman, who was so pretty and blonde that she seemed like a supernatural creature to May, poured herself a glass of orange juice.

'Come, May,' Clive said.

Errol bent down to her. 'You won't forget where Tasmania is now?'

He is my father, she thought.

'Wait—' he said and went over to a bowl of Otaheite apples on a table. He picked one out and brought it for her. 'Come back and visit again. All right?'

242

She nodded. The blonde woman chuckled, and May thought the man looked slightly annoyed.

Clive took her arm and hurried out with her. When they reached the pool, she stopped, wanting to look at it again, but he pulled her along. She looked behind and saw the man standing in the doorway watching her.

They got to the boat, and Clive was just about to give her a good telling-off when he noticed that her face was wet with tears. He sat her on his knee and tried to comfort her. 'Is all right. Hush.' *Poor little thing*, he thought, *I can't help her. She needs her mother.*

20

Across the Water

'Cubans!' Eli Joseph shouted as they arrived at the harbor in Father Reynold's church van.

Castro's army had taken over Cuba. Refugees had begun sailing over to Jamaica, and their arrival had choked the twin harbors of Port Antonio. For days a crowd of curious and officious Jamaicans had met them: policemen, newspapermen, priests, nuns, nurses, and self-appointed guides. Others came down to the harbor just to peer across the water as if the winds from Havana might bring news of what was going on there.

To seven-year-old May, they looked like fallen sea-birds, the Cuban boats. Some of them were just rafts, lurching and tossing on the waves. She had no thoughts as to the cause of their plight. What impressed her was the escape itself, the adventure by sea. She imagined herself desperately clinging to her own handmade raft but, unlike these people, fleeing in the opposite direction toward the open sea.

She saw a boat tip to one side as some refugees landed and scrambled onto the pier. They came with nothing in their hands, shouting among themselves, '*Habla con ellos en Ingles! Pide un doctor!*'

May was not there because of the Cubans but to meet her mother, who was arriving on the *Louisiana*. The massive white passenger ship made the Cuban vessels seem even more flimsy. Yet May was more certain of the refugee boats bopping up and down on the waves than she was of her mother's arrival. Even now, as she saw the *Louisiana* at anchor, she was prepared to learn that for some reason or other her mother was not on board.

She was curious, though. She'd been told that her mother's husband was arriving too. Did that mean her father? Would he be the same man she had met months ago on Navy Island or someone else? She was tired of not knowing who her father was; everyone had a father, even if he were dead or in another country.

Policemen were clearing a walkway through the crowd so the passengers on the American ship could disembark. A group of Cubans, confused by the policemen's orders, began to panic and shout hysterically. There was a scuffle, a tide of humans all pushing forward, and everyone on the pier seemed to be part of it. May heard a woman scream. Had her mother been injured? She held on to the little folding chair where her grandfather sat.

'What happen? You see her?' Eli asked Father Reynold.

'You see anything, Derek?' Father Reynold shouted to Derek, who stood on a wall, peering across the crowd.

'I think is a fight or something. Police down there.'

'I wonder if I should go help since I can talk Spanish,' Father Reynold said.

'No, man, stay. Ida soon come,' Eli told him.

'I think I see her. I see her,' Derek shouted. 'She wearin' a white hat.'

'Yes, is her.' Father Reynold said and began shouting, 'Ida! Baroness! Ida!'

He swooped May up into his arms. 'You see you mama? You see her?'

At first May couldn't distinguish anyone who looked like the mother she had seen in the pictures. Then she made out a pretty woman in a white hat and a blue dress that clung to her figure like fish scales on a mermaid. Her white-gloved arm held on to a man who was much taller than she was. The woman saw her, raised her hand to her lips, cried out, and began waving.

May began wriggling in Father Reynold's arms; she wanted to be put down. Father Reynold thought she was excited and about to run to her mother. 'Wait—' he began as she got free of him. Instead she ran in the opposite direction, back to her grandfather.

May saw the couple approaching and she clenched the back of her grandfather's chair. Then she squatted down, trying to hide.

'Papa!' Ida cried and hugged her father, whose face and hands trembled.

She heard her mother: 'May? Oh, my, you're so big now. Come give me a hug.'

Father Reynold pushed May forward.

Her mother wrapped perfumed arms around her. May hadn't realized that her mother's eyes were so dark. They were wet too, and May wasn't used to seeing grown-ups crying. It was upsetting. As her mother hugged her May looked across at the large blond man who had arrived with her. He was a complete stranger to her, this father.

Ida looked out at the night sea. She and Karl had been back in Jamaica for three months, and they had rented Montevin

Villa, a few miles east of Port Antonio. It was everything the word 'villa' suggested to her, both grand and restful, with a lot of land and a manageable number of servants: cook, maid, laundress, and gardener. The house stood on a cliff overlooking the sea, and it had been built in a Mediterranean style with terraces supported by white columns and parapets. There was an arbor where someone had tried to grow grapes; the dead, heat-shriveled branches still clung to the latticed arches. Stone steps led down to the small beach, which was too rocky for swimming. But up on the cliff, just a minute's walk from the terrace and sharing the sea view, was a swimming pool which had entranced May the moment she saw it. 'Is you house this?' she had asked in the bad English she had grown accustomed to speaking. '*Our* house, at least for now,' Ida had answered, and May had looked astonished. But the pool had been the only thing that had really impressed her; she had not seemed interested in the cheerful bedroom, painted her favorite color, yellow, nor had she seemed enthusiastic about her mother's return.

May had been wary of Ida that first day — exploring the place furtively on her own like a nervous kitten, disappearing from sight, then reappearing now and then to check on her grandfather. Ida had gone to May's room that night to tuck her in and sing her to sleep the way she used to, but May had already fallen asleep. Her old teddy bear, 'Lassie,' was in bed with her along with a plastic sword and a big illustrated copy of *Treasure Island*. Ida hadn't been able to resist curling up beside her, pressing her cheek against May's cool skin and soft hair. And she'd cried because it was May at last, but in a way it was not.

'She'll adjust,' Karl said. 'Give her time.'

Eli's presence had helped. His happiness at being with Ida

had shone out on them all. Ida would watch him and Father Reynold on this veranda playing dominoes late at night the way she remembered. One day she'd gone to her father with the news that Karl was going to buy back the Palace Theatre, and he had held her hand. 'I proud a you, darling,' he'd said, and she'd felt as if it had been her own accomplishment, not Karl's.

Then, two weeks later, Ida had gone into Eli's room to wake him and found that he'd died in his sleep. At the funeral, people had tried to comfort Ida, saying things like: 'He was just waitin' for you to come back home.' Yes, it was generally agreed, he had been living merely to see Ida again, and so he had died a contented man. Father Reynold had cried as he'd buried his best friend and recalled their last evening together playing dominoes. They had been friends for over fifty years.

Eli's death had stunned May. She'd grown more distant, hardly ever talking.

Ida had taken May from the school in Port Antonio and sent her to her own former school, Pringle's. The headmistress called one day because May had disappeared. Not quite eight years old, May had gotten on a bus and found her way back to Port Antonio. She had gone to Miss Gloria's yard looking for Derek, forgetting that he no longer lived there. Ida and Karl had arranged for him to go to boarding school in Kingston. She had then gone to Clive's repair shop, and Clive had brought her home to Ida. 'She not a bad child,' he said. 'She jus' need a little civilizing.'

May told Ida that she wanted to go back to Miss Gloria's yard.

'I should never have left her at that place,' Ida told Karl. 'It scarred her.'

Karl was examining some slides from an excavation site in Guatemala, holding them up one at a time in the lamplight. 'She reads remarkably well for her age,' he said.

She supposed this was his attempt to show an interest in May, but she wondered if he'd even been listening.

She sat out on the veranda now. Karl had already gone in to bed, and she knew he was waiting for her. It was a lovely night, he'd said, and it was. The scent of jasmine came and went with the breeze; the sea was calm. He'd looked at her as if he saw the whole fragrant night in her face, and he'd kissed her. 'I'll come soon,' she had promised.

There was a light out there in the sea. She saw it every night and knew it was Navy Island. During the day, the island was barely visible from the veranda, but every night it showed itself as this starry light on the water. She thought of Errol all the time. How could she not? May was the very image of him.

Since that time in New York when Errol had telephoned, Ida and Karl had avoided talking about him. It was awkward now that they were back, especially since Ida knew that Karl visited Navy Island. He was careful never to say he was going to see Errol; instead he would say, 'I've got some business over on Navy Island today,' and Ida would try to look as if she weren't interested, as if it didn't matter to her. She knew Karl had invested in a film Errol was making in Cuba, and she had a notion about some financial or legal matter Karl was helping him with. She imagined that when they were together, the two men avoided talking about her, pretending that the whole affair with Ida hadn't happened. Karl would require that evasion from Errol, just as he required it from her and from himself too.

Ida thought of Karl waiting for her. *Go in to your husband.*
She knew she should be grateful to him. What a muddle. She
felt as if she kept making one mistake after another. *Are you
a mongoose or a girl?* she could hear Madda Oni asking her.
Choices. Had she chosen badly? Should she have stayed in
Jamaica with her daughter and never have gone to New York?
Stayed at Plumbago Road and been content with little? She
hadn't wanted that.

And marrying Karl? Was that what she'd wanted? She had
been so determined not to be his mistress that she hadn't
properly considered what it would mean to be his wife. He
was good to her. She was a baroness. There was splendor
around her. But not within her. She felt as bewildered as
May.

All the avoided thoughts came together now like a cloud
in her brain. To be a sorry unwed mother or the well-cared-
for wife of a man whom she admired but didn't love – had
those been her only choices? It was exhausting to constantly
fall short of loving someone you shared your life with. Now,
letting her eyes rest on the dark water ahead of her, she
realized she'd been trying to live with the destruction of her
most earnest hope.

She and May belonged on that island. She knew it; her
daughter felt it.

The memory of her own mother's distress came to her.
Ida remembered sitting in the room with Esme as she lay
dying, the years of disappointment closing in around her. At
the time Ida hadn't understood the cause of her mother's
bitterness. It had seemed to her that no one could have loved
Esme more than Eli had. ('Is you I love, Esme,' Ida had heard
him say. 'Not that woman in Kingston who call herself Mrs
Joseph.') But that hadn't been enough. Esme had felt cheated

of something she'd deserved: marriage and the self-assurance that it gave to a woman of her time and beliefs. *You must ask you father for what you want* . . . She realized now that at the end her mother had been worried about her, Ida, the illegitimate daughter, the 'outside child.' *That's why I saved* . . . And Esme's worrying had impressed itself upon Eli too. Ida remembered her father, after he'd learned about her pregnancy, saying, 'Your mother wanted more for you.'

And now, May deserved more. Ida didn't know exactly what that 'more' meant, but she felt a distant, estranged hope stealing across her. Where her own happiness lay, there with Karl or on that island across the water, she couldn't tell, but she would try her best to ensure May's happiness. She didn't want May to ever feel she must choose the lesser over the greater, to shrink back overwhelmed and frightened in the shadow of a disappointed mother. *You must ask* . . . *for what you want.*

21

Errol, up to His Old Tricks

Errol and Brenda decided to have a party for their houseguests. Marilyn Monroe, Tony Curtis, and some other Hollywood friends were visiting Navy Island. Everyone of importance along the north coast had been invited, including Baron and Baroness Von Ausberg.

Karl didn't want Ida to go.

'Look, Karl,' she said, 'we have a saying — "When water t'row way it cyan pick up again." What happened happened. It can't unhappen.'

'By "it," I suppose you mean—'

'May is Errol's daughter. I'm not ashamed of her.'

'This is not about May. You want to see him again.'

In the past she would have reassured him, but she was getting tired of his jealousy. He was generous, but she felt she had now earned his generosity. All those months in South America when she had wanted to go back home and see her daughter, she had stayed with him. She had never complained, not even when he'd asked her to go up into the mountains with him to look at some broken old pots he'd dug up instead of going to Jamaica for Myrtle's funeral.

She told him now: 'If you don't want to go the party, I'll go by myself.'

A few days before the party she took May with her to visit Oni. May had no memory of going up the mountain. She climbed the steep path quickly and ran around looking at Oni's chickens and pigs. She swam and caught crayfish in the river.

Ida sat under the big cotton tree with Oni and told her, 'I'm going to see him again.'

Oni was now eighty, and she was having some pain in her legs that day. It took her longer to move from place to place. She was thinking how long it would take that afternoon to feed the animals and do the weeding, so with Ida she wasted no time: 'What you want me to do for you?'

'I 'fraid,' Ida said quietly.

'You talk like this Bakra Flynn have something over you.'

Ida was startled by Oni's using the old slave word for 'master.'

Oni went on, 'You think him have anything over you?'

Ida didn't answer.

'I see. Is *you* want to have something over him.' When Ida didn't answer, she went on, 'Is a fightin' thing or a lovin' thing you lookin' for?'

'I not fightin' him.' Ida looked down at her hands and played with her ring.

'Wait a minute. You want tek him 'way from that other woman?'

Ida didn't answer, but she was thinking about how that other woman, the teenaged girl Errol lived with, did not have a child, nor had she known him as long as she, Ida, had. *Ida-Rider. Dear girl, you are saving my life* . . . Ida had heard rumors that even though he was living with Brenda, Errol still had affairs with other women. Obviously, he wasn't that happy.

Oni said, 'You stubborn like stubborn-self. I could give you some oil-a-fall-back. But no, no, no!' She shook her head. 'No trouble trouble till trouble trouble you.'

'Then just give me something for myself. Something—'

May was coming toward them, asking Oni if there was any more coconut cake.

Ida lowered her voice: '—for courage.'

'Chu!' Oni said to Ida. 'Stop this nonsense.'

Stubborn like stubborn-self. She was, and she couldn't help it. She had grown up hearing about oil-a-fall-back: it brought back straying husbands, made debts disappear, confounded enemies. She didn't stop to think about whether or not she believed in obeah. When she found the little bottle of oil among Oni's containers, she took it with her.

'You might not recognize him. He's changed so much,' Karl said, fastening the hook of her dress as she looked at herself in the mirror.

'You mean the weight he's put on?'

'He's changed.'

They both gazed at her reflection. For weeks she'd worried about what to wear; she had so many fine things now, and she didn't want to appear overdressed. She'd noticed that people in Jamaica didn't dress up that much nowadays. Some ladies even went out without a hat. She'd finally chosen a black décolleté dress that showed off her curvy figure – a 'heavenly body,' Karl had once described it. Her hair was pinned up, baring her neck. Karl leaned in and kissed her.

'We don't have to go,' he whispered. 'I could make a

reservation at Blue Mountain Inn — we'd have a nice dinner alone—'

'It's our royal duty. We're the only baron and baroness around here.' She looked one more time in the mirror. 'Are the diamonds too much? You think it's too formal?'

An hour later, by the poolside of Bella Vista, the flash of more than one camera reassured her: a photograph of the baron and baroness with Tony Curtis would appear in the *Jamaica Gleaner* and maybe even in *Life*. Ida did not allow the flashing cameras to interrupt the flow of her conversations and smiling introductions. Did Princess Margaret or Princess Grace ever stop to look at the camera? Her years of studying foreign magazines had prepared her, but she was made uncomfortable by the memory of that other party nine years earlier. She saw now how out of place she must have looked then, all dressed up 'like poppy show,' as Jamaicans said, in a floor-length evening gown, satin heels, and her mother's sapphires, and the only colored guest. She'd overheard a man asking, 'Who's she?' And someone had murmured, 'I don't know, some Jamaican girl.' No one would say that now. North-coast society had heard about her marriage and wanted to befriend her.

'I know those are real,' her cousin Antoinette Levy said, looking at Ida's diamond necklace. 'There was never anything fenky-fenky about you, Ida.'

Bella Vista hadn't changed; there were the same potted plants around the patio, and there were the Jolly Boys, Flynn's favorite little band (as opposed to Flynn's Swamp Boys, who used his name but were dreadful musicians). They'd just finished playing 'Big Bamboo' and had begun a calypso they'd become famous for called 'Mother and Daughter.' The beach

below was lit with torches, and the sight of the waves breaking in the distance was one of many luxuries offered to the
party guests. Men in white shirts and black bow ties brought
out trays of champagne and hors d'oeuvres. She had heard
that Errol was having money trouble, but one wouldn't have
believed it from all this.

Marilyn Monroe had an entourage with her, including an
Arab sheikh who seemed to grow more sober as she grew
more drunk. Peter Finch was there with his Jamaican wife,
both of whom Ida liked right away. 'They're so nice and
down-to-earth. Let's invite them over,' she whispered to Karl.
She saw Tony Curtis sitting back on a lounge chair in
conversation with a woman sitting on a lounge chair beside
him; they looked like a middle-aged couple on a cruise. Nigel
and Denise were both there. 'Just like old times,' Denise said
with the usual sarcastic point, and she pretended not to
notice Ida's necklace.

Errol looked awful, Ida thought. It was not just the
weight he had put on or the unhealthy color of his face but
the fact that he seemed to have no energy, physical or
otherwise. There was no more mischief in his face. But it was
Errol. There was no other voice like his, and hearing him
unsteadied her.

For most of the night he remained on a patio chair in a
relaxed pose that she saw as fatigue. His girlfriend, Brenda,
seemed devoted to him and never left his side. She even
hand-fed him hors d'oeuvres. Ida had to admit that she was
beautiful in a pale, fairy-tale sort of way.

He greeted Ida with the same somewhat drunken smile
with which she had seen him greet others. Ida thought his
hand lingered an extra moment in hers and that she saw a
flicker of self-pity in his eyes. It was a look she knew well.

She wanted something else, something that included her, Ida-Rider — some brief, private acknowledgement of their history together. But he turned away from her and began talking to Karl.

It was horrible, just standing there while the two men ignored her. From where she stood she could see the lights of Port Antonio and partially make out the neon letters of the Palace marquee. It should have comforted her or filled her with pride, but on top of everything else she felt a pang of grief: she no longer had her father.

'My dear nymph!' Nigel appeared suddenly and rescued her. 'Let's go find you some more champagne.'

She was grateful for his attention, but she found it hard to give him hers. She was overwhelmed by memories of the place and felt unbalanced, like a top that had just stopped spinning.

Nigel was telling her some funny story about going crab-hunting with his son Ian, and he was saying that May and Ian really ought to get together to play. Out of the corner of her eye, she saw Karl and Errol leave the patio, then reappear a few minutes later on the upstairs balcony, where they continued talking. She asked Nigel to excuse her so she could go 'powder her nose.' She had to find somewhere she could be alone for a few minutes. She went inside the house.

Going upstairs, all she kept thinking about was that she had a handkerchief in her evening bag with drops of obeah oil. She could leave the handkerchief somewhere in the house; maybe the obeah would work, maybe not, but there would be something of hers in this house. She imagined Brenda finding it, another woman's handkerchief in Errol's bathroom. It would upset her; they might quarrel. She remembered exactly where Errol's bathroom was, and she went in.

There were Brenda's things resting beside his things – everyday belongings – bedroom slippers, bathrobes. The bathroom smelled of sweet, feminine soap and she saw bottles of pink nail polish and a pair of gold hoop earrings, cheap-looking things. Ida could see that Brenda really was just a girl – how old did they say she was – sixteen, seventeen? There was an eye-shadow palette left open by the sink with about a dozen different colors.

Ida stood in front of the brightly lit bathroom mirror, looking at herself without seeing herself, delirious with thoughts of the damage she might do. After a while she began to notice how lustrous and unreal her own face looked to her. She sat down on the bathroom stool, ashamed.

She had thought that she belonged here tonight, among these people, but here she was behaving like some idiotic country girl. (*Look, the country girl.* Who had said that about her? Her half-sisters, the day they'd come to take her father back to Kingston and she'd learned for the first time that her parents weren't married. *What you have there, a juju?*). What did she have in her evening bag? Something that would put obeah on her lover, make him come back to her. What if some harm actually came to Errol because of what she'd done, or someone found out? Obeah was illegal. She had May to think of. She was a baroness.

This bakra have something over you? Oni had asked her, and at the time Ida had wanted to protest. But there was truth in it; she still had too much feeling for Errol, as if he had been the one to put obeah on her. She smiled a little at the thought.

She didn't want to go back down to the party. She felt fraudulent and out of place. *Stop this nonsense*, she heard Oni saying. Or were they her mother's words? She composed herself and went downstairs.

She saw that Karl and Errol had been joined on the balcony by Brenda. Karl saw her standing alone and came down to her.

'It's late. Maybe we should go,' he suggested.

She thought he looked annoyed, but not with her. She glanced up at Errol and was surprised to see him looking at her.

'Yes,' she said; she was ready to go.

Later that night at Montevin Villa, Karl found her alone on the terrace. He decided not to disturb her and turned to go back in. But she called to him, saying, 'Stay with me a little,' and they stood quietly looking at the dark waves below.

'I think he's sick,' she said after a while.

'I'm sorry,' Karl said.

She leaned against him, tired. The night air was at its finest, and they stayed there enjoying it for a while longer.

Ida came home from shopping the next day and the maid told her, 'Mr Flynn, him did phone again, ma'am.'

'What you mean, "again"?'

The maid looked worried, as if she were about to be blamed for something. 'Him did phone before an' I give the message to Mr Karl.'

Ida looked hard at the maid to see if she was a troublemaker or just plain stupid. 'You gave the message to Mr Karl? Did Mr Flynn ask for Mr Karl?'

'No, ma'am, for you.'

'Next time somebody calls for me, give *me* the message.'

'Yes, ma'am.'

Ida was mystified. Errol wanted to speak to her? She

remembered how he had seemed to look at her as she was leaving the party.

She sat on her bed, ridiculously happy. For the rest of the day she expected his call and thought about whether or not she should call him. When Karl left the house the next morning, she did.

The phone rang unanswered. She tried again several times and there was still no answer. She was stirred up by the thought of seeing him. It was hard to imagine how or where they would meet. She could only picture being with him on Navy Island.

Then he called again. 'Ida, let's meet.' He spoke in a hurried, matter-of-fact way, but his voice, even though it had no ardor in it, drew her.

She agreed to meet him at the bar of the Silver Sands. It was forty miles away, near Ocho Rios. When Karl came home, she told him she was going to visit her cousins the Levys the next day.

Ida waited for him at the hotel bar. Actually, she didn't sit at the bar itself but at a nearby table. She was twenty-six and had never gone to a bar, having been brought up to believe that only promiscuous women did things like that. She knew from her years in New York that this wasn't really true; she'd met nice girls who went out drinking on a Friday night after work. Still, this rule had been ingrained in her and she felt unlike herself sitting there. The lunch crowd had already left. There was only the bartender, who looked over at her occasionally, a few waiters wandering in and out from the restaurant across the way, and a couple of foreign men, guests at the hotel, who'd stopped for a Red Stripe; one of them smiled at her. She would have felt much better if the bartender had seemed puzzled by her appearance, but instead he seemed to have come to his own conclusion about her.

She drank a Coca-Cola. It was not easy for her, waiting there, looking up when she heard footsteps thudding closer or a door opening, then recovering herself, taking another sip of the melted ice which was soon all that was left of her drink. The effort to conceal her embarrassment became too wearying, and after an hour and a half she left.

Errol was waiting for her, not at the Silver Sands but at the Silver Seas, a new restaurant-bar in Oracabessa.

Nigel Fletcher happened to see him there. Errol had the remnants of a curry-goat lunch on his plate, and to Nigel's surprise, he was surprisingly sober, drinking what looked like lemonade. Nigel ordered himself a gin and tonic.

'You here alone, old chap?' Nigel asked. 'I didn't see your car outside.'

'It's in the garage with a broken axle. Took a taxi.'

'What brings you to Oracabessa?'

'A date.' He took a cigarette from the pack Nigel held out to him, and Nigel noticed a slight shaking of his hand. 'With our lovely Jamaican friend, Ida. But she stood me up.'

'Baroness Ida?'

'Ida-Rider.' He smiled, reached for his glass, realized it was empty, and beckoned to the waiter to refill it. 'Coconut water,' he told Nigel. 'Supposed to be good for the kidneys.' He went on, 'I lied like the devil to Brenda so I could get away. Cost me a fortune in taxi fares – and no Ida.'

'Careful,' Nigel said. 'She's married now.'

'I know, I know. But I've got some damn important things to say to her.'

His voice had suddenly become louder, and the other people in the bar looked over at them. He drank quickly as if terribly thirsty, and then he spoke more quietly: 'I was looking forward to having a chat with her; it's been such a long time. She was—' He hesitated, looking for the right words. 'For a while she was in a bit of trouble, but it seems to have worked out all right. Worked out well for her. The child—'

'Have you seen May?' Nigel asked.

Errol looked blank.

'Ida's daughter,' Nigel said.

'I saw her once.' He drained the coconut water from his glass.

Errol began to smile. He'd found a new mood to put on. 'Did you see her with Karl the other night?' He raised his eyebrows and with palms in the air drew the outline of a womanly, hourglass figure. 'I didn't get a chance to talk to her, what with Brenda and Karl and everyone else around.' He began tapping the table with his fingers and looking around.

Nigel decided to change the subject. 'They're showing *Too Much Too Soon* at the Regal this week.' The film, about Diana Barrymore, had come out a year ago in the States, and he'd heard that its one redeeming feature was Errol in the role of John Barrymore.

'Typecasting. Played myself.' Errol smiled. 'But they won't let you drink on the set. That's the hard part.'

'What's next on your list?'

'*Cuban Rebel Girls* comes out in a month,' Errol said, and Nigel tried not to wince.

By all accounts it was pure drivel, the stupidest thing

Errol had ever done, a film about Castro that he'd written and directed himself and that starred his girlfriend, Brenda.

'I might do some television,' Errol said and glanced across the room as the door opened. A stout Jamaican man entered. Nigel thought he had never seen Errol look so forlorn.

Nigel told him, 'I heard once that it's awfully good luck for a man to be stood up by a pretty woman. Apparently the more attractive the offending *femme*, the better your luck. Good day for a game of poker.'

'It's not what you think, you know.' He reached for another cigarette from Nigel's pack. 'It was just to have a chat with her and clear the air. Be friends again. Why the hell not? We used to have a good time. All of us. Karl watches her like a hawk now. But it's up to her, isn't it?' He stopped. After a while he said, 'I wanted to see her.'

Why do you want to stir things up? Nigel wanted to ask, but then he realized that he didn't need to worry. Errol couldn't cause any more harm to Ida; he seemed barely capable of stirring up whatever lay at the bottom of his own heart.

Finally Errol said, 'A woman's got to be what she is, and a man's got to do what he does.'

Nigel looked at him.

'The game, Nigel. Men, women, love, sex.' He lifted his glass to his lips and took what looked to Nigel like a very unsatisfying sip of his coconut water. Nigel half expected him to throw the glass across the room and get himself a real drink.

'You're not expecting me to say something to cheer you up, are you?' Nigel asked.

'I threw pearls to the swine—'

'Come on, I'll drive you back to West Harbor.'

On the way Errol rattled on, not about Ida but about

himself, how he'd been having chest pains and was thinking about marrying Brenda as soon as she turned eighteen, and he didn't regret sleeping with any of the fifteen hundred or so women he'd gone to bed with in the course of his life, not even his first wife because in spite of her being a royal pain in the you-know-what she'd given him a wonderful son.

'Christ, it's going to be 1960 in a couple of months. I'm half a century old. Maybe I won't make so many mistakes in the next half. It's not too late, you know.'

It would be months before Ida heard about this from Nigel.

The day after the thwarted meeting, she went to see Clive Goodman.

'Do me a favor, Clive.' Ida held out an envelope to her friend. She had put embarrassment behind her and decided to send a note to Errol arranging another meeting. 'Could you take this to Errol for me?' She knew that with Clive she didn't need to explain more.

He had never refused her anything before. She remembered the day he'd run ten miles to fetch her shoes, and he had been good to May while she'd been away. But now instead of taking the envelope from her, he stood looking at her, perplexed.

'He's gone,' Clive said.

'Where?'

'California, I think. He left this morning on the *Zaca*.'

She looked out at the horizon. Just like that, he had sailed away? It took a few moments for her to recover, to become aware of herself standing there like every 'lass' in those songs about sailors leaving port and the girls in sad calypsos. She knew the songs so well that she felt all their sadness and bad luck tumbling down on her, and it was she who was being left again and again.

Later Karl mentioned to her that Errol and Brenda had headed out to the Pacific. He also told her that Brenda was pregnant. Errol was broke and going back to California to try to find work in television.

A month later, Ida was at home mending May's torn pants at the sewing machine. Sewing was the only domestic task she was any good at and she enjoyed it. She heard swords all of a sudden – May and Nigel's son Ian playing at sword fighting, she thought. But the children's swords were plastic; these sounded real. She got up to look, then suddenly sank back down.

She saw shadows dueling against the wall, Errol's shadow and another. Daydream, apparition, flash of memory, she wasn't sure; it played before her like a scene from Errol's movie *The Adventures of Robin Hood*. The swordsmen's shadows darted back and forth across the walls. Then Errol emerged, victorious and, for a moment, no longer a shadow. He bowed to her, and she sat quietly suffused with sadness.

So it didn't shock her when Karl brought her the news. Errol had sailed to Vancouver because someone there had offered to buy the *Zaca*. While they were there negotiating the sale, Brenda miscarried, and a few days later Errol had a heart attack and died.

'The thought of losing her, that's why his heart failed,' Ida said.

'Losing who?' Karl asked.

'The *Zaca*. You know how he loved that boat.'

His death had the effect of not only unlocking memories but ending her silence about them. She talked about him now, irrepressibly, not like a rejected lover but like a widow. She was upset to learn that Errol's body was not being brought back to Jamaica.

'He told me he wanted to spend his last moments looking out on the Caribbean,' she told Karl. 'He would have wanted his grave on Navy Island.'

But apparently there was not enough money left in his estate, even after the sale of the yacht, to bring his body back to the island.

'Couldn't you help with the cost, Karl?'

'I don't want to interfere. It's up to Paulette.' He felt the need to remind her of Errol's widow. 'Anyway, I don't believe in spending a lot of money on the dead.'

'You've always been jealous of him,' she said.

'I'm not jealous of him now.'

He looked on quietly for weeks as she privately and publicly mourned Errol. He saw that she needed to proclaim this lovesome kinship since she'd been deprived, during Errol's life, of a legitimate one. Karl tried not to wince at the indiscretions – an obituary to the local newspapers in which she spoke of Errol as 'beloved' and mentioned 'his daughter May.' The Palace ran a month of Errol Flynn movies and lost money to the new theatre in town, which showed *Ben Hur*.

They had been living at Montevin Villa for six months when Flynn died. Though May had gotten used to living with her mother and stepfather, she hadn't grown affectionate toward either of them. She tolerated Ida's devotion but was skeptical about everything she said or did. Under the skepticism was a well-hidden curiosity. She was intrigued by her mother's life, her air of sentimental longing, and that unsinkable quality of hers. 'Buoyancy' wasn't exactly the word; she had seen her mother look sad and preoccupied, and it was not 'adaptability' because that would suggest effort, and to May, Ida seemed to accomplish everything effortlessly.

Ida, for her part, worried about how Errol's death affected May. She began spending more time with her daughter, trying to get closer. It wasn't easy; May resisted. So Ida spoiled her.

'Is it May's birthday again today?' Karl would ask when he saw Ida buying her so many new things.

Ida even tried cooking; she knew May had a sweet tooth, so she attempted making desserts. May wondered how anyone could spoil Jell-O. Ida put strange things in it, like corn.

May didn't trust Ida. She seemed fickle, unpredictable. The way she said the name 'Errol,' like a secret she couldn't help blurting out, irritated May: 'Your father and I . . . we used to ride our horses in the sea . . . and then, one day . . .' Sometimes when they were in town together, with Navy Island in view, Ida would bring up the subject of Errol, and May would say dismissively, 'I know that already.'

It seemed to Ida that May was more interested in learning about Navy Island than about her father. She asked questions like 'Did the whole island belong to him?' and 'Who does it belong to now?'

One day Ida took May horseback riding at the old Equestrian Club. For all her athleticism, May wasn't comfortable on a horse. It surprised her to see her mother riding so well and to see that, for once, Ida wasn't merely trying to impress her; she was enjoying herself. Here was something she was really good at. And she looked so attractive, riding. Always, everywhere, so attractive. May suddenly became glum and guarded. Everything came so easily to Ida, and it was all because of that beauty which she, May, felt she'd never have. As she began sinking into this well of self-pity, she heard 'Hee-haw!' and noticed that Ida was doing circus-like tricks, leaping on and off the horse. May couldn't help smiling. She remembered then what Clive had told her about Ida being full of 'mirth.'

Karl didn't try to befriend his eight-year-old step-daughter. He would have preferred it if Ida had sent her to boarding school. May viewed him as a boring foreigner, hard to ignore only because of his large body and the blondness that seemed to crown him in a world of darker people. But one day at dinner she heard her mother saying something about Karl's 'searching for treasure,' and she looked at her stepfather curiously: 'What kind of treasure?'

He thought carefully about how to answer her. He was reluctant to stir up her enthusiasm in case she'd grow inquisitive and even want to handle some of his artifacts. Many were fragile.

'Ancient treasure,' Ida told May, 'and sunken ships.'

'Shipwrecks?'

'You should take May with you to St Ann's Bay,' Ida told Karl. She turned to May: 'He's looking for two of Columbus's ships – the *Capitana* and what's the other one? *Santana?*'

'*Santiago*. I'm not actually doing any diving myself – and there's not really anything to see yet.'

'Is there gold?' May asked.

'Possibly,' he answered.

'There's no gold in Jamaica,' Ida said.

'Columbus thought so. He saw gold ornaments on the Arawak Indians.' Karl added, 'He wrote about it in his diary.'

'You read his diary?' May was impressed.

'But—' Ida said again, 'no gold has ever been discovered in Jamaica.'

'The Arawaks may have brought it here from the mainland,' he said, 'and now it's vanished – like them.'

'It's in those ships at the bottom of the sea,' May said. 'Columbus took it from them!'

'Maybe. Or they may have hidden it from the Spaniards in caves up in the mountains.'

He saw her raise her eyebrows. Her whole face had become alert and excited. She looked incredibly like her father – the same longish, handsome face printed on a little girl.

'It's in the ships,' she said.

'I hope you're right,' Karl told her.

'Do you want Navy Island?' Karl asked Ida a few months after Errol had died.

'Navy Island?'

'I'm one of the executors of his estate. Paulette doesn't want it, and I think I can afford it.'

She looked preoccupied, and it annoyed him that she hadn't leapt at this generous offer. After all, this was Navy Island he was offering her.

'Was there anything in Errol's will about May?' she asked quietly.

'No.'

She heard the exasperation in his voice. But she had to ask another question.

'Or me?'

He shook his head.

'What about Brenda?'

'Nothing. Her mother wants to go to court.'

'Oh, God.'

'I hope it's the last one of his messes I have to clean up.'

Of course she wanted Navy Island — for herself and for May too.

She walked over to Karl and put her arms around him. 'I would love it.'

There was a Jamaican expression about fate: 'Wha' fe you cyan be un-fe you.' That was what Mrs Goodman, the hairdresser, said when Ida told her she'd be moving to Navy Island, adding, 'What a way everything turn out good.' Father Reynold was also pleased. As a religious man, he knew he should not harbor vindictive thoughts but he remembered how much money Errol had owed Eli, not to mention the hurt and disappointment Errol had caused — Ida deserved Navy Island.

The only one who didn't seem happy was Oni, who cautioned Ida about moving to a place where she'd have to come and go all the time by boat, especially since she hadn't learned to swim. Hadn't she already fallen off a boat once and almost drowned? 'Stay a-land,' she told Ida.

Ida told Karl, 'That woman putting goat-mout' on me.'

He looked at her, fascinated. He'd noticed that she reverted to patois whenever she spent time around Oni, and also whenever she was annoyed. It was one of the pleasures of being married to her, the dusty, unusual little treasures that turned up on her tongue. *Goat-mout'? Goat's mouth?* His thoughts flitted now from ancient Greek amphitheatres to West African divination ceremonies and on to the gastronomy of Bedouin herdsmen. 'What do you mean?' he asked.

'If you tell somebody they goin' catch a cold because they not wearin' a sweater, an' then they catch a cold, that's puttin' goat-mout' on them. If I drown one day, it's going to be Oni's fault.'

'You could take swimming lessons.'

She shook her head. 'Oni talk a whole heap a nonsense. I not payin' her no mind.'

The property was run-down. Many repairs had to be made; new fixtures and furniture bought. Also, new servants were hired because, according to Karl, with the exception of Winston, the old gardener, the former servants had been stealing things.

Ida enjoyed all the work involved in the move: the plans and renovations and the going back and forth by taxi-boat every day. Often Clive Goodman would take time out to sail her across to Navy Island. He would listen quietly to all her plans and now and then make workman-like suggestions — the outdoor lighting needed rewiring, the kitchen sink could be taken out and replaced by a much larger one. She had forgotten how handy he was. Ida wanted things at Bella Vista to remain basically unchanged. The walls and plantation-style shutters were given a fresh coat of paint in exactly the same shades of pink and white. New, lush potted plants replaced those that had withered on the veranda and by the poolside. Someone suggested a new, modern-style roof to replace the terra cotta, but she wouldn't hear of it. Both she and Karl rather liked the style of the house, a mix of California ranch and Spanish colonial. She noticed that May was very quiet and attentive throughout these preparations. She seemed overwhelmed rather than excited and stayed close to her mother or to Clive during these trips back and forth.

Most of Errol's things were still there. Ida gave some of his clothes to Winston the gardener and left a lot of the household items where they were: clocks, mirrors, and those unusual things of his that were familiar to her from years of visiting the house, like the carved prow of a canoe from New Guinea which Errol had hung on a wall and the painting of one of Errol's favorite horses, Gentleman Jim. Ida remembered Gentleman Jim. So many memories. She felt like a widow who had just gotten remarried, deciding what, for the new husband's sake, to put away and what to keep in sight. The odd thing was that at times it seemed as if it were Errol she was now finally marrying and Karl who was dead. Then Karl would come into the room and she would be shocked and ashamed. *Is mad me just mad, or is Errol' duppy mad me?*

She and Karl were going to occupy Errol's old bedroom. They went to examine it after it had been emptied of all its furniture. It was spacious with jalousie windows and doors opening onto a terrace. Two sconces, like eyes wide apart, were set in the wall on either side of the place where the bed had been. An open archway rather than a door led to the adjoining bathroom, where there was a huge sunken bath. Some of the tiles on the bathroom floor were loose. Everything had been cleaned and cleared away except for a blue bar of soap at the sink and a full bottle of perfume, something Brenda must have disliked and left behind. There was a ghostly feeling about the place, an atmosphere of interrupted, ordinary pleasures. She and Karl walked about quietly and separately and then stood together by the doorway for a moment.

'I always liked this room,' Karl said carefully and even gently. 'And you?'

The slight emphasis on *you* wasn't lost on her, nor was the note of consideration with which he approached but did not tread upon the memories the room had revived. It was one of those moments when she found herself appreciating him. He understood, she thought. Then she remembered that he too had been close to Errol, something she'd been jealous of before but could be gracious about now.

'I think it will be very nice for us,' she said, smiling warmly at him.

Karl had his own reason for moving to Navy Island. The estate gave him better access to West Harbor, which was useful to him in the artifacts trade. Karl was on friendly terms with the customs inspector, who was very compliant about the crates arriving from overseas and also about the team of divers and archaeologists, who often came and went by boat; he rarely bothered about their papers. Living on Navy Island, directly across from the harbor, would make these comings and goings even easier.

He converted the lowest level of the house into a study and wine cellar. He took out the old ceiling fan and put in an air conditioner to preserve his artifacts, his wine, and his jazz recordings. The servants would not be allowed to dust any of these things or even to go down there without his permission.

Ida was amused; she imagined him occupied for hours down there with his ancient objects and boxes of slides. 'You used to be a playboy,' she teased. 'Now look at you.'

'I promise to come up for meals,' he said.

As long as he had dominion over his study, he was content to leave all the decisions about the rest of the house to her. 'Whatever you like,' he'd say. The only thing they disagreed on was the bar in the living room. Karl wanted to take it apart and build a bar outside by the pool so people wouldn't come in with wet feet.

'It still smells strange in here,' Karl said to her as they

stood in the living room. It was about a week before they were to move in. He thought it was the bar; years of spilled liquor had soaked through the wood, and there was something else too, the smell of garden dirt or mud.

Ida sat contemplating the bar with its dark wood panels and stonework; it had been a big part of her teenaged years. Not that she had spent a lot of time in the house, but she remembered when it had first been built, how the luxury of having such things in one's own home – a bar, a swimming pool, a room with nothing in it but a pool table – had impressed her.

She recognized the smell Karl was talking about. It was Errol. 'I want to leave the bar the way it is,' she said. 'It matches the rest of the room.'

'Well, we could sand and revarnish the wood. And we'll get some new things for it, a new bar set, don't you think?'

Ida didn't object, though she knew Errol had been fond of the silver-plated bar set engraved with his initials. It didn't matter, however, because the new set mysteriously disappeared soon after Karl bought it. Karl thought it had to be one of the many workmen coming and going through the house. Luckily, Ida hadn't yet thrown out the old set.

Finally she told Karl, 'The bar is haunted and there isn't a thing we can do about it.'

It was the only way to explain the smell and the other peculiar things that kept happening in that part of the house. They would find things on the bar counter first thing in the morning: a glass of half-melted ice, a bottle of scotch, or the ice bucket moved from one place to another. Sometimes there would be the smell of a cigarette when no one was smoking.

'It's Errol,' she said, 'up to his usual pranks.'

She began leaving a drink out for him every night before she went to bed. Libations for the spirit, Ida said, an old West Indian thing.

'Don't pretend you don't see him too,' she said to May about Errol's ghost. 'And you,' she startled Karl. 'Just because you're a white man doesn't mean duppy cyan frighten you.'

Karl wanted to say that May's resemblance to her father was ghost enough.

Just before they moved, May heard her mother ask Karl, 'What happened to that funny map of Errol's, the old one with the drawings? It would look nice framed over the bar.'

'I don't know. He probably sold it.'

'You mean it was actually worth something?'

'It was an antique.'

May knew they were talking about the map her father had shown her. *It's very old and very valuable*, she remembered him saying. She had never told her mother about the day she'd met her father.

'Well, he certainly seemed to treasure it,' Ida said. 'And he didn't like to part with his things.'

May paid special attention to this. She had taken something from Bella Vista that day when she'd seen her father. She had been worried for weeks after that someone would find out and she'd be in trouble. It was a strange-looking coin that had been lying on his desk. It had looked to her like some pirate thing – a piece-of-eight maybe – but had learned later that it was just some small change left over from a trip he'd taken to Italy.

After months of preparation and renovation, Ida, Karl, and May installed themselves.

May was solemn the first few days there. Ida went looking for her one afternoon and found her down by the servants' quarters: Cassava Piece was what they called it because of all the wild cassava growing there. It was late afternoon and she was sitting by the coal-pot with Florence, the new cook they'd hired. A breadfruit was roasting.

'Come for a walk with me,' Ida said to May. They followed the river down to the beach and Ida told her stories about Navy Island, about the buccaneers who had hidden there and Captain Bligh and the legend of the ghost, Sabine, and about the very first time she'd come there with May's father.

May listened quietly and then asked, 'Who owns Navy Island now?'

'Karl.'

'The whole island?'

'Yes.'

May thought for a while. 'If Karl dies, who will own it?'

'If Karl dies?' Ida repeated.

'Can we go on living here if he dies?'

The thought of Karl's dying had not occurred to Ida, and she was a bit shocked by May's question. May was waiting for an answer.

'Nobody's dying,' Ida said.

22

Treasure Cove

She was safe. She belonged there. When she grew older, May would look back on those first two or three years on Navy Island as the only untroubled time of her life. Trouble was there, of course, spots of trouble, eating away the perfection like moths in cupboards. But she was too busy to see it, busy enjoying ownership of every rock, tree, and vista that Navy Island provided. No, she didn't see trouble, not until around the time of her eleventh birthday, and she would remember that birthday because of the invasion.

It was April 17, 1961. The Fletchers were coming for the birthday lunch. Ian Fletcher had been visiting May all week, and the two children were outside playing. By eleven there were balloons on the poolside terrace. Ida had just finished her bath and was getting dressed. Florence was in the kitchen decorating a birthday cake. No one on Navy Island had any reason to suspect that just fifty or sixty miles north of them, American ships and submarines were about to attempt an invasion of Cuba.

May and Ian playing pirate down by the water heard no sounds of naval warfare other than those of their play world.

The two were now as 'close as twins,' people said. They were the same age and height; they both had straight, short brown hair, and though Ian was much paler than May, people mistook them for each other from a distance. Ian and his brother Martin went to school in England, so May only saw them during the long school holidays. Most of all she liked being around their father, who'd taught her how to sail and fish. Nigel's sons were not the avid sailors May had turned out to be, so he was more than happy to have her around.

When Ida was planning the birthday party, it had occurred to her that her daughter had almost no friends. May was taller and more athletic than the girls in her class. She played like a boy, climbing trees, sword fighting, stick fighting, wrestling, even boxing; she preferred wearing boys' clothes and keeping her hair short. Ida would get flustered when they were out together and strangers asked about her 'little boy' or called May 'he.' Ida tried to convince May to grow her hair. May's solution to the problem was to take on the name 'Mason' and for a while that was how she introduced herself to people. Finally Ida came to an agreement with her: she could keep her hair short but had to get rid of the masculine name.

Ida was grateful that May at least had Ian Fletcher for a friend. He was a strange, sullen child, and it had taken Ida a while to warm up to him. May was the faster, stronger one and the leader in games, and this sometimes upset Ian. He had artistic talent and was happiest sketching while May read aloud to him from her pirate books.

Karl, who had never liked Ian, was especially annoyed with him that day of May's birthday. He couldn't wait for the Fletchers to come and take the boy back home. Ian had locked May inside a shed earlier that morning and had left her there for over an hour.

They had been at May's favorite place, Treasure Cove. It was sheltered and leafy, a good hideout for pirates. The bent coconut tree, stretching across the water, made a good perch for them as well as a diving board. There was an old shed nearby with fishing nets and a canoe which they sometimes took out to sea. May was pretending to be a lady pirate, Lucy Sharp. Ian was a Spanish pirate chief by the name of Benito Diaz who wanted to leave her behind on the desert island.

'You won't leave me here, you scallywag!' Pirate Lucy shouted, drawing her sword. 'I'll fight you like a man.'

'You'll be sorry, Lucy Sharp.' He rushed at her and pushed her into the shed. 'You'll rot in the dungeon!' he shouted and in the excitement he snapped shut the old padlock hanging on the door.

He immediately realized that there was no key. 'I'll go for help,' he cried.

There were no windows and she began to be afraid of suffocating before Ian got back. She heard scraping sounds on the walls outside and thought about the ghost, Sabine, who was said to haunt Navy Island. Once, walking along the beach, May had thought she'd seen Sabine with her long white hair staring at her through the trees, but it had only been a white bougainvillea swaying in the wind.

She began to pound against the door of the shed.

Ian wasn't sure what to do, whether to run away and hide or try to get May out himself. He was afraid of getting into trouble. So he sat on the garden wall, worrying about it until Karl found him there.

Karl broke the latch. He hadn't known about the shed before. He looked around carefully and told them it was dangerous for them and that they must never play in there again. He would get a new padlock to keep them out, he said. His stern voice frightened them.

After birthday cake and the opening of presents, the children went back outside and the grown-ups sat on the upstairs veranda.

Martin, who was fourteen and only interested in childish games if he could boss the younger ones around, sat in a tree with a spyglass and interrupted their adventure by shouting things like 'Rocks ahead! Avast! Steer windward!' May and Ian had the advantage of knowing the island better than he did. But they were in awe of the older boy, so they allowed him to take charge and explain things: 'It's volcanic,' he would say for instance of a large rock with a hole in the center, 'millions of years old.' There were some relics and ruins of the eighteenth-century English navy, including a cannonball. Martin instructed the younger children in warfare, bullying his brother until the younger one cried and May intervened: 'Stop bossing him.'

'What are you going to do? Tell on me?'

'I'll box you down.'

'Girls don't box; they scratch.'

'I'll box you and scratch you.'

'Maybe I'll hold you down and kiss you.'

'Maybe I bite you tongue off.'

Karl left the veranda for a few minutes, and Nigel began telling Ida about the plans to film his spy novel, *Change of Latitude*, in Jamaica. He had made a lot of money not only from that novel but from a series of them about an English secret agent named Jack Blaze. He'd recently bought a chateau in Switzerland for Denise, hoping it might change her opinion of his writing, but she continued to despise the novels ('rubbish,' she called them).

'You could make money writing sensible books.'

'But Nigel enjoys what he writes,' Ida told Denise.

Nigel gave a quick bow. 'Thank you for that.' He suddenly wanted to tell her how pretty she was in that bright red dress; she was hard to look at only because one couldn't look long enough. 'Why on earth don't you visit us in Switzerland?' he asked. 'May would love to go skiing with the boys.'

Karl came back. 'The US Navy is invading Cuba. It's on the radio.'

'For heaven's sake,' Denise said, lighting a cigarette. 'They'll provoke the Soviets, and here we are in the line of fire.'

'Don't be so gloomy,' Nigel said, also lighting a cigarette.

'Well, I suppose that's the end of Castro, then,' said Denise. 'He can't stand up to the Americans, can he?' It was a rhetorical question and it seemed to hang in the air with the smoke.

Ida was the only one not smoking. Karl looked at her. The late-afternoon sunlight caught her long hair which she'd let out for a change. He remembered her washing and drying it earlier – an elaborate ritual that involved the boiling of mint and hibiscus leaves and her sitting for a certain time in the sun. She wore a new sundress that was gathered softly and intricately around her breasts, something she'd made herself that bared her shoulders. She looked primitive and regal to him, like an Aztec princess He wondered as he sat there whether she'd let him make love to her later.

'Don't underestimate Mr Castro,' Nigel was saying. 'I'll bet fifty pounds he will.'

'What? Defeat the Americans!' Denise, suddenly bored by her husband, turned to Karl. 'What do you think?' She had thrown her head back slightly as she puffed on the cigarette; it was a sensuous move meant to draw attention to her body.

Ida looked at Denise's sunburned arms and wrinkled cleavage and wondered why men found her appealing. She was known to be unfaithful to Nigel (though people said he had affairs too) and was currently having an affair with a famous English sculptor.

'The invasion? I just hope it will be over soon, one way or another,' Karl said, emerging from his secret reverie and rejoining the conversation.

'They would have done better going in with the air force,' Nigel remarked.

'You should have advised them,' Karl said.

'Speaking of the air force,' Nigel turned to Karl, 'I was with some old RAF friends last month in London. Do you remember Lloyd Bixley?' He paused for a moment. 'Had a summer place on the Swiss-Austrian border. He knew your family before the war.'

Ida glanced at Nigel. She sensed something probing and less than friendly in his question.

'I don't recall the name.' Karl said.

'Are you sure?' Nigel persisted. 'He remembered meeting you and your sister. Yvette?'

'Eugenia,' Ida corrected. She knew Karl didn't want to talk about the war or Austria.

'Yes. Eugenia,' Nigel said. 'He remembered a picnic, and even a Bordeaux you brought along—'

'That sounds like Karl,' Ida interjected and hoped, when everyone laughed, that the subject was closed.

But Nigel continued, 'He spoke about a friend of yours, someone named — Max — I think?'

'Max was Karl's friend,' Ida said. She remembered Max from a photograph she'd seen. He had made a strong impression on her because he looked like Errol. She had also seen an inscription in a book of poems and though she hadn't been able to read the German words, she'd gathered that it had been a present from Karl to Max — or from Max to Karl. She believed Karl had suffered deeply from the loss of this friend because of the way he avoided talking of him. 'He died in the war,' was all he'd ever said to Ida.

'Yes, he was my friend,' Karl told Nigel, 'but I don't remember the picnic or Lloyd Bixley. Coffee, anyone? We have your favorite, Nigel, Blue Mountain.'

Ida exchanged a quick look with Karl, and he sent back the hint of a smile. They had a long-standing banter about coffee: Karl insisted on drinking imported Italian espresso in the morning and Ida would nag him — 'How can you dislike Jamaican coffee? Nigel says it's the best in the world.' 'What do Englishmen know about coffee?' Karl would say.

'Tea for me, please,' Denise said. 'Do you remember when Errol tried to grow tea here? Tea trees from New Guinea, or was it Tahiti?'

'Didn't he grow coconuts too?' Nigel said. 'What was he going to do with all those coconuts?'

'He planted a lot of things, most of the things in this garden—' Ida began quietly.

'Yes,' Denise cut her off and took on a slightly nostalgic, slightly amused tone, 'fancied himself the big plantation massa as well as the world's greatest stud. Well,' she swept her eyes across the garden, 'he did leave you with some nice things.'

Ida felt as if she had been jabbed. She had been thinking about Errol all day, maybe because of May's birthday, and now in this awful way because of Denise.

She was relieved when the children's shouts broke in.

'A grave! A dead person!'

She saw May running across the lawn toward the veranda. Her clothes were dirty. She looked earnest and happy. Ida wanted to turn to Denise and say, 'See what he gave me.'

May slowed down just long enough to see her mother send her a strange, conspiratorial smile. She wasn't sure what the smile meant but it intrigued her.

Breathlessly the children described a grave they'd found.

'It's covered with moss.'

'And weeds and grass.'

'I think it's a lady's grave.'

'Come look. It's true.'

'Isn't this up your alley,' Nigel asked Karl, 'digging up things?'

Denise and Karl stayed behind. Ida and Nigel followed the children and on the way they talked about how close Cuba was to Navy Island, and that you could see the Sierra Maestro from Bella Vista sometimes with binoculars.

'Fascinating,' Nigel said when they reached the grave. 'Someone went to the trouble of making a headstone, a nice one too. I can see why you think it's a woman's. Look at the engraving.'

May was cleaning it off, trying to make out the badly eroded letters.

'Martin wants to dig it up and see the skeleton,' Ian said nervously.

'I wonder who she was,' May said. 'Maybe it's Sabine.'

'The ghost of Navy Island,' Ida explained to Nigel. 'Some say she was the daughter of the pirate Ann Bonney, and some say she was here with Captain Bligh.'

'I know who Captain Blight is,' May said with enthusiasm.

'Captain Bligh,' Ida corrected.

'Martin said her duppy might get mad and come get us,' Ian told his father.

'Martin knows everything, does he?' Nigel said as a way of comforting Ian, who seemed scared by the talk of graves and ghosts.

'Don't be frightened of duppies, Ian,' May said.

'Ian's frightened of everything,' Martin said.

'I'm not!'

Nigel said, 'I've always thought this place had a certain charm.'

'You're a writer. Write a book about it,' May said.

'It's your island. You do it,' he shot back.

'All right. I'll write a book about Sabine and Captain Blight,' she told Nigel. Then she turned to the two boys. 'Race you to the lookout.'

'I'll be Captain Bligh,' Martin said. 'May, you're second-in-command.'

'Who am I?' Ian cried out.

'Sabine.'

'I don't want to be the dead lady.'

'Last one to the lookout is the dead lady,' Martin shouted as he and May took off, racing each other.

'Look at her,' Nigel said, watching May. 'She's so bloody fast. And strong. Did she tell you that she caught a baby shark the other day?'

'Yes, and I wasn't too happy about it. It's too dangerous, Nigel.'

'If you'd seen how proud she looked—'

Ida saw May put her arms around Ian, comforting him. He was upset about getting to the lookout last. 'They're such good friends.'

'They're more than that, nymph.'

'What? Don't tell me you believe that nonsense?'

'It's not nonsense. Denise told me.'

'Told you what?'

'He might be Flynn's boy.'

'She said so?'

'We were having a row and it came up.'

'Nigel, why do you stay with her?'

They had begun walking back to Bella Vista. The children were collecting sticks, under Martin's supervision, in order to build a fortress.

'I suppose I'm afraid of what would happen to her and the children. She's always been been – well, a bit high-strung.'

Ida was not surprised to hear him say that; she'd always thought there was something out of control about Denise. She remembered bringing up the subject of the Fletchers' marriage with Karl after a particularly dreadful visit with them in Oracabessa. Denise had insulted everyone: Nigel and his 'shoddy writing,' Karl's Austrian background, and Ida's taste in jewelry. Ida had worn a large emerald ring Karl had given her for her birthday.

'I think precious stones should be in a more delicate setting,' Denise had said.

'Really?' Ida had replied. 'I like mine to have some weight.'

Afterward, with May sleeping in the back of the car, Ida had asked Karl, 'Why on earth does he stay married to her?'

'I told you, he's queer. She helps him look like he's living a normal life while he goes out chasing boys.'

'Why do you dislike him?'

'He dislikes me. He was in love with Flynn, you know.'

'Oh, for heaven's sake. Do you know that Nigel said the exact same thing to me once about you? That you were in love with Errol.'

'Because he's always been jealous of me. I tell you he's queer and he hides behind Denise and her enormous tits.'

Ida didn't think there was any truth to Karl's theory. She'd heard stories of Nigel's playboy years and often sensed — now, for instance — that he found her appealing.

'So you take care of her?' Ida asked Nigel.

'And in her own way, she takes care of me. We used to be great friends before we got married. Why do you stay with Karl?'

The question surprised her. She thought her marriage looked perfectly happy to others.

'Why do you ask?'

'Because he's cold and secretive, and you're not.'

'You don't know Karl. You two have never gotten along, and I've never gotten along with Denise.' She laughed and linked her arm in his. 'Shall we run away together?'

He smiled. 'I'm sorry Errol never got to know May. She's a splendid child.'

'He's still here, you know,' she said with conviction.

'Hocus-pocus.'

'—watching us.'

'He's not the one watching us, nymph.'

She followed Nigel's eyes and saw Karl on the veranda looking at them. They both waved to Karl at the same time.

Someone else was watching them: May. The unusual smile her mother had tossed out to her earlier lingered in her mind. Now she noticed Ida walking arm in arm with Nigel, looking more at ease than she ever looked with Karl. To May, Ida was like tropical weather: so balmy and pleasant that it was easy to forget the force of the hurricane; her mother's unpredictability was intriguing but also worrying. For once May was happy with the way things were; she didn't want anything to change.

I Sabine will tell you how I came to be alone on this desolate island. She began writing the story of Captain Bligh (whom she renamed Blight) and Sabine the next morning. She was often praised for her extensive vocabulary and 'command of English,' but the truth was she was something of a parrot. It was her gift, a mind like a mimeograph, a memory that sucked in and spewed back words – the fine phrases of her favorite writers: Daniel Defoe, Robert Louis Stevenson, and Sir Walter Scott.

She carried her notebook with her now to the breakfast table.

'Can I try your coffee?' she asked Karl. She loved the smell.

'When you're older,' Ida said. 'It's too strong for you.'

'Not this morning, it isn't.' Karl grimaced. 'I'm not even sure that it's coffee.'

Ida took no notice of him. 'What's that?' she asked, seeing May's notebook. 'Homework?'

'I'm writing a book about Captain Blight and his whore.'

'May! Where did you learn that word?' Ida asked.

'Martin. He said that lady in the grave was—'

'Never mind. I want you to call her Captain Blight's – I mean Captain Bligh's – well, we don't even know if she knew Captain Bligh. What about "the Captain's lady"?'

May thought for a moment. 'I'm going to call it *Treasure Cove*. I'll show it to Nigel since he writes books too.'

Karl made a derogatory sound.

'Well, he was right about the Cubans,' Ida said. 'The Americans had to turn back.'

May looked up. She had heard everyone talking about the invasion. At first she had misheard and thought it was a festival that was being talked about – Day of Pigs – something involving lots of pork. Even after bossy Martin had corrected her and told her it was the Bay of Pigs she still couldn't help imagining some sea adventure that had to do with shipwrecks and castaway pigs. She had peered through her mother's binoculars, trying to spy on the invading Americans.

'They should have invaded by air,' Karl was telling Ida. 'It would have been a different story.'

'Isn't that what Nigel said?' Ida pressed the point.

'Yes. And I didn't disagree.' He got up, and looking at Ida he said, 'I'm going to Panama next week. Why don't you come along?'

It seemed more like a demand than a request and this irked her.

'I have the Parent-Teachers supper next week,' she said. She turned to May. 'Read me your story. You know, your father wanted to be a writer as well as an actor—'

'Please ask Florence to make my coffee stronger; this tastes like dirty water,' Karl said on his way out.

'Young Gloria is in the kitchen this morning. I gave Florence a few days off to visit her niece in hospital.' What she meant was: *You are not the only one in charge here.* 'Go ahead, May, read to me.'

May read, 'I Sabine will tell you how I came to be on this

desolate island. My father was the infamous pirate, Cayman Jack. I never knew my mother. They say she was a pirate too. I grew up in the taverns of Port Royal . . .'

She stopped as soon as Karl was out of hearing distance and told her mother, 'You can go to Panama. I don't mind.'

'I don't want to go to Panama.'

'Karl wants you to.'

'What are you worried about? Karl?'

No, she wasn't worried about Karl, but she knew that if it weren't for him, they wouldn't have Navy Island. 'He wants you to go with him,' she said again.

'Chu!' Ida said. 'Karl knows I'll be here when he gets back.'

But Karl didn't go to Panama because the day he was to leave May fell from a tree and broke her leg. Karl had to take her to the hospital because Ida wasn't home. She was in Port Antonio doing various errands.

May couldn't swim because of the cast on her leg, so she spent the weeks of convalescence writing about Sabine:

Before my father died, he entrusted me with a map.

'If any ill fortune should befall me at sea, my girl, as will likely happen to an old sea-dog like me, you'll find your inheritance in the treasure marked here.'

I hid the map in my room at the Three Bells tavern. One night Blackbeard and his cutthroats went on a drunken rampage through the streets of Port Royal, setting fire to the tavern, and the map was destroyed.

However, its lines were etched securely in my memory . . .

Karl told her she looked like a real pirate now with her crutches and one good leg. He'd been nice to her, helping her with the spelling for her stories and eventually buying her a dictionary. Winston the gardener helped her build a thatched shelter down by Treasure Cove, and she hobbled down there, sometimes with Ian. While she read aloud to him from her book, Ian would sketch or do watercolors.

One day May told him about how her real father had shown her a map.

'Do you remember if there was an X on it?' Ian asked her. 'That's the sign for where the treasure's buried.'

'No. It had pictures of ships and funny spelling.'

'Don't tell anyone. Especially Martin. He'll try to find it before we do. Promise you won't tell him.'

'Awright.'

That night in her room she wrote:

There were many rumors of my father's having buried treasure and so, fearing myself in danger, I fled Port Royal and went to a little town on the northern coast named Port Antonio.
There I became—

May stopped to look up a word in the dictionary.

—proprietress of an inn, not a cheap tavern for drunkards, but a respectable establishment for traveling merchants and sea captains. From the inn, which was set on a hill, I could espy that tiny island where my inheritance lay buried . . .

Another night, thinking about the map, she decided to look for it down in Karl's study, where there were still many of her father's belongings.

She often went down there to look at Karl's collection of artifacts. There was one she was especially intrigued by, a shaman-like fetish carved from wood that he kept locked behind glass. The shaman's eyes bulged and his heart protruded through his chest. It seemed alive to her; sometimes she thought she saw the wood sweating.

She didn't have a clear memory of what the room had looked like when she'd been there with her father, except that it had been messy. It was now very neat. A Persian rug covered the floor, and there were other colorful rugs and cloths hanging on the walls and covering the furniture. Ancient pottery decorated the shelves along one wall. There was a trunk where Karl had put some of her father's things. It was locked, but she knew Karl kept keys in a brass jar on the desk.

She opened it and saw boxes and containers of various sizes. Some were filled with slides. Another one had photographs. She didn't recognize anyone in the photographs until she came to one in which she saw Karl, a much younger Karl, with another man and a woman. They were out on a sailing boat. The woman was dark-haired and wore sunglasses; the other man looked remarkably like Errol Flynn except that he was shorter and thinner. On the back of the photograph, she read, *Max, Eugenia & Karl, Salzburg 1934.*

'What are you doing?' Karl's voice startled her.

'Sorry.'

He switched off his flashlight and approached the lamplit corner where she stood.

'I was looking for something.'

'What?'

'A map.'

'What map?'

She was a terrible liar and always regretted it when she was dishonest. So she told him about the day she'd met her father and about how he'd shown her Captain Bligh's map. Karl didn't seem shocked to hear about it.

'It's not here,' he said.

She wanted to ask how he could be so sure, but he was looking at the photograph in her hand.

'Is he the friend who gave you those German poems?' she asked.

He took the photograph from her. 'Yes.'

'Where does he live?'

'He died – in the war.'

'And your sister?'

'They both died.' He put the photograph back and locked the trunk. 'There's no map here.' His face softened. 'Let's go upstairs.'

He suggested that they make some hot cocoa. She watched him swirl condensed milk on top of his; he liked sweet, creamy things.

'Were you and Max best friends?'

'Yes.'

'Like me and Ian.'

He nodded.

'If Ian died I would feel sad talking about him.'

He didn't respond.

She thought back on the picture of Max. She knew that Karl and her own father had been friends, and she wondered if Karl had cared for her father as much as he'd cared for Max. And where did her mother fit into the story?

'Are there any pictures of my father and mother together?'

He put his cup down. 'You should ask your mother.'

May frowned.

Karl looked at her. At times it was almost as if her father inhabited her. But she was so different in other ways, he thought: less impulsive, more a thinker than a doer. She was, he thought, a clever child.

May looked up and saw him watching her. She felt strange suddenly, intimidated, not by him so much as the whole knowledgeable world of grown-ups.

'Yes?' He sensed a question.

'Is there going to be another invasion?' she asked. 'In Cuba?'

'I don't know,' he said.

She actually hadn't been thinking about the invasion. It just seemed like the right thing to ask about. Her mind was billowing with mysteries and inconclusive stories: the map her father had shown her and its disappearance, Karl's youthful friendship with that man who had died, and the death of an unknown woman centuries earlier whose grave happened to be in her own back yard.

23

A Flag on Her Island

May wrote:

Ship's Log, Captain W. S. Blight
Wednesday July 15
I have been keeping a watchful eye on this island's inhabitants as they make preparations — whether for feast or war, I cannot tell. There appear to be different tribes dwelling here, the largest being the Black Caribs and second largest the Veranda tribe. There is also a small band of mountain warriors called Maroons and another group, generally quiet and peaceful, who call themselves Rastafarians.

'Let us be clear,' Father Reynold spoke in the sonorous tone he used in the pulpit even though he was now sitting by the pool at Bella Vista. 'Jamaica isn't *getting* independence. Great Britain is *granting* Jamaica independence. You see the difference?'

May looked up from her writing. It was the summer of 1962. She was twelve, and in less than a month Jamaica was officially getting its independence from Britain.

They had just finished a poolside lunch of cold

marinated red snapper and were resting a bit before dessert. Father Reynold, Ida, and Karl sat under the shade of a patio-table umbrella; May was on a lounge chair in the full afternoon sun.

'What can we do when we have independence?' May called over to them.

'Good question,' Father Reynold said.

'Fly our own flag,' answered Ida. 'Why you have that devil look on you face?'

May glanced at Karl. He had seen the skull-and-crossbones flag she'd hoisted earlier down at the boathouse.

'No more Union Jack,' Ida continued. 'And it's about time.'

'Hear, hear!' Father Reynold raised his glass.

May had been listening to these conversations for months. There were people, like her mother's cousins, the Levys, who thought Jamaica was simply better off having Britain in charge. Then there were those like her mother and Father Reynold who were fed up with the whole drawn-out process and palaver among the politicians. After all, Britain didn't even want West Indian colonies anymore.

Down at Cassava Piece, May had heard Winston and the others talking about 'brown man's rule.' That was what they called independence. They said 'brown man's rule' would be no different from 'white man's rule.' 'Brown people,' as they called the light-skinned, prosperous Jamaicans, had been lording it over poor black people like them for a long time. All the same, Winston said, independence was a step forward. 'Sooner or later black people go rule.' Florence, the cook, wasn't sure she was quite ready for that: 'Easy, man. Tek time.'

About a week before independence, there was a disturbance in Port Antonio. Princess Margaret was visiting the town and a delegation of Maroons came down from the mountain to speak to her. They said they had business to clear up with the queen's representative. It had to do with the treaty they had signed with the British in 1739 that had given them self-government. The new Jamaican parliament had told the Maroons that their treaty with Britain was meaningless and that they had to be governed by Jamaican laws. This had upset the Maroon leaders.

'You mean the Maroons want to have their own separate country?' May asked. She was concerned because of Oni's being a Maroon.

'Well, yes. Sort of,' her mother answered.

'Oni too?'

'Oni doesn't care about any of this.' Indeed, Oni had dismissed the whole thing as 'Politricks!' That was what she had told Ida when she'd recently come to Navy Island. She had brought them an 'independence goat' to start fattening up for Karl's fiftieth birthday, which was also to be celebrated that August.

When the Maroons weren't allowed to meet with Princess Margaret, they protested in the town square, shouting, 'Burn the new flag.' Disturbances then broke out in other Maroon settlements. The outgoing British governor met with the Maroon leaders, promising to work out some degree of autonomy for them, and the trouble calmed down.

But then the Rastafarians grew worried about their position. They believed their true homeland was Africa, not Jamaica, and wondered who was going to represent them in the new Jamaican government. The Rastafarians also requested a meeting with Princess Margaret, and they too were turned down. There were more protests and some Rastafarians were arrested.

May heard Father Reynold say, 'It worries me, man, to see Jamaicans divide up an' we not even a nation yet.'

'It's natural,' Karl told Father Reynold. 'Independence. Self-rule. Plant a new flag anywhere and it brings a new set of problems. The Americans had their Civil War.'

'There's going to be a war?' May asked.

'No,' Ida told her, 'it's just how men talk. Come help me plan the party.'

As president of the Port Antonio Women's Club, Ida was in charge of the children's Independence Day party. All the children of Port Antonio, rich and poor, were invited. There would be cake, ice cream, and a movie at the Palace Theatre.

On the afternoon of August 6, as Independence Day was being celebrated throughout the country with parades and official ceremonies, about fifty children were shown to their seats inside the Palace Theatre. May was among them. As usual, she was the only one who was not black and not poor. None of the better-off families sent their children. For years she had been attending these kinds of events. Every Christmas the mayor gave a party at the Palace, where he handed out ice cream and treated the town's children to a movie. Because Port Antonio was proud of the fact that Errol Flynn had lived there, the movie was usually one he'd starred in, like *The Adventures of Robin Hood* or *The Sea Hawk*.

Now, on Independence Day, May had told her mother she was getting too old for these children's parties. But Ida had insisted: 'Your grandfather built the theatre; it's our theatre. You have to go.'

It wasn't the movies usually being her father's that troubled her – actually, she had become more and more interested in his movie roles – it was being with those other children. At least this time it would be a little different. Her mother planned to show *Blue Hawaii*, with Elvis Presley, which May hadn't seen yet.

Ida had at first wanted to show something relevant to Jamaica's independence. She had talked it over with Karl. 'What about *Jamaica Inn*?'

'It doesn't have anything to do with Jamaica.'

'Remember that Ray Milland movie – *Jamaica* something?'

'*Jamaica Run*. With Arlene Dahl diving for sunken treasure.'

But Ida had problems getting the film from the distributor. 'I give up,' she said. 'Elvis Presley. I like Elvis Presley.'

The children rose from their seats as the new national anthem was played and a picture of the new Jamaican flag – green, black, and gold – came on the screen. Then the movie started.

It was not *Blue Hawaii*; it was *Captain Blood*. (Later May heard Ida saying, 'Well, it's got Jamaica in it – you know – pirates and Port Royal, and the children love the sword fighting.')

For May sitting there, Independence Day drained away. It was like all those other town events of her childhood where she'd been gathered up with the rest of the children to watch Errol Flynn. Maybe because she was getting older, she felt more out of place than ever. She told herself, *I'm going to write in my notebook when I get home, not about Sabine or Captain Blight but about me.*

She knew she could get up and leave if she really wanted to. The sea was right across the street; she could take a walk along the shore. But everything, even the sea, seemed distant compared to the mesmerizing clamor on the screen. Cannons were being fired. Pirates were scrambling up the rigging and leaping with daggers. A map of the Caribbean burned. Treasure chests teeming with jewels were thrown open, ship after ship plundered, and against all this, Errol Flynn's face spread wide across the screen like a flag of victory.

May sat in the last row because she was the tallest of the children. The tall one, the white one. There in the darkness, she felt for the first time not how different she was but how different they were. Some of the children tittered. A romantic scene had just begun. They laughed when they saw Captain Blood seize the governor's daughter roughly by the shoulders and kiss her, and they laughed louder when the governor's daughter slapped Captain Blood.

Why are they laughing? May asked herself, exasperated. She looked at Captain Blood's smile, which seemed more alive to her than anything or anyone in that whole theatre, and it struck her that he was the cause of everything – he, the movie star. Because of him she was here now with these others. Because of him, one of them but not like them.

Later, all north coast society made its way to the Levys' mansion for the Independence Ball. The Von Ausbergs' Mercedes-Benz was part of a cavalcade of expensive cars with well-dressed people speeding along the winding mountain road at sunset.

'Why are we going so fast?' Ida asked Karl.

'Because the cars in front and behind us are.'

'If you slow down—'

'I'll seem like a bad sport.'

'I don't think it's too fast,' May said. She was enjoying being part of the procession. The cars only seemed faster than usual that day because there were more of them on the road and also more pedestrians. And because there were no sidewalks, every time a car whizzed by, the pedestrians had to stop and stand back as close to the edge of the road as possible.

'She doesn't look happy,' Karl said as one woman pulled her little boy quickly out of the way.

Karl slowed down to see if they were all right, and the little boy ran up to the car curiously. The woman pulled her child back and took out her anger on Karl: 'Oonu t'ink oonu can run down black people? A fe we country now!' A man nearby repeated what she'd said: 'A fe we country!' Others came running toward the car, curious, some of them now also yelling.

May drew back against the seat. She was relieved when Karl rejoined the line of cars.

'She's got a point,' Karl said.

'What you mean?' Ida asked. 'This is our country just as much as hers.'

'I meant about the cars running them down. There should be sidewalks.'

May wrote in her notebook before she went to bed. Not, after all, about how she'd felt that day at the movie or what she thought of the Maroons and Rastafarians having their own countries, or the poor people not having sidewalks. She wasn't ready to write about that. She was glad that Navy Island was a bit like a separate country. She loved her home, her room, the smell of good wood, the cool walls that she liked to press her palms against, the mosquito net that was soft as air, and the frangipani outside the window that filled the room with sweetness. She continued with *Treasure Cove*:

. . . whether feast or war I could not tell. If war, I feared for Sabine, for she was alone and unprotected in that remote seaside town. But my fears were misplaced. It was not the Blacks, Browns, Maroons, Rastafarians, or any other Native people who posed a danger to her. It was that scallywag Thames rat turned pirate, Peter Flood! And he had already incinerated—

Dictionary.

—insinuated himself into her heart!

A month later May sat at the top of the stairs and heard Ida and Karl talking inside their room. Ida was packing to go to New York. Her Aunt Carmen had died and Ida was going to the funeral.

May was worried about her mother's leaving; it brought back the years she'd been left in Miss Gloria's yard. 'I'm just going for a little while,' Ida had said. May didn't like the sound of 'a little while'; the last time Ida had left for a little while, she had stayed away for four years.

Another school year had begun, but May was at home. She had thrown a soda bottle at another student, cutting her quite badly above the eye. The child had needed stitches, and May had been sent home for two weeks with the warning that if she were to repeat such behavior they would have to expel her. May wished they would.

Karl wanted to go to New York with Ida, but Ida said that because of the trouble May had been in, she needed to have a parent at home with her.

She heard her mother tell Karl, 'I don't see the point in suspending her. Being home isn't a punishment for May.'

'Maybe the school meant to punish us,' Karl suggested.

'She's not allowed to go swimming.' There was silence for a few seconds. 'Well, I have to take something away from her. Otherwise she'll just be here having a good time. She needs discipline.'

'From me?'

'She listens to you more than to me.'

'Should I whip her or just lock her in the dungeon if she disobeys?'

May had never spent any time alone with Karl and she was curious to find out how they would get along without Ida. Maybe he would let her drink espresso.

Karl knew that Ida wanted him to show more affection for May. But neither he nor May was demonstrative and it would have felt artificial. He left all the decisions about May to Ida and never intervened in their arguments, except once. May had grown attached to one of the skinny, flea-ridden dogs in the servants' compound. The dog grew sick and May secretly brought her into her bedroom to care for her. When Ida found out, she had the dog, who was suffering, put to sleep while May was at school. It caused a fight, one that went far beyond the subject of the dog. The animosity continued for several days until Karl suggested that a puppy might be a nice pet for May. He pointed out to Ida that she'd had a horse when she was younger. Why shouldn't May have an animal of her own? Ida, who could not bear the idea of depriving her child of anything, even when she was upset with her, relented. Karl brought home not one but two white Alsatian puppies for May. He doted on the dogs as much as May did, giving them ice cream for dessert every evening, and they were allowed to sleep in the house in spite of Ida's objections. Ida, noticing that the dogs were one of the few interests he and May shared, had gradually accommodated herself to the canine infiltration of her home: the dog smell, the special dog blankets and dog toys.

So while Ida was in New York, Karl remained at Bella Vista with May and the two dogs, Hans and Olga.

One afternoon he found May looking miserable in her room. She was doing schoolwork. 'What's wrong?'

'Can't write.'

'You write all the time.'

'This is a *description*. I have to write a description of something in nature. I won't be able to swim on the team if I fail English.'

'Fail?' He brought a stool up to her small desk and sat down beside her.

She thought he looked like a giant in a fairy tale. He was too big for the stool, and he seemed out of place not just with the furniture but with everything in the room; she found it moving.

He read her description of the egrets that lived on the island, how at evening she'd see them resting on the eucalyptus trees which her father had planted, trees he'd brought specially from Tasmania. Her sentences were knotted, but each knot was in itself rather marvelous, he thought. 'It's wonderful.'

'Wonderful' was a favorite word of Karl's. She had noticed that and didn't think it was much of a compliment.

'But the punctuation—' he began.

'I don't like punctuation.'

He looked at her. 'How many kinds of swimming strokes can you do?'

'All of them. Backstroke, breaststroke, butterfly . . .'

'Why not just jump in the water and paddle to the other side like a dog?'

'It would look stupid.'

'Precisely. There's more to swimming than paddling, and more to writing than words. Do you want me to help you with your punctuation?'

'How long is it going to take?'

'Three lessons. The first will be right now. After each lesson we'll go to the pool.'

Her eyebrows shot up. 'Mama said—'

'She said no swimming. She didn't say anything about diving.'

During their final lesson, Karl asked her why she had thrown the soda bottle at the student.

'She bothers me. Says things.'

'Like what?'

'She calls me a white witch and then the others do it too. They don't tease the other white girls. Just me. Because I'm not really white. I don't talk like the white girls or— you know.'

When Ida came back, Karl brought up the possibility of May changing schools. He had visited the Port Antonio Secondary School, where Ida's old friend had been a deputy headmistress just before her death.

'There's nothing shabby about the Port Antonio school, and it's so much closer.'

Closer? Ida was surprised, considering Karl had not too long ago wanted May sent to boarding school in England.

'Is it cheaper?' Ida asked. Karl was sometimes surprisingly thrifty.

'No,' he said. 'Not when you consider the donation we might make to expand their library. You wanted to do something in memory of your friend. The Myrtle Tate Library is a name you might suggest.'

'I might suggest? You surprise me sometimes, Baron Von Ausberg.'

'Do I?'

'You and May seem to have been quite happy without me.'

'We were inconsolable. Even the dogs missed you.'

She didn't say it but she was glad to be back — not just back at Bella Vista but back with him.

But what on earth was wrong with him? It was a few weeks after she'd come back. He'd woken up long before her, as usual; the early morning was his favorite time of day, but there he was now waiting moodily for her at the breakfast table, looking like thrown-out lettuce. 'What happen?' she asked. 'You sick?'

'American troops landed in the Dominican Republic yesterday.'

After a short silence in which she tried to imagine what this had to do with them, she said, 'You have friends there. That man at the museum, what was his name? He was so nice to us on our honeymoon.'

'You went to the Dominican Republic for your honeymoon?' May asked.

'It was beautiful. Wasn't it, Karl? Is it another missile crisis?' she asked gently.

'Is there going to be a war?' May asked.

'I hope not,' he said in a voice that sounded like a book suddenly being closed.

'Of course not,' Ida assured May, but May sensed tension in both her parents.

Karl finished his coffee but ate nothing, and then he went back down to his study.

Ida continued her breakfast quietly. Every now and then

she found herself wondering about Karl. He was the kind of man who didn't want to be wondered about, and she appreciated that. But he had looked so grim when May had asked about war. It wasn't as if troops had landed in Jamaica.

'How close is the Dominican Republic? Look it up in your atlas, May.'

Maybe it was just the mention of war, Ida thought. After all, he had lived through a terrible war and seen his home and family destroyed. She didn't know much about it. He had nightmares that sometimes caused him to call out in his sleep. What had he suffered? He had walled off his past, from himself even. There was no nostalgic mention of family or friends, never a glimmer of that younger Karl to help her understand the Karl she had married.

But maybe his worrying now wasn't anything to do with war but rather with his shipwrecks, the *Capitana-Santiago* project. There had been some trouble there lately; thieves had broken into the place where the archaeological equipment was kept.

Her attention floated back to the table and she noticed that May had eaten several bananas, a number of hard-boiled eggs, and a whole dish of bacon. Yet she never gained weight; she just grew taller and taller. A band of sunlight fell across the table's empty dishes. She noticed May getting up, saying she was going upstairs to look in her atlas. 'Don't take too long,' Ida reminded her. 'We're going out.'

She went on thinking about Karl. He took his work too seriously. She thought of it as his work, even though it was really just a hobby, a passion of his. He made quite a lot of money at times, selling some old pot or carving, but then he'd spend it buying another in its place. She didn't know what it was he actually did all day long. Her eyes had sometimes fallen upon the notes he kept in his tiny, almost indecipherable handwriting. There would be something, now and then, that made sense to her, like 'large pre-Columbian water vessel.' She had the feeling that these notes weren't even necessary, that they were just his way of keeping himself busy.

'May!' she called upstairs. 'We goin' Port Antonio.'

May came downstairs slowly with the big atlas open in her hands. She didn't want to go on errands with her mother. Lately her mother had been dragging her along with her, saying things like, 'Now that you're growing older . . .' May was not interested in clothes or shoes or in being her mother's companion on shopping trips. 'Can I bring the atlas?' she asked.

'No. It's too big. Why you draggin' you feet? Come!'

'Can I bring my book?' She meant *Treasure Cove*.

'OK.'

They went down to Karl's study to say good-bye and found him setting up his slide projector. They'd be back at three, Ida said. Did he want anything from Port Antonio?

He shook his head and didn't look up from what he was doing. Ida imagined he would be surly like this for the rest of the day. She was not merely annoyed by his aloofness; she was disappointed. Upon her return from New York, she had felt a new closeness and playfulness between them. Last night they had made love, and now today he had shut himself off, reminding her of the Karl she'd first met and disliked, the man who had made her feel so irrelevant. Sunlight poured in through the study windows, making even brighter the yellowness of his hair and the pale, fine hair on his forearms. Who was this man, this foreigner, she had married?

'Come, May,' she said.

The uneasiness in the household that morning was not lost on May. The talk of invasion worried her too. Even at the best of times, she was alert to hints and threats of instability; it was a kind of dormant anxiety she had not been able to shake since the days of Miss Gloria's yard, as if any day she might wake up without home or parent. But to Ida and Karl she now said, as if to reassure them both, 'I found the Dominican Republic. It's far. But not too far.'

Sitting on the ledge of the shop window, waiting for her mother, May opened her book and read, *Being a woman of means and moderate beauty* . . .

Ida interrupted her. 'May, come look at this. It has peacocks on it. What a heavenly blue.'

May got up reluctantly. They were in Brook's Fabric and Sewing Supplies. Ida loved buying cloth. She would stroll in a peaceful little rapture among the tightly wrapped columns of linen, cotton, chiffon as if she were in a park full of beautiful trees. When May grew older, many of her dreams about her mother took place in the aisles of this shop. By then she was able to look back somewhat nostalgically on the Saturday shopping trips, but at the age of twelve it was her least favorite thing to do. Ida held up the bright cloth against May's body. 'What you think?'

'No,' May said. She pointed to a bale of khaki nearby. 'I like that.'

At the dressmaker's house, May had to wait even longer while her mother got measured and fitted, but at least here she had a more comfortable place to sit.

Being a woman of means and moderate beauty, I attracted many suitors. I knew I should exercise good judgment in choosing a husband, but, alas, like many others of my sex I let my feelings and not my best interests guide me. Reader, I fell in love with a penniless rogue . . .

Her mother called, 'May, come. Mrs Peters is ready for you.' She was to be measured for new school uniforms. Mrs Peters had been Esme's and then Ida's dressmaker. A kind of genius in her day, she had once been able to copy any dress Ida showed her from *McCall's* or *Vogue*. But now her eyesight was failing. She stuck pins in May and always felt entitled, as dressmaker, to comment boldly on May's shape and size. 'Eh, eh?' she said now. 'Little titties! You soon need a brassiere.'

May hadn't realized that they were meeting Nigel for lunch and wondered about her mother's not mentioning it to Karl. Nigel had great news: the cast and crew for *Change of Latitude* were arriving in a few days, and the shooting of the movie would finally begin.

'Speaking of movie stars—' Nigel began, and they saw Paulette Flynn come into the restaurant with her daughter.

Ida hadn't seen Paulette for a while; their paths crossed now and then at charity events, but Paulette led a very quiet life on her ranch outside Port Antonio. She also had a home in California.

Nigel said, 'I'll just pop over and say hello.'

Paulette turned around while Nigel was greeting her and smiled at Ida and May.

'That's Tara Flynn, looking so grown-up,' Nigel said when he came back. Then, to distract May, who was staring at Tara, he asked about *Treasure Cove*.

'Last time you read it to me your Captain Blight had some wild person living in his attic.'

'I changed that.'

'Good show.'

'You think she could write books when she grows up, Nigel?' Ida asked.

'That reminds me—' He pulled something out of a bag for her. It was a book called *True Accounts of Sea Robbers*. 'Everything you could possibly want to know about pirates is here. Some of these stories were actually written by pirates.'

On the front page was an illustration captioned 'Walking the Death Plank.' She decided that Nigel was the nicest person she knew, and that the next time he visited Navy Island she would show him the thatched shelter she'd built at Treasure Cove. Suddenly she got up from her seat and gave him a hug, which surprised him; she'd never done that before.

She turned to the chapter titled 'The West India Pirates' and read aloud, ' "A tropical climate is suited to a roving life, and liquor, as well as dissolute women, being in great abundance—" ' She looked up. 'What's "dissolute"?'

Both adults answered at the same time.

Nigel said, 'Lonely.'

Ida said, 'Lazy.'

'Whores, you mean.' May went on reading to herself.

'Well,' Nigel turned to Ida, 'how are Karl's shipwrecks? I heard about the break-in.'

'He gets so wrapped up in his work.'

'Anything stolen?'

'There's nothing to steal.' She stopped for a moment. 'I hope it works out. I mean, the ships are down there, aren't they?' She looked at Nigel for some assurance.

'Well, the experts seem to think so, and the historical facts suggest— I dare say, if that's where the ships sank, they must still be there, more or less.' He saw how worried she looked and made a mental note to find out more for himself about Karl's activities, but to Ida he said, 'The discovery will be staggering. You'll be richer than the Pope.'

'And you?' she asked with a warmth that made May look up from her book and follow their conversation. 'You're happy about this movie they're making?'

'It's terribly exciting, don't you think? And I've started a new book.' He paused. 'Denise has decided not to live in Jamaica anymore. She'll visit once a year in winter.'

Ida thought that was already their arrangement and said so.

'Well, not really; she's been coming and going, you know. Now I'll be the one doing all the traveling back and forth if I want to see her.' He played with his coffee spoon as he spoke.

'Well, I hope we'll be seeing a lot of you,' Ida said. 'Don't forget about us just because you've got all these Hollywood people at your beck and call.'

'You can be in the movie, Ida. Would you like to?'

'Oh, no.' She smiled, 'I almost drowned last time, remember.'

On the boat ride home, May asked her mother, 'Is Nigel lonely living by himself?'

'I don't know. Ian will be here in summer to keep him company.' She wondered what her daughter was getting at and asked, 'He's nice to you, isn't he?'

'He's nice to you too,' May said.

When they reached Navy Island, Ida said, 'May, what is that?' She had suddenly noticed the skull-and-bones flag flying from the lamppost. 'If you goin' to make a flag, make a nice one. You could have gotten that cloth with the peacocks on it.'

Ida watched May leap from the taxi-boat onto the pier.

There was so much joy in her body now. She wondered what would happen to all her tomboy exuberance as her body developed, and, more importantly, what would happen to her developing body if her tomboy exuberance didn't go away. It was hard to imagine skinny May ever becoming curvaceous. And what about boyfriends?

May jumped and ran across the planks, waving the pirate book and singing:

I'll drink whiskey when I can
Whiskey Johnny
I'll drink it out of an old tin can
Whiskey for my Johnny

As she passed an oleander bush, she tore off a sprig of the bright pink flowers and stuck it behind her ear.

'May, don't pick the oleander!' It was poisonous; how many times had she told May that?

'I not putting it in my mouth!'

The child's head was hard like rock-stone. She didn't listen now and she probably wouldn't listen when she became a teenager.

When they reached the house, they saw Karl outside playing with the dogs. The two dogs saw May and ran over to her as she loped across the lawn to talk to Winston. Winston was cutting back the bougainvillea and there was a younger man helping him.

Suddenly May ran back to her parents. Her face was heated and angry.

'Why is that man here?' she asked.

'I hired him to help Winston,' Karl said.

He was one of the boys who had abducted her and taken

her to the Folly ruins that day in Port Antonio. She was sure of it.

And he knew her. He had looked up slightly from his work and smiled – not with his mouth but with his eyes – as if they shared some secret.

She had never told Karl and Ida about that day; they looked at her astounded as she told them now.

'Ask Clive if you don't believe me,' she said.

'Of course we believe you.'

'Make him go!'

The dogs looked up at her, perplexed.

'I'll take care of this,' Karl said.

May went with him, not paying attention to her mother calling after her, 'May! Let Karl handle this.' After a moment, Ida followed.

May stood apart, kicking a stone back and forth with her foot, while Karl talked. She heard the man mumbling that he was being treated unfairly, that he hadn't done anything wrong.

'You wut'less liar!' May said, sounding not at all like a child. 'You have a lot of nerve coming here.'

Winston looked at May, astonished.

'He did something to me!' she explained to Winston.

The dogs began growling. Karl spoke to them in a calm voice, but they wouldn't stop. The boy backed away, afraid of the dogs. He started complaining, first in a low voice, then louder, that May was lying and now he was going to lose his day's wages. Karl gave him some money, and after taking it, the boy continued complaining: 'Me neva see her before dis day. Is grudge she grudge me because me a black man. A lie she a tell.'

Karl said firmly, 'You have your day's wages. Now go.'

The boy started walking away, and then he turned and spat in the direction of May.

The rock-stone hit him before anyone realized she had thrown it. His face bled where the stone had cut him. May picked up another stone, and the boy looked at her, dazed.

The dogs barked more furiously, and Karl held them back by their collars as the man turned and ran down the hill.

Karl said quietly, 'You know, May, that's a good way to make enemies.'

'He was already my enemy.'

Ida said, 'But May – stones?'

Winston watched the man hurrying down the hill. 'You run him gone, Miss May. Like David an' Goliat'.'

Ida, beginning to recover, said, 'Now he's going to tell everybody how the white people on Navy Island stoned him. Na true, Winston?'

'A true,' Winston said. 'You ha fe careful nowadays. Jamaica gettin' to be a devious place.'

Ida felt she should say something to May but wasn't sure if they should be words of reprimand or solace.

Later she stopped by May's bedroom to say good-night. May was not reading or writing, as she usually did at bedtime, but just lying there.

'That was bad what I did today,' she said.

Ida said, 'Yes, but—' She saw May look at her expectantly. After a while she said, 'You know, Father Reynold is a good person to talk to about these things. That's what priests are for—'

'No. I just want to hide,' May said.

'From who?'

'Jamaicans.'

'We're Jamaicans.'

'The other Jamaicans.'

That night Ida asked Karl if he agreed with Winston about the country becoming 'devious.' Karl thought it was too strong a word to apply to an entire nation. But it struck Ida as being precise. *A fe we country now . . . because me a black man . . .* where had all this anger come from? She felt that things were changing in Jamaica, but she couldn't imagine the outcome. There were hidden grudges and unforgotten hurts. Unfortunately, it was that way with May too. She hadn't known until now that May had experienced such a horrible thing. What else had May been through? It was too much for Ida – May growing, Jamaica changing.

Part Five

He was surprised and pleased, supposing that now he would have a mistress to himself; but he was greatly mistaken and found that it was necessary to court her for his wife. Being a man of indecent adventures, that is, a pirate, he was ignorant of the subtler arts of wooing. He knew only two things: conquest and defeat, and so he arrived in Port Antonio intent on conquering Sabine and plundering her inheritance.

Treasure Cove

24

'Bastard — *That Is Not a Nice Word*'

'Who's bringing you back home?' Karl asked. 'Derek or the Fletcher boy?'

'The Fletcher boy' was Martin; that was what Karl had begun calling him.

May was sixteen, and this was the first time she was going out dancing. Derek had invited her, and there were a number of them going: Ula, who still lived at Miss Gloria's yard, Ian, and Martin.

Martin Fletcher had been in Jamaica that past Christmas after not visiting for a few years, and he'd found May 'all grown up and awfully frisky,' as he put it.

She thought he was quite frisky himself.

They'd gone swimming and sailing together and though she found him attractive, she thought he was a bit of a show-off with his sports car and polo trophies. He wore a large gold watch that his mother had bought for him in Switzerland for two thousand pounds. What bothered her most, though, was that he went around with people who weren't her type, or rather who thought she wasn't their type — the horse-riding teenagers, mostly expats from England

and Canada; she thought of them as the horse-people.

One day she went to see Martin in a polo match. She hadn't wanted to go, but Nigel had invited her, and she thought with Nigel she wouldn't feel too out of place. When she got there, she discovered that it was Martin himself who was considered the trophy, at least in the eyes of the unattached girls of the horse-people. As usual, none of them paid her any mind. But Martin did. He seemed genuinely happy to see her and stayed by her side before the match. Later, when she saw him charging ahead on horseback, she thought he looked like some ferocious prince in battle, and indeed, he was almost an earl: his real father, his mother's first husband, had been Lord Fitzwilliam-Grey. The day after the polo match she made him chase her down a sandy beach and when he caught her she let him kiss her.

They had kept up what she thought of as an exquisitely painful romance after he went back to England – exquisite when letters arrived, painful the rest of the time.

It wasn't Martin but Derek who was picking her up that night. The last time May had seen Derek he had been twelve and she had been nine.

'He's here!' May hurried downstairs. 'I don't believe it! Derek, man, look at you!'

Ida and Karl came downstairs too.

'Who is this good-looking man?' Ida asked.

Derek stood before them smiling, the same broad, shy smile they remembered. He was over six feet now, slender but broad-shouldered. There was still his boyish ease, as if he might squat on the ground for a game of marbles or begin kicking a ball around. His dark skin was smooth-shaven, and the compelling features of his face were still his eager, often mischievous-looking eyes.

'I like you shirt,' May said. It was a blue denim shirt with the top buttons undone. She could see part of a gold chain underneath.

'My God, I can't believe this is the little boy who used to ride him mash-up bike up an' down Port Antonio,' Ida said.

'What are you driving these days? A Benz?' Karl asked.

Derek smiled. 'No, man, I have a secondhand Mustang. I not into big car an' t'ing.'

Karl shook his hand. 'It's been a long time,' he said with fondness.

Derek was about to go on tour in England as part of the backup band for Desmond Dekker and the Aces.

Karl and Ida had helped with money when Derek had first gone to Kingston to attend high school. By sheer luck Derek had met a man there who would become his mentor – the school's music teacher, who, though trained in classical music, had his ear close to the new sound coming from the slums of West Kingston, a music called 'ska.' Derek made friends with two other students at the school, a trumpet player and a drummer. The three of them, under their teacher's guidance, started experimenting with a slower version of ska. The music caught on and was called 'rock steady.'

'We proud a you,' May said now.

'I like some of the songs but I don't like the new dance,' Ida admitted. 'It's not happy. People should look happy when they dance.'

Derek smiled as Ida went on, 'And the words aren't happy either. Rude boy an' shootin' an' lootin'. What was that you were playing the other day, May?'

' "Prince Buster," ' May said.

'I thought somebody had broken into the house. Let me tell you, I never heard anything like that before.'

May and Derek began laughing.

'I sound like an old lady,' Ida laughed at herself, 'but really, what is all this *rude boy* thing in the songs nowadays?' She hadn't thought of herself as belonging to an older generation until now. After all, she was only in her thirties and still enjoyed dance parties, especially when there was steel-band music or Harry Belafonte songs. But here was her teenaged daughter going out on the town and listening to musicians she'd never even heard of before.

Before May left, Ida examined her. She wore a short red dress with spaghetti straps. The dress was feminine, but Ida observed that nothing else about her was. Her hair was almost as short as a man's; she wore no jewelry except gold bangles and no makeup.

'Put on some lipstick or some earrings at least,' Ida told May. 'What you think, Derek? Doesn't she look like a boy?'

He studied May for a moment and smiled: 'May don't need no ornament.'

They met the Fletcher boys at East Harbor. Someone else joined them, a man May had never met before who had apparently driven up from Kingston with Derek. He was crude-looking, someone Karl and Ida would have described as a 'rough type.'

'This is Brasso,' Derek said, introducing him. 'He used to live here in Port Antonio. Your parents know him.'

Brasso acknowledged her with his eyes only, nodding his head slightly.

They stopped at Parrot Lane to pick up Ula. She and May went to high school together now in Port Antonio. She wore a miniskirt, a very tight top, and high white boots; her eye shadow and lipstick were the same frosty pale color. May had never seen her look so dressed up and sexy and she could see that Martin was having a hard time keeping his eyes off her for the first few minutes that she was in the car.

The club, aptly named Back-a-Wall, was a large, dark dance hall concealed by high bamboo walls. It was roofless with an unpainted concrete floor, and there was a wooden platform for the sound system. It was already crowded with dancers, and there were a few stares when they entered because there were no other white people. Music boomed from the speakers; nothing else could be heard, and the air was pungent with ganja.

May danced with Martin, Derek danced with Ula and her miniskirt, and Ian wandered around. Brasso didn't dance. May noticed that he had a bad limp. She remembered her mother saying rock steady was not a happy dance. It wasn't. And wasn't meant to be, May now thought. Men in dark glasses wore expressionless faces and tipped their bodies backward and forward while staying rooted like a tree. The women danced more expressively but also seemed rooted. It was all about roots, May decided, and she caught on to the movements easily, unlike Martin, who danced like he was watching himself in a mirror.

If you no treat de rudie right
You a go see 'im ya tonight
It call de rude bwoy skankin'
Cause 'im a de highya rankin'

Because Port Antonio was a small town, there were a number of people who recognized May. But toward the English boys, Martin and Ian, there was hostility, and it seemed to build rather than dissipate as the night went on. This wasn't tourist territory. Their look said: *We didn't ask you to come here; watch yourself.* The bartender seemed to sneer as he served them, and Martin felt the need to apologize several times to people he bumped against. He was hot and sweaty and a bit fed up, so he sat down for a while, and Derek danced with May.

'I think you boyfriend wants to go home,' Derek said, indicating Martin.

'After the next one,' May said. She was enjoying herself. Derek smelled so good; he didn't wear cologne like most men; she wondered if it was just the nice smell of the soap he used. She moved closer so she could whisper in his ear, 'You think Ian is high?'

Ian was beside them, dancing with Ula; he had a large spliff in his hand, and May had just seen him lick Ula's face.

Derek grinned. 'Him not comin' back down anytime soon.'

May laughed and let her head fall against Derek's shoulder. She knew Martin was getting jealous. He was looking down at his beer bottle, trying not to look in her direction. She wasn't sure why she liked to aggravate him.

They got ready to leave and went looking for Ian and Ula, who had wandered off together. Outside there was an argument going on. It was Ian and some other man, stocky and about twice Ian's weight. The man shoved Ian, almost knocking him over. Ian regained his balance and began arguing back.

'Wha' g'wan?' Derek asked somebody, and some of the onlookers started to explain.

The man had made some derogatory remark to Ula, and Ian had defended her by making some even more derogatory remarks back to the man. Now the man was threatening him.

Ian, far from flinching, was daring the man while Ula was doing her best to pull him back. Ian's eyes were red and intense; he was definitely stoned.

Suddenly the man broke a bottle and lunged at Ian. Everyone moved at once in every direction, and the next thing May saw was Brasso appearing from nowhere, holding a knife against the man's throat.

'Ease off. No blood tonight-iya! Seen?'

'Awright. Seen.' The other man let go of the broken bottle.

'I see you've got a bodyguard,' Martin said to Derek later in the car, trying to relieve the tension.

Brasso, looking out the window, cursed quietly.

'You have to kind a keep you cool 'round these people,' Derek offered in the way of advice to Martin and Ian. Ian had fallen into a slumber, his head lolling on his brother's shoulder.

'Right,' Martin said in a tone that was just short of saying, 'Piss off.' He didn't say anything, not even to May, the rest of the way to the harbor.

'Derek says he'll take you home,' Martin told May stiffly, not even kissing her good-bye. He drove off in his sports car with his brother.

She decided he was being ridiculous and thought, *Let him go, then!*

She was happy to spend time alone with Derek. They caught the last taxi-boat to Navy Island, then walked up the dark hill. It was a country darkness that felt very friendly to both of them. Fireflies sparked here and there. The road up to the house was quiet except for their footsteps, and they could smell Otaheite apples faintly. When they got to Bella Vista, they found leftovers and cold ginger beer, and they sat out by the pool eating.

'Boy, I tell you, Florence can cook!' Derek said, eating a piece of chicken. 'So Martin is you boyfriend fe true?'

She had food in her mouth, so she just nodded.

'Well,' he said, 'all grown up. So what you going do when you finish school?'

'Ma wants me to be a doctor, but I can't stand the sight of blood.'

She was stronger in academic subjects than Ida had ever been, so Ida had big hopes for her.

'What you want to do?'

'Swim. That's all I ever wanted to do. Swim and coach swimming.'

'So where you go to learn coaching and that kind of thing?'

'There's a college in Switzerland Karl knows about where I could get a degree in sports education.'

'You were always a good swimmer,' he said.

'I read that eighty percent of Jamaicans don't know how to swim. How can people live on an island and not know how to swim? Is a shame.'

'Maybe you can do something about it.' He smiled. She noticed that he still had those long, lazy smiles that looked as if he were having a good dream.

'What you mean?'

'I don't know. Sound like you have some good ideas. Maybe after you get your degree you should get involved in politics or some kind of government thing.'

She looked thoughtful. 'You think people would ever vote for somebody like me in an election?'

'What you mean somebody like you?'

'You know, somebody my color?'

'Michael Manley is your color.'

That was true. But Manley's father had been one of the founders of Jamaican nationalism. The Manleys were to Jamaicans what the Kennedys were to Americans.

'So what does your boyfriend, Martin, think about you going to Switzerland?'

'Well, I'll be closer to him there than I am now. He's at Oxford. He wants to go into politics.'

'Then he shouldn't smoke so much ganja.'

'Ian is the one who smokes a lot.'

'Be careful around those boys, you hear?'

'I'm a big girl now, Derek. I can take care of myself.'

He smiled. 'You been saying that since you were three years old.'

'Well, you be careful around that Brasso. I get a bad feeling from him.'

'Chu, him awright. Jus' tryin' to help us out.'

'Jamaica's changing, don't you think so? People gettin' rough.'

Derek nodded in agreement.

'Even the movies they show now at the Palace. Nobody wants to see nice movies anymore like *Doctor Zhivago*. If we don't show Charles Bronson movies we go out of business,' May said.

'True-true,' he agreed. 'But don't worry. Is Jamaica still.'

They sat quietly together for a few more minutes, staring into the darkness and watching fireflies.

May raised her head toward the second floor, where her parents' bedroom was. 'Those two havin' a good romp,' she said.

Derek's thick eyebrows came together in a frown. 'May Josephine Flynn! You out of order.'

'Don't be such a prude.' She laughed.

~

Upstairs in their large four-poster, plantation-style bed, Ida and Karl lay naked and entwined. Karl stroked Ida's hair. It had been a long time since they'd made love like this.

Earlier that evening he had brought up the possibility of their living somewhere else.

'Leave Navy Island?'

'Leave Jamaica,' he clarified.

'What about May?'

'It's May's future I'm thinking of. If we sold Navy Island there'd be—'

'Sell? You must be joking.'

'The economy's in trouble. Things will just get worse if Manley wins the election.'

'Oh, politics, economics! I don't want to hear about it. And where would we go?'

'I was thinking of the Cayman Islands, Bermuda – somewhere less volatile. I could still collect and trade occasionally.'

'You. You. You.'

'What does that mean?'

They had just come upstairs and were getting ready for bed when the discussion had started. On one side of the room was Ida's closet, which she always forgot to close, and her dressing table, cluttered with jewelry boxes, powders, old and new perfumes, and knickknacks she'd had since she was a girl; on her bedside table was a photograph of her and Karl and a pile of women's magazines. On the other side, Karl's side, there was an expanse of polished wood floor and practically nothing else. He kept all his toiletries in the bathroom cabinet and his clothes, shoes, and accessories neatly arranged and hidden from view inside a built-in closet.

There was a photograph of him with Flynn aboard the *Zaca*, placed on the bureau by Ida. The only other furniture on his side was his favorite armchair.

Ida sat up rigidly on her side of the bed, and he stood on the other side of the room, buttoning his pajama shirt.

'You and your damn artifacts.' She stopped but clearly had more to say.

'Go on,' he said mildly.

She wished she could sound as reasonable as he did. She began slowly, 'When we first got married, you knew how much I wanted to come home and see my daughter, but you had me traveling all over South America with you looking for God knows what. It's always where *you* want to be, what's best for *you*. Now you want to drag me off somewhere else.'

'I didn't know traveling with me was such a burden.'

'No, you didn't. You were too busy with your ancient pots and pans to notice.'

'They helped pay for this house.'

She walked over to the mirror and began vigorously brushing her hair.

'Jamaica, Cayman Islands – maybe it's all the same to you. Not to me.'

'I know what Bella Vista means to you.'

There was a silence.

'What you mean by that?' she asked. 'Just say whatever it is you're thinking.'

'You always wanted to live in his house.'

'You wanted it too.'

'I wanted to please you.'

'You did please me. Until now.'

The words fell out of her mouth before she'd thought about them.

'What does that mean?' he asked.

'If you want to go – go.'

They had finished getting ready for bed. Ida sat up on her side of the bed. Karl sat across from her on an armchair. Neither of them spoke for a while; neither of them felt they could.

Finally Karl spoke quietly: 'And take my pots and pans with me?'

He saw the anger receding from her, and he continued, 'Ida, I just wanted to discuss – the possibility of going some-place a bit more stable. We don't have to if you don't want to.'

She looked at him and said, 'Come to bed.'

Sex had never been a straightforward matter for them: she would hold herself back from him; he never pressed her. He was not the kind of man who needed snacks between meals, and when it came to making love to his wife, he'd found that restraining his appetite was no hardship when such a feast lay ahead. Their lovemaking was nearly always stimulated by verbal struggle and capitulation, the combustible exchange a kind of foreplay. He adored her.

After she fell asleep beside him, his worries returned.

There had been another break-in at the *Capitana-Santiago*, so American security guards had been sent over. Now there were rumors and accusations that the site was going to become an American naval base like Guantánamo Bay. Threats had been made against him and others involved in the project. Karl hadn't told Ida that someone had even called Bella Vista, threatening violence if he and the Americans didn't leave. 'Tell me what's troubling you, Karl,' she had said before falling asleep. 'Why you keep so much to yourself?' He had reassured her, telling her that he just had a lot of boring financial details on his mind, nothing else.

But something ugly was stirring. There was an election coming; the two major political parties had begun a nasty campaign involving gangs. The violence was for the most part in Kingston, far from Navy Island, but he was becoming increasingly worried about what would happen across the water – 'over a-land' – and how it would affect them.

'Fuck! do you have to do it right out here in the open?' Ian shouted, finding them by the gravestone.

His brother was lying on top of May. They were both still wearing their clothes, not actually 'doing it.'

Martin rolled off her. 'Why don't you knock before you come in?' he asked.

Ian grinned. 'Look what I've got.' From his pocket, he extracted a giant spliff of ganja.

'It's almost as big as my dick. Light it up!'

The three of them sat smoking well into the night, laughing and singing Beatles and Rolling Stones songs. Martin started fondling May again, working his fingers under her clothes, and Ian was too high to notice. He went into the bushes behind them to pee.

'What's that light over there?' May asked, pointing to a glow near the beach.

'Extraterrestrials,' Martin whispered, and he started kissing her again.

'No, really.' She stood up.

Martin followed her down a narrow, rocky path. They heard footsteps.

'Wait!' Martin whispered and pulled her down with him behind the bushes.

Just then Ian came toward them, singing 'Under My Thumb' at the top of his lungs.

'Sshhh.' Martin tried to hush him and pull him down into the bushes, but it was too late. A flashlight shone on them.

'What are you doing out here?' It was Karl. He switched off the flashlight. The three young people all stood quietly in front of him. 'It's almost four in the morning.'

After a while Ian said, 'Just hanging around, looking at the st-st-stars.' He burst out laughing. May and Martin looked as though they wanted to choke him.

'Hanging around with an illegal substance, I think,' Karl said.

Ian continued laughing; he couldn't control himself.

Karl said, 'You two boys can spend the night in the downstairs guest room.'

They turned to go.

Karl spoke again: 'Martin, stay for a minute, I'd like to have a word with you about May's blouse.' He saw the surprised look on Martin's face. 'It's unbuttoned.'

May began to say something.

Karl stopped her. 'It's Martin I want to speak to. I'll let your mother deal with you tomorrow.'

The next day Martin told her he'd been 'run over' by her old man, though he'd tried to assure him that the two of them hadn't 'done anything.' Karl had warned him that if May got pregnant, Martin would be dealing not with his wrath but Ida's.

'I know about birth control,' she hissed at Karl.

She kept to herself, silent and indignant, for a few days. She was terribly annoyed with Karl. Here she finally had a boyfriend, not just any boyfriend but one of the most desirable, popular boys around. She was being invited to go places, even by the horse-people. It was very gratifying to be known as Martin Fitzwilliam-Grey's girlfriend. She didn't want Karl and Ida to scare him off. As for her mother, she expected a lecture from Ida and that would mean a blowup between them because May didn't intend to listen and obey. She was ready for Ida. There were phrases already planned in her head – 'I'm not like you' – 'I don't see why I should take your advice.' But Ida didn't say anything to her about the incident, and May realized after a few days that Karl hadn't told her about it.

She went out with Martin the following Saturday night. He took her to the Equestrian Club in Port Antonio for drinks. She had a whiskey sour, and then he had her try the single-malt scotch he'd ordered for himself. He told her about the Scottish island where his great-uncle lived, of the smugglers who used to roam there and of the famous distillery nearby. He seemed older and more interesting to her than before and reminded her of Nigel.

They were supposed to go to a party after the club. But instead they drove to a beach where they sat kissing.

Martin badly wanted her, but he remembered Karl's warning.

'Your old man's scary,' he said.

'I'm not scared of him.' The drinks had made her bold. She unzipped his pants and put her hand around his erection the way he'd shown her.

'Oh, God, May.'

'I don't want to be a virgin anymore,' she said.

'We can do something about that.' He took off her panties, pulled down his pants, and got between her legs.

'Wait. Where's the condom?'

'I don't have one.'

'What?'

'It's all right. I know what to do.'

'You're not doing anything without a condom. I mean it, Martin.'

They drove all over Port Antonio looking for somewhere that might sell condoms. Finally they found a little Chinese grocery shop open and he went in while she waited out in the car.

They went back to the same beach.

'How'd it feel?' he asked afterward.

'Fabulous. What's that smell?'

'It's us. It's the smell we make together.'

'My mother said it would hurt, but it didn't really.'

'That's because I know what I'm doing.'

'Show-off.'

'Where're you going?' he asked. She had started gathering up her clothes.

'It's windy. I'm getting sand in my eyes.'

'But I'm not finished with you.' He began kissing her again.

She suddenly thought about what she'd done. While she didn't feel different, she imagined that now her life would be different. She'd been brought up to think that there were consequences when a girl started having sex, sometimes good, sometimes bad.

'Martin, do you love me?'

'Madly.'

'Really?'

'I'll prove it.' He rolled onto his back and grabbed her hand so she could feel his erection.

'That doesn't prove anything,' she said, giggling, but she kept her hand where he had put it and began stroking him again.

'Sit on me,' he said. 'I'll show you how much I love you.'

She laughed.

'Do you want to get married?' he asked.

'What?'

'Sit on me, May, and say you'll be my bride.'

'Idiot!'

'No, really; I'm head over heels in love with you. Marry me.'

'OK.'

On the way home, she said, 'Now we'll miss each other too much. Do you have to go back to England?'

'I've got to finish my degree, my darling.'

She pouted.

'I'll get you an engagement ring before I go.'

'Am I old enough?'

'To be engaged? 'Course you are.'

He bought her a diamond ring before he went back to Oxford, and she loved all the shock and excitement it caused when they announced their engagement.

Karl was upset.

'She's too young,' he told Ida.

'But you know how she is. If we try to stop this, she'll run away with him. And I suppose if she's really in love—'

'She's not even seventeen!'

'I know. I know.' She didn't say what it was she knew — that at sixteen or seventeen you could love a man as truly and faithfully as you ever might again.

'I've never liked that boy,' Karl said.

'Why not? He's doing well at Oxford and—' She seemed to be trying to convince herself.

'He's weak-minded. And I don't like his watch.'

'What?'

'It's flashy, and he's a fool, wearing something like that in a country where people are so poor.'

'Actually, I don't like his watch either,' she said. 'But let's just wait and see.'

Martin returned to Jamaica that summer. Marvin Gaye had just released 'Mercy, Mercy Me,' and the song played continuously in their rooms, their cars, and inside their heads, the vanished blue skies of the lyrics part-warning and part-beatitude. To May, looking back, it was a time when saving the world was sexy, and having sex seemed like a way of saving the world. All the conversations they had, the ganja they smoked, and the records they listened to were squeezed in between hours of sex.

'My parents are going to Kingston for a few days,' May would call and tell Martin. 'You can stay the night.'

'Dad's gone,' Martin would tell her. 'Don't bother to bring any clothes.'

Ian got used to seeing them both walking around naked; it felt very hip to all three of them.

One day Martin asked her, 'Is your great-grandmother really African?'

'Pure African — a Maroon.'

'So our children could look black and have that bushy hair?'

'They'll probably look like us. Does it matter?'

'No, 'course not.'

'Will we live in Jamaica some of the time when we're married?' she asked.

'Depends. Will you inherit Navy Island?'

May thought for a moment. She'd never imagined living anywhere else, so she said, 'I suppose.'

'Then we'll have two grand estates, one here and one

there. So what do you call yourself if you're not really white?' he asked.

'I don't know — off-white?'

'I think you're a Creole. That sounds right. You'll be my Creole wife.'

He was supposed to come back that Christmas but went skiing with friends. He surprised her, though, by arriving for New Year's Eve and staying a week. May spent the week with him in Oracabessa. Nigel and Ian were there as well. 'Lucky girl,' Ida teased, 'three handsome men all to yourself.' But it was less than ideal. Martin was distant. It hurt her when he took off without her for a whole day to spend time with his old polo-playing friends. It was rainy so there was no sailing or swimming for her in Oracabessa. Ian was busy painting. Nigel played cards with her and asked about her upcoming exams. He was thrilled to hear that she was studying the Romantic poets and read some of his favorite poems out loud to her. Over the next few days, she and Nigel bandied lines back and forth ('Hail to thee, blithe spirit' — ''Tis sweet to win, no matter how'). Martin looked befuddled, and May, still feeling hurt, was glad that he felt a little excluded. 'What are you two on about?' he asked one day, looking from May to Nigel. Then he grabbed May and pulled her onto his lap with an air of proprietorship rather than playfulness.

He went back to England and after a month or so stopped writing to her. Her seventeenth birthday came and went, and she didn't hear from him. She knew nothing had happened to him. Ian wrote to her frequently and he would have told her if anything were wrong with Martin. Her final exams began, but she was too fretful to study. She failed all her subjects except English literature, and that was because

Nigel's favorite poem, *Don Juan*, was on the exam and they'd read it together. She didn't turn up for her biology exam. She didn't want to study medicine anyway. All she wanted to do in life was swim, and so she swam furiously every day, from Navy Island to Port Antonio and back.

Ian visited her one afternoon and suggested a walk along the beach. He told her that Martin was in Jamaica but that he'd been spending a lot of time with Tara Flynn, whom he'd met in London. Tara had become a model, Ian said. May was hurt. Tara, when she was on the island, was one of the horse-people. It was bad enough for Martin to be unfaithful, but it seemed especially mean to shut her out in this particular way, with Tara of all people.

'He asked you to tell me about him and Tara?'

'Well, he knew I was coming to see you and he didn't ask me not to tell you,' Ian said, his eyebrows bunched together as though he were trying to figure out something. 'I think he's mixed up right now about a lot of things. I know he doesn't want to lose you.'

'He has.' She tugged the ring off her finger and threw it into the sea.

'Jesus, May! That's a diamond ring!' He rushed to the edge of the water and then just stood there, the sea soaking the bottom of his pants.

May was sitting with her head in her hands when he came back.

'Look, he's no good for you. All he cares about is himself.'

'He used to care.'

'Yeah, but he's gotten more and more selfish. Part of him wants to be a barrister and settle down with a family and the other part wants racing cars and tarts—'

'Tara's a tart?'

'Well, no, but you know what I mean – sexy models, the clubs, all that. My mother spoiled him to death.'

He lit a spliff and handed it to her.

After a while he said, 'What you going do now? I mean with your life. Dad thinks you should study literature at Oxford.'

'And chance bumping into Martin? No, thanks. I'm going to that sports institute in Switzerland. What about you?'

'Travel for a few months. I always wanted to see Tahiti, you know, like Gauguin—'

'Tahiti,' she said dreamily. 'Land of the Otaheite.' And she felt miserable thinking that all that time she could have been planning a trip to the South Seas with Ian instead of wasting time with his self-centered brother.

'—then I'll come back here and do some more painting.'

'This is good,' she said, exhaling a pungent stream of smoke. 'Where you get it?'

'Sensemelia – special supplier – a friend of Ula's.'

'Ula?' To May, Ula had always seemed so meek. Now it looked as though she had a whole other life of sexy miniskirts and drug connections.

'Why did we have to grow up?' she asked. 'I was happy playing pirates with you, and I don't really want to leave home.'

'I know what you mean,' he said, relighting the end of the spliff and inhaling deeply.

'Don't finish it all off by yourself. Gimme some,' she said, reaching for it.

When they finished smoking, May looked out at the sea.

'That diamond is out there,' she said.

She thought about it for a while and then stood up. 'Let's get our gear. It's worth a try.'

'You're insane,' he said, jumping up and following her to the boathouse to get the diving gear.

'The boy's an idiot,' Nigel remarked some weeks later.

Martin had written to May, explaining nothing and asking her to always be his friend. He didn't mail it to her directly; Nigel brought it to her. She read it quickly and then threw it in the wastepaper basket.

'You know,' Nigel said, 'I've never actually heard Martin say anything intelligent—'

May kissed him suddenly on the cheek. 'I'm fine,' she said and walked wet-eyed over to the bar. 'I'll make you a drink. Scotch-and-soda?' She poured out two glasses. 'Another hot day,' she said.

It was a very hot July. The temperature rose to a hundred degrees and stayed that way for days in spite of brief thunderstorms. May and Ian spent a lot of time in the swimming pool. It was comforting to have Ian there; she knew she'd miss him when he went on his trip to Tahiti. She realized that when she and Martin had been engaged, she had been slightly estranged from Ian. Now he'd pop unannounced into her bedroom as he'd done when they were children, or May would hear a splash in the pool and realize Ian had come over. There was a joke among them all at Bella Vista: one night Ida thought she'd seen Errol's ghost in the kitchen, but it was just Ian, who no one realized had come by, helping himself to something from the fridge.

Ian gave May quaaludes. He was taking them along with other drugs. She tried some of the others but preferred the quaaludes, which he sometimes called 'mandies.' The drug wasn't addictive, he said.

'Martin didn't really want to live in Jamaica,' she told Ian, 'so it wouldn't have worked out. But I still hate him and you can tell him that.'

He hadn't thought she was good enough. She knew that was the reason. One day she had overheard something.

Ida and Nigel were out on the veranda. She was about to go out and join them when she heard Nigel telling Ida about a conversation he'd had with Martin. Martin had been upset about May's being colored and illegitimate; he was worried that marrying her would interfere with his political aspirations.

May went out. 'That bastard called me a bastard?'

'May!' Ida said.

'Thanks for letting me know,' she said before turning around to leave.

'You're welcome,' Nigel said.

That night Ida went to May's room to talk to her.

'The things Martin said about you being colored — it's hard to believe there are stupid people like that in the world.'

'I don't want to talk about it.'

'Well, don't talk. Just listen.'

She was sitting on the edge of May's bed, and it occurred to her that this was the very room where she'd once made love to Errol.

'Do you think color was the reason your father didn't marry me?'

May was actually interested in hearing about this, though she continued to act as though she were indifferent.

'He was a wandering man, an adventurer. I knew that, but I was so determined to have what I wanted that it made me act stupid. It wasn't about color.'

'Martin said I was a bastard.'

'That is not a nice word.'

'You know what it feels like, what it means to be an outside child.'

'I know.'

'But your father was there. It's different for me. All my life. Outside. That means I don't belong anywhere—'

'I thought it meant you're not shut in. Really, May, stop feelin' so sorry for you'self. You know what? We wouldn't have a country or history if it wasn't for so-called bastards. From way back we mix-matchin' black, white, Chinese, Syrian, and every blinkin' race. And it hasn't ruined us, far from it.'

'How you know it hasn't ruined us? How can you say it hasn't hurt us? He didn't want to marry me because I have black blood—'

'No—'

'And my father who was white didn't marry you. And the white man who was my grandfather, bless his soul, I loved him, how come he didn't marry my black grandmother? Don't tell me color has nothing to do with it! It does!'

25

Nigel and the Eleventh Jack Blaze Novel

Those hot July days, Nigel usually joined May and Ian at the pool. Ida was there too because Karl was traveling on business, but she rarely went into the water. Nigel called her 'Miss Dry Clean.' She lay in the shade wearing a big hat and sunglasses, reading historical romances. They got into a routine: indoors during the morning, swimming in the afternoon, scotch-and-soda or rum-and-colas before dinner.

Nigel read to them every night from his work-in-progress. This would be his eleventh Jack Blaze spy novel. Like his first, it was set in Jamaica.

'But it's not the real Jamaica,' May complained. 'Come on, where've you seen Jamaican *beauties* sunning in the nude?'

'It can't hurt the tourist industry,' he replied.

'If you want Desiree naked, then have Jack undress her back at the hotel. And the thatched huts – that's not Jamaican either. Galvanized iron.'

'That's right,' Ida said. 'Zinc roof!'

'I must say, you're hard to please. One of these days I'll write a sensible book about Jamaica and dedicate it to you both. But Jack Blaze is about glamour and daring—'

'And sex,' May said.

'No, my dear: the opportunity for sex. There's a difference.'

May went with Nigel to see Ian off at the airport. On the way back, he let her drive the new Jaguar.

'If that son of mine hadn't been such a complete ass—'

'He wasn't a complete ass; he just had ass-pirations.'

'Ha! Well said! It would have been nice to have you for a daughter-in-law.'

'There's still Ian. He doesn't want to become prime minister of England, does he?'

She heard him chuckling and turned to look at him. The breeze ruffled his graying hair. She'd convinced him earlier in the summer to stop using brilliantine in his hair – 'It's old-fashioned,' she'd told him – and he'd let it grow a bit longer.

'You're much too smart for him,' he said. 'My God, if I were younger I'd marry you.'

She stole another glance at him. She had never believed the rumors about him being queer. All the time she'd spent around him, there'd never been any indication of his liking boys. She'd always suspected he was in love with her mother.

'No, you wouldn't. You'd marry Ida.'

He seemed to consider this. 'I used to think that I was in love with her, but the feeling I have for Ida is a sort of cousinly infatuation. She's just too beautiful. I'd never get any work done.'

'But you would with me; I'm plain enough.' She laughed.

'Don't you ever look in the mirror?'

'Not much. You don't know what it's like having such a beautiful mother.'

'You're every bit as lovely as your mother, you know, and a man can actually have a good time with you. I mean, sailing and fishing and all that. Ida needs to have someone sit still and admire her. It would be impolite to do otherwise.'

' "Perfect she was, but as perfection is/Insipid in this naughty world of ours," ' May recited Byron.

He smiled. 'I don't think anyone could call Ida insipid.'

'True. Do you get on with Denise?' She realized it was an odd question.

'Oh, Denise and I manage all right because we leave each other alone. That's the secret of our well-bred marriage.'

'Strange.'

'Why strange?'

'Because when you're not writing, you don't really like being alone, do you?'

'You've always been a clever one.'

Karl returned from his business trip. He and Ida spent the evenings quietly at Bella Vista while May and Nigel began getting together almost every afternoon in Oracabessa.

Nigel would write in the mornings until May arrived, and then they'd have lunch together and go snorkeling or fishing. Nigel's cook, Beryl, still worked for him. She'd known May since she was a girl and liked feeding her because she was such an appreciative eater. So sometimes May stayed late and had dinner there too, and she'd read over what Nigel had written that day and make suggestions. Then they'd take a night drive along the coast with the roof of the car down and he'd see her onto the boat at East Harbor.

She was still hurt over what had happened with Martin. Being with Nigel helped, and the pills she'd gotten from Ian helped too.

'I didn't think that breaking up with Martin would affect her so much,' she overheard her mother say to Karl.

'She's drinking a lot. Have you noticed?'

'Maybe we shouldn't keep so much liquor in the house.'

'Where would we keep it, then?'

They were right; she was drinking a lot, especially at night. She'd lie awake feeling horrible.

She was supposed to be getting ready to study at the sports institute in Switzerland, but she felt unenthusiastic. She remembered her talk with Derek, how he'd encouraged her to work with the government in sports training once she got her degree. He actually thought she could make a difference. She wasn't so sure.

When she was fourteen she had briefly been a member of a swimming club. It was a club for wealthy teenagers whose parents could afford swimming pools and who wanted to swim competitively. She was so used to not fitting in that she hardly talked to the others at first. But they admired her athletic strength and team spirit and made overtures of friendship. She had been thrilled to belong to something. The team represented Jamaica in competitions against foreign clubs, and once when competing against a Venezuelan club, May broke a regional swimming record for her age group. She was in the newspapers and there was even talk of a future Olympic tryout. But when the reporters talked to her they always asked about her famous father. 'Are you *really* his daughter?' one of them asked one day, and she replied, 'I *really* hate it when people ask me that.' Her response was printed in the newspaper; it came up on radio shows and, it seemed to May, on everybody's veranda. People were saying *really* all the time about everything and mocking her. She wanted to hide. Her desire to swim competitively ended after that.

She had visions sometimes of starting a swimming school or club for poor children, or of one day working with the ministry of education on mandatory swimming lessons for all schoolchildren. Actually doing something. But people saw her as an item of curiosity, not just because she was a movie star's daughter but because she was the child of an illicit romantic affair involving a man who was famous for his illicit affairs. She had read the books by and about him. She knew about his rape trials. 'In like Flynn' – people actually said that to her and thought it was funny. No, she didn't want to do anything that might involve the local newspapers again. She really wished she could stay on her little island away from everyone else, or have a life at sea. Unfortunately, there was no navy she could join.

Nigel had dinner with them one night at Bella Vista. She had been looking forward to his visit and was going to suggest that he go with her for a nighttime swim or boat ride. After dinner they were all having cognac on the terrace and listening to some of Karl's favorite records – Valaida Snow singing 'Until the Real Thing Comes Along.'

Nigel got up. 'If you don't mind, I'm going to dance with your wife,' he told Karl.

May watched the ease and pleasure with which he held Ida. And Ida who loved dancing, especially with Nigel, seemed delighted to go on dancing to the next song and the one after that. May began to feel out of place, like a child among the grown-ups. She got up.

Ida said, 'You going to bed already?'

'I'm tired,' May said. She didn't look at Nigel as she left.

Upstairs she heard the music and their laughter. She was going to Switzerland in less than a month, and it seemed as if no one would miss her. She took not one as usual but two of the quaaludes Ian had given her.

She went down to the bar and poured herself a drink. She noticed that Karl had left, and only Nigel and her mother were on the terrace, laughing and talking. She pulled herself back upstairs with her drink in hand. The pills worked delightfully fast. She felt cushioned all around; even the pale-blue walls of her room seemed soft, even caressing. Too tired to undress, she finished her drink and lay down in her T-shirt and jeans.

She sensed him there in the room before she saw him, her father. And then she felt the weight of him, sitting on the bed beside her. Was it really him? He seemed older and less attractive than he was in all the pictures and movies she'd seen. There was a big red-and-white towel around his waist as if he'd just come in from a swim.

'Daddy,' she whispered, testing the word because she'd never uttered it, and then she wished she hadn't because it felt infantile, humiliating.

Because Ian had told her quaaludes weren't addictive, she didn't think she was addicted, not even when she found herself in Oracabessa searching through Ian's drawers for any pills he'd left behind. She found an old green container with a few. Then she remembered that Ula knew the supplier. So she telephoned her.

Ula told her to go to the Paradise Natural Juice shop in St Ann's Bay and to ask for Clayton. Clayton had everything: ganja, quaaludes, cocaine, hash. 'Tell him Ula sent you. Don't forget to say that.'

The juice shop, which really did sell fruit and vegetable

juices, was on a busy strip known for prostitutes, gigolos, and people who hustled and harangued tourists.

Clayton, a wiry man with an afro and goatee, talked to her in a fake American accent until he realized she was Jamaican. 'You from here, me did t'ink you was from foreign. Come, mek we go siddung a back.' He buzzed her into a back room and insisted that she smoke some ganja with him. 'Yes, man, sekkle an' smoke a while. No-hurry, no-worry.' She began to get a bad feeling about what else he expected from her as payment. When she told him she had to leave, he didn't seem to hear her and relit the spliff. It was at that point that Ula came in. She had her own key. She talked with May for a few minutes, then May took the opportunity to get out. She wondered whether Ula had come by on purpose to rescue her. The whole experience had been troubling, but she had gotten the drugs.

Yet the drugs weren't making her feel that good anymore or even helping her to sleep. Every day she grew more depressed.

It helped to go diving. There, beneath the water's surface, the solitude was infinite but never sad. Everything was so alluring: the schools of fish like agitated streams of color; the things that trembled as she went by and the things that fanned out; motions that were alien to her but not alienating. There was the oxygen tank on her back that would fail if she wasn't careful. She could die a hundred feet down, just by staying a minute too long. It almost happened one day. The air was practically used up, and, crazily, knowing she had less time left than usual, she pulled the lever open and started swimming back up. There were a few seconds when she wondered if she would make it. She did, and she'd never felt more alive. It was even better than Ian's pills.

'That was stupid,' Nigel said when she told him. He was so angry he barely spoke to her for the rest of the afternoon.

She began to feel the sheer idiocy of what she had done. She didn't want to die; she wanted to be happy. How could she be happy if she lay dead at the bottom of the sea?

'Sometimes I think I'm losing my mind, Nigel, honestly.'

She looked so crumpled. He opened the liquor cabinet and took out his best scotch: 'Here, this is good medicine. I'll have one too.'

She asked him why he locked up the really good stuff. Did Beryl, his cook, have a craving for fifty-year-old Armagnac?

No, Beryl didn't drink, not even rum. He thought maybe he was hiding it from himself.

'But you have the key,' she pointed out.

'Yes, so I do.'

The sight of the little key reminded her of the day Ian had locked her in the shed while they were playing pirates. She told Nigel the story. 'I actually thought I might die there and become a ghost like Sabine.'

'I think Ian said something about that one day but I thought he was making up things. It must have terrified him, thinking he'd suffocated you.'

'We had a lot of adventures.' She thought back. 'We were always coming across my father's old stuff in strange places – fancy sunglasses, even his underwear – but we never found any buried treasure.'

'You know, you should write about your childhood one day. It would be very piquant.'

'Remember—'

'—*Treasure Cove?* How I remember! You'll have to leave it for me as a memento when you go to Switzerland.'

They hadn't spoken about it, but they had both been thinking how much they were going to miss each other when she went away.

'I think you'll like it there,' he said now.

She frowned. She was supposed to be going in less than a month and had done nothing in preparation. She reminded herself that Nigel had a house there ('a castle,' as Ida liked to say) and he'd invited her to visit him there, so it wouldn't be so bad.

'You going to Nigel's again?' Ida asked May the next morning. 'You spend all your time there. What about us?'

'So why don't you come too?' May said. But she hoped her mother would not come along.

A shift had occurred but so gradually that it was hard to tell when or how. There had been all those times when May had asked Martin and Ian, 'Is your dad coming along?' And when Nigel had come along, May had been elated. When she and Martin had announced their engagement, May had looked quickly at Nigel, not Karl and Ida, for a sign of approval or concern.

'Nigel, here's an idea: Why don't you pull the shark all the way in for a change instead of letting it go? They're probably all down there laughing at you.'

They were out far, almost in Cuban waters, and she was watching him knot the lasso.

'Why should I? The fun is catching it.'

'I think that's gotten too easy for you.'

'Oh, you do, do you? Well, go ahead, you try pulling one in.' He threw the lasso over to her.

She couldn't help herself; she swung the lasso and caught him.

It was so like her, he wasn't that surprised.

'What do you propose to do with me now?' he asked.

She came in closer. 'I don't know. Are you ticklish?' She touched his waist. 'Here?'

He didn't respond.

'What about here?' She tickled behind his ears. 'No? Fascinating.'

'What?' he asked.

'Human flesh.'

'You're fascinating,' he said.

'So now I've caught you, can I do anything I want with you?'

He mouthed the word, silently and emphatically: 'No.'

She wrote about Nigel in her notebook. For some time now, she had been keeping daily entries. She used the same blue ledgers she'd once used for her pirate stories.

He's forty years older than me. But why does that have to be a problem?

It wasn't as if she were seeing something for the first time but more as if something that used to seem fuzzy had become clearer.

We're always together now. We eat together, read together, sail and take walks on the beach, and sometimes we sleep together. Not sex. We just lie down on the bed under that big fan because it's so hot and there's no better place to be, and sometimes we fall asleep. Though, to be honest, we don't really sleep well.

I don't want this to end badly. Actually, I don't want this to end at all. Maybe it doesn't have to.

But what did she actually want? she asked herself. Did she want Nigel to leave his wife for her? Yes. It would cause a huge shock and scandal even, but all that would eventually wear off. Denise had never been any good for Nigel, in May's opinion. She was a selfish, self-centered woman who belittled everything he'd accomplished. Nigel would be happier with her, May, and he would write better than he ever had. She even imagined taking care of him in his final years. She didn't care if he felt too old to have more children; she could live without children. She didn't even care whether they got married or just lived together. He could grow old and infirm; he could be rich or poor, write well or badly – she loved him.

She thought more and more about the kind of future she would have with him: Nigel would always want to live in Jamaica. He had a special and revered place among Jamaicans, the way her own father had once had. She, being Jamaican, would be a conduit for him into that less accessible Jamaica which had so far eluded him, the secret geography and spirit of the country, so that one day he would be able to write that serious book he wanted to write. Being with Nigel made sense to her, made sense of the miscellany which was her own life. With him, she wouldn't ever feel out of place.

May woke up one morning in Nigel's room remembering bits and pieces of the night before. It had gotten late and was raining heavily so she'd stayed the night.

He had lent her a pair of his pajamas, and she'd said, 'I like wearing your clothes.'

'They suit you,' he said. 'How tall are you now exactly?'

'Five foot ten.'

'You'd better stop growing or I'll have to cut you off at the ankles.' He picked her up in a burst of romantic energy. 'But you weigh nothing, nothing at all.'

'Do you think I'm too skinny?' she asked as he got into the bed beside her.

'For what? For reeling in large aquatic animals? No you're perfect.'

She nestled beside him. 'Thanks for letting me stay. I don't like you driving all that way on a rainy night.'

'I happen to like it when you stay.'

He said no more. There seemed to be an unspoken agreement between them that no more should be said. They had achieved this perfect balance; to disturb it would be devastating. The desire was there, all around them. It saturated them, seeped through their bedclothes and into their veins. Her knee would accidentally brush against his crotch, or his hand would fall across her thigh and rest there ambiguously for a second. Each night their restless bodies wound up closer, her head against his chest, his head against her breast, until they could hear one another's heartbeats and see the rise and fall of each other's breathing like big, bountiful sails.

Awake now, she saw the tangled sheets, the indentations in his pillow and the fan whirling above her like the question: What will we do?

'Where were you last night?' Ida asked when May came home the next morning. 'We were worried.'

'Helping Nigel with his book. It got late, so I stayed over.'

'Oh,' Ida said, and it sounded like a question, which May decided to ignore.

~

Nigel drove her back to Port Antonio one night after she'd spent the afternoon with him. She'd decided not to stay over. They both slept so badly when she did. Then they'd wake up late, and that ruined Nigel's writing schedule. For some reason, on the way she found herself telling him about the time she'd hidden on Clive Goodman's boat and gone to see her father, and how he'd shown her that map.

'I don't know why he wanted to show it to me.'

'Most likely he wanted to give you something, a remembrance.'

'But he didn't give me the map. He didn't give me anything except an Otaheite apple.'

'What did you do with the apple?'

'Ate it.'

'My dear girl, an Otaheite apple is not to be scoffed at; it's the pomegranate of the tropics. Fruit of gods and goddesses.'

At East Harbor, they waited in the car because the taxi-boat wouldn't be there for another half an hour. There was a steady gentle breeze and the water softly slapped the pier. Over on Navy Island it was completely dark except for a tiny glow by the boathouse.

'Were you close to him?'

'Errol? Not really. He worked like the devil, you know. So no one ever got that close.'

'Not even my mother?'

He thought for a moment. 'Karl was closer to him, I think, than your mother.'

'Really? That close?'

'You rarely saw one without the other.'

After a pause she asked, 'Did you like him?'

'Your father? Yes, as a matter of fact I did.'

'Even though—'

'—he slept with Denise?'

She didn't answer, and he went on, 'He slept with everyone. You couldn't take it personally.'

He saw the beginning of a frown on her forehead.

'But I do believe he felt something deeper for your mother; it wasn't a one-night thing. Doesn't Ida talk to you about him?'

'She does, but she's so besotted with him. I can't stand it.'

He burst out laughing. ' "Besotted." That's a good word. Haven't you ever been besotted with anyone?'

'No. Though I'm not sure what "besotted" means.'

'A sot is a drunkard. So to "be sotted" means to be in a bloody stupor from drinking—'

'—or passion for someone?'

'Or passion for someone.'

'Well, that's it. That's why I can't talk to her about him. She's besotted. Here's the boat. Good-bye. See you tomorrow.' She planted a quick and tender kiss on his lips.

Ida and Karl were concerned.

It was shortly after lunch. May was about to head out the door to visit Nigel when they spoke to her. She had been home the night before, but it was the first time she'd slept in her own bed in a week.

'You've been spending a lot of time in Oracabessa. It doesn't seem right—' her mother faltered.

May looked her straight in the eye, daring her to go on.

'Is something happening that we should know about?' Karl asked, getting to the point.

'Something like what?'

They were silent.

Her mother began again on a different tack: 'We've known Nigel for years, even before you were born. He's a good friend to all of us.' She stopped and looked at Karl for a moment. 'I'm not making judgments about you – or Nigel. But try to remember that he's almost like a father to you. At least, I know that's how he feels—'

'How do you know what he feels?'

Ida and Karl shared a troubled look.

'There are only a few weeks left before you go away,' Ida began. She looked mournfully at Karl. 'And we'd like you to spend more time with us.'

'Oh? So this isn't about Nigel? Don't be hypocritical. Say what you're thinking.'

Ida lost her patience. 'He's married and you're too young for him,' she said.

May's lips curled as if she were about to laugh. 'Everybody knows what you were up to when you were my age.'

The slap stunned her. Ida had hit her hard. May felt the side of her face stinging. She walked out the door, leaving it open behind her.

She decided not to say anything to Nigel about the quarrel with her parents. They went snorkeling and then out to the market for some vegetables. Beryl was cooking spicy black-crab soup for supper that night, and Nigel invited May to stay.

'You look a bit run-down,' he said. 'How about a scotch-on-the-rocks before dinner?'

She had two. Then they shared a bottle of wine with dinner.

Afterward they went out on the patio, where they could

hear the sea below them and watch the breeze threshing the coconut trees; it was a beautiful tropical night.

They had their after-dinner drinks with them and were sitting quietly in big rattan chairs. Nigel was smoking Craven As. He'd cut back to just three cigarettes a day. May had taken a couple of pills just before dinner, and she felt as if her head were part of the night, floating at large.

She went over to Nigel and sat on his knee. They sat like that for a while, not speaking. He put out his cigarette and took the glass from her, placing it gently on the table beside them.

'Are we going to talk about this?' he asked.

'About what?'

'Well, to begin with,' he spoke slowly, 'the fact that I've known you since you were an infant, and I'm old enough to be your father, but nevertheless, I seem to be in love with you, and you with me.'

'What else is there to say, Nigel?' She felt old saying that, like a fifty year old, not an eighteen year old.

His fingers smoothed the fine, almost invisible hair on her forearm. 'Like so many wonderful things, it feels a bit wrong, doesn't it?'

'But is it wrong?'

'I'd hate it if you began to hate me.'

She touched his face. 'Never.'

'How can you be so sure?'

She kissed him, and he responded, at first hesitantly and then like a man risking everything to kiss a woman.

She began to cry, short broken cries, and he kissed her soothingly on her cheek and forehead. 'Let's go inside,' he said.

She told him so many things as he sat on the edge of the

bed, still kissing her soothingly – things that were all broken up: 'I'm so happy with you – I don't want to leave – make love to me – I'd never hate you.'

She cried and cried.

When she woke the next morning, she saw him beside her already awake. Pain split her head.

'You must feel awful,' he said.

She noticed he was wearing his robe and that he smelled fragrant, as if he'd just had a shower. She was wearing his pajama shirt.

'What happened?'

He smiled. 'You make yourself entirely vulnerable asking that. Do you really want to know?'

She looked anxious.

'You had a good cry, then fell asleep.'

'We—?'

He shook his head.

'I wanted to,' she said.

'So did I.'

She looked at him, wondering what would happen now.

'I'm too old for this,' he told her gently. 'It's been almost thirty years since I was in love with anyone. Do you have any idea how I've felt these past few weeks? Don't look injured. It would be better for you in the long run if I said I didn't want you. But of course I do. I've been living with the possibility of making love to you, hating and loving every minute of it. Maybe it will happen one day. But not now.'

He saw her eyes brimming with tears.

'I'm too old to reorganize my life,' he said gently, pleadingly. 'I don't dislike Denise enough to divorce her. And you deserve more attention than an old married man can give you.'

He held her close. 'Don't forget me.'

She cried and he let her go back to sleep. He woke her a bit later with a cup of coffee in his hand.

'The antidote for everything. Drink it. Then you must get dressed my dear, and go home, and I must get back to writing my novel.'

Back at Bella Vista, after a few days in bed, May went for a walk. But even the slightest exercise felt wearying. She sat down to rest under the shade of the poinciana tree by the tennis court and was surprised to see Derek walking across the lawn toward her. She'd thought he was still away on a world tour.

He sat beside her and handed her a bag of plantain tarts, her favorite sweet. He had heard that she wasn't eating.

'My mother called you?' she asked.

'She's worried. I'm kind a worried too.'

Tears suddenly threatened to roll down her face. It was so embarrassing to be always crying or about to cry.

'You using drugs, May?'

She nodded.

'What?'

She told him.

'And drinking too? What about Switzerland and college?'

She could barely get up in the morning, much less get on a plane. Karl had managed to have her place at the institute held open for her.

'You have to stop feelin' sorry fe you'self.' Derek smoothed back a lock of her hair. 'Show some gumption.'

He stayed at Bella Vista for two weeks. At six-thirty every morning, he woke her and made her swim laps. They went running together every evening. He mixed concoctions of coconut milk, mangoes, and guavas, and he grilled fish for her on the coal-pot. They played pool.

He was there whenever she looked around but not in a stifling way. And when she didn't see him, she'd hear the sound of guitar chords coming from the guest room, parts of a new song, she supposed.

Though her appetite and energy began to come back, she still cried uncontrollably at times and sank into periods of lassitude. He was tough on her when she slid, expressing disappointment rather than sympathy. 'I thought you had better sense than to mope around like this. So, you fall in love and lose all you ambition?'

Ida watched all this and pondered. There was very little she could do to help May. Since the day she had slapped her, she and May had barely spoken. Ida spoke to an old schoolmate in Kingston, a psychiatrist, who sent a prescription for Valium, but Ida's instinct told her that the last thing May needed was more drugs. She sent a message to Oni, who sent back sour-sop leaves to make a bush-bath, but Derek was the only one able to get May to take the baths.

'You want go Blue Mountain?' he asked May one day. 'Why we don't go see Oni?'

'Me no born a-mountain,' Oni told them.

Derek and May sat in her kitchen drinking bush-tea. Rain crashed on the tin roof and poured down the corrugated eaves and windowpanes, muting Oni's voice and changing the world outside. An oil lamp glowed from the center of the table and held them together in a flickering yellow light.

'But me did always like it up here. Too much nize an' excitement for me in town. You know wha' me mean?'

Derek leaned all the way back in his chair, his long legs crossed at the ankles. He seemed to May to be completely at home in Oni's house though he had never been there before.

'So how you come to know 'bout bush-bath an' all that?' he asked Oni.

'Obeah? Some of it you born with, an' the rest you learn. Ida, she have it, but she no want it.' Oni was quiet for a while, thinking, and then she added, 'Ida's heart is light-light. Like a bird. She fly far an' see whole heap but she no wan' carry whole heap.'

Thunder suddenly boomed around them and left the room silent. Nothing could be seen through the windows except the great wash of rain, as if a wave had consumed the little house. But May felt safe. She was in a warm, dry space, a ship, an ark. And Derek was there, as if they were once again sitting together in that wooden crate in Miss Gloria's yard.

'You know, you father, Errol, come to see me once.'

Ida had told May about it, but it was one of those stories May had not wanted to listen to.

'Me never know a white man fe get himself in a so much trouble. No matter where you put him down, him manage to lose him way.'

May stood outside the next morning looking at the view. The rain had finally ended and had left the air cool and clean. 'It was a good idea to come here,' she told Derek.

'Yeah, man, the air sweet. Country sweet,' he said.

'It feels like nothing is going to change up here, not even Oni.'

'You frighten of change, May? What you think could happen that would be so bad?'

'Everything and everybody disappearing.'

'But why would that happen? That not goin' happen.'

'I have bad dreams, ever since I was a little girl I've had them, about being stranded somewhere dark-dark, and there's all this — I don't know — wreckage, like after an explosion, a lot of broken things—'

'You read too many shipwreck stories, man.'

'I hear the sea but I can't see it because it's that dark. Maybe you right. It's a shipwreck dream.'

The time came for Derek to go back to Kingston.

'Why you don't come?' he asked May.

'To Kingston?'

'Maybe a change will do you good.'

'I need to keep swimming.'

'They have swimming pools there, you know? Big ones.'

She laughed.

'All right, country gal. Stay here. You na mek fe de city.'

The day he left, May hurried down to Cassava Piece to eat lunch with Winston and Florence. While Derek had been there, he'd made her drink raw vegetable juice and eat lean, saltless meat — *Ital* food, he called it. She was dying for something greasy and delicious — jerk chicken, fried breadfruit, fried plantain, fried dumpling.

Back in Kingston, Derek wrote and recorded his first solo single, a funny reggae song that became popular, called 'Country Sweet.'

~

It would have surprised May to learn how badly Nigel was doing. She imagined him immersed in his spy novel. But he wasn't writing at all.

He was shocked to find himself, at his age, heartbroken. He wavered between stoicism, when he congratulated himself for having done the right thing, and hours of bewilderment, when he did nothing but mentally retrace the steps of their romantic adventure. He decided that letting her go was a tragic mistake. Why not spend what was left of his life with her? Why had he thought of her as a disruption? It was Denise with all her demands and comings and goings that had been a source of chronic irritation, like some rash he couldn't control.

He telephoned May, wanting to tell her all this. She sounded like a weak, unrecognizable version of herself, and then she started to cry uncontrollably. He tried to speak with her several times after that and was always told that May wasn't there or wasn't 'able to come to the phone.'

One day Karl asked him to stop calling: 'You're ruining her life.'

Nigel, who had never liked Karl, began to despise him.

'Life is just too short,' Ida told Karl and May at breakfast one morning. 'I've invited Nigel to come over on Christmas Eve.'

'Because life is short?' Karl asked. 'Isn't that a good reason not to ask him?'

'For heaven's sake, Karl! May's leaving for Switzerland in a few weeks. Time we put this bad feelin' to rest.'

He said nothing more. May didn't say anything either.

Fortunately, there were a lot of other people for May and Nigel to talk to, so no one noticed the awkwardness between them or the animosity between Nigel and Karl. Derek came, and so did Ian. Some of the archaeologists and divers who were working at the *Capitana-Santiago* site were there too; Ida tried to chat with them but they seemed unable to socialize, like big turtles who wanted to find their way back to the water.

May spent most of the evening chatting with Clive. He usually didn't come to parties at Bella Vista, declining invitations with the excuse that he was busy. May suspected that Clive had never let go of his resentment toward her father, Errol Flynn, and that it still made him uncomfortable to be at Bella Vista. 'Garage busy right now. I even working Sundays,' he'd say. Old Mrs Goodman, his mother, complained, 'He making so much money, you would think he has time for a little fun now, but no.'

But to everyone's surprise, Clive had finally gone away on a holiday; he'd gone to Europe and was now telling May about it. He had brought back an extravagant present for Ida – an antique clock, decorated with porcelain figures, a beautiful thing that even Karl had to agree was finely crafted. But it had bothered Karl that Ida had accepted such an expensive gift from another man. 'It's something for the house, not just for me,' Ida had reasoned. 'It's not as if it's jewelry.'

Denise came, unexpectedly. She'd surprised Nigel by arriving for the Christmas holidays.

'I bet you anything she knows about the whole affair,' Ida had privately told Karl. 'She and Nigel have some kind of arrangement where they tell each other these things.'

'Don't we?' Karl asked.

'I think she's checking up on him,' Ida said. Ida guessed that Denise, who had never worried about Nigel's infidelities before, must have sensed Nigel's anguish, smelled divorce in the air, and didn't want to lose her husband to an eighteen-year-old.

But at the party there was no hint that Denise knew anything; she was just as rude and abrasive as usual ('She's got as much tact as a Portuguese man-of-war,' Karl said about her after the party).

When Nigel visited Bella Vista by himself a week later, May wouldn't come down from her room. It distressed him.

Ida could imagine how hard it was for May. She thought about herself and her own disappointments, how hard it was to fail at love, and how long it took to forgive someone, much less oneself, for the failure. She went to May's room and told her, 'What happened between you and Nigel isn't something to feel sorry about. I've been through enough to know these things aren't as simple as right and wrong. You have a good friend in Nigel, and that's worth plenty.'

May came downstairs. Ida left them alone together on the upstairs veranda.

'Denise told me you're not writing,' May said.

'The eleventh Jack Blaze novel? I think the world can do without it.' He smiled weakly. 'I know I can. But I'll start something else soon.'

'I hope so. Actually, what I read of number eleven was quite good.'

'No, it wasn't. It was redundant. It's time for me to write something different. Maybe get back at Denise and all her literary friends.'

'Write something true, then.'

'Meaning?'

'Something true about Jamaica, about yourself—'

'About you?'

'Maybe. Me, my father and mother. You know enough about us and what you don't know, you can make up.'

'I've actually thought about that. *Lolita*, *Lady Chatterley's Lover*, and *Rebecca* all mixed together and set in Jamaica.'

She smiled.

'What about you?' he asked. 'When are you going to write something true?'

'I did. *Treasure Cove*.'

'Isn't it time you joined us here in the present century?'

'I'm leaving for Switzerland next week. Will you come see me off at the airport?'

'I'd like to.'

The drive from Port Antonio to the airport in Kingston began pleasantly, like other country drives. They traveled along the twisting mountain roads for two hours, then began the gradual descent, past proud suburban houses, to the shanty-littered streets of the capital. It was 1972. Political slogans were painted across the walls and billboards: TIME FOR A CHANGE — VOTE PNP — NO CIA — VOTE LABOURITE — PNP IS A CASTRO PLOT. The PNP's color was orange; the JLP's was green. For months partisan gangs had clashed and fought for control in the poorest parts of the city — Trench Town, West Kingston, Tivoli Gardens, Vineyard Town — and one of the two colors, either the orange or the green, would take over the other, multiply, and sprawl across everything like some strange weed. In those still unclaimed districts where no party color was visible, soldiers patrolled the empty streets in jeeps. May had never seen soldiers before except in parades.

No election campaign had ever been so ferocious or so

crucial. If Manley's PNP won, it would bring big changes and 'power to the people.' Seaga's conservative JLP would bring closer alignment to the United States and 'change without chaos.' So the politicians and their slogans claimed. No one knew what to believe.

About five miles from the airport they were stopped at a roadblock. Karl rolled down his window to speak to a policeman: 'What's happening, Officer?'

There had been a funeral procession for the leader of a political gang and members of the rival gang had attacked the pallbearers with machetes, killing one of them.

There was a long line of cars ahead and behind, many probably on their way to the airport.

'This doesn't look good,' Ida said.

'Is awright. Police have things under control,' Derek said.

He sat in the back with May. He knew Kingston well and explained to them that these policemen were a special force 'from Harmon barracks.' May noticed their automatic rifles and bulletproof vests.

Men were being herded, some of them dragged along the ground, into the back of a police Jeep. The dead man lay covered by a blood-soaked sheet. A crowd of onlookers had gathered and the police were shouting harshly to them, even to the children.

Until then May had been taking in everything on the drive through Kingston, trying to imprint the city on her memory, even its impudent graffiti. But this scene at the roadblock was different; she had a part in it.

Men walking by the car fixed hostile eyes on May and her family; policemen gazed at them with the same hostility and, in addition, with far too much assurance of their power. She didn't want to be an enemy of the people, yet more and more she felt as if she were being given no other choice.

On one side of the road was a vacant lot fenced off by barbed wire. There, among tall grass and bushes, two donkeys began copulating. The male donkey had succeeded after several attempts to mount the female, who stood under him, alert and subdued. She seemed so delicate, May thought. A group of boys stood by the fence, jeering and flinging stones at the animals, who continued helplessly mating. Others came and went from the fence as if unable to decide which was more interesting to watch, the actions of the police or the donkeys. Children passing the Von Ausberg car gazed in at them, and one boy made a clownish face at them, his eyes widening and his mouth in an exaggerated frown. The other children laughed.

Suddenly Karl said, 'Columbus was dead wrong.'

'About what?' Ida asked.

'There's no gold here.'

No one said anything for a moment.

'No Arawak gold, no indigenous precious metals whatsoever.'

A policeman signaled to him to move the car on.

'How can you be sure?' May asked. She was the one most familiar with this quixotic side of Karl. They'd had many conversations about Columbus's sojourn in Jamaica and the conquistadores' attempts to get gold from the indigenous people. Karl had always cherished the belief, disproved by all experts, that if Columbus had seen gold ornaments on the natives' bodies, then gold had to be somewhere on the island. She wanted him to go on believing what Columbus had believed.

Karl didn't answer her; he just drove on.

When they got to the airport they learned that the flight

had been delayed. So they all sat drinking in the air-conditioned lounge. May tried not to show disappointment over Nigel's absence.

Ida was nervous. 'Maybe you shouldn't have packed your coat. Suppose when you get there, your luggage is lost. You'll freeze.'

Derek recalled how cold London had been on his tour. 'Man, even the toilet seats are ice-cold, and what you can do 'bout that?'

The flight was finally announced. As they got up, Nigel arrived. May was very happy to see him and couldn't hide the fact.

'I was afraid you weren't coming.'

'Almost didn't. I got held up in the roadblock traffic.'

Everyone took turns hugging her and saying good-bye. Nigel and Karl avoided each other.

'I'll see you in March,' Nigel said. 'Remember, our house is just an hour by train.'

'House? You mean the castle?' Ida remarked.

'It's not really a castle. There's no moat. It's just a stupendously large estate.'

'Write that book,' May said to him and turned to give her mother another hug.

Karl had a special VIP pass that allowed him to walk almost all the way to the plane with her. He had become sullen as soon as Nigel had appeared.

She was glad to have this extra bit of time with him. She noticed that he was beginning to show his age. He was in his sixties, still healthy and good-looking, but he seemed somehow weighed down by things and less energetic. She was truly sorry for all the worry she'd given him and her mother.

'Take care of yourself,' she said to him.

'I'll be all right.'

He and Ida had not been getting on so well lately, she'd noticed. Ida had become more impatient with him, and he had grown more distant.

'And take care of Bella Vista.'

'Of course. Don't worry about anything.'

She could see the nose of the plane. The noise of the engines was distressing. She knew that her mother and the others would be up at the waving gallery shouting her name and waving to her as she walked across the tarmac.

'Don't give up on the indigenous gold, I mean on Columbus and what he saw. He was right about that other thing.'

He enveloped her in a hug that showed great love for her but a complete disregard for what she'd said.

'I wish I could stay and vote in the election,' she said, shouting through the noise of the plane.

All the other passengers had crossed the tarmac and boarded the plane. Karl was trying to hand her two overpacked bags and she seemed not to notice. All this talk suddenly about voting and elections – she was afraid, he realized; she was once again the girl who didn't want to go to school, and being her father, he told her, 'You have to go.'

26

Switzerland

May 3, 1972

Dear Ian,

It's finally safe for me to go out. The snow has melted.

I heard you were back in Jamaica, just in time to vote. Vote for Manley, please. He's a real leader, and aside from everything else, quite handsome, don't you think?

Write and tell me everything about your trip to Tahiti. Was it like our dear isle? Are there lots of Otaheite apples? Did you paint while you were there?

I'm about fifty miles from Zurich, in a little village with cobblestone streets. It reminds me of children's stories like 'The Pied Piper.' There's even a well in the village square and people still pull up water from it. Maybe there's a frog-prince waiting for me there.

Speaking of princes, I saw your brother in Lausanne a few weeks ago. Your parents had a house party, you know, everyone staying the whole weekend. I couldn't avoid him. Actually, it's worse than that. You're the only one I can tell these sorts of things to because I know you won't go tut-tut.

I slept with Martin. It was just one night. Then Martin called when he got back to England and wanted me to meet him in Paris. I almost did but then I realized it was Paris I wanted to see, not him. He's not even that much fun in bed anymore.

It was nice seeing your father. We had some good conversations about books and things, in spite of your mother. She wants to set me up with the son of a count named Campolieri. I suspect she just wants me out of the way so I won't mash-up Martin's career or spend too much time chatting with Nigel.

I heard her telling your father that this Campolieri fellow was 'tall enough for May.' And your father said, 'Yes, with a brain the size of a pea and a face like a dinosaur.' So mean, but I had to laugh.

Anyway, it's very kind of your parents to introduce me to some people my own age. I haven't made many friends here at the college. Maybe because my German is so bad. But maybe too because everyone is very competitive. Some of the athletes here are hoping to make it to the Olympics. There are two other foreign students in my class, both African and both of them runners – a woman from Mozambique and a man from Uganda. The Mozambique woman, Tsawunda, showed me how to wrap a cloth around my head African-style. The first time I did it the Ugandan guy sneered and called me a half-caste! One day when he saw me putting sugar in my coffee he asked me if sugar didn't remind me of the cane fields where my white ancestors forced my slave ancestors to work. He looks at me as if he'd like to chew me up, then spit me out.

I spend a lot of time writing at a little café in the village. The café owner and his wife speak English very well. I've also made friends with the hairdresser who cuts my hair every two or three weeks. In fact, I made some Jamaican jerk pork for him the other day. You should see how short my hair is now. I think having only about an ounce of hair makes me swim that much faster than the other women.

Your father says you're doing a lot of painting and are going to try to sell some of your work. You're a good painter, Ian, so I think you'll succeed. Just don't sell that one of East Harbor. It's my favorite.

Oh, East Harbor! I miss home, and I miss you too.

Love, May

July 10, 1972

Dear Nigel,

It must be good to be back in Oracabessa. Lucky you.

Your long letter was wonderful. I enjoyed every bit of it, even the part that bothered me. I'll get to that, but first – do you really think that Manley's government is going socialist? I can't imagine anything so drastic happening in Jamaica.

I've tried to like it here, and of course the mountains are beautiful, but it's like the beauty of a movie or postcard for me. I really just want to finish my education and go home. Mama says I need to try harder to adapt and make friends. I miss the sea so much; I think about it all the time.

Your friends, the Forwards, invited me to the South of France. I took some nice walks in the countryside with Mr and Mrs Forward. They're amazing! I could barely keep up with them. I also went on some excursions with their son John and his friends – all in their twenties, very rich and sporty. I tried not to be awestruck by their surnames – Cunard, DuPont, Picasso! I didn't even know Picasso had children, much less grandchildren. And I suppose the word spread about my father. I get curious looks but these people are too well brought up to pry, thank God. Still, I can see the unasked questions in their eyes (are you *really*...?) and especially behind their parents' eyes. They all rave about my Jamaican accent and keep asking me to say certain things again and again, like 'duppy,' and to translate Bob Marley's songs.

By the way, Campolieri invited me to visit him in Tuscany next month and I've accepted.

All this is to answer your question: Am I going out and trying to meet people? I am.

As for your other question: Have I fallen in love with anyone? I know you have my best interests at heart, that you want me to be happy. But do you really want to hear about my love life, Nigel? Wouldn't you rather I just said something vague like 'I've been going out and having a good time with friends'?

You said I probably mean more to you than anyone you've ever known. Part of me loves your saying it, part of me says, please don't. It was hard seeing you in Lausanne, hard not to misbehave and do something very improper with you. But it was also wonderful. If I had to stop talking to you, I would be miserable. So I think it's worthwhile trying to behave ourselves.

I will *try* to get out more, see all of Europe, have boyfriends, and not just to please you.

Love always, May

P.S. Here in Switzerland, people actually think of me as *la femme noir*, which is quite an interesting change for me.

April 12, 1973

Dear Nigel,

I'm worried about what's happening in Jamaica. I read in the overseas *Guardian* that the violence is getting worse and people are lining up outside the American embassy. Is the trouble mainly in Kingston? Please send me news.

I'm in Paris right now visiting a friend. All right, not really a friend, a man I met recently.

Being in this city reminds me a lot of my grandfather. He used to tell me all about the places he'd been, London, Paris, as if he had landmarks like the Eiffel Tower stamped on his brain.

I went to the Luxembourg Gardens, where he used to work. He used to clean the park, washing benches and emptying wastebaskets. It was at the beginning of the First World War and he told me that although he wasn't fighting, he felt that he was playing an important part, maintaining the continent's splendor.

It is a splendid continent, and I thought I would feel something deeper for it. The Luxembourg Gardens, Notre Dame, the Seine, Mont Blanc – all the places I've read about. My mother says I'm here to broaden my mind. But I feel like I'm at the narrow and not the wide end of the funnel. The wide end was my childhood in Jamaica.

Feeling a bit depressed and trying not to misbehave. Spending a lot of time in the water. I find it's not the amount of laps so much as the speed that lifts my mood. I did the 200-metre freestyle in just a little over two minutes the other day. Thanks for recommending those books. The Graham Greene started well but then I lost interest. Rebecca West – yes! How's your novel coming along?

Love, May

September 20, 1973

Dear Mama,

So it's official then about the country going socialist. I read parts of Manley's speech in the newspaper. I wish people wouldn't panic; it seems to me that he plans a very different kind of socialism than the Soviet or Cuban kind.

Glad to hear that everything remains the same on Navy Island. I sometimes think the government's forgotten we're even there.

One more year, then I'm coming home. I like the course I'm taking this term in sports education. It's given me some ideas about work I want to do when I'm back.

I can't tell you how much I miss everyone and how much I *'fraid a winter*. How is Oni?

Love, May

P.S. Are you still going to give riding lessons? Where? And how much will you charge? Tell me all about it.

January 1, 1974

Dear Derek,

I had a dream that I was by the boathouse on Navy Island waiting for the taxi-boat, and I looked across at Port Antonio and saw those ruins at the Folly estate.

You remember something bad happened to me there when I was little. I dream a lot about that place, bad dreams where sometimes I escape and sometimes I don't.

But this was very different. It was a little before dawn. No one was with me. At first I saw the ruins and the trees surrounding them from a distance. Next thing I was there with the broken walls and trees around me. There was a blue glow around everything, the first light of morning. It was so beautiful in the dream. The mangoes looked like moons on the trees and there were a lot of tamarind pods on the ground. The earth smelled good.

In the dream I realized that the bad men were not around anymore and that they weren't coming back. It felt peaceful, and this might sound strange, I felt I had misjudged the place. The land never did anything to me; it was those men. All the bad feeling I used to have drained out of me, and Derek, when I woke up, I had a vision!

My grandfather built the first movie theatre in Port Antonio; why shouldn't I try to build something right there at Folly? There was talk about fixing up the ruins as a tourist attraction, but why spend time and money on broken walls? The Jamaica National Sports Institute — doesn't that sound great? I think it's time for something like this in Jamaica. I don't know whether it would be through the government or a private thing. Karl would know. What do you think of this idea?

Your friend, May

July 1974

Dear Karl and Mama,

I'm trying not to be too worried but, as you said, things are more worrying when you're at a distance. I can't believe they shot down the plane. I know nobody was hurt, but what will this mean for the *Capitana-Santiago* project? Things have been hard enough and I doubt that anyone wants to go on working somewhere where they're getting shot at, never mind if it's an accident. What's going to happen now?

Nigel told me that the army thought it was some drug

lord's plane and even now they won't apologize. Don't they realize how important your project could be for Jamaica?

Is the ganja trade so bad now that the army's shooting down private planes?

I know Karl didn't like my sports institute idea and I can see why he might not have much faith in the government. But I think it's worth proposing. Do either of you know anyone in the Ministry of Education that I could get in touch with? I think Father Reynold has a friend there.

About my staying here another year. I don't want to, but I see your point. Some work experience would be good, and I never had a place of my own — that might be exciting. I'll have my own kitchen and can cook some Jamaican food!

I've been going out with a Frenchman who lives in Zurich. His name is Alain Masson. He's a film director but I doubt you've seen any of his films. They're in French and very strange. He's been to Jamaica and wants to visit it again with me. He's very smart, especially about wine. I think Karl would enjoy talking to him.

Please don't let any planes get shot down over Navy Island. What a thing! Say hello to Florence and Winston and the rest,

Love, May

November 1974

Dear Ian,

My parents said I should stay for a while in Zurich even though I've finished my diploma. I'm to get experience and broaden myself!

I'm working with the city government in their department of recreation. I'm learning a lot that will be useful when I come back to Jamaica. There's a club near my flat. Private. Somebody spread the word about who my father was so I'm allowed in. It is pitch-black in there, really, and there's a lot of American disco music playing all night. I think it would be more fun if you were here. Sometimes I meet interesting people there, men I mean, and that's where I met Alain, my new boyfriend. I'll tell you about him another time.

Your father came to see me here in my little flat. We had a good time and talked about his book. He's written over four hundred pages.

Here's something I wanted to ask you. Why can't your mother be more encouraging to him? Can you talk to her? He's trying to write something serious and quite different from the Jack Blaze novels. The other day, right in front of him, your mother told me, 'He might have once, but it's too late now.' She's like a grater, grating away at your father.

I wish you'd come to visit me here before I come back home. But I know you don't like leaving Jamaica. Tell me about your paintings and Oracabessa and everything. Is there some fascinating woman in your life these days? Have you seen Ula recently?

I think about Jamaica constantly. Beautiful thoughts. That impure whiteness of the spider lilies; it was you who showed me the purple veins of the petals, and the smell of the frangipani outside my bedroom window. I imagine myself eating Otaheite apples, enormous amounts of them. As I write all this it sounds like I'm describing some Garden of Eden. But it's true, isn't it? We grew up in a physical paradise. The view of the sea from the north of the island, remember we called it the Cuban Sea, and looked for refugee boats with my telescope? We never spotted anything, just a whole lot of blue. How come we never got tired of looking?

I know you've been a bit down. Remember that Navy Island is your other home. Your paradise too, Ian. Swim in the saltwater pool; that always revives you.

Love, May

February 1, 1975

Dear Nigel,

Mama told me you've been ill. Is it your asthma? Let me know what the doctor says.

Will you be coming to Switzerland this spring?

I really am lonely. I'm just not a city girl, and I don't make friends easily.

There were times in Jamaica when I used to feel like a foreigner. Now I really know what 'foreign' means.

I think I told you that I took a train ride last autumn from Paris to Budapest. At each of the borders I showed my passport and they would always have something to say about it – '*Jamaique? Oui! Comme le Bob Marley!*' – '*Jamaika, Yamayca, Iamaica bella!*' It was quite charming. In Prague I met some Czechoslovakian students at a café and they invited me back to their apartment, where they played outlawed Peter Tosh tapes for me, and one young man got out his guitar and sang Jimmy Cliff – 'The Harder They Come.' When I got to Hungary the border officials hadn't seen a Jamaican passport before. I told them, 'It's near Cuba.' They got out an atlas so I could show them where it was. 'Ah! *Jamaika*. Such a small island. No charge for the visa.'

Here is a secret about me: I feel strange saying it but I've always been madly in love with the land of my birth – the land, not the nation or state – it's not patriotism; it's *landscapism*, which is both a passion for the land and a kind of escape. I used to wake up earlier than everyone else when I was a little girl just so I could be alone with the view and have no one intruding between me and the morning air.

I thought I didn't have the right to love the place as much as I did because I was not a typical Jamaican, whatever that is. In the yards and streets I felt like my whiteness made me suspect. I even suspected myself of the sin of not really belonging. What right did I have to imbibe all that loveliness? So I loved it secretly, in daydreams and long walks by myself, and by writing those stories about pirates just like Daniel Defoe and Robert Louis Stevenson. I copied their way of writing and hid behind it like a mask. I didn't think I was entitled. I don't know why I'm telling you all this. You just seem like the person to tell.

I hear terrible news about Jamaica now, and, don't get me wrong, I believe that what's happening is terrible. At the same time, I know that Oni's all right, and so is everyone at Bella Vista; great music is being made and no earthquake or hurricane has hit the island. Is Jamaica really changing like everyone says, or has it just outgrown the old stories about itself? It's frightening and chaotic to have all that feeling and finally be able to express it in one's own way. Like Pandora opening the box she thought was full of gifts.

You poor man, having to read my ramblings. Probably hoping you'll come to some pleasant thing that actually concerns you. Well, you have: I'm dying to see you. I want to show off my new, mod haircut. Honestly, it would be great to visit you in Lausanne or be visited here, but get well first.

Love, May

March 10, 1975

Dear Ian,

Thank you for the Burning Spear tape. It's irie.

I can't remember whether or not I told you about my boyfriend, Alain. It feels funny calling him a *boy*friend since he's forty-two years old. My lover, then. He's a big fan of my father's acting, and he's been to Jamaica and loves it. He's even said the 'm' word, you know, 'marriage.'

He's bisexual, which he told me about right away, and that's OK as long as he isn't sleeping with anyone else while he's with me. He's also manic-depressive and that's no problem either, as long as he takes his medicine.

The other night, after we finished making love, he looked at me and said, in French, which I'll translate for you, 'Incredible.' I thought he was talking about the sex, but he said, 'You look just like Flynn but you're a Negress!'

That was it. I wrote to my parents and told them that I'm through broadening my mind. Enough of this citizen-of-the-world crap. Time to be a citizen of my own country now. You'll see me next month.

Love, May

Part Six

I was persuaded to take passage to Jamaica. What I should find there upon my return, peace or great confusion, I could not begin to imagine.

Treasure Cove

27

From Kingston to Jamaica

The violence in Kingston had become so uncontrollable that a special prison called the gun court had been built; people could be arrested, tried, and sentenced all on the same day. May drove past the wood-and-barbed-wire structure on her way in from the airport. It looked like something that had been quickly constructed. Its watchtower reminded her of prison camps she'd seen in movies about World War II.

That was Kingston. The rest of the country was relatively peaceful, but even there people were growing discontented. Food was scarce; staples like rice and flour were unavailable or rationed. Public services had broken down: firemen on strike, running water shut off, electrical power constantly failing. But May noticed that there were more children in school uniforms – thin children who walked to school on the main country roads where there were still no sidewalks. Manley had kept one of his promises: free education for the first time in the country's history. There was a benevolent idea, May thought, behind all the hardship and disruption, and she placed her faith in the idea.

Ida felt she had to show her support for Manley simply

because she had voted for him. Her cousins, the Levys, and a number of the big property owners along the north coast had too. But now they complained that Manley was destroying the country. The servants at Bella Vista thought so too. 'How poor people suppose to eat?' Florence said. 'No flour or rice in de shop.' Manley's government was even blamed when a plant disease ravaged the coconut trees throughout the island. It caused the foliage to wither and fall off, leaving miles of tall, decapitated tree trunks.

'Chu!' Winston said. 'Dem no know how fe run de country. Look how dem mash-up de place.'

There were fewer tourists on the north coast and almost none to be seen in Kingston. The new faces on the island were those of Cubans. Castro sent workers to Jamaica to build schools and clinics. The Cubans worked quickly and efficiently, and their discipline made people suspicious. In spite of all evidence to the contrary, people said these Cubans were really soldiers and that communists were 'tekin' over' the island.

Karl showed his usual disinterest in partisan politics. One government was as bad as the other as far as he was concerned. He didn't say a word against the Manley regime even though the army had mistakenly shot down a plane he had chartered for his archaeologists. But he found it amusing to test Ida's faith every morning at breakfast.

'The Kingston Sheraton is closing,' Karl said, reading the morning paper. 'Looks like everyone's closing down and leaving.'

'Only white people are leaving,' she said. 'I'm not white. May's not white.'

May looked up from her breakfast at her mother. 'When did you become black? When Manley came to power?'

'Don't be fresh. I've always been proud of my color.'

'What color?' She exchanged an amused glance with Karl.

Ida wagged a finger at May: 'Ah-ah, little mongoose. Don't forget where you come from.'

'It's nothing to do with color,' Karl said, still reading the paper. 'It's the violence that's scaring everyone.'

'Don't you think the newspapers exaggerate?' May asked.

'No,' he answered.

Ida gave a little sigh; she had to agree with Karl. 'It's not just the killing – it's the *way* they're killing. Savage,' she said.

The stories of violence reached them, but the violence itself hadn't. Ida would look over at the Blue Mountains and say it was because Oni was up there watching over them. It seemed that way to May too, that the mountains were a barricade, the only thing between them and the troubles in Kingston.

With her diploma in sports education, May got a job teaching PE at her old high school. She taught all the swimming classes and a required class called physical hygiene – everything from hand-washing to birth control. She took a taxi-boat to Port Antonio every morning, and on her way to work she'd look across at the unused land that jutted out between the two harbors – the old Folly ruins. That was where she imagined the National Sports Institute would be built.

For the first time, she used her connection to the wealthy and important Joseph-Hannas in order to arrange a meeting with the deputy prime minister. He had gone to school with Peter Hanna, one of Ida's cousins. Another of the Joseph-Hanna cousins, Keith Joseph, was chairman of the Olympics committee ('handsome Keith' was how May thought of him, and they had started going out).

It happened that the government wanted to host the next Commonwealth Games. A sports institute like the one she proposed, one that would train West Indian athletes and physical education teachers and also provide Olympic-sized facilities, was appealing. The government had no money for the project. However, the Cuban government had the manpower and technical resources. Within three months of meeting May, the deputy prime minister consulted a team of Cuban architects and engineers.

Karl advised May, 'Governments come and go. Try to get private financing.'

'Do *we* have the money?' she asked him. 'Do I have an inheritance I can borrow from?'

'You'd spend your own money on this?' he asked, astonished.

'Did I say something wrong?' she asked her mother later. 'Was it tactless to ask about inheritance?'

'I've asked Karl about it before – everything he has will be yours.'

'You mean I'm an heiress?' May smiled. Memories of historical novels absorbed her for a moment. *Miss Bottomsworth, a Creole heiress, had just arrived in Bath. She was supposed to have a considerable fortune, including her father's West India estate . . .*

'Of course. Who you think he was going to leave this place to, the dogs?'

The violence in Kingston grew worse. There were reports now even in the foreign newspapers. May saw a clipping from the *New York Times* of men in paramilitary uniforms shooting automatic rifles on a Kingston street. It seemed unreal to her, a mistake, a picture taken in another country.

'It makes no sense,' Ida said one morning. 'How can people go on living in Kingston?'

Karl said, 'Having to lock yourself in and hide in your own home isn't living.' Then he saw how troubled she was. 'Maybe you should stop reading the newspaper, Ida.'

'People are still going about their lives just like always,' May said. She'd been in Kingston just the day before to see handsome Keith. He'd invited her out to dinner; she'd stayed over at his apartment. Yes, life, dinner, sex, and other good things were still possible in the capital. 'We can't let the news frighten us.'

But then there was news that did frighten her. Florence, who always had the radio on in the kitchen, came out to the breakfast table: 'Gunmen kill 'bout twelve people at the Trench Town concert last night.'

Derek had been performing there. It was a reggae concert for peace.

Florence brought the radio into the dining room and they all listened throughout the morning. Derek called May later. He hadn't been on stage at the time of the attack. But it had shaken him. Four musicians, friends of his, were dead.

'I not staying here no longer,' he told May.

He left Kingston and rented a house in Port Antonio.

'It's not even politics anymore, it's just brutality,' he said

May was still optimistic. She told him, 'They started building the sports institute.'

The Cubans had come with trucks and machinery to Port Antonio. The land had been cleared.

Derek said, 'Dem start, but dem no finish yet.'

'He's right,' Karl said. 'Don't get your hopes up.'

But the Cuban builders were diligent; they worked even

on weekends. From the upstairs veranda at Bella Vista, May could see the new walls going up near the Folly ruins. She was helping to build something. Something she could actually see from there, a new thing that slightly changed the view.

'What happened?' May asked. She found Ida and Karl sitting on the upstairs veranda looking worried. Saturdays there was usually a huge breakfast that went on till about noon. Sometimes friends like Father Reynold would come by; there'd be mimosas, Bloody Marys – typical Jamaican dishes like escoveitch fish, green bananas, ackee and salt fish, breadfruit, johnnycakes. All of it prepared the day before because Florence had Saturday morning off.

'Those two Americans,' Karl said. He meant workers from the embassy who had been kidnapped. 'They found them murdered.'

'They might close the embassy,' Ida said. There was something else.

Karl and Ida looked at each other, and Ida said, 'Tell her. We're all in this together.'

'The investors want to pull out,' Karl said.

She knew he was talking about the *Capitana-Santiago* project. 'What you going to do?' May asked.

'Try to convince them to stay or find new investors. I'm leaving for New York in a few days.'

'It seems like a bad time to try,' Ida said.

'I know.'

'Maybe hold off for a while,' Ida suggested gently. 'Wait till things are more settled.'

'I don't want to lose the divers or the scientists. They're committed.'

'You really believe the ships are there?' May asked. She had never had the heart to pose the question before.

'In bits and pieces maybe, yes.'

'Why is it taking so long?'

'Well, there's the depth and lack of visibility—' He saw May looking at him questioningly. 'And the sargasso, lots of it,' he explained.

'Sharks too,' Ida said.

Later, after Karl had gone down to his study and May had gone to the beach with the dogs, Ida put on a sunhat and a pair of gardening gloves and went outside. Some dead poinsettia leaves caught her attention and she was glad to have a task to occupy her while worries and questions flapped around in her mind. She picked the shriveled brown leaves from the stalks and noticed how hot it was and that it hadn't rained for two or three days. Not a drought coming on, she hoped; the country was in enough trouble. She'd tell Winston to turn on the sprinklers.

Karl was a good man, she told herself. She would hate to see him fail at anything he'd put so much time into, but something didn't feel right to her. One piece of an old ship – an English galleon, not Columbus's – was all that had been found in seven years. Karl had more than enough money. He owned valuable things and was still buying and selling artifacts. Just the other day he'd had a shipment from – where was it? – Colombia. It had included a gold container, quite beautiful, she thought; he had said it was worth about five thousand dollars. Why wasn't he content? When she tried to picture the *Capitana-Santiago* project, all she saw was murky water and divers tangled in monstrous seaweeds. Sometimes it was Karl she saw like that, all tangled up, drowning — a horrible picture. No doubt Columbus's last two ships had sunk there, but now they were lost. Some things were meant to stay lost. She wished she could convince him.

Sometimes Karl reminded her of her father; both men had entrepreneurial energy, but they also each had a shell they drew themselves into where they seemed to dream up the most far-fetched things. Men were so unstable. She remembered when her father had lost everything. A terrible time. She had come far from that; she was the wife of a baron, and they lived on an island worth millions of dollars. She reminded herself that even if one project failed, it wouldn't be the end of the world. On the other hand, if Karl was right and Columbus's ships were found, it would be like finding Noah's ark.

She saw May returning from the beach and reminded her that they had a dinner invitation at Nigel's.

'Is Karl coming?' May asked.

'No, he says he's busy.'

May and Ida knew that wasn't the only reason. There had been an incident involving Ian.

Since May had returned from Switzerland Ian had come frequently to Navy Island, turning up unexpectedly at all hours like before. He didn't need a key. Doors weren't locked at Bella Vista, a fact Ida was proud of at a time when people were putting iron grillwork around their verandas in Kingston.

But one morning Karl and May, following the barking dogs, found Ian on the beach with two men. They had sleeping bags, the remnants of a meal, and ganja. It looked as if they'd camped out all night.

One of the men with Ian was Brasso. May hadn't seen

Brasso since that night long ago when she had gone dancing with Derek at the Back-a-Wall club. Brasso's eyes were bloodshot; he was high.

'Baron,' he called out to Karl.

The other man with them looked nervous.

Karl ignored Brasso. He turned to Ian. 'Ian, you've always been welcome here. But not in this state, not with these people. I'd like you all to leave.'

Ian walked up to Karl and attempted to look threatening. He was so stoned that he had trouble standing up straight.

May said, 'I'll take you home, Ian.'

Ian told Karl, 'Manley say no more private beach in Jamaica. This is the people's beach now.'

May reached for his arm; he pulled away from her.

'Come, *amigos*,' he said to the other two.

'Don't come back here again like this,' Karl said, and then, less harshly: 'Go clean yourself up, Ian.'

'No more private beach!' Ian shouted as they left.

'Is that true?' May asked. 'About the beaches?'

'It's just talk. Until it's made law, they're trespassers.'

Karl watched them walking toward the boathouse: 'Rascals.'

'Should I talk to Nigel about it?' May asked.

'Yes. Maybe he'll stop giving him money. Force him to get a real job.'

Ian had sold one painting in three years and he'd been so discouraged that he'd stopped painting. Now and then he made and sold tie-dyed T-shirts to the tourists along the north coast.

When he was just on his own with May, Ian behaved like his old self. They sat at Treasure Cove one day and Ian sketched as they chatted.

'Why you hang around with Brasso?' she asked. 'He seems a bad type.'

'Karl brainwashing you.'

'No, he isn't. I can tell bad from good. You know Brasso gave my father a lot of trouble once.'

'You father?'

'Flynn. Brasso threatened him. He threatened to burn down Bella Vista.'

'Chu, Brasso awright, man. Him check fe me,' Ian said, sliding easily into Jamaican dialect. He looked up at her from his sketch. 'You writing anything these days?'

She laughed. ' "I Sabine will tell you how I came to be on this desolate island—" '

'I thought it was irie. Dad says you should write a book about your life.'

'I've only been alive for twenty-five years.'

'Write a children's book. About our adventures. Remember that map we kept lookin' for, the one you father showed you?'

'Yes.'

'Suppose—' He stopped for a moment to look at his sketch. 'Suppose it's really here someplace. Even if it's not a treasure map, it might be worth something.'

She shook her head in disagreement. 'Was there anywhere on this whole island we didn't look?'

'Maybe it's not *on* the island.'

So Karl stayed at home while Ida and May headed out to the Fletchers' for dinner. Ida drove. May was in a bad mood. She was peeved at having just ended things with handsome Keith. It had lasted almost two months; then she'd discovered he was sleeping with another woman and, worse, lying about it. 'A lying, conniving snake,' she told Ida now.

'I was worried he might be a womanizer. Warm hands. Too warm,' Ida said. 'But I thought maybe — well — if anybody is a match for that kind of man, it's you.'

Ida really had hoped Keith would 'turn out better.' She wanted May to settle down with one person and have some joyfully distracting children. There was a destructive, depressive side to her that was like her father. She chose the wrong men, older men, married men, unmarriageable men.

'You talked to Nigel?' Ida asked.

'A couple days ago. He cheered me up.'

'You tell him about handsome Keith?'

'No.'

Since she'd come back, May had talked to Nigel on the phone almost every day. Talk, that was all it was, all it would be. But five minutes of conversation with him was more satisfying to her than any time she'd ever spent with a lover in or out of bed. Sometimes she thought she'd given him up too easily, that she should persist even now. 'Look, Nigel,' she could say, 'I'm giving you another chance — choose me.' Or she could offer unconditional love: he didn't have to divorce Denise for her; she didn't need him to make any big changes.

One day she joked with him: 'Nigel, why don't you let me — you know?'

'I'm sixty-five and wheezing.'

'You wouldn't have to do anything—'

'My dear, the word is *couldn't*. Old age is a terrible thing — but it's nice of you to ask.'

'What about a game of Scrabble, then?'

He was the one to keep the wall in place between them. 'Love then, but love within its proper limits' was one of the sardonic lines from *Don Juan* they tossed back and forth. But if a few days passed and he hadn't heard from her, he'd have to call. After a minute or so, they'd be laughing or at the very least making each other smile.

In the car now, May was telling Ida about the book Nigel was working on.

Ida said, 'I see you always writing in that diary. Maybe you should think about being a writer like Nigel.'

'Writing spy novels?'

'You could write something historical like *The White Witch of Rosehall*.'

The White Witch of Rosehall was a popular story of a white Jamaican slaveowner named Annie Palmer who was said to have practiced obeah, tortured slaves, and murdered three husbands. The book, one of the earliest Jamaican novels, was sold in souvenir shops at the airport, and Annie Palmer's plantation house had been restored as a tourist attraction.

'That's not history,' May said. 'It's a lie.'

'Annie Palmer was a real person.'

'She was a woman trying to run a sugar plantation all on her own; that's why they made up those stories about her.'

'Where you get these ideas?' Ida asked. 'You don't think she had sex with her slaves?'

'So did all the men who owned plantations.'

'You have a point. But it's still history.'

Nigel had disheartening news for them that day. He was leaving Jamaica. He'd been diagnosed with emphysema and the only way to prevent its getting worse was to leave the humid climate.

It shocked May, not just the news but the way he told her with Ida there as a buffer between them. Ian was there too but in that airy way of his that didn't seem to register changes.

She found it hard to be there with Nigel and Ida. After dinner she went down to the jetty with Ian to smoke a joint and then took the boat out with him, sailing upwind till Santiago de Cuba was in sight.

It wasn't just because of his health, Nigel told Ida; the political climate worried him.

'That's in Kingston,' Ida said. 'Nothing's changed here on the north coast.'

'It's all changing,' he said. Through the window he saw Ian and May heading out on the boat. He kept looking until he couldn't see them anymore on the water.

She found herself blurting out her own concerns: 'Karl is worried too, but he's not saying anything. I don't see how the project can go on. It's hard enough believing in this country the way things are, much less in some old bruk-down things at the bottom of the sea.'

She saw Nigel smile at her calling the prized shipwrecks 'bruk-down things.' His breathing sounded labored; he was having a bad day.

'Don't worry about Karl,' he said. 'He's practical. If he doesn't find new investors, he'll stop.'

'You think so?'

Nigel nodded. 'I've never liked him but I wouldn't call him stupid.'

'You're right,' Ida said.

They were quiet for a while, then Nigel asked, 'So you and Karl are going to weather things out here?'

'I can't imagine living anywhere else.'

'Neither can I,' he said.

Later, as Ida and May were leaving, he squeezed May's hand and assured her, 'We'll talk. I'm not going for at least a month.'

'It's his health,' Ida said to May on the way back to Navy Island. 'He'd never leave if it wasn't for his health.'

They saw army jeeps on the road, heading in both directions. When they got back to Bella Vista, Karl told them that a State of Emergency had been declared.

Three months went by. Christmas came and went; the year 1975 ended, and Nigel kept delaying his departure. Denise came in the first few weeks of the new year and finished the packing herself.

'I know he doesn't want to go,' she said. 'But he's got to. He'll die if he doesn't get to a better climate.' Ida and May agreed that it was the first time they'd seen any sign of Denise caring about anyone else. She'd even given up smoking because of Nigel's emphysema. After she arranged the shipping, she was to go back to Switzerland to wait for Nigel, who would follow in a few weeks. 'Maybe I should stay and travel with him, just to be sure.' She said this with a tinge of exasperation, as if she couldn't stand herself in the role of concerned wife.

'Don't worry, Mum, I'll make sure he gets on the plane,' Ian said.

May went to Oracabessa to spend a day with Nigel. 'I'm coming to take you sailing,' she'd said. But when she got there he said he had 'a million things to do' and suggested that she go with Ian. He'd been letting her down like that more and more, pulling back from her, practicing distance.

'Just you an' me left,' Ian said to her on the boat. They drifted near the coral reef, keeping the house and Oracabessa's cliffs in sight.

'You ever think of living in England like Martin?' she asked.

'No, man, when I go 'way I miss Jamaica too much.' His Jamaican accent had finally conquered the English one.

He still smoked ganja but had promised May that he'd stop using other drugs. Both he and May had recently had shocking news about people they knew. Ula's body had been found washed up by the sea, and the autopsy had shown a cocaine overdose. It turned out that she'd been working as a prostitute to pay for drugs. Some people thought her pimp had killed her. Poor, quiet Ula was how May thought of her from the days when they'd shared a room in Miss Gloria's yard. Ula's mother had never come back from the States to be with her as May's had.

Tara Flynn had also died young; officially the cause was heart failure.

May thought about how all three of them – she, Ian, and Tara – possibly shared the same father, like kittens from the same litter, raised in separate families. When she and Ian were about ten, Martin, in some vile mood, had told them, 'I know a secret about you two buggers. You've got the same father – you're brother and sister.' They'd made a pact, she and Ian, not to let their parents know they'd found out.

'Life in the tropics!' It was a lighthearted expression meaning – what exactly? Things not working out in the proper fashion the way they did in the temperate, industrial world. Putting up with malfunction, intemperate climate, intemperate people. 'Life in the tropics' seemed applicable to this kind of family muddle too, or at least to the unspoken acceptance of it. Maybe it was 'all the fault of that indecent sun,' as Byron had written, as if on arriving here white men shed their scruples along with their warm clothes. And what about the children they left scattered about?

What did Ian actually do? May often wondered. How did

he occupy himself? She'd once heard a rumor that he smuggled drugs. May didn't believe it. Ian wasn't brave enough for that sort of thing.

But that day on the boat, he did tell her a secret. He was gay.

'But I've seen you with girls.' There'd been Ula for a while and – she tried to think of others but realized there had been very few.

'You know what they do to us in Jamaica? You hear the songs they sing 'bout "batty-man"? I could tell you stories.'

He was scared, yet it seemed to May that he took such risks. He was telling her about picking up men on hotel beaches.

'Is it a want or a need?' she asked him.

'Both,' he said. 'Isn't it that way for you?'

'Yes. But I wouldn't want to if I had to hide it or be afraid.'

'Yes, you would,' he said. She'd told him about her one-night stands in Europe, men she'd met on trains and in bars, and recently, men at hotel bars along the north coast.

'Maybe you're right,' she said.

She sat quietly, thinking about how they'd been friends before they'd even learned to talk. Now she felt like they were both a hundred years old.

'I feel so worn out here.' She pointed to her heart.

He lit a new joint and looked out at the horizon as he smoked. He seemed peaceful for a change, maybe because he'd finally told her. It was the same face she'd known practically all her life except for the stubble on his cheeks He had become so thin. His stomach caved in from not eating. He was always on some health diet, which was a joke considering all the dope.

She remembered how they used to have the same-sized feet as children and would play a game in the sand, stepping in each other's footprints.

'Ian,' she said, 'if we get old and haven't found the right one, you know, let's live together and keep each other company.'

'Yes, man, on Navy Island, and live off the fat of the land.'

'Maybe we'll find the buried treasure.'

'You Nazi father knows where it is.'

'Stop.'

He flicked the end of the joint into the sea, angry now at the thought of Karl.

Before she left, Nigel said to her, 'Look after Ian when I'm gone, will you? He's a bloody idiot, but I'm fond of him.'

28

The Republic of Ida

There was a going-away dinner for Nigel. Ida invited Father Reynold, Derek, and Ida's cousins, the Levys. Because of the State of Emergency's curfew, the guests arrived early that afternoon and were all staying the night at Bella Vista.

Florence made Nigel's favorite Jamaican meal: black-crab soup as a first course, followed by roast pork, baked plantains, rice with gungo peas, creamed callaloo, and for dessert a guava bread pudding. May chose a white Bordeaux for the first course, and Karl, unpredictably, opened a Rioja for the main course; he was usually faithful to French wines.

Everyone was being nice to everyone else; even Karl and Nigel seemed to be making an effort with one another. Karl was in a cheerful mood; he'd told Ida a week earlier that he'd found a new investor, so the *Capitana-Santiago* project was continuing. There had been protests, however, in the newspaper and on radio shows about foreigners trying to rob Jamaica of its heritage. 'How can we steal what we haven't even found yet?' was Karl's response.

Things were not working out as well for May. The building of the sports institute had stopped almost as soon as it had begun, and the Cubans had returned home. An election was coming up and there had been pressure on the government over the presence of so many Cubans. Some Cuban doctors had remained but all the construction jobs, which would have meant schools and clinics, had been brought to a halt. Whenever she'd look out from the veranda now, she'd see the unfinished concrete walls – new ruins next to old ruins.

'Karl was right,' she'd said one day to her mother. 'You can't trust any government.'

'Maybe, when things settle down a bit, you can get some private investors,' Ida had suggested. 'The idea is good; it's just the timing.'

Ida looked across the dinner table at her daughter and noticed that May had put some effort into looking pretty tonight. She wore lipstick for a change and gold hoop earrings, Mexican antiques that Karl had given her for her twenty-first birthday. She *seemed* happy, sitting between Derek and Father Reynold. Was it all for Nigel?

And Nigel, when he looked across at May, didn't seem to Ida like an aging man who had resigned himself to this parting; no, he seemed like a young man expecting an answer. Back and forth between them, hanging on glances and the avoidance of glances, there seemed to be some question, unknown to everyone but them. Was there actually a question, Ida wondered – a question of staying, leaving, will-you-come-with-me – or just her own imagination, her fear?

She worried constantly about May. It was always the same worry – that May would end up a wreck. Ida felt that May's beginnings had put her at a disadvantage – fatherless, illegitimate, left in a tenement yard – and that she, Ida, was to blame. She had done all she could to raise May's standing in life, and she had succeeded: May was the stepdaughter and heir of a baron. But there were things beyond Ida's control; she had seen a frightening side of May. Like her father, May had no clue how to rescue herself from sadness; she let it drive her into disarray. May entered the most unstable kinds of relationships when, in fact, she needed a loyal, committed man to look after her. When May had fallen for one of the Cuban engineers, Ida had asked her, 'What's the point? Are you going to go live with Juan in a communist country?' May had shot back, 'Was there a point when you fell in love with my father?' Ida had convinced Karl to invite one of the divers from the project for dinner one day – a man about May's age, unmarried, a lover of water sports. But May had refused to meet him; she'd gone to see Nigel that day. 'Well, I give up,' Ida had told Karl. 'Good,' he'd said. 'You worry too much.' Yes, and she worried now because she knew how wrongheaded a woman in love could be.

'These things aren't random. They're all well planned.' The voice of her cousin, Aaron Levy, interrupted her thoughts.

There had been new horrors in Kingston in spite of the State of Emergency's curfews and roadblocks: the Peruvian ambassador and his family had been murdered in their home.

Aaron continued, 'They get these boys, organize them into posses – that's what they call them now – pay them fifty dollars each—'

'Fifty dollars?' Ida looked astonished.

'You can hire a killer for less nowadays,' Antoinette Levy told her. 'A coffin is worth more than a life now, let me tell you.'

'They give them drugs so they turn savage,' Aaron explained.

'Jamaicans are not an intrinsically violent people,' Nigel said.

'That's what I'm saying. It's the drugs.'

'Drugs don't explain it. The sadistic nature of the attacks — it's so un-West Indian,' Nigel insisted.

'It's the CIA,' Father Reynold said.

'Chu! That makes no sense,' Aaron Levy said. 'It's in the best interests of the United States to keep things safe here.'

'Not if they want to overthrow Mr Manley's government,' Derek suggested.

'Ah, you've been reading Nigel's novels,' Karl said. 'You think Jack Blaze will parachute onto the prime minister's lawn one night?'

Nigel leaned back in his chair, amused. 'I'd call that a very weak plot.'

'And he knows a thing or two about plots.' May smiled across the table at him.

'Let's drink to Nigel and to Jack Blaze,' Ida said.

Everyone drank.

'It's not just Jamaica,' Antoinette Levy said mournfully. 'Look at the Middle East. You remember Brian Hanna?' She turned to Ida. 'Your father's brother-in-law who owned the duty-free stores. He couldn't stand the violence here anymore so he and his wife went back to Lebanon after being here fifty years. A week after they were back in Beirut, bombs fell and destroyed the house next door to them. Now they're thinking of migrating to Canada.'

'Shame,' Aaron Levy said. 'You work hard, save up you money, and can't find nowhere to spend you old age. Jamaica was a promising place when our parents came from Lebanon. This is where they chose to live, this place, over France and America.'

'Jamaica spoil.'

'It's the drugs, man.'

'Well,' Father Reynold said, 'we have Navy Island. Maybe we should migrate here! A peaceful republic with good food, good company, and Ida as president.'

'Hear! Hear!' they cheered.

Ida smiled. The dinner party was going so well. There were no bad feelings, no food too tough or oily for the digestion, no stains on the silverware or cracks in the soup bowl, not even a creaky chair at the table; the tiles and furniture gleamed around her. Everything at Bella Vista was running smoothly. But she felt as though something were wrong.

Was it because Ian hadn't come? Ida thought Ian had put that incident with Karl behind him. He'd promised her over the phone that he would be there. Nigel seemed to still be expecting him; he'd tried to call him in Oracabessa and he kept checking his watch. 'I hope he's all right. It's a bit worrying, you know, with these roadblocks and everything,' Nigel told Ida.

Ian hadn't visited the house since the day Karl had turned him and that troublemaker Brasso away. But May had seen Ian; she had gone swimming with him down at the beach a few times. 'He's just avoiding Karl,' May had said.

Ida remembered the incident between Errol and Brasso years back. She had felt a bit sorry for the man; after all, he'd been attacked by one of those reptiles while working on Errol's film. She remembered that part of his bottom had been devoured, and there'd also been that humiliating rumor that the crocodile had castrated him. A calypso song had been made up about it — 'Brasso's ass-o' or some such thing. Ida wondered if it was true that the man's testicles had been bitten off. That would make anybody bitter, she thought. He had demanded a lot of money from Errol and had threatened him. Karl had eventually given him some money to go away. Now Brasso was back with bad Kingston ways, hanging around Ian.

Antoinette asked Ida, 'So you really don't have any burglar bars anywhere? Even in Ocho Rios, we have to close off the verandas.'

Karl answered, 'We have the dogs, and we've always had a night watchman.'

'I can't imagine burglar bars at Bella Vista,' Ida said. 'I would rather get a rifle and learn how to shoot than shut myself in like that.'

They drank a lot of wine and champagne, except for Father Reynold, who had given up drinking. Ida thought sobriety was very bad for him; he looked shriveled, like some poor animal that had been shorn for no good reason.

Since he wasn't drinking or playing dominoes, Father Reynold had no reason to stay up late with them. He went to bed early, and the Levys soon followed. But the rest of the party went out by the poolside to continue drinking and chatting. Karl put on an Ella Fitzgerald record. Nigel and Ida were recalling the 'old days.'

'I remember when they used to park donkeys outside the shops in Port Antonio,' Nigel said.

'They still do sometimes,' Ida said. 'They ride them down from the mountains.'

Derek proposed to May that they go upstairs to the game room and play pool.

'OK,' she said. 'But hold on a minute.'

' "Oh, Lady Be Good!" ' had just started playing. May went over to Nigel. 'Señor?' She'd had a good deal of wine and champagne and was feeling a little reckless.

'Señorita?'

'Dance with me.'

She put her arms around his neck and they danced, a little bit away from the others but within sight of them. Ida, Karl, and Derek had no idea how much they helped by simply being there. For May and Nigel, it was a relief to embrace in this accepted, open way rather than trying to snatch at some confused intimacy.

She was a little drunk and stumbled as they danced. 'Are you all right tonight, my dear?' he asked.

'Besotted,' she told him.

He smiled. 'Sleep it off.'

'Like hell! I goin' beat Derek at pool.'

'You awright, May?' Derek asked as they went upstairs to the game room.

'What? You think you can get out of this?'

He smiled. 'You goin' to be so sorry.'

He had taught her to play the game when she was about seven. She had to admit to herself that he was still the better player.

'It's your birthday soon, no?' May asked.

'Yeah, man, almost thirty.'

He had bought a house in Port Antonio, and he was about to release his first solo album. His dreadlocks reached beyond his shoulders and he had grown a goatee. He was such a good-looking man, it seemed strange that he remained single. She remembered that there had been someone a couple years ago – Reeza, Riza, Ariza? – a singer.

'You still not checkin' anybody?' May asked.

'Chu, I workin' all the time. Not everybody has time to play around like you.' He stood there grinning at her – boyish dimples and innocent, bushy eyebrows.

'Don't insult me in my own house. I have a job.'

'You know what I mean. You're a playboy.'

'*Girl*.' She bent over the pool table and lined up her shot. 'Anyway, what you talkin' 'bout?'

'Your reputation,' he said.

She hit a three-ball combination and sank two of them.

'For winning,' she said.

He smiled. 'You can't fool me with you tough act. I know the real May — just a sweet country girl, searchin' — searchin' for her place in the world.'

She laughed. 'It almost rhymes. Write a song about that girl.'

'I have. Several.'

She looked at him.

'Who else I goin' write 'bout? I don't have no family,' he said.

She knew what his childhood had been like, but she spoke harshly: 'What's family? They put us down in some yard to grow up by ourselves. An' look at us. Look what happened to Ula.' She stopped playing and looked seriously at Derek. 'You know who I blame?'

'Who?' he asked.

'Our parents. That whole generation. All they cared 'bout was sex an' power an' now that's all we have. We can have sex anytime we want. We have power to blast ourselves to pieces.'

'I never knew you had all this speechifying in you, May. You should go into politics.'

'I'd rather drown,' she said.

'That's the problem. You want to blame. But you don't want to take responsibility.'

'Because I'm not responsible.' She felt she could use a drink or some herb right now and wondered how Derek remained so pure in an industry full of ganja-heads. 'Let's go swimming.'

'Now? At night?'

'It's not against the law.'

'I don't have swimming things.'

'We have extra.'

Ida came in. 'Who won?'

'Nobody,' May said.

'A draw?'

They didn't answer. Ida opened the jalousie doors to the veranda.

'What a night, eh?'

May and Derek followed her. Nigel and Karl were downstairs about to take a walk. Karl was telling the dogs to 'stay' because they wanted to follow him.

'Those two look like they're finally getting along,' May said.

'Yes. Nigel suggested a walk. I'm a little worried, though – Karl's cigar and Nigel's emphysema.'

'He'll be all right. We're going to the beach. Come on,' she told Derek.

Left alone on the upstairs veranda, Ida looked across the water. Clive's taxi-boats were in for the night. Except for a few policemen who seemed to be strolling rather than patrolling, there was no sign of the State of Emergency there at the harbor. For the first week there had been the whole commotion of army and police jeeps pouring dozens of uniformed men onto the streets and the wharf. Completely unnecessary, Ida thought. There was no violence, no partisan ugliness in Port Antonio; it was a quiet, old-fashioned place.

At West Harbor a ship was at anchor, a rare sight these days, and Ida could make out a scraggly line of women under the wharf lights, all of them carrying bananas on their heads. It was so different from the noise and bustle she remembered as a child. Port Antonio had been a vital place then. Now hardly anyone knew about the town.

She could see the figures of some sailors going down the gangplank and moving among the women. There was a burst of laughter, so out of place in this spiritless scene. And then another burst of laughter – but this one was nearby. It was the children (she still called them that in her mind), May and Derek, walking by Cassava Piece and exchanging some humorous words with Winston.

Winston sat on a little stool outside his room. Ida remembered him getting quite angry one day when May and Ian were children; he had brought them to her, roughly holding each by the wrist: 'Dem pull up all the red ginger in de yard, ma'am.' 'What you think we should do with such bad children, Winston? Beat them?' 'No, ma'am. Mek dem plant back every single one. Dat will teach dem to tek care.' That seemed such a long time ago. Was age catching up with her? She was only a little over forty. There wasn't a gray hair on her head.

Ida-Rider, his voice crept up suddenly, a sound more real than the fading murmurs of May and Derek and the footsteps of Karl and Nigel on the gravel. She felt as though she'd been called out there tonight to hear and to witness the scene – the big foreign ship and the yielding beauty of the harbor. The night seemed to have a question for her. What was it?

Something wasn't right, May thought, as she passed Nigel and Karl on the way down to the sea with Derek. The two older men, sitting on the bench near the tennis courts, did not seem to her to be having a pleasant chat, but it was hard to tell whether they had been confiding in each other over some troubling matter or arguing. Nigel managed to smile weakly at her. Karl looked solemn. She wondered if they were discussing Ian's problems.

At the beach, May and Derek took off their shoes and walked through the cool sand.

'You serious about swimming? It's so dark.' Derek looked out at the sea.

'It's the best time. You'll see.'

'What you doing?'

She had taken off her clothes and stood before him, stark naked.

'May, have some respect.'

'Chu man, in Europe everybody swims nude,' she said.

'We're not in Europe.'

'What happen? You shy?' she reached out and pulled teasingly at the waist of his pants.

He held her firmly by the shoulders. 'Why you actin' like this?'

'I just playin' with you, Derek. Why you have to screw up you face at me?'

He let go of her and walked away. She went into the water, angry. *Let him go, then*, she thought; she was tired of all his self-righteousness. Who was he to judge her? She saw him heading across the sand, about to disappear from sight, and she felt sad. It was an ugly way to end their evening.

'Derek!' she called out. 'Come back, no?'

He turned back and sat on the beach. After a while, he joined her in the water.

'I'm sorry,' she said as they both floated on their backs

looking at the stars. She wondered if he felt better now, if he were pleased that she'd called him back here where he could see the whole sky above them.

'Is awright.' His voice was soft and forgiving.

The night air billowed around them like a dark cloth. She sensed him not far from her and thought about how weightless their bodies were on the bobbing water, and he thought about how fearless and unguarded she was in the water and how different she was on land.

Winston sat outside his wooden house, drinking a Guinness, wondering how long he was going to go on living at Cassava Piece. His transistor radio was playing, and he could hear Dennis Brown singing, 'Money in my pocket, but . . .' He usually didn't listen to the young people's music, but this song had an old-fashioned sweetness.

His mind drifted from the words of the song to the things worrying him. Yes, it would soon be time to stop working at Bella Vista. He was sixty-two, and he missed his wife, who lived twenty miles away. Also, he was losing patience with the young people nowadays; they had no respect. This time it was Young Gloria, the maid (they called her that because there used to be an older woman working there also named Gloria). The way she cussed all the time was getting to be quite unpleasant.

He was waiting for Florence to finish washing dishes up at the house so he could have a talk with her about Young Gloria. He hoped she wouldn't be too tired. Then again, maybe he shouldn't bother the poor woman; she had her own troubles. She'd had news that her sister in America was sick in hospital. Well, maybe he would stay up and see if she wanted some solace from an old friend.

~

At the gatehouse, the new night watchman was chatting with Young Gloria and had the same Dennis Brown song on the radio. She had brought him some dinner and wore shorts that hugged her bottom.

'I like you structure,' he told her.

'Chu man, tek it easy,' she said. 'Me hear seh you 'ave woman over deh a-land. Me no wan' ketch in a fight.'

Florence had warned her about this watchman – 'Him have a long eye an' a quick mouth.'

Young Gloria walked away from him knowing his eyes were fastened on her behind. He was a strong, good-looking man; she smiled to herself, imagining the weight of his body on top of her. How long before he would be in bed with her? she thought. Two, three days?

Ida was still on the veranda. The scent of jasmine and frangipani drifted up. May had remarked that Nigel and Karl seemed to be getting on well. Ida wondered about that. She wished she hadn't told Nigel her worries about Karl's project. She was afraid Nigel might bring it up now and that their walk would turn awkward. Karl would be upset if he knew she was talking to Nigel about him.

'Good-night, ma'am.' It was Florence going home.

'Good-night, Florence. Thank you for the delicious dinner.'

Downstairs the dogs waited for Karl, cocking their ears now and then, anticipating him. They had grown old, Hans and Olga. Hazy and Lazy, she'd nicknamed them, for Hans was blind in one eye and Olga was much too fat. But they were sweet dogs. They were devoted to Karl and to May and had even come to expect their share of affection from her, coming over and resting their chins on her lap.

Somewhere out in the water, May and Derek were swimming. Her thoughts went out to them. Were they chattering away and laughing like they used to do as children? She hoped so. What she couldn't know was that at that very moment, Derek was trying to disregard May's nakedness, telling himself it was some inoffensive attitude she'd brought back from Europe, this nude swimming; still, it bothered him; and May, floating on her back, her nipples small dark points on the water's surface, was feeling horribly self-conscious and silently berating herself. From where she stood, Ida couldn't see or hear May, but May permeated her.

Motherhood: it was like a fire that had melted her down and recast her. She had done everything she could for May — even that hateful absence from her had been done out of necessity, and this place, Bella Vista, was for her too.

A single flame was burning down at Cassava Piece. Florence and Winston sat outside talking by the light of a kerosene lamp. They talked about the things that vexed them: food prices, the rudeness of certain young people, where they would go when they stopped working at Bella Vista, and whether they would be able to manage with their little bit of savings. 'Long time ago, me sister tell me to join her in America,' Florence said. 'Now Manley 'im mash-up everyt'ing, an' de money me 'ave in de bank wut'less. Can hardly buy bus fare much less plane ticket.'

'An' we not as bad off as some people,' Winston reminded her. 'At least we have place fe live an' food fe eat.'

About a hundred yards away from them, on the bench by

the unlit tennis court, Karl and Nigel were quietly talking, Karl smoking a Montecristo and Nigel, against doctor's orders, a Craven A.

Ida continued to stand on the breezy upstairs terrace, the highest point of the little island, wondering why life hadn't turned out more simply for her. Why couldn't she be standing here now with the man she'd fallen in love with so long ago?

It couldn't have been a more perfect tropical night, with the sweet, fresh air and the calm sound of the waves, and yet every human being on that island was agitated.

When Nigel left two weeks later, he asked that no one come to the airport to see him off.

He told May, 'Let's not bother with all that airport dreariness.'

May wasn't sure whether he was avoiding an emotional good-bye or if it was vanity. He was in poor health. He'd fallen on the jetty while getting out of his boat one day and broken his hip. His emphysema had also taken a turn for the worse. He had arrived in Jamaica in 1947, an energetic, handsome former World War II officer. Now, thirty years later, he was leaving in a wheelchair with a tube to help him breathe, disenchanted with his adopted country.

And so without fanfare or proper good-byes, Nigel left the country. One local journalist, a man of the old school and former World War II soldier himself, noted Nigel's parting and wrote about him in an editorial: 'His Jack Blaze novels brought glamour to the island.'

May was struck by the word 'glamour.' It was a favorite word of Nigel's. 'Glamour,' he'd once told her, was an ancient

Scottish word for 'grammar,' and in former times both these words, 'glamour' and 'grammar,' had meant the ability to decipher symbols, cast spells, bewitch.

The word suited men like Nigel and her father, she thought, both of them drawn to the tropics, residing here for years, then leaving behind ghosts of the high life: anecdotal nights of drinking, pool parties, beach parties, yachts, idolized lives of wealth and pretty companions. It did seem like a kind of charm or spell. But had the island cast a spell on the men or had the men cast a spell on the island?

29

Karl's Shipwrecks

There was a reggae song called 'Two Sevens Clash' that played often on the radio in 1976. It invoked a prophecy uttered decades earlier by the Jamaican black nationalist, Marcus Garvey, that apocalyptic violence would occur on July 7, 1977. The song followed May everywhere. Even when it wasn't on the air, she heard its predictive wail. It seemed to saturate the fears of the whole population. And yet it was personal, like a warning Oni might have given her: 'Bamba yay!'

1976 was an election year, and Jamaica was in a state of undeclared civil war. One faction strove ferociously to get rid of Prime Minister Michael Manley and the other to keep him in power. Neither of the two political parties took responsibility for the violence, and it was hard to trace its origins back to the politicians. It was easier to blame the ubiquitous, nameless 'gunmen.'

There were other hit songs around that time, lamentations from Trench Town and the poorest parts of Kingston, with titles like 'Tenement Yard' and 'War Ina Babylon.'

Even in peaceful areas like Port Antonio and Navy Island it was hard to ignore the sound of Kingston's dread, blasting out from jukeboxes, shop doorways, and car radios. Sometimes it seemed to May that the pounding reggae was the only thing keeping pandemonium at bay.

It was hard to tell rumor from fact. Had there really been an attempted coup? Was the American embassy shutting down? There were so many stories of rape that it seemed to May as if the country were at war against women. Mothers begged gunmen to take them instead of their daughters. She'd heard that rich people sometimes bargained with the gunmen to spare the lives of at least one person in the family. Unimaginable stories like that reached May's ears.

The reports from Kingston upset her so much that she stopped reading the newspapers and would switch off the radio unless the station was playing Motown hits.

To calm herself, May took up gardening. She put in some new hibiscus plants, the kind they called coral hibiscus, with lacy red petals. She started a vegetable garden. 'You growin' enough callaloo to feed us forever,' Ida said. On Saturday mornings, May worked alongside Winston, digging, pulling up weeds, or pruning. Now and then Winston would say something like: 'Dem burn down a man's house in Morant Bay an' tek him wife—'

She would hold up her hand in a plea for silence.

'So much trouble over so, Miss May,' he would mumble.

'I know. But not here, thank God.'

Karl was more occupied than usual with his *Capitana-Santiago* project. Every day he was either at the site or on the phone to people about something concerning it. 'Something must be finally happening,' Ida told May. 'I might actually live to see those shipwrecks.'

Ida was full of strange, bustling, almost shrill energy. She was planning a big celebration in honor of Father Reynold's eightieth birthday. 'Yes, man, a big fete like we used to have.' There would be 'a whole heap a people,' she said, plenty food, rum punch, and a steel band.

'It's a dance party?' Karl asked one morning as if he hadn't been listening to these plans for weeks.

'What you mean?' Ida asked. 'Of course we goin' dance.' She was noticeably annoyed with him. They had been disagreeing with each other about everything lately, and she was in no mood to quarrel with him now about the party arrangements.

He watched her as she walked away.

May was on her way out the door. 'Father Reynold's a Trinidadian,' she told Karl. 'You can't give a party for a Trinidad man without calypso – even if he's a priest.'

'I suppose not,' he mumbled.

Karl loved music but hated to dance. He knew that for Ida dancing was a sensual pleasure. Nigel, her favorite dance partner, was gone. Obviously she didn't expect him, Karl, to dance with her. Was there someone else? Her friend Clive Goodman? He didn't believe this was all for Father Reynold – all this anticipation and expense and a steel band too? He hadn't been paying enough attention, he realized. There were urgent matters he had to attend to regarding the *Capitana-Santiago*, things he hadn't shared with Ida. He stood by the open door and watched her in the garden with Winston, her beautiful hand with its emerald ring pointing out something. There was nothing he would have liked more in that instant than to walk beside her, to roam pleasantly about this island with her free of all cares. But he was not without cares. Too many years of hope, effort, and money had been invested, too much to back out of right now. He continued to look at her talking to Winston and felt an indescribable sense of fear. She meant more to him than anything or anyone. He told himself that soon he would make up the lost time with her. Maybe even surprise her by dancing at the party.

Though the party was not until June, Ida had started preparing for it months in advance. She wanted to show Bella Vista at its best. There were two kinds of parties at Bella Vista: the small dinner parties of up to twelve people where there would often be a little dancing to favorite records toward the end of the evening. The second kind, the kind they were having for Father Reynold, was what Ida called a 'fete': anywhere from thirty to a hundred people roamed about the grounds. Invitation was by word of mouth; friends brought friends; there would be live music, vats of rum punch, and great big iron pots of food – curry goat, fish tea, rice-an'-peas, and so on.

One day May saw Ida inspecting the grounds with Winston and making a list of what needed to be done: the gate and garden walls needed a fresh coat of paint, cracked patio tiles needed to be fixed.

'While we're doing all this fixing up,' May said, 'don't you think it might be a good idea to put up some grillwork, just on the downstairs windows and doors?'

'I'll look into it,' Karl said.

'No,' Ida said. 'I don't want to live like that. We have the dogs. We have a watchman. And anyway, who's going to sail all the way over here to trouble us? Chu! You know how Jamaican people 'fraid a water.'

May felt reassured. Her mother spoke so confidently, and what she said made a kind of sense. The sea between Navy Island and Port Antonio was a bit like having a moat.

There was reassurance also in the unbroken routines at Bella Vista. Every morning, without fail, there were fresh flowers on the breakfast table, and the sounds of *Calypso Corner* and local news filtered in from the kitchen radio. Every evening after supper Karl gave the dogs each a bowl of vanilla ice cream; Mondays the washerwoman came to help Young Gloria with the laundry; Thursday nights Florence came in and watched *Bewitched* with Ida; Friday mornings fishermen sailed up to the island to sell them fresh fish.

Then one morning, about two weeks before the big party, the flowers were on the breakfast table, the radio was playing in the kitchen, but neither Karl nor Ida was there.

May went upstairs to find them. She heard them arguing so she hesitated before knocking.

'Come in,' Ida said.

Karl was fully dressed and sitting in his armchair; Ida was still in her nightclothes. Her hair was out and her skin looked very pale.

'Breakfast,' May said.

Karl spoke for them both. 'We'll be down soon.'

But they didn't come down. May ate her breakfast alone and went to work: she was having students try out for the intramural swimming team that morning and then there would be the usual scheduled swimming classes.

She left work earlier than usual that afternoon. She'd had to rescue a panicking twelve-year-old from the deep end of the pool. It had taken so long to calm the child down that May had decided to cancel her last two classes.

Driving to East Harbor, she saw Ian on the side of the road, looking as if he hadn't shaved or washed in ages. His hair was matted. He was very thin, and his baggy pants were tied with a piece of cord to hold them up. He was waving down cars, and she couldn't tell if he was trying to get a ride or to sell the bundle of tie-dyed T-shirts that he had with him.

'Wha' 'appen?' she said pulling up.

'Tryin' fe get a likkle transport. How far you goin?' He had completely absorbed the Jamaican dialect and looked like he was just one step away from becoming a Rasta.

'What happen to you car?' May asked.

'Me sell it las' week.'

'I not goin' that way. You need some bus fare?'

'Yes, man. Cyan sell no shirt today.'

'Buy you'self a patty and soda too.'

'Peace an' love, sista. Irie.' He kissed her on the forehead.

'You haven't been over in a long time. Come stay a few days.'

'Chu, Karl—'

'Is my house too. An' I'm inviting you, all right?'

A bus came around the corner.

'Run catch you bus,' she said.

She watched him waiting to board the bus, a head taller than everyone else in the robust little crowd, and it occurred to her how Jamaican he had become. The only remnant of his Englishness was the color of his skin.

When she got home, lunch was ready on the stove. There was no sign of either Karl or Ida, but Florence said, yes, they were both home.

May went looking for them. On her way down to Karl's study, she heard them speaking quietly. It sounded to May like a very private conversation or maybe another argument. She was worried when she went back upstairs.

She ate lunch in the kitchen with Florence, and they

chatted about the high prices and food shortages. They stopped when they heard Ida come up from the study and continue up the stairs to her room.

'They arguin' all day?' May asked.

'Me no know if is argue-dem-arguin' or jus' talk-dem-talkin'. Young Gloria couldn't clean the bedroom because dem upstairs all mawnin'.'

May took a walk after lunch, then took out her scuba-diving gear and swam out to the reef.

When she got back, Ida was down in the study again with Karl. She was used to them disagreeing, but this wandering from room to room all day long, so engrossed that they didn't seem to notice anyone else – this was unusual.

May went downstairs to them.

Ida turned to her: 'We have nothing left. He spent everything on those damn shipwrecks that don't even exist.'

The phone rang. Karl picked it up and spoke as calmly as usual. 'It's for you, May.'

May hesitated. She was still trying to absorb what her mother had just said.

'It's Ian,' Karl said.

'I'll take it in the living room.'

'May, you can lend me some money?'

'This isn't a good time, Ian.' She wondered why he hadn't asked her earlier when they'd seen each other.

'Jus' fe help me out likkle bit. You know how it go.'

He didn't sound quite like himself. She felt somebody was with him. 'How much?'

'Two hundred US.'

'I don't have any US dollars.'

'Ten thousand Jamaican, then. Yes?' He was making an

effort to sound nonchalant. 'I can come over early tomorrow an' pick it up.'

'I don't have that kind of cash here.'

'Borrow some from you old man.'

'It's not a good time, Ian. Some heavy t'ings goin' on here. Call you parents and ask them to wire some money.'

He hung up on her.

She decided to sit for a moment in the living room.

It was an odd name for it, living room, since it was the least lived-in room in the house. The sofa was hard and uncomfortable because no one sat on it. The bar was in the corner, and people came in and out of the room to mix drinks and take them out to the patio or the upstairs terrace. But it was precisely because the room was so neutral and characterless that it felt like the best place for her to be at that moment.

'We have nothing left,' her mother had said. How could there be *nothing?* That was ridiculous. Her mother had to be exaggerating. How often had she heard that Karl had millions? How could he suddenly have nothing?

She stretched her body out on the sofa. It was not a comfortable place to lie down. She remembered sitting in that room as a tiny girl the day she had met her father and sinking into a huge leather sofa. It was gone now, replaced by a yellow-cushioned, angular Danish sofa with matching armchairs. Karl and Ida thought it looked posh and modern, but it reminded May of the nondescript furniture in airports.

Ida came in. She went past May into the kitchen. May heard her speaking quietly to Florence. Then she went by again and walked purposefully upstairs.

'*Nothing left.*' What did that mean, exactly?

May went upstairs to her. She found Ida lying on the bed, gazing up at the ceiling. Ida, hearing her enter, said, 'I need to be by myself for a while. I have to think.'

May went to the kitchen for a glass of water, thinking she would take some water down to Karl too. Young Gloria was standing in the doorway, making no effort to hide the fact that she had been listening to all that was going on in the house. She stared at May as if expecting her to fill in the missing pieces.

'You don't have anything to do?' May asked.

Young Gloria cut her eye at May and went back outside to finish the laundry.

'Some lemonade mek this morning,' Florence told May.

'Good.'

Florence continued rinsing vegetables at the sink, her back to May.

'Too much bad feelin' in dis house today,' Florence said.

May sat on the stool by the stove.

Florence continued, 'I tell you, trouble everywhere in dis country. Me sister in New York ask me fe come, but me too ol' fe move.' She breathed heavily and then went on. Something was weighing on her: 'Mr Karl, him love Miss Ida. Me no know what him do her. Me no judge fe dat. Me only know wha' me know.'

May poured a glass of lemonade for Karl and went downstairs.

He was leaning back in his desk chair gazing up at the ceiling.

'What's going on?' she asked.

He looked exhausted. 'I'll tell you later, if you don't mind.'

'OK.'

For days the house was steeped in angry, hopeless silence. Karl slept in the study. He and Ida avoided each other and they also avoided May. No more meals were taken together in the dining room. Florence left food on the stove and they helped themselves, each at different times. Finally Ida roused herself and made phone calls canceling the party. There was a renewed sense of purpose about her but nothing had mended between her and Karl. She was frozen around him.

May found her on the upstairs veranda one evening watching the sunset. She didn't seem to mind May joining her. Across the water, the lights of Port Antonio were being turned on, including those of the Palace Theatre marquee, which could be partly seen in the distance.

'These men and their cockamamie dreams,' Ida said. 'They live in another world. Even my father. Thank God my mother had her head on straight.'

'Mama, we have to talk.'

'Yes, sit down,' Ida said. 'I've given notice to the tenants at Plumbago Road and I'm going to go there for a while, at least until I decide what to do. I can't stay here with Karl.'

'Why are you doing this to him?'

'You don't know the facts and you're taking his side.'

'What are the facts?'

She seemed unable for a moment to give words to what had shaken her. 'There were never any other investors. He's been lying all this time.'

May tried to absorb this. 'How do you mean "never"?'

'You don't know half of it.' She stopped and looked out again across the water. 'I still have my mother's house. That at least is mine. And yours too. You can come with me if you want.'

'Leave here?' May was shocked by the very suggestion. 'There must be something we can do?'

'There's no *we*. He didn't consult us when he put Navy Island up for sale. He plans to sell the Palace too. Go ask him. Let him tell you himself.'

Ida left the next day, taking just one suitcase of clothes and the clock that Clive Goodman had bought for her. The Plumbago Road house would not be vacant for another month, so she would stay with Clive's mother until then.

May spoke to Karl. 'Ma says you want to sell Navy Island.'

She tried to keep accusation out of her voice, but this was her home.

'That would give us the money to move somewhere more peaceful.'

'More peaceful than here?'

'Navy Island isn't a separate country, May. Things are getting worse all over Jamaica.'

'Where on earth would we go?'

He said nothing, and it occurred to May that the word 'we' was painful for him to hear just as it had been for Ida.

'I was thinking of the Cayman Islands,' he said.

'There must be something we can do for money.'

'I've already got a buyer.'

'Who?' When Karl told her the name of the prospective buyer, she laughed bitterly; she'd heard of the man, a Jamaican businessman who lived in Florida, rumored to have shady connections. He wanted to build a casino resort on Navy Island.

'There must be something less drastic we can do,' she said.

'I know you never considered leaving.' He looked at her sympathetically. 'But you should.'

'I don't want to.'

'Then you're as stubborn as your mother. We're not the only people in Jamaica facing this kind of thing. Hundreds of people are leaving their homes.'

'But not because they invested in sunken ships.'

He looked as though she'd hit him. She was sorry and she told him she was.

'It's all right,' he said. 'I know — it's a lot to think about.'

'We can work this out,' she said. 'And Ma will be back. She's just mad like hell right now and she wants you to know it.'

She stood on the upstairs veranda. It was just before sundown, and she could see the familiar outline of Port Antonio: the almost derelict harbor, the rows of dilapidated Georgian houses, and, set back among the trees, the ugly ruins of the Folly mansion. It was called that because of the foolishness of the builders, who had mixed the cement with saltwater. A New York millionaire, an heir to the Tiffany fortune, had built it as a holiday home for himself and his new wife. But like the proverbial house built on sand, it had collapsed. Near those ruins, May could make out that other fiasco, the unfinished walls of the government's sports institute project.

Directly ahead, facing her, were the cannons of Fort George, where Admiral Nelson had given orders to defend the country and empire. Teenagers went there at night now to smoke ganja and have sex; beggars and vagrants slept there, and the old, neglected fortress smelled like a public toilet.

Was Karl right about her being stubborn? Why did she want to hang on to it all, this house, this vista?

Two weeks went by and Ida didn't return. Winston and Young Gloria seemed distracted and apathetic. The household depended entirely on Florence, but even she looked glum and could not help starting or finishing whatever she said with the phrase 'since Miss Ida gone . . .'

Florence told May, 'This is not a happy place. It come like duppy live here since Miss Ida gone.'

Each day May's sense of the catastrophe deepened. Karl was looking into ways of keeping the property by mortgaging it to the bank, but the Jamaican banks were not doing well themselves. In the meantime there was that Jamaican mafioso millionaire, as May thought of the prospective buyer, eager to transform her home into a casino. The place would revert to its piratical origins, she thought, but with modern-day *boucaniers*.

One afternoon she was on the sofa, listening to the rain coming down hard. Karl was in Kingston for the day. The servants were sheltering under their own roofs. The dogs were asleep on the floor nearby. She could think of no reason to get up, and so she lay there for hours, her body inert but her mind striving, striving for a feasible plan. She imagined the rain outside beating the low stone walls of the garden, beating the mangoes and Otaheites on the trees. A hurricane would have made more sense to her than the human error that had brought them to this state.

Karl had once said that she was his heir, but what immediate claim or right did that give her? And was it just his word, his good feeling for her, or was there something legally binding? He'd been unforthcoming about the actual state of his finances when she'd asked for details. *How much do you have left in the bank? Do we have enough to pay Florence and the others?* It was so overwhelming. Her mind went blank like someone suddenly forced to evacuate a building.

She looked at her limbs hanging over the couch and at the floor tiles gleaming around her. Gray tiles. Cool under bare feet. They got slippery when people came in from the pool to get drinks at the bar. They were not supposed to do that ('How many times I tell you not to come inside with wet feet?' her mother used to say) but everyone did it all the time. It was silly to have the bar right there.

She remembered how enormous the tiles had seemed to her when she had first walked into this house.

'Where did you come from?'

'Port Antonio . . . I'm Eli Joseph's granddaughter . . . Where you come from?'

'Tasmania.'

Across the wet tiles, down the stairs, he led her to the cool, dark room.

'. . . show you something.'

A map — old and full of mistakes. 'This is Captain Bligh's map. He brought breadfruit trees to Jamaica.'

The map was valuable, he said. To whom? Not to her, seven years old. What did an old map have to do with him being her father? She had come there to see him.

Mutinous sailors and scallywag pirates, familiar faces from the pages of her childhood darted about in her mind. Was there nothing more to be inherited on the paternal side than legends of misbehavior?

That was what all her striving came to: lying down with an old memory, revisiting daydreams in which she dueled with charismatic men and tried to tear the secrets from their hearts.

~

Ida called May: 'I runnin' out of clothes. You can bring some things for me tonight?'

There was to be a party at Clive's new house. Ida was there helping him get ready.

'But when you coming back?' May asked.

'Karl and I are finished.'

It confounded May – her mother's ability to part from people she cared about when she thought it necessary, the way she had been able to leave May when May was only three, and now her husband. But what was also true was that Ida had come back that other time, to Jamaica and to her; and so May told herself that Ida would come back this time too. She kept these thoughts to herself and wrote down the list of things her mother asked for.

'What time you plannin' to reach here?' Ida asked.

'Around nine. I invited Ian to the party. Is that all right?'

'Of course. But come earlier. You can help me put up my hair.'

That was the last telephone call made to Bella Vista.

30

Besieged

This was what May remembered later when she spoke to Police Inspector Perkins about that night.

It was eight-thirty when she looked at her watch. She had been writing in her notebook and had lost track of the time. Derek was meeting her at East Harbor. She wasn't dressed yet and she still hadn't looked for the things her mother had asked her to bring.

In her mother's room, she noticed two things (this was what she remembered, not what she told the inspector as it didn't seem relevant to the case): it looked as though Karl had moved permanently to his study since Ida had gone. There were none of the usual signs of him: no robe, bedroom slippers, or indentation in his favorite armchair.

The second thing – something she hadn't realized before – was that her mother had a lot of crimson lingerie, not various shades of red but the one vibrant shade; it was a remarkable collection. Ida had said, 'Bring some nighties and brassieres' (Jamaican women of her mother's generation always said 'brassiere,' never 'bra'). May had hurriedly picked through the silky things, some of them slipping over the edges of the drawers onto the floor, things that smelled like Ida, that had cupped and clung to Ida. May thought with embarrassment about her own underthings: sensible white cotton and nylon things that she kept till they were completely worn down.

After her bath she couldn't find her dress, a white halter-neck gown that fell to her ankles (her mother had seen it in a magazine and had gotten the dressmaker to copy it. 'You look like a swan,' Karl had said when she'd first tried it on).

She had taken the dress down to the river that morning, where Florence was standing knee-deep in the water washing her own clothes.

'Do me a favor, Florence?' May had asked, handing her the dress. 'I want to wear it to the party.'

Florence had tested the fabric between her fingers.

'It should dry quick. Pray no rain come.' She had put the dress on top of her pile. Her skirt was hitched up between her legs, and the water on her dark hands glistened.

For a few moments, May, squatting down on the riverbank, had wondered what it would be like to have a life like Florence's, a life that was purposeful. She knew it had not been easy for Florence. She'd never married, and she worked hard to support her parents and many nieces and nephews. May admired her.

It was after nine when May walked down to Cassava Piece and knocked on Florence's door. 'Florence, you know where my dress is?'

'Oh, Lawd, me did forget to iron it. Wait mek me come do it now.'

'No. Is OK,' she said, though disappointed.

'No, no. It will jus' tek five minutes. Come.'

They went together to the laundry room, and that was when they heard the sound of a blast.

'Cedric bus'-up a tire,' Florence said. Cedric was the driver, boathouse keeper, and handyman.

May groaned. If it were a flat tire, she would be so late.

About five minutes later the electricity went. This happened at least once a week all over the country.

'Power cut!' Florence sighed. 'An' look, the iron was jus' heatin' up.'

May looked at her watch. It was nine-thirty. Derek would wonder what had happened to her, 'I'll just wear something else.' It looked like it would rain anyway and the long white dress would get muddy.

She put on jeans and a dressy black top, then went downstairs to say good-bye to Karl.

He was lying on the daybed listening to music on his portable record player.

'What time is it?' he asked.

'Almost ten.'

She had tried to call the boathouse to let Cedric know she would be late but hadn't been able to get through. She remembered the sound of the busted tire. Well, if Cedric didn't come for her, she'd drive Karl's Peugeot down to the boathouse.

'Going out?' Karl said. 'Be careful; it's so dark.'

'I think it's going to rain. By the way, something's wrong with the phone.'

He gazed at her but seemed to be considering something else. *He must miss my mother so much*, she thought.

'The first time I saw you – you were trying to hide behind your grandfather.'

'We didn't like each other.'

'No. Not at first.'

She thought he seemed especially distressed and wondered if she should leave him alone.

'This place really is your home,' he said.

She looked at him, not sure what to make of his sentimental tone.

'Go,' he said. 'We'll talk about it another time.'

She grabbed an umbrella and went out to the Peugeot. Karl was right about its being dark, much darker than usual, with the electricity gone and the strident breeze promising a storm.

She drove past the gatehouse wondering why Grant the nightwatchman was not there. No Cedric, no Grant. You would think a hurricane was coming, she said to herself.

She turned on the car radio; Dionne Warwick was singing 'Do you Know the Way to San Jose.' May sang along:

'Wuh-wuh-wuh-wuh-wuh-wuh-wuh-wuh-wuh-waaah-'

She pressed hard on the brakes. Winston was inches from her headlights. Had she hit him?

'Miss May, turn back! Gunman!'

'Get in.' She made a U-turn and headed back to the house.

'Dem kill Cedric down at the boathouse. Him tie up on the ground, dead.'

Through the rearview mirror she saw black shapes. The gunmen were on the driveway behind her.

When she got inside the house, she locked the door and pushed the sideboard against it. Karl came up from the study. He'd heard the dogs barking around the back.

'I'm going to bring in the dogs.' She started for the door. But then there were two gunshots, and the dogs were silent.

May felt faint. Through the jalousies, she saw the dark

shapes again, swift and ghostly, stepping in and out of the night. Karl and Winston were pushing furniture up against the doors.

'How many out there?' Karl asked Winston.

He shook his head. 'Five or six.'

'All of them have guns?'

'Me only see dem machete.'

They heard a scream that seemed to come from Cassava Piece. Florence? Young Gloria? There were more screams, prolonged and horrible.

Karl thought the phone at the boathouse might still be working. He told Winston to stay with May while he tried to make it down there, but Winston said no, he'd go. He knew a shortcut. He slipped out the kitchen door.

An upstairs window seemed not to break so much as blow apart. They heard movement up on the terrace, and a minute later the sound of something heavy being rammed against the front door.

'The dogs—' May wanted to believe they were still alive.

'Go down to the study,' Karl said.

'What about you?'

'I'm going upstairs for my gun. I'll be down soon.'

'Here.' She gave him her handbag which was still on her shoulder. 'Let them take everything.' She pulled off her gold bangles; they clattered on the floor. She'd heard that if you gave the gunmen enough money or jewelry they wouldn't kill you. 'Ida's jewelry,' she said, 'give it to them.'

'Go downstairs,' he said. He was calm, and that somewhat reassured her.

She went down and locked herself in the bathroom. Above her were the slow, irregular footsteps of people who enter an unfamiliar place. Now and then she heard a voice yelling out a question or maybe a command. She wondered where Karl was.

The handle of the door leading downstairs rattled. She prayed they would not manage to get downstairs, that she wouldn't come face to face with them. She could not bear the thought of their faces.

'Where de key?' someone growled. There was a pause and then the sound of something or someone falling hard on the floor above her, a sound that made her almost cry out. She was sure they had done something to Karl.

She felt that she couldn't stay there. She had to get help. There was a window in the bathroom. It was high up and seemed too small for her to fit through. She could hear them battering the study door. She heaved herself up and squeezed through.

Cassava Piece was on fire. Two men stood across from the blaze drinking beers. One of them threw something into the fire and there was an explosion. The fire grew, fitfully lighting up everything around her. She moved alongside the house and saw Karl through a window, sitting on the sofa, and she thought she saw his head bleeding. A man, vaguely familiar, stood over him holding a machete.

She inched nearer to the broken-down front door, not sure what she was doing, only feeling that she had to help Karl. He saw her, and then the man standing over him turned and saw her too. It was Brasso.

Karl stood up suddenly and lunged at Brasso, knocking him down.

'Go,' he shouted to May, but she couldn't move. She saw Brasso swing the machete at Karl and heard Karl shouting out to her again: 'Go!'

At the gatehouse, she saw Ian on the ground. He was holding his leg, which was bleeding.

'They shot me,' he said.

She helped Ian up, half dragging him along with her into the bushes. She knew a path that would take them down to the water.

'Quiet,' she whispered because he was crying. 'Get up. I can't carry you.' She kept pleading with him as she continued to help him along.

'Get on my back,' she said. He was heavier than he looked, and at first she almost stumbled. But he kept his arms tight around her neck. She was heading for Treasure Cove. There was usually a canoe tied up there.

Ian dropped onto the sand as soon as they reached the cove.

The canoe was not there.

Ian started to wail. 'I'm sorry. I'm sorry.' If she left him there, they would find him.

'We have to swim.' She pulled him into the dark water.

'I can't. I'm in pain. I'm in bloody pain,' he cried, but he began to swim, following her.

They had only gone a little way out when she heard him call out to her. She swam back to him. 'I can't. I'm going back,' he cried.

His face contorted suddenly with pain. His eyes rolled back, and he lost consciousness. She grabbed him and swam. Carrying him by water was easier than carrying him on land.

She saw the small, steady light of a boat moving on the water. It seemed to be heading for Navy Island. She shouted for help. There was a roll of thunder, and the waves suddenly rose, tossing her back. She shouted again.

Someone on the boat shone a flashlight out toward the sea. She stayed where she was, holding Ian and treading water.

Ian came to consciousness: 'My leg, I can't feel it.'

The rain began to beat down on them and the waves rose, tugging Ian. She grasped him tighter, but he had given up and she was pulled under with him. She pushed back up to the surface still holding him.

The boat's light came nearer. It was the only thing she could see. Ian's limbs flopped heavily around her.

'Here. Over here!' she cried but it was futile against the noise of the sea. She was treading water and still holding Ian. The boat's motor shut off suddenly and a flashlight shone out. She began swimming again, pulling Ian with her. The rain blinded her.

'Over there!' It was Derek on the boat.

She stopped and began to tread water again. A wave swelled up, taking Ian from her. She tried to grasp him, but he was pulled farther out. Then she lost sight of him.

'Ian!' she shouted.

'You swam,' was all her mother said when May woke up in the hospital. The words sounded strange, almost like a reprimand.

By the time the police had arrived at Navy Island, they'd found everyone dead except Karl. Now he was in a coma and there was very little chance that he'd survive. The doctors said that even if he came out of the coma, he would be completely paralyzed and never be able to eat or digest food properly again. He was also susceptible to pneumonia because of his injuries. They waited for him to die.

'They say he hears when you speak to him,' Ida said to May one day.

They were sitting in the waiting area outside his room. Nurses came and went along the hallway; attendants wheeled things in and out, all strangely unquiet compared to the despondent hush of patients and visitors. As far as May knew, Ida hadn't spoken to Karl, but she had been attentive, replenishing the flowers in his room, making sure the hospital staff were doing their best.

'You think he's worrying – about us?' Ida asked.

May didn't know.

'When you talk to him, tell him I'm all right,' Ida said.

'Why don't you tell him?' May asked.

'You don't understand.'

May was silent for a moment, and then she said, 'He disappointed you.'

'Yes,' Ida answered. There was more, of course, that she could try to explain. She could tell her daughter, *I came to trust him even more than I trusted my own father*. What May had said about disappointment was true. But that was only part of it. Yes, Karl had deceived her. But she had been false too and was now ashamed to think of the years of idolatry, the passion for Errol that she had secretly clung to, the shipwreck of a love that had never promised love in return. She had squandered her heart. But she wasn't ready to talk to May about these things. It was enough to feel them.

They sat quietly, not like mother and daughter but like two survivors of the same catastrophe.

A few days later Karl emerged from his coma.

May told Ida, 'He wants to go back to Bella Vista. So do I.'

31

Her Father's Map

It looked like a hurricane had swept through. The front door was down, furniture turned over and broken. But it was worse than a natural disaster because it was the destructiveness of men. Something heavier than the machetes, like an axe, had been used to smash things. One of the jalousie doors had been ripped off its hinges. May saw bloodstains on the sofa and graffiti-like writing across the walls, righteous-sounding oaths: BURN, SUFFER. Books had been pulled from the shelves, even photographs taken out of their frames, torn and scattered about.

'Good God!' the nurse said. Her name was Mrs Donovan and she had accompanied them back to Bella Vista.

She stayed for the morning and showed May how to care for Karl: the intravenous tubes, morphine, catheter, gauze dressings. To quench his thirst, May had to use strips of sponge soaked in icy water. But the refrigerator wasn't working; neither the electric lines nor the phone had been repaired since the attack. May would have to use the freezer down at the boathouse and make several trips there every day. She was grateful to Nurse Donovan for not mentioning what was obvious: that Karl would soon die, and that the house was unfit even for healthy people.

May washed him – not washing really but wiping, handling his body like a breakable object – and, to ease the embarrassment, she avoided eye contact with him. His spine was broken. There were stitched-up wounds on his neck, chest, arms, and hands, which May cleaned with peroxide and then rebandaged, and there were internal injuries she could do nothing about which were causing him to die.

That first night, she sat up awake in the room with him as he slept. She was glad that she had brought him home. He'd fought the intruders, killing two of them while suffering their machete blows and bullets. He had prevented them from setting fire to Bella Vista and had earned the right, she thought, to die peacefully in his own bed.

A little after midnight she was startled by the rooster's crying. The hen coop at Cassava Piece had been destroyed in the blaze of the attack; only the rooster had survived. She'd noticed that the creature had taken up residence on the downstairs veranda. Now she heard his agitated crowing and flapping of wings. Then footsteps along the gravel driveway. She sat up rigidly, listening. Someone entered the house.

There was a soft rap against the door before it opened. It was Derek. He whispered so as not to wake Karl, 'You rooster, him in a panic.'

Derek stayed two nights, taking turns watching Karl so she could get some rest. He didn't want to leave her alone there but he had a concert in the Bahamas. As he said good-bye, he held her a long time and said, 'May, May, May.'

Down the hill, then back up again, twice a day, with the ice for Karl. It would seem at times as though nothing around her had changed: the sea sounds, the white bougainvillea, and other landmarks insulating her from the shock of what had happened and the decisions she'd eventually have to make.

Clive Goodman brought Ida over on the boat every morning. She brought supplies – clean sheets, food, batteries, and news from Port Antonio. But she refused to leave the boat. May thought there was more fear than fury now in the way her mother acted. Ida considered the place a blight. 'I done with Bella Vista,' she told May. But now and then May noticed her gazing out at the island, her face smooth and quiet like a shell.

'May,' Ida said one day – and she spoke quietly so Clive, absorbed in his newspaper, wouldn't hear – 'you need to fix up you'self. When last you had a bath?'

May kept her hands clean like a nurse's hands but couldn't remember when last she had showered or washed the clothes she was wearing. Her hair was beginning to grow out and look matted. 'Maybe I'll turn Rasta,' she said.

'And that's another thing – is ganja I smell on you?'

'Karl waitin' for me up at the house,' May said, annoyed. 'You have anything else for me?'

Ida fixed her big, dark eyes on her daughter for a moment. 'I wonder if you goin' mad. You need to put this mash-up place behind you.'

Everyone thought Karl would pass away within a few days of returning to Bella Vista. 'Try to make him comfortable,' the nurse had said, and during those first days back May had moved about with a kind of insomniac lightness and energy.

But Karl had grown stronger.

The doctor came to see him; Father Reynold too. 'You missed you true calling, May. You could a been a nurse,' Father Reynold said, looking around the room.

She had made it pretty with fresh flowers and bright cloths.

'Coconut water? That's what you feedin' him?' the doctor asked.

Actually, she had begun giving him other things. But she thought carefully about what she should tell the doctor.

She had noticed how thirstily Karl sucked at the little sponges of ice water she placed at his lips. It had reminded her of the way he used to suck the marrow from bones — oxtail, fish, anything with meat around it — and of the enormous appetite he'd once had. She'd wondered if he still had his sense of taste, if he was perhaps hungry. So she'd sent for coconut water first, then papaya juice, and later, from her fingertips, because she was afraid the sponges might mar the flavor, she'd given him drops of fish broth, Italian espresso, honey-sweetened bush-tea.

'Bush-tea,' she told the doctor.

'What kind a bush-tea?' the doctor asked.

'Plantain leaf and other things we grow 'round here.'

'Ganja?'

She didn't answer, and the doctor laughed softly. 'You turning bush-doctor, eh? Well, good-good. He has a strong heart. Who knows?'

Two weeks passed, three weeks, a full month. Karl improved; it did not seem as painful for him to speak. One day she mentioned to him that she'd found a 1938 Château Lafite downstairs. His eyes rested on her for a moment, hurt.

'What do you think?' she asked him after he'd had a drop.

'Sumptuous.'

She was good company, reading *Treasure Island* and Coleridge to him. She brought his portable gramophone upstairs and played his favorite records.

'The high life,' he said.

~

Ida thought the opposite: 'So you small-up you'self.' That was how she described May's hand-to-mouth existence — carrying baskets of food up and down the hill like a countrywoman and cooking 'out-a-door' on a coal-pot. 'For God's sake, use some deodorant. You don't smell good.'

She handed some letters to May one morning and said, 'Nigel called. They're having a memorial service for Ian in Switzerland. Maybe we can have one here too — later.'

The police and coastguard had stopped looking for Ian. They'd expected his body to wash up and when it didn't, they assumed sharks had taken him. The first night she was back, after Derek had taken over watching Karl and she'd fallen asleep, Ian had appeared in her room, whether a ghost or part of a dream she didn't know. Now and then she'd hear him walking along the gravel driveway or out by the pool. Strangely, these apparitions didn't disturb her. She kept expecting him to walk into the room, any room.

One day she smelled ganja and saw some movement through the coconut trees down by the beach. Ian? She heard a man's voice and went to look closer.

Two men had sailed up in a canoe. She was afraid at first but then saw that they looked like fishermen, not gunmen.

'This is private property,' she said.

They didn't move but sat facing the sea, smoking spliffs, barely looking at her. It reminded her of the big croaking lizards that appeared on the walls at night, how hard it was to make them budge.

One of the men took a spliff from his pocket and held it out to her. He said, 'Ten dollars.'

What did they think — that she was some hippie tourist

camping out here? 'I said this is private property. You have to go now.'

'Awright. No problem,' one of them said, but they still didn't move.

'You have a five dollar you can give us? We don't eat all day.'

'Sorry,' she said.

'Maybe you change you mind.' He held out the spliff again. 'Buy some goods from me no dawta. I gi' you fe jus' five dollars.'

'Go before I call the police.'

'No problem.'

No problem. When they said that, then you knew there *was* a problem. She watched them as they rowed away, and they watched her.

Buy some goods. She had her own, Blue Mountain-grown, and she sat on the upstairs veranda smoking some of it later that day. Oni had sent the ganja. She'd written on the packet, 'Tea or smokes,' and a list of the things it could be used for: 'lungs, blood pressure, nerves, pain, but not too much.' The tea seemed to help Karl's coughing; May kept the 'smokes' for herself.

You turning bush-doctor?

She'd brought a wrought-iron table out on the veranda, and that was where she'd write in her diary and read her mail. There was a small pile of mail in front of her now, unopened. The only letters that ever interested her were the ones from Nigel but there were none from him that day.

There were some official-looking things to do with the prospective sale of Bella Vista. That casino man still wanted to buy Navy Island. She still didn't know much about Karl's finances except that one dreadful fact: that he'd spent and lost everything on those shipwrecks. What claim she had, whether or not she had the right to sell or not sell the island, she didn't know. 'What you goin' do after Karl is gone?' someone, maybe Clive Goodman, had asked. 'Where you goin' get the money to repair and keep up the place?' May didn't try to answer these questions. As Oni might have said, *Today fe dis, tomorrow fe dat.* Karl needed her full attention. She felt like a nurse in a refugee camp with no time to think about where she was or should be.

'Do not stay there on any account,' Nigel had warned in a letter.

Ida said, 'You just refuse to leave, eh?'

No, it hadn't come to that yet. But, sitting on the veranda now, she began to picture what that would mean, to never leave, to go on living there in a smaller and smaller way without money and with even less human company. *May, fix up you'self.* The lizards and bush would take over. The place would go back to its origins – a deserted island . . . *That mash-up place.* She'd grow white-haired, shriveled, finally a thing merely sensed in the air, not pleasantly, like the jasmine she smelled now, but something miasmic, putrid. *You don't smell good.* People would wonder: Was she still alive on that island or a ghost now, haunting the place? *White witch. White witch.* Duppy. And they'd make up stories about her like they did about Sabine: 'Errol Flynn's daughter . . . his outside child, you know the story.' People like those two fishermen would sail by, then tell of having seen her, papery-skinned and white-haired.

She would peer at them and frighten them away: *I Sabine will tell you how I came to be on this desolate island.*

I goin' mad fe true, she told herself. It was getting dark, and the ganja made her eyelids heavy. A moth landed on the table beside her. 'Who are you?' The sound of her own voice shocked her.

She heard Karl coughing and remembered she hadn't yet given him his morphine. She went in and attended to him, and the smell of rubbing alcohol roused her.

'Imagine, I'm twenty-six and this is the first time I've ever taken care of anyone other than myself.'

She was not sure whether she'd just thought this silently or said it out loud. The moth had followed her inside, and it rested on the wall above Karl's bed.

Inspector Perkins's visits were the only interruption in her routine. He'd been assigned to investigate the attack. She liked the inspector. He was a country gentleman who always stood up whenever she came into the room, and he brought her plantain tarts. He moved about the house quietly and respectfully, asking her permission before touching anything, prefacing his questions with phrases like, 'If you don't mind my asking, Miss Flynn . . .' He used old-fashioned words like 'slew' ('That man Brasso, yes, your stepfather slew him').

'Let me know if I can do anything to help, Miss Flynn,' he said.

She told him she felt unsafe, frightened that the gunmen would return. She was thinking too about those fishermen who'd turned up. Inspector Perkins arranged for the police to check on her every night.

Soon it was not just policemen's faces she saw but soldiers too. It was August 1976 and a State of Emergency was again declared. There had been an attempted overthrow of Michael Manley's government. A deputy minister had been shot.

This time it wasn't just soldiers' Jeeps across the harbor; she heard and saw helicopters. One day a helicopter circled the house, descending lower and lower. Then it left suddenly, accompanying a patrol boat heading out to sea. Later she saw the same boat drift in to one of the coves of Navy Island. Some soldiers got out, looked around a bit, and then sailed away.

'Could you do something for me?' she asked Inspector Perkins the next time she saw him. 'The soldiers. I don't want them coming here.'

'That's out of my hands,' he said sadly. 'State of Emergency. They have to secure these outlying cays. Boatloads of weapons have been arriving. From Cuba or Miami, maybe drug lords, who knows?'

'Pirates,' she said.

'Yes, buccaneers.'

Derek returned. It was a great relief for her when he was there. She got some rest. She showered and washed her hair.

She made up the daybed for him downstairs. Karl's study was the only part of the house that the gunmen had not entered. His collection of ancient objects remained unharmed on the shelves, the more valuable ones inside a glass cabinet. She and Derek sat there among the strange, primitive objects, chatting and drinking beers. She wasn't sure why she started talking to him about old love affairs.

'The father and the son, May?' Derek had known about Martin but not about Nigel.

'Don't look at me like that. Anyway, I never had sex with Nigel because I was too drunk.' She asked him about a former girlfriend of his: 'What about you and Riza? Was that her name?'

'Rizna. Chu! She was too much into material things, you know, a shine-eye gal.'

Shine-eye gal. May remembered the ring-game and song from childhood: *A shine-eye gal is a trouble to a man . . . for she want an' she want an' she want everything.*

'So you don't have a new girlfriend?' she asked. 'What happen, you don't like sex?'

He found her annoying when she talked like this.

She realized she'd gone a bit far. 'Sorry,' she said.

'You think I wan' leave pickney all 'bout the place like my father?' he said. 'No, man.'

'You ever met you father?' she asked him.

'He could walk in here right now, an' I wouldn't know him from Adam.'

From Adam. They laughed, then grew quiet, as if the name of that father of fathers said it all. She wondered though if it were true, what Derek said about not recognizing his own father. In this room, now full of artifacts, she had sensed hers — seen, heard, felt him — rather than known. How long ago? Twenty years. She had gone to so much trouble — hiding, stowing away on Clive's boat. And in the end there had been no acknowledgment or assurance that he was indeed her father, only that sensing, maybe the same way Karl sensed, when he held the ancient objects on these shelves, that they were the authentic things he sought.

She looked around the room. What would she do with all these things after he died? The thought of Derek's unknown father, her real father, her dying stepfather, the sight of the fetishes in the cabinets and the smell of preserved metal, all felt burdensome. Nothing had actually been bequeathed, neither land nor name, and yet the burden of it was there — in the excavated pieces, the debts, the whole inventory of things, facts, truths.

~

If any ill-fortune should befall me at sea, my girl, as will likely happen to an old sea-dog like me, you'll find your inheritance in the treasure marked here.

If it were only as clear for her now as it had been in her story about Sabine.

One day Ida brought up the will.

'Not Karl's will,' she said. 'Your real father. Karl was in charge of your father's will. I never saw it with my own eyes, and I wish to God that I had. Ask him about it.'

But May didn't have to; Karl brought it up.

'We need to talk about Bella Vista,' he said.

'I know.'

He seemed distressed and weak. She'd noticed that his cough sounded worse.

'I have a safety deposit box at Barclays in Kingston. All my papers—'

Maybe it was the thought of him actually dying. Or maybe it was his worried expression. She wasn't ready to face unpleasant facts and the unavoidable decisions those facts were certain to lead to, like the loss of Bella Vista.

She joked with him, 'Just put an X where you've buried the treasure,' and she was sorry right away. He looked distraught. 'I ruined everything for you,' he said.

'Don't say that, Karl.'

The crazy rooster downstairs began making a racket. He'd become like some old grumpy watchdog, alerting them when anyone or anything came near the house.

'Your young man is downstairs,' Karl said. He meant Derek.

'He's not my young man,' she said. 'You know that.'

~

May and Derek went out together in the canoe the next morning, hoping to catch some fish. May rowed.

He noticed that she had cut her hair even shorter than usual; it looked like a well-mown lawn, completely exposing the shape of her head and her long neck. The gold hoops in her ears caught the sunlight as she rowed. He didn't understand how she could be so unconscious of her beauty. She looked primitive and strong to him.

'You mother want me to talk to you 'bout leaving here.'

'Go ahead. Try.'

'I understand what you doin' here but – you not afraid?'

'Of course I 'fraid.' The answer surprised him; he hadn't thought she would admit fear.

'I 'fraid the gunmen goin' come back an' kill me,' she went on. 'Chop me up in my bed like the White Witch of Rosehall! Or soldier-man goin' come shoot me.'

'There are other places you could go. You don't have to stay here worryin' 'bout gunmen an' all that.'

She shook her head.

'Why you want to tek so much worry on you'self?'

'Look.' She turned her head toward Navy Island. 'You don't think it's worth the worry?'

He looked, not at the beautiful islet but at her. Why did she always have to choose the hard way? Always fighting, fighting, ever since he'd known her. He changed the subject and decided to tell her something about himself for a change.

'I have a big tour comin' up,' he said.

'Where?'

'Europe.'

She didn't say anything.

He went on, 'You haven't left this place for two months. A nurse could stay with Karl. You could even just go to Port Antonio an' stay with your mother for a little.'

She looked at him, puzzled. 'You askin' me to go with you to Europe? Or you suggestin' I go stay with my mother?'

He smiled his big, lazy smile. 'I know you not goin' Europe with me, but I would worry less when I'm gone if you would tek a little break – even jus' across the water.'

He could see she was working herself up into a refusal.

'You not thriving, May,' he said.

'Go to Europe or wherever else you want. But don't give me no lecture.'

'So I must only tell you what you want to hear?'

'What you want from me, Derek? Why you bother to come here?'

He looked at her with something just short of anger, and he thought, *As soon as we get back to shore, I'm gone.*

She realized she had been too sharp. 'I'm sorry.'

'I tired of you sorrys,' he said.

'I'm havin' a hard time. I don't need you mekin' me feel worse.'

'You act like you the only one who ever had a hard time.'

'What you want me to do, leave Karl to die by himself? Give up the place?'

'I haven't asked you to give up anything.'

'What you askin' me, then?'

'I not askin' anything.'

'Well, don't come here an' judge me like some high-an'-mighty priest.'

He looked at her with disbelief.

'I didn't mean it—' she began, then changed her mind. 'Yes, I did mean it.'

'High-an'-mighty priest?' He looked at her with his eyebrows raised.

'Don't judge me, Derek,' she said softly.

She was rowing more willfully now, farther out to sea. Sometimes he thought he could detect the change in her face, in her body, as she went from tough to tougher. *She's in some kind a shock. She won't listen,* Ida had told him. *May's strong,* he'd assured Ida, *a born soldier.* But he was afraid that she was growing a bit savage here, unbalanced.

While Derek and Karl listened to a Django Reinhardt recording, May did some sorting out downstairs in the study. She had begun going through Karl's and Ida's things.

Around midnight, after Karl was asleep, Derek joined her.

'Find anything interesting?' he asked.

'This—'

She showed him the photograph that she'd seen once before of Karl, his sister, Eugenia, and their friend Max.

'I don't know why he keeps it locked away.'

Derek held it up. 'Is this your father with Karl?'

'No. It's Max – Karl's friend who died in the war.'

She placed the photograph on the desk and studied it. Max did have a resemblance to her father except that his body was smaller, thinner. It was remarkable too that the picture had been taken on a sailboat, like the one of Karl and her father on the *Zaca.*

Derek yawned and stretched out on the daybed.

She asked. 'You goin' to sleep now?'

'No. I thought we could go out on the town, see a show, have dinner.'

It took her a moment to realize he was joking. He was grinning at her with his eyebrows and everything.

He said, 'Come, mek us get a Red Stripe upstairs.'

They stayed up late again, chatting and drinking beers. He didn't seem to mind hearing about the love affairs she'd had in Europe. She'd read somewhere that her father had slept with hundreds of women. She didn't think she could compete, she told Derek, half joking. She felt worn out, like someone who would never have sex again.

'Maybe I've had enough,' she said, and she saw his eyebrows coming together as though his head ached.

'So how old are you now, 'bout ninety?' he asked.

'Twenty-six. Isn't that old?'

He saw a tired smile on her face, and she seemed perturbed. He asked her, 'You want children?'

'I don't really care.'

He stayed another night and it was the same thing – beers and late-night talking.

'I'm glad you're here,' she said. 'It makes me feel like a normal person.' She told him about her vision of becoming a weird, crazy, old lady like Sabine, 'Like somebody in a ghost story.'

'So you would be a swimming ghost?' he asked.

She laughed and let her body collapse exhausted against him. He was glad he had been able to make her laugh at her worries.

She asked again about his former girlfriend Rizna and he told her a little about the relationship, how it had kept ending and starting up again until he'd realized he didn't really love her.

'Love.' He said the word easily, she thought, like the songbird that he was. She'd once teased him about the lyrics of his love songs ('Chu man,' he had said, 'I can write love songs without being in love'). She brought up the subject again, but this time she wasn't teasing. She wanted to know.

'That line in "Country Sweet"?'

'Which line?' he asked.

' "I can wait to want" – to want what?'

He ran his fingers through her short hair and looked steadily at her: 'What you think?'

He had been kinder to her than anyone had ever been. But she thought of herself as too reckless a lover, not the lover he deserved.

'We grow up in the same yard,' he said, 'almos' like brother and sister. But is a long time now I don't feel like a brother.'

She looked away from him at the blank wall across from her; it seemed impossible that he was saying this.

'You remember the night when I took you dancin',' he said, 'an' I hadn't seen you in about five years?'

She remembered. Slow dancing. He in a denim shirt, smelling good. And the walk up the hill afterward, the fireflies, and the quiet. When quiet had felt safe.

'I think that's when it started to change for me,' he explained. 'That night. But you had Martin. After you broke up with him—'

'I must have frightened you.' She laughed nervously. 'I mean with all my bad behavior.'

'You still frighten me, May.'

She understood, and she didn't want to become a trouble to him, like the shine-eye gal in the song. But did it always have to be so dire?

She thought about her affair with Nigel. One night, when they'd been so full of uneasy desire for each other, they had taken a walk along the beach in Ocho Rios. A hustler had approached them, trying first to sell them ganja, then offering cocaine, and finally just begging for money. They told him they hadn't carried along any money, which was true. The man wouldn't budge and they began to feel threatened. He seemed to be sizing them up – the older Englishman, the young Jamaican-voiced white girl. Then after a while he said, 'Walk in peace.' And that, she realized, was what she and Nigel had done. The affair had come to nothing – all that heat, gone – but they had been 'walking in peace' ever since.

'I think, no matter what, we'll be able to look back as easily as we look forward,' she told Derek.

He looked surprised to hear her say that.

The next day, he had to leave, not for the big European tour but for a week of concerts in Negril and Montego Bay. 'I jus' up the road if you need me.'

Karl caught pneumonia. The doctor said there was no point giving him antibiotics. 'You can increase the morphine,' he said. 'Let him go as comfortably as possible.'

May didn't increase the morphine. She stayed up all night placing cool, damp cloths on his forehead. 'He's not ready to go,' she told Ida.

'Lime will cool down his body,' Ida said. She had brought bottles of limeade, and she also handed May some antibiotics. 'Give them to him. No care what the doctor says.' She was strangely flustered, distraught. 'Oh, I forgot the batteries for your radio,' Ida said. 'Clive will bring them by later or send somebody with them.'

When May made a second trip down to the boathouse that day to pick up the batteries, she came across the note and the newspaper clipping. For a moment she thought she was imagining it. The note was written on brown paper torn from a grocery bag and placed on top of the freezer. The words were properly spelled but the handwriting like that of an illiterate: 'Wickedness shall be judged.' The clipping was from that week's paper. Right there in Port Antonio, a family tied up and tortured in their home and then the house set on fire. Children. Grandchildren.

The antibiotics helped Karl. His fever went away, but the painful coughing remained. She was exhausted, having been up with him for several nights without rest.

Between the soldiers across the harbor, the news of brutalities every day on the radio, and the note left for her, she was on edge. It wasn't just death she was afraid of; it was atrocity. She didn't want to be humiliated while she was being killed. She didn't want the face of a callous stranger to be the last thing she saw on earth.

'It's some prankster trying to scare you,' Inspector Perkins said when she told him about the note. 'Probably schoolboys. Don't worry. The policemen will check on you at night.'

He looked down at his notebook, indicating that he had some questions to ask her.

'I have to ask you about Ian Fletcher. The boat that the gunmen used, it was registered to Ian's father, Nigel Fletcher . . .'

Finding themselves desperate, the captain and his crew, armed with cutlasses, rounded the little island and fell aboard their prize in the dead of night . . .

She thought about how when she and Ian were children, he had listened to every word of *Treasure Cove*.

'Karl, what you think Ian was doing here that night?'

'He wanted money for drugs.'

She waited a while, then asked, 'Did my father include Ian in his will?'

'And not you?'

She didn't answer. Finally she had brought up the will.

His eyes lingered on her, a steady gaze that was interrupted by a horrible cough.

'We need to talk about things,' he said. 'I stole what should have been yours.'

She noticed how unequivocal, how solid it sounded, like a key placed in her hand. He didn't say 'squandered' or 'lost' but 'stole.'

His breathing sounded horrible. She propped him higher on his pillows. 'Don't talk. Rest,' she said.

He was miserable for the next few days, coughing and in terrible pain. He took no pleasure in anything, not the smell of coffee, or his jazz records, or the sight of her. She gave him extra morphine so he could sleep.

For three days it stormed, with noisy winds tugging the doors and windows, blowing patio furniture about, and stretching the tree branches taut. Ida was unable to come over with supplies. Derek was still away in Montego Bay. She missed him.

May spent the rainy days in Karl's study. A bowl of Otaheite apples on the desk grew riper and riper and scented the room.

She had come across a box of her father's things – old movies, letters. One letter was to Errol from his father, addressed from Hobart, Tasmania.

Tasmania. No place seemed farther from the Caribbean than the South Seas. *The Antipodes* – she had always liked the sound of that word. She pictured a white explorer making his way through huge, dense tropical plants. At the end of a long day of hacking away the bush, he would swing restfully in a hammock. And he would dream. What dream, she wondered, had brought Captain Bligh, then Errol Flynn, to this tiny, unmapped island where she lived? What romantic impulse had swung them from antipodes to antipodes?

The rain and wind slowed down, and the quiet made her feel somehow lonelier, vulnerable. To distract herself, she decided to watch one of her father's old movies, *The Sea Hawk*. It was right there among his things. She set up the projector and turned out the light.

The King of Spain gazes at a huge map of the New World. He wants the Americas all for himself. But the English are in the way, especially that indomitable pirate, Captain Thorpe, played by Flynn. While the Spanish King plots against England, Queen Elizabeth and Captain Thorpe are busy plotting against Spain. On the wall of the English queen's chamber is a map as large as that of the Spanish king. The queen asks Captain Thorpe what's brewing in that piratical brain of his. He is a favorite of hers, even though she knows he is a rascal. He bows and strides over to the map, his whole body edgy with risk and excitement. He points to the Gulf of Mexico and unfolds his plan.

May suddenly realized why, of all her father's movies, this was her favorite; it was the maps — those naive, inaccurate, and audacious maps from the age of New World conquest.

The rain ended. Hazy sunlight shone through the jalousies, throwing pale shapes across the screen. She saw herself at the age of seven in this room with him, her father.

'It's old,' she said, looking at the map.

'Very old — and very valuable.'

The map interested her, with its strange little drawings of ships. But he frightened her a little. He seemed eager to make her understand something.

'Do you like breadfruit?' he asked.

'I want to go,' she said.

But he hadn't wanted her to. He had one more thing to impress upon her.

'Let me show you something quite special.' He picked her up and held her on his knee again. 'This —' he pointed to Tasmania, 'is where I was born. And this —' he drew his hand to the other side of the map, 'is where you and I are right now.'

It was Navy Island.

'Captain Bligh drew this in himself after he got here. There's no other map like it anywhere in the world. Not anywhere.'

She put on her rain boots and sloshed up and down the puddle-filled path. She walked, walked, walked all across the island in the weak afternoon sun, unaware of the rocks, the slippery hillside and dripping leaves, like a woman in a dream, absorbed only with what she sought: the map, her father, her father, the map. There was no real purpose to her walk, only a need to press her feet into the ground, to leave tracks like exclamation marks and somehow claim her share of an elusive inheritance.

She got back to Bella Vista. In the fading daylight, the cracks in the patio tiles looked like veins. She noticed new vines clinging to the jalousies and imagined the place in a few more months completely overtaken by bush.

'Karl?'

He opened his eyes.

'My father's map of Captain Bligh's voyage—'

'Yes.'

'You know where it is?'

'Yes.'

~

She would not find it buried like the treasure of her childhood stories, he said; it was not anywhere in the house or on the island. Something that valuable — and it was valuable, more valuable than any of Karl's artifacts — was with his important documents in the bank's safety-deposit box in Kingston.

May gave the information to Ida, and Ida went to Kingston and brought the contents of the safety-deposit box back to May.

She sat alone at the desk in the study. The map seemed smaller than she remembered. How could something so small and inert be so telling? She saw the lines of navigation presumably used by Bligh himself when he'd sailed on HMS *Providence*. There were the illustrations of the ships and Pacific tribesmen, and then the islands: Tasmania, New Guinea, Otaheite. At the opposite side, to the west were the islands of the Caribbean, which, on this strange map, seemed to mirror the South Sea Islands. Everything that lay between the two sets of islands was compressed, skinny. Navy Island was there, obviously drawn in later, and marked by an illustration of a slave holding a breadfruit.

'Was there a reason to keep it from me?' she asked Karl later.

'I had a reason.'

She sat down, tired, tired of things being kept from her. There were those years when she hadn't known who her father was. Then she'd found out, but never with certainty. To this day, she couldn't write her surname without feeling slightly fraudulent. Now Karl, it seemed, had been keeping something from her — this thing, this map. Why on earth?

She had thought of it as having only sentimental value to her, something that confirmed a tenuous memory of fatherly grace.

She looked at Karl lying there. His curled, atrophied hand seemed to claw the sheet.

'It might help—' She was barely audible, and so she began again. 'It might help if you told me everything.'

32

Opere et Omissiòne

'Toward the end of the war, I went to America. I made new friends there. Many of them famous, wealthy people, and I moved from place to place, everybody's houseguest. There were a number of us – refugee princes. The Hollywood people especially liked having us around.

'I got tired of doing nothing, so I went with a friend of mine, an anthropologist, to Libya. I liked the fieldwork, studying the people, but I was even more fascinated by the things their ancestors had used, especially the old metals. When I went back to New York, I began studying archaeology at Columbia. One of my professors took me on an excavation with him to Bolivia. I did very well on that expedition, and afterward I was offered a permanent job.

'Searching for artifacts, you learn a lot about what's going on in a place. So it happened that while I pursued the things that interested me, I was paid well to keep my eyes and ears open to other things. Do you understand? I became an agent for the United States government.

'I was assigned to the Caribbean. There was a list of people here in Jamaica and some of the other islands. I was to make friends with them. Your father was on the list.'

He was quiet for a moment, as if waiting for her response, but she was silent.

'He'd made some stupid remarks in public. He'd also made some bad acquaintances. At one time he was suspected of being a Fascist sympathizer, and later of being susceptible to the Russians. He wasn't at the top of the list by any means, but I enjoyed being in Jamaica. The country intrigued me, offered things I was genuinely interested in. And your father made the job easy. He liked me.'

'And you liked him.'

'He reminded me of someone.'

'Max.'

'It wasn't just that they looked alike; they had the same love of adventure.'

The sun had gone down and what was left of the day clung depressingly around them.

'I didn't notice your mother until the day I found them together. He never forced himself on her – he wasn't a rapist. She – desired him. When I learned she was pregnant . . .'

She desired him . . . Ida's stories came to her, the intimate recollections she'd tried to share that May hadn't wanted to listen to – *This was our spot – we discovered it the first time we came to Navy Island – we liked to ride here . . .*

'I can't tolerate men who are careless about other people's lives. And it was such a betrayal of your grandfather. There was no malice in what Errol did to people, just thoughtless galloping over everyone, like a princeling.

'He'd just been through a trial involving a young woman when he found out Ida was pregnant. He wasn't in the mood to be accused again. He thought some other man might have made her pregnant, maybe even me.'

He stopped and stared ahead for a moment, remembering.

'There was a lot of mischief going on between here and Oracabessa, a lot to keep track of.'

'Nigel?'

'No, Nigel didn't take part, but he tolerated the whole mess. Errol was already sleeping with Denise when he seduced your mother. Denise knew about Ida and thought it would be amusing to include her in one of their little games – I won't go into the details. She suggested getting Ida drunk or giving her tranquilizers. Errol didn't want to do that to Ida, and that's to his credit. Denise teased him, though, told him he'd miss the fun—'

'Did you – take part?'

'Of course not. But he probably thought I did. He saw us together. I let him come to his own conclusions. We had shared women before and stories about women. He liked telling me about the concubines he'd had in New Guinea—'

'He didn't think about my mother that way.'

'There wasn't much *thinking* about her or anyone else. Everything was about him, how he saw himself – a demigod who could dive into sultry waters with the savages and come up just as white as before. He felt as though he had some sort of moral immunity.

'When he saw Ida with me he thought the worst of her. He had a complex about women using him.'

'And you didn't dissuade him.'

'No, I didn't. What good would it have done? He wouldn't have married her or given her any assistance.'

'How do you know?'

'He went to Europe to make a film and to get away from

the whole mess. Ida sent him a letter asking for help after her father's stroke. I knew he wouldn't do anything about it. He was such a miser. So I sent her money and let her believe it was from him.

'When your mother wrote back thanking him, he had no idea what she was thanking him for and thought it was the biggest joke – that's what he told me – a woman thanking him for sex. It amused him so much that he wrote back to her. You ask about him marrying her? Do you think he deserved her?'

He was silent. They both were for a while.

'Why did you do it?' she asked.

'Spy?'

'Yes.'

'So I could go on being Baron Von Ausberg.'

He was quiet as though reflecting on this for the first time.

She felt somehow that he wasn't finished. The air was taut, as if everything he'd said had merely been like the tuning of an instrument.

'Nigel—' he began slowly, carefully, and she felt alarmed at the sound of his name, '—found out something and threatened to tell Ida.'

'Why did he care? He used to be in the Secret Service.'

'Not that. He wasn't interested in that. It was before. In Austria.'

May sank deeper into the chair. It had become dark outside and in the room. She had no desire to turn on the lamp. She wanted the night around her.

'We went for a walk one evening – Nigel and I—'

She remembered when she had seen them walking and talking together. It hadn't been so long ago. Bella Vista had been itself then, intact.

'—and he told me that he'd found Clara Von Ausberg. I had thought she was dead.'

She had never heard the name. She knew only of Eugenia and Max, the two people in the photograph with Karl.

'What happened in Austria?'

He was silent.

She asked even more gently, 'What happened to your friend Max?'

She heard his deep, wheezy breathing and was about to say, *It's all right; we can talk later.*

'I'm Max,' he said simply. 'Karl Von Ausberg was shot by the Germans.'

It was as though something thick had fallen. For a moment she couldn't breathe.

'I was born Max Weiss. My father died when I was six and left the family without an income. My mother was hired to tutor the Von Ausberg children – three of them: Eugenia, Karl, and Clara. Clara was the youngest, a deaf-mute.

'My mother and I were given a home there on the Von Ausberg estate. When my mother died, the Von Ausbergs took me in to live with them. They were very kind. Karl especially was like a brother.

'He was brilliant, full of marvelous energy. The sort of person you never picture sitting down. Karl sailed. He flew. It was impossible not to admire him. He could make the simplest things memorable. We'd go on fishing trips and stay in an old broken-down cottage, a place with a dirt floor. He'd roast the fish on an open fire and it would seem like the most elegant meal we'd ever had. He learned Arabic on his own so he could read *The Thousand and One Nights* in its earliest printing.

'What we shared, above and beyond everything, was a love of jazz. We'd get in the car, the three of us, Karl, Eugenia, and I, take a picnic basket, and drive all day to see Armstrong or Django Reinhardt. When jazz was banned, we found our way to the underground clubs. We tuned in to the BBC jazz programs even at the height of the war. Duke Ellington was easier to believe in than the Führer.

'And then a singer, a lovely woman Karl knew and admired, was sent to a concentration camp. Karl changed after that. He got involved. And so we all did, even the baroness. Helping people escape, getting them false documents. Karl was heroic. I'm not trying to discredit him when I say that he did it for the excitement. He once helped someone across the border in his own car. It was the greatest adventure of his life.

'Then the baroness was arrested. She was tried and executed. The baron sent Karl, Eugenia, and Clara to a house near Switzerland, and he asked me for my help. I was to take him there to the rest of the family. He had prepared for the possibility of his arrest and given me all the papers to take to Karl if that happened. And true enough, when I went to get him, I found out he'd been arrested.

'I set out for Karl and the girls just as he'd asked, but I never got to them.'

'What happened?' May asked

After a moment he said, 'I crossed the border on my own. I don't know – fear – some overwhelming sense of the opportunity. It didn't seem like a decision at the time. It was more like a hesitation.

'I stayed on a farm in Switzerland until I learned what had happened to them. The baron died in prison, Eugenia too. Karl was executed. I never knew what became of Clara until Nigel Fletcher found her in a French convent.'

May could imagine Nigel doing this, digging things up not only out of animosity but because he could, because he had the time and resources and probably saw it as material for a book.

She heard Karl's strained breathing as he went on, 'The agency knew when they recruited me. As Karl Von Ausberg I impressed them. But Max Weiss impressed them even more.

'I tried to explain to Ida about being an agent. She hates me, not because I lost all that money but because of all the lies. But she knows my feelings for her have never been a lie. She knows that, doesn't she?'

He closed his eyes. She thought he was too tired to say any more, but he began again: 'Let me tell you something about your father.' He saw distress in her face and said, 'No, listen. We were out on the *Zaca* one day. There were strong winds, and we saw another boat in trouble. A fisherman and his boy. The boy went over. Your father swam out and rescued him. Of course he enjoyed telling an exaggerated story of the rescue, and there was a report about him in the newspaper. But he hadn't been thinking about any of that when he dived in. It had been instinct. Even with all his selfishness and theatrics, he was able to do something like that without the slightest hesitation.'

'Did he ever say anything about me?'

'He began writing another will soon after Ida and I came back to Jamaica, but he never signed it. It wasn't legal. He wanted you to have the map. And he talked once about leaving you the island. But he never followed through with that.'

'Why didn't you tell my mother?'

He didn't answer.

'It would have meant a lot to her. They might have had a chance, even just to be friends.'

'I removed all chance.'

'Why? What was it to you?'

'I removed all chance,' he repeated with finality. 'I made an unforgivable mistake, and I lived with it. He made so many and thought he could redeem himself just by giving away his possessions.'

She looked across the room at him. His chest rose and fell rapidly, the lungs willful and anxious. Who was he? He was Max; he was Karl. He had become the man he'd betrayed and betrayed the possibilities of the men they could both have become. She had always wondered why he kept that photograph hidden. Now she wondered why he had kept it at all. She asked him.

'I needed a past,' he said, 'even a bad one.'

The next morning she found him awake but lying more rigidly than usual. His skin had changed to a dusty, grayish color that worried her. He didn't speak to her. For two days he didn't speak, and he avoided looking at her. He seemed confounded, alarmed even, that after all he had said and done she'd still take care of him. He seemed ready for her to abandon him as Ida had, and that he would think so saddened her.

He'd been a good father to her, and these past few months had hollowed out something even deeper around them. He'd had to become a man-child, too weak for modesty, as she'd fed, wiped, dispensed, relieved. There'd been embarrassment in that, but no disgrace. The disgrace had come only now, in the secrets he'd confessed. But these were now laid bare between them, and she would tend them with the same uncringing care with which she tended his exposed, and even most intimate, flesh.

Gradually his eyes began to accommodate her, at first with a look of gratitude, then faith.

'Hot outside,' she said one afternoon, dabbing his face with a cool sponge. 'How we goin' survive this heat, eh?'

'I won't,' he said and waited for her to smile.

They heard a commotion outside. It was the traumatized rooster again, crowing. She opened the jalousie doors onto the veranda. Derek was walking up the driveway with a large box.

'What's that?' she called down to him.

He opened the box, and three fat hens shook themselves out. The rooster grew quiet, watching them. The adaptable, self-interested hens immediately made themselves at home, pecking and scratching at the gravel.

'Derek brought us some hens,' May shouted across to Karl.

'Laying hens,' Derek told her. 'You can have eggs for breakfast now.'

'Wait,' she told him. 'I comin' down.'

Later she went back to Karl's room to check on him. His cough had become unbearably painful, and she could see that it hurt every time he took a breath. She offered him morphine. He shook his head and looked over at the box of cigars on the bedside table. Tomorrow, maybe, she told him.

She went down to the study to say good-night to Derek. It had been sweet of him to bring the hens.

She was surprised to find him already in bed, undressed under the sheets, waiting for her. She remembered how he'd reacted that time when she'd stripped off her clothes on the beach and so she sat now on the edge of the bed, a little flustered.

He gave her his long, lazy smile, and she was relieved because it seemed to invite playfulness.

'Derek.' She spoke in a slightly reprimanding tone. 'You've got no clothes on.'

'And you have on all yours – for a change.'

'Yes. I'm always worried now about shocking you.'

'You can't help it.'

Beneath the teasing and bantering, she really was worried, not so much about herself as about him. 'So you're not afraid of me anymore?' she asked.

'I look afraid to you?'

She looked him in the eye, and he could see she was about to say something. He reached for her without any awkwardness, as if they were already lovers.

The next day, from the upstairs veranda, May saw the boat coming. There was something peculiar about the way it drifted in slowly with the motor shut off. Then something even stranger happened: Ida got off the boat. She stood on the pier for a while looking up toward the house, and then she started up the hill.

Karl. May rushed in to him. At first he seemed just to be sleeping but then she saw that his face had broken loose from all pain.

It was too late but she told him anyway, 'Ida is here.'

'I didn't want you stayin' here alone with a duppy, ' Ida said as soon as she got to Bella Vista. 'God have mercy on him.'

May didn't ask how she'd known. She left Ida in the room to attend to her husband. Ida washed and dressed him.

Clive came back later and helped them carry Karl's body down to the boat.

May noticed that Clive had brought the canoe instead of the motorboat and sensed it had to do with some superstition about the dead. It tipped as they got in. Karl's body took up nearly all the room. Ida sat at one end of the boat with Clive, facing the Port Antonio dusk; May sat at the other end with Derek, facing the oars and backwash, watching Navy Island recede.

33

Mongoose or Girl?

May had no childhood memories of Plumbago Road. Ida pointed out things: 'See, you old swing is still there. You and Derek used to play 'round that tree.'

Derek was on tour now. He'd left soon after Karl's funeral. They'd spent nights together before he'd had to leave, gratifying nights, but their days had been unsettling, filled with vacillation. 'I not sure this is the right thing for us,' he'd said to her, and she had appreciated it as an honest admission, not an excuse to back down. They were edgy, quick to suspect each other of new, impossible demands, and insecure about their own flaws in a way they hadn't been before. May didn't know what to expect.

But she was aware of a change in herself. She took better care of herself now. She was more cautious when she went swimming alone and had a new feeling of benevolence toward her own body.

Two months had passed since Karl's death. She sat on the steps of her mother's house. where she had been visiting for a week, and watched Ida plant a rosebush. 'Did my father come here to visit you?'

'Yes. He ate with us a few times. My mother would cook up rice-an'-peas an' t'ing. He liked Jamaican food.'

Ida patted the soil with her gloved hands. She was fully protected from the heat, dirt, and dust: straw hat, sunglasses, gardening gloves, and a big jug of ice water on the veranda ledge.

'We lucky to have this house. My father always said Oni was smart when it came to property. And you will have this house too. No matter what you decide to do about the other.'

'It's a pretty house,' May said, looking at the freshly painted fretwork.

'Yes. A pretty little place,' Ida agreed. 'When I was a girl, it seemed small to me. I wanted a modern house with swimming pool and an upstairs, you know. I wanted to big-up meself. But now it seems quite enough. Life is funny, eh?'

The day that May was going back to Navy Island, Ida invited a few people over for lunch. To everyone's relief, Clive did the cooking: roast beef with onions and thyme. His mother, Mrs Goodman, was there and so was Father Reynold.

After the meal they sat on the veranda till almost twilight. Father Reynold had gone back to drinking rum and seemed in much better shape than before.

'When I wasn't drinking,' he explained, 'I was forever catchin' colds. The rum purify me blood, man.'

'I glad to see you don't follow fashion, Ida, an' barricade you'self behind burglar bars,' Mrs Goodman remarked.

'No, man, I not livin' in a cage.'

'Better safe than sorry,' Clive said, disagreeing with her.

'Where dem get so much gun?' Mrs Goodman asked.

'CIA,' Father Reynold thought.

'Drugs,' Clive said.

'Oh, ganja.' Mrs Goodman shook her head sadly.

'No, worse than ganja. Cocaine, heroin. Drugs tek over. If is not criminals, is police an' soldier. Soon we cyan walk 'round safe in our own yard,' Clive said.

Father Reynold said, 'Port Antonio used to be peaceful and prosperous.' He allowed Clive to fill his glass with more rum. 'You know, many years ago, me and Eli had the opportunity of meeting Lorenzo Dow Baker.'

'The United Fruit Company man?' May asked

'Same one.'

'Nobody knew 'bout Port Antonio before the banana boats,' Ida said.

'We met Lorenzo Dow Baker,' Father Reynold continued, 'when Ida was a little girl.'

'He must have been an old man by then,' May said.

'Older than that,' Clive said.

'Old like old-self,' Father Reynold confirmed. 'Could barely mek it down the gangplank by himself. The United Fruit Company had set up a big fairground over by the cricket oval, a Coney Island kind of thing with Ferris wheels and all that. You remember, Ida?'

Ida smiled. 'It was the first time I ate cotton candy. I remember Papa introduced me to Mr Baker and the old man sent a whole bunch of hula hoops to the house for me. Dozens and dozens of hula hoops in all different colors.'

'I remember them all lying around you yard,' Clive said.

'My mother would get so mad. Hula hoops messing up her garden.'

'Esme,' Father Reynold said, remembering her.

May looked at her mother. Ida had put on a bit of weight in the last few months; there was fullness and peacefulness in her face. She rarely talked about Karl now, but when she did it was without regret or malice: 'All in all, we treated each other good, me and Karl.'

May left the party early to catch a boat back to Navy Island. Clive wanted to drive her to the harbor but she insisted on walking. After a rainy morning, there was now a sunset of thinly spread clouds.

'How these young people can carry everything in those little bags is a mystery to me,' she heard her mother say as May strapped on a backpack. 'They really know how to travel light.'

'Walk good.'

'Keep safe.'

'You sure you don't want me to take you to the harbor?'

'Nobody goin' trouble her with so much soldier an' police 'bout de place.'

'Well, get home before the curfew.'

'Chu! Nobody goin' trouble May.'

She heard the veranda talk continuing behind her as she went up the road.

Port Antonio was quiet, as if the houses and roads knew that it was Sunday. She didn't see any soldiers on the way. That was how it was a lot of the time now: nothing for days, then the big military vehicles would appear, a sudden reminder of the government's desperation. But not this evening.

The harbor, like the rest of the town, was lifeless; no ship was anchored or even in sight, and there were not the usual stragglers and sleeping bodies. A few canoes were tied to posts and she could make out a fisherman in one of them, cleaning his net. He turned, hearing her coming, and she remembered having seen him around town.

He was an albino with a mass of rust-colored dreadlocks

bunched under a striped knit cap. His skin was patchy, raw pink in places, smooth and yellow in others, and his clothes held the pungent smell of ganja. She saw the words 'Lion of Judah' painted in bright yellow on his red canoe.

'Yeah man,' he agreed to take her across for ten dollars as soon as he finished what he was doing. He squinted as he pulled bits of weed and sea scum from the net. He was horribly nearsighted, maybe stoned too.

'So you de lady who live over so?' he asked, pointing his chin in the direction of Navy Island.

So he's heard of me, she thought. *White witch. White witch. White like duppy.*

'Yes,' she answered.

She saw him nodding as if he too were affirming something, and he continued pulling at the net with big leaden fingers.

It was a little after sundown when they left, an opulent hour for both the sea and sky. Across from her was the familiar shape of Navy Island and at its easternmost point, the dark waterway that led to the rest of the world.

The canoe drew near the boathouse.

'We reach,' the fisherman said and looked at her expectantly with his heavy-lidded eyes.

She handed him a ten-dollar note and leapt onto the dark pier, already smelling the night jasmine from there.

34

Treasure

I've inherited the Island.

Karl left it to me along with everything else he owned: the Palace Theatre, his artifacts and books. I have the map too. My mother is relieved that Karl was finally honest with me. But she wants me to sell the place to some yacht-club owner from the Bahamas. 'Let them turn it into a marina. It was meant for boats, not people.'

Clive has warned her against hastiness. But she's in a strange, airy mood: 'Chu!' she said. 'Sell the Palace too. I can pass by every day and the memories won't cost me a thing.' She has the house on Plumbago Road and her jewels and says that's more than enough.

A white moth just landed on my pile of papers. That's unusual. They usually go for the walls. And this one isn't pure white when you look closely; it has fine green lines like veins.

I've made some repairs, and I'm growing vegetables outside the kitchen. My mother said, 'But so much duppy 'round there.' Yes, but there are duppies everywhere. And I can live with them without turning into one, can't I?

I took a walk down to that old gravestone today, that grave that we decided was Sabine's. That's where I go to lay flowers for Ian. I remembered the hours and hours we played there. We were so serious about looking for buried treasure. There are huge indentations where we dug with our shovels. We didn't expect to find the glittering coins and jewels we'd seen in storybooks. No, we were practical and knew that after years of being buried in the dirt or in some cave, the loot would be spotty and rank-smelling, not a pretty sight.

I remembered too the day we both went looking underwater for my engagement ring. Ian, I wish you were here so I could tell you: those things are really lost, but we were not so lost. I think the real treasure was our own spotty childhood here.

On the way back I picked an Otaheite apple; I didn't eat it right away because I like to hold it and enjoy the smell as long as I can. There are more Otaheite trees than I can possibly count and new saplings growing. They spread with the wind and thrive in the salty air. Captain Bligh's trees.

It used to give me a ghostly feeling to hear stories about the days when men like Bligh and Admiral Nelson were in Jamaica. Not that they were ghostly but that I was, creeping around their big, conspicuous ruins. I'd feel ghostly too when I'd hear stories about my father. Because women like my mother, Sabine, the White Witch of Rosehall, women like me, are usually heard of only in legends about haunted places. But it's not a haunted house that I've inherited; it's history.

It's lonely here, but Derek will be back from his tour in a week. I'll finally tell him what I couldn't bring myself to say over the phone. My mother, who has already guessed, says the baby will be a boy. If so, I'll name him Joseph after my grandfather, and if a girl, Oni.

That view! You would think I hadn't already seen it a thousand times.

May closed her notebook, got up, and took one last look around before going in. To the north was an undisturbed view of the Caribbean. With a good telescope, she would be able to see Cuba's Sierra Maestro or, turning slightly east, the sea passage to the Atlantic. But at that moment, with the naked eye, it was all edgeless blue.

A warm breeze touched her face and gently rattled the

wooden jalousies. She stopped and inhaled the lively air before pulling the doors closed and thought, *Let the winds come from the sea and blow seeds about, seeds of the north, south, east, and west. Let moths beat their wings against the windows and fishermen cast curious glances. Let them come, let them return, let them reach.*

Epilogue

Par Avion

A package with a Port Antonio return address arrived at Nigel Fletcher's home in Switzerland. His wife took it in to him. He'd been bedridden for weeks with emphysema.

Pages from his novel-in-progress lay in a neat, neglected pile on his bedside table. If he ever finished it, it would be his twelfth book and, he hoped, different from all the others. He knew whom the package was from and began opening it even before his wife left the room. He didn't hear her say that lunch was on its way.

Inside was a typewritten manuscript.

On the title page he read, *Treasure Cove.*

On the next page he read, *I'm joking.*

He smiled.

Finally, after reading some rather sentimental words dedicating the work to him — words that made him shamefully happy — he turned to the page that said, '*Untitled* by May Josephine Flynn,' and then he began to read:

This is a story that could only have taken place in the tropics, where the climate draws sea rovers, pirates, and desperadoes from all corners of the world. They come and go, these adventurers, bedazzled and dazzling, and they leave women behind, lovers, who repeat outlandish tales, murmuring to themselves unheard, and if heard, not believed. This is one such tale, a tale of swashbucklers and of the women who were besotted with them.

I will never be able to separate all the strands — her story, his story, theirs, mine — or properly connect the ruminations of twenty years in which I searched for my father and tried to pierce the elusive glamour, or is it grammar, that he cast on us like a spell. Well, here it is, then, as promised, not tidy but true: the notes of a pirate's daughter.

— *Navy Island, December* 1976

Acknowledgments

I wish to thank first of all my dear friends Trudy Smith and Marilyn Sides; without their help, advice and encouragement over the years, I could not have completed this book. Thanks also to my aunt and uncle in Jamaica, Isobel and Charles Smith, who gave enormous help in my research and traveled with me throughout Jamaica. Deep appreciation also goes to the following friends for their help with the manuscript, their support and encouragement: Luther Tyler, Rufus Collins, Laura Peters, Venita Datta, Steve Bold, Urs and Joanne Berger-Sweeney, Jodi Mikalachki, Byron Loyd, Julie Donnelly, Claire Fontijn, Amanda Clay Powers, Adlai and Judy Murdoch, Michelle Morgan, Rosemary Robothom, Jean Fuller-Stanley, Judy Clain, Jesse Browner, Zia Jaffrey, Marjorie Dobkin and Phyllis Fleming. I thank my father Dudley Thompson for his astute reading, advice and inspiration and his wife Cecile Eistrup who has been a dear friend and support to me. To my mother, Genevieve Cezair-Thompson, I also say thank you for years of rich anecdotes and for taking me to Errol Flynn movies, all of which contributed to this book. Thanks also to my brother

Anthony Thompson for suggestions especially regarding music. I thank Yonald Chery for building a terrific computer for me. Appreciation also goes to the wonderful, dependable people of the Wellesley Community Children's Center, especially Mary Kloppenberg, for taking such good care of my son Ben while I was busy writing; and to Ben's outstanding 1st grade teacher Christina Cooney who helped more than she realized. My colleagues, students and former students at Wellesley College have also been a great support, and among them I'd especially like to acknowledge former student Genevieve Brennan; Vicki Mutascio, director of the Copy Centre; Lindy Williamson, Kathryn Lynch, Margery Sabin, Timothy Peltason and William Cain of the English Department. I'm grateful to Wellesley College for awarding me faculty research grants to help with this project. A special acknowledgment also goes to Alison H. Vanvolkenburgh for the splendid map she drew for the book.

Several books were helpful in my research, among them Errol Flynn's autobiography *My Wicked, Wicked Ways*. I also drew upon numerous seafaring stories of the eighteenth and nineteenth centuries including Robert Louis Stevenson's *Treasure Island*, Daniel Defoe's *Robinson Crusoe*, Lucretia Parker's *The Female Captive* and stories collected in *The Pirates Own Book*. Certain films starring Errol Flynn were also invaluable, especially *The Sea Hawk*, *Captain Blood*, *They Died With Their Boots On*, and *Cruise of the Zaca*.

My agent Sarah Burnes has been extraordinary. I thank her for her insightful, smart reading of so many drafts, and the great care she has shown toward me and my work. I also wish to thank Chris Parris-Lamb for his meticulous reading of the manuscript and his suggestions. I am deeply grateful to my editor Greg Michalson for bringing such wisdom, thoughtfulness and appreciation to the project, and to Mary-Anne Harrington at Headline Review for acquiring the British rights and bringing the book to a wider audience.

Finally, I would like to thank two very young, vivid individuals for their enthusiasm and inspiration: my goddaughter Lucy Sides, who asks such very good questions and my son Ben, an avid baseball fan and lover of books, who has shown a capacity for devotion, support and encouragement way beyond his years.

If you enjoyed reading *The Pirate's Daughter*, read on to find out more about the author and the inspiration behind the novel. Also included are topics for discussion and suggestions for further reading.

My Adventures with Errol Flynn

Margaret Cezair-Thompson talks about how she came to write *The Pirate's Daughter*

Readers often ask me: are there autobiographical elements in *The Pirate's Daughter*? I'm not the daughter of a pirate or a swashbuckling movie star; I'm the daughter of a Jamaican barrister, a man well-known for his legal victories in East Africa and the West Indies, and later for his role as an ambassador. Like May Flynn, the 'pirate's daughter' of my novel, I grew up with a charismatic father who led an exciting, public career. I recall several times during my teenage years checking the newspaper in order to find out exactly where my father was: Zimbabwe? New York? Havana? So while I never set out to write anything that drew on my own experience, I do share some of the sentiments of May Flynn — on one hand, a fascination with my father's life and, on the other, a need to be recognized as a person in my own right, not just my father's daughter. Something else: like May Flynn I belong to that generation of Jamaicans who came of age at the time our country was coming of age, emerging from colony to independent nation. What I have in common with the other female protagonist, Ida Joseph, the young woman who falls in love with Flynn and gives birth to May, is less obvious and more complicated. So while there is nothing blatantly autobiographical about the novel, I do have strong affinities with both these characters, and on that basis, I'll go ahead and talk about my life as a pirate's daughter and my hitherto undeclared affection for Errol Flynn.

To be a pirate's daughter is to have your heart wandering back and forth between two places: land and sea, or to be more exact, where you are and where you long to be – a sensible place and a risky place. For May Flynn, this is tied to the longing for her unknown father (as was possibly true for the daughters of real pirates). When May, at the age of three, asks her mother about the whereabouts of her father, Ida is speechless and painfully reflects, 'If only she could point to a place on a map and call it "Father".' But the underlying truth in *The Pirate's Daughter* is that May *can* point to just that place: Navy Island, the lovely islet off the coast of Jamaica which Errol Flynn bought.

During those difficult years, when May is semi-abandoned and roaming the streets of Port Antonio, she becomes intent on getting to that island, having heard rumors that the man who lives there might be her father. In her young, imaginative mind Navy Island is also associated with the islands of literature and legend – with *Treasure Island*, *Robinson Crusoe*, castaways, buccaneers, treasure and desperadoes. It becomes a symbol of loss and belonging, and of escape from a bewildering world. Who among us has not dreamed of such a place – an island of our own, a place of peace? The island promises May what a good parent would: safety, a home.

The story May creates under the title *Treasure Cove* is

about abandonment and inheritance; it is her own story in the guise of an eighteenth century adventure. '*I Sabine will tell you how I came to be on this desolate island.*' Writing it, she will discover her own voice; and the writing will eventually define her. Here we come to the other thing I share with May. I didn't realize it at the time, but in the same way that the island becomes profoundly important to May, writing *The Pirate's Daughter* became an urgent, vital thing for me. I'm not a full-time writer: I have a demanding job, and all the responsibilities of raising a child. It was not easy to get to my writing desk; in fact it would have been altogether more sensible not to have tried. I cannot tell you how I found the time except to say that often I felt the desperation of someone outfitting a raft and heading out to sea. I know I'm not unique or alone in this, that there are others, some of them mothers of small children, who cling to their own rafts as they doggedly make their way to the place that defines and fulfills them.

Now Ida is another kind of adventuress, quite different from her daughter. Ida can't sail or even swim; in fact, she's afraid of water. Yet Ida is not a timid person. While May is physically brave and daring like her father, Ida has emotional resilience. She makes a grand mistake falling in love with Errol Flynn at such an early age, and the rest of her life is spent dealing with the consequences. There's a sense in which Flynn doesn't see Ida except as part of a beautiful, tropical landscape. Indeed, in his real life, Flynn once compared Jamaica to the most beautiful women he'd known. He's not unlike some other famous men who have ventured to far-off worlds and involved themselves with native women in a quest for self-renewal. But it was important to me not to make Ida an ignorant, helpless girl taken advantage of by a powerful white male; that would be stereotypical and not much fun. Ida is willful and bright. She has many advantages: education, a doting father, a wise mother who warns her against choosing the wrong man. She also has a fearful, warning voice inside her, reminding her of ill-fated Jamaican women in legends, folksongs, and in her community. Still, she *risks* loving Errol Flynn.

In doing this, in taking such a risk, Ida has a lot in common with the pirates themselves. Subconsciously, May understands this about her mother: '*she was a pirate too*' May writes about Sabine's mother in *Treasure Cove*. There are only a few well-known women pirates: Ann Bonny and Mary Read, for instance, who were both caught and tried in Jamaica. What made women leave family, society and tradition for a life of adventure on the high seas? It may have been a combination of disturbing events. But I like to think that at some point they were faced with a choice: land or sea; a roof over their heads vs. a dangerous, uncharted life of adventure. To go off to sea is one thing, but to *remain* at sea facing all the perils of a buccaneering life suggests that these women were dazzled by something; they had a vision of themselves not as conquered but conquering – a man-pirate or a ship laden with treasure. Ida is dazzled too, not just by Flynn but Flynn's world and the belief that she can be a meaningful part of it. Other women had tried, why shouldn't she? It is a self-confident, optimistic Ida who sets out to capture the heart of this famous man, a young woman who sees herself not at the edge of a more glamorous world but at its center.

Even after she's realized her mistake and suffered, Ida continues to hope. She doesn't want to become estranged from her youthful dreams. There are many things that can come between oneself and one's aspirations, and so I can't help admiring Ida, first, for wanting more from life and later on for her honest self-questioning and the earnest wish that her daughter will make happier choices.

Why Errol Flynn? I'm often asked.

Growing up in Jamaica, I'd heard stories about Flynn and his home on the north-eastern shore of the island. But the novel didn't actually begin for me with him. It began with the image of a young Jamaican woman looking out at the sea from the veranda of a beautiful but ruined house. And then, once I had the opening images and the setting, Port Antonio, in mind, it was as if Flynn just stepped forward and said, 'Remember I was there too.' My mother told me how women in Jamaica fainted when they saw Flynn because he was so handsome. That story amused and fascinated me as a child without my realizing why. Now I think it's something to do with the impact of two very different worlds colliding: glamorous, mesmerizing Hollywood and small Jamaica, which was still a colony at the time and more susceptible to outside influence.

But the main point is that Flynn was actually there. That is what makes all the difference for Ida. Many adolescents become infatuated with movie stars, but in Ida's case he was right there, a family-friend. Novels are often founded on the question 'what if?' What if an irresistibly handsome, famous older man seemed to take a sincere, reciprocal interest?

Like Ida, I first knew Errol Flynn superficially from movie posters, magazine pictures, movies like *The Sea Hawk*, anecdotes and rumors of his life in Port Antonio. When I began writing this book I came to see him up close, like Ida. I took the time, as she does, to wonder about him. That he didn't deserve so much of her attention, not to mention adoration, is something Ida herself soon realizes. But it doesn't stop her from loving him. As a writer, I was similarly unconcerned with making a moral judgment on Flynn or any of the characters and more interested in what lay hidden. I spent years looking at and listening to him and he began, in a sense, to inhabit my home as well as my mind. My little boy knew him, recognized his face, his voice as he watched films like *Captain Blood* and *The Adventures of Robin Hood* with me. Gradually, I came to know a lot about Flynn: he grew up on the island of Tasmania and was passionate about the sea; he was afraid of heights yet did most of his own stunts; he suffered from a lack of self-esteem, a profound feeling of failure and was at the same time an exhibitionist and an outrageous prankster. He never stopped seeking the approval of his parents, the brilliant, pre-occupied father whom he adored and the critical, self-absorbed mother with whom he constantly fought. He had literary aspirations. Darwin and Huxley were among his heroes. He never quite grew up. His longing to recapture and perpetuate his own youth went awry and turned into a misguided attraction to much younger women. He worked terribly hard, put body and soul into his films but never felt appreciated as a serious actor. There was much about himself that he was ashamed of; he wanted most of all to feel at peace with himself.

What do I think finally of Errol after spending all that time with him? He was a poor listener, but he was never boring. He liked a good time and enjoyed his children, his women, his dogs and cats and most of all his boat. Most endearing of all, he had a sincere love for my homeland, Jamaica. His writing suggests that he grasped the unique beauty of the place and appreciated the vistas his coastal home offered. And that is one of the things about Jamaica, not only the abundant loveliness that lies within but the splendor of what you see from its promontories. I was able to imagine my own country again through his eyes, just as Ida does in the novel. I kept pictures around me as I wrote, of Navy Island, the Port Antonio harbor and Blue Mountains. So it has not been unpleasant, my time with Errol Flynn. And I like to think that he appreciates the chance to live again in my book, to enjoy the Jamaica that he knew, Navy Island with its frangipani trees and view of the turquoise sea.

At first, I had wanted the title to be *Notes of a Pirate's Daughter*, but that seemed long and ponderous for a work of fiction. Although I settled on this shorter title, the idea of May writing something remained central to me. I imagined her writing out of necessity – a declamatory act – claiming the right to her name, the right to her history and most of all the right to be happy. Her being a writer seems to me entirely compatible with the idea of a pirate's leaving everything behind to embark on a sea adventure. There's a similar kind of leap into the unknown that one takes as the writer of a novel. Long nights of watchfulness. Many souls on board. Doubts. Even fear. But now the book is on the shelf, complete; it was a great adventure, and a new novel awaits me. Land or sea? I wonder where it will take me.

Discussion Points

1. *The Pirate's Daughter* is in many ways a novel about heroes. How does the desire to prove themselves influence the men in the novel, and how do their exploits compare with the struggles of the female characters?

2. How has Margaret Cezair-Thompson brought the character of Errol Flynn to life on the page? How does the interplay of fact and fiction add to your enjoyment of the story?

3. The Hollywood Margaret Cezair-Thompson describes in *The Pirate's Daughter* is that of a vanished age – how does she create a sense of nostalgia for this more innocent time? In what ways are the Hollywood icons of that era viewed differently from the celebrities of the twenty-first century?

4. How does Margaret Cezair-Thompson develop the pirate theme in the novel: do the *Treasure Island* motifs of antique maps and buried treasure encourage us to reflect on

the legacy of colonialism, and Jamaica's journey to independence?

5. How does Jamaica change, between the time Errol Flynn first sets foot on the island, and the end of the book? How are these political and social shifts mirrored in the plot and atmosphere of the novel?

6. May is shocked when Martin implies she is a 'bastard'. How does the notion of illegitimacy, of being an 'outside child', resonate in the story?

7. *The Pirate's Daughter* is a novel full of passion and seduction. Would you describe it as a love story, or something more self-aware?

8. The book opens with May at work at her typewriter, and ends with Nigel unwrapping '*the notes of a pirate's daughter*'. For a novel with no shortage of action, *The Pirate's Daughter* is full of references to reading, and to writing. What role do these play in the story?

For more reading group questions on *The Pirate's Daughter*, please go to www.readingcircle.co.uk

Suggestions for Further Reading

Ida Joseph recommends:

Herbert G. Delisser, *The White Witch of Rosehall*
Anya Seton, *Katherine*
Jean Plaidy, *The Thistle and the Rose*
Ian Fleming, *Dr. No, Live and Let Die, For Your Eyes Only*
Daphne Du Maurier, *Rebecca, Jamaica Inn*
Pamela Jeckel, *Sea Star: The Private Life of Ann Bonny, Pirate Queen*

May Flynn recommends:

Robert Louis Stevenson, *Treasure Island*
Daniel Defoe, *Robinson Crusoe*
John Pearson, *The Life of Ian Fleming*
Jean Rhys, *Wide Sargasso Sea*
Marion Patrick Jones, *Pan Beat*
V. S. Naipaul, *A House for Mr. Biswas*
Orlando Patterson, *Children of Sisyphus*

VICTORIA HISLOP

The Island

On the brink of a life-changing decision, Alexis Fielding longs to find out about her mother's past. But Sofia has never spoken of it. All she admits to is growing up in a small Cretan village before moving to London. When Alexis decides to visit Crete, however, Sofia gives her daughter a letter to take to an old friend, and promises that through her she will learn more.

Arriving in Plaka, Alexis is astonished to see that it lies a stone's throw from the tiny, deserted island of Spinalonga – Greece's former leper colony. Then she finds Fotini, and at last hears the story that Sofia has buried all her life: the tale of her great-grandmother Eleni and her daughters, and a family rent by tragedy, war and passion. She discovers how intimately she is connected with the island, and how secrecy holds them all in its powerful grip . . .

'Passionately engaged with its subject' *The Sunday Times*

'A moving and absorbing holiday read that pulls at the heart strings' *Evening Standard*

'Hislop carefully evokes the lives of Cretans . . . but most commendable is her compassionate portrait of the outcasts' *Guardian*

'Wonderful descriptions, strong characters and an intimate portrait of island existence' *Woman & Home*

978 0 7553 0951 1

headline
review

MAGGIE O'FARRELL

The Vanishing Act of Esme Lennox

Edinburgh in the 1930s. The Lennox family is having trouble with its youngest daughter. Esme is outspoken, unconventional and repeatedly embarrasses them in police society. Something will have to be done.

Years later, a young woman named Iris Lockhart receives a letter informing her that she has a great-aunt in a psychiatric unit who is about to be released.

Iris has never heard of Esme Lennox and the one person who should know more, her grandmother Kitty, seems unable to answer Iris's questions. What could Esme have done to warrant a lifetime in an institution? And how is it possible for a person to be so completely erased from a family's history?

The Vanishing Act of Esme Lennox is a stunning depiction of a life stolen, and reclaimed.

'At the heart of this elegant, spare novel is a horrifying story of jealousy and betrayal . . . [O'Farrell] tenderly shows how the past can haunt the present with devastating consequences. Mesmerisingly good' *Daily Mail*

'O'Farrell's subtlety and delicate touch have never been so finely demonstrated . . . a triumph' *Independent on Sunday*

'Gripping . . . her best novel to date' *Elle*

'This novel has the pace, revelations and strategically dropped clues of a psychological thriller . . . utterly compulsive' *Scotland on Sunday*

978 0 7553 0844 6

headline
review

EMMA DARWIN

The Mathematics
of Love

'Convincing and involving . . . a book to lose yourself in'
Daily Mail

'This sweeping tale of nineteenth-century war and
courtship and twentieth-century teenage rebellion has a
real flavour of its own that will grip you to the end . . .
An accomplished, vividly realised debut' *Marie Claire*

It is 1819 and Stephen Fairhurst wants only to forget the
horrors of Waterloo and remember the great and secret
love he lost. But, despite his friendship with the clever
Lucy Durward, he cannot tell her about the darkness in
his past.

In the summer of 1976 the teenaged Anna, hot, bored, and
lonely in the Suffolk countryside, becomes entangled in
two men's lives: Theo, a photographer in exile, and the
forgotten Stephen Fairhurst.

Acclaimed, gripping and extraordinarily moving, *The
Mathematics of Love* is one of the most powerful novels you
will ever read of war and suffering, the heat of passion
and the redemptive power of love.

'A beautifully written, intelligent book . . . as historically
graphic and passionately romantic as Sebastian Faulks's
Birdsong' *Waterstone's Books Quarterly*

'A daring debut novel . . . Emma Darwin's prose is golden
and convincing. Addictive' *Daily Express*

'The reader is spellbound . . . electrifying' *Independent*

978 0 7553 3064 5

headline
review

LALITA TADEMY

Red River

It is time for a new journey: I have told you of CANE RIVER, and the story of my mother's family – of what slavery and the American civil war did to their lives. Now it is time to tell the tale of my father's family.

From Sam Tademy, the son of a runaway slave, and his fiercely strong wife Polly, to the father and son who witness unspeakable crimes, this is a story in which courage and hope do battle with almost unendurable suffering; where real lives collide with history.

Astonishingly powerful and compelling, Lalita Tademy's RED RIVER is an extraordinary novel of true lives in the Deep South. It will break your heart, give you hope, and never let you go.

'Entertaining . . . compelling . . . Lalita Tademy has every right to be proud' *Washington Post*

'*Red River* is a remarkable historical fiction, illuminating a shameful episode of American history and giving voice to people who might otherwise never have been heard' *Boston Globe*

'One of America's most promising new writers . . . Bold, controlled . . . a remarkable feat . . . Tademy has rewritten the history books. A book of grave importance' *Scotland on Sunday*

978 0 7553 3270 0

headline
review

SUE GEE

The Mysteries of Glass

'Unashamedly romantic and sensual, but also so sparely written that the economy of her writing is often breathtaking . . . a beautiful, redemptive book' *Glasgow Herald*

Hereford, winter 1860. Mourning his beloved father's death, Richard Allen takes up his first position as curate in a remote country parish. Vulnerable and lonely, he has ideals of serving his priest and his parishioners, but there are those who do not welcome the newcomer, or his views. Then he falls helplessly in love, and ignites a scandal that will rock a quiet Victorian community to its foundations.

'Written with the delicate fluency of a storyteller utterly at ease with her craft . . . rippling, sinuous prose, alive with the cadences of the natural world' *Times Literary Supplement*

'The reader is held from start to finish by the mood . . . *The Mysteries of Glass* casts its own spell, which is the essential requirement of a novel' *Daily Telegraph*

'Gee's gentle and restrained story celebrates the sanctity of the ordinary and the beauty of holiness . . . Writing of surpassing beauty brings commonplace objects into a clear, melancholy light' *Independent*

'This exquisitely written novel transports you to the simple beauty, poignancy and hypocrisy of the Victorian era in a way that makes you feel you've been there. I cannot recommend it highly enough' Katie Fforde

978 0 7553 0309 0

headline
review

MANETTE ANSAY

Vinegar Hill

'A place for everything; everything in its place. The house is as rigid, as precise as a church, and there was nothing to disturb its ways until three months ago when Ellen and James and the children moved in because they had no place and nowhere else to go.'

When Ellen Grier's husband loses his job, she has little choice but to agree to his suggestion that they and their children move in with his parents on Vinegar Hill. Their new home is more stifling than she feared – a loveless place where dark secrets lurk behind a façade of false piety, and calculated cruelty is routine. Ellen's spirit is close to crushed: how is she to protect her children from their grandparents' bitterness and disapproval? Will her love for little Amy and Bert give her the strength to find a way for them to escape?

'Magical . . . A satisfying journey to freedom . . . Ansay writes in a lovely voice' *Vogue*

'One of the best books of the year' *Chicago Tribune*

'Ansay transcends both feminist epic and midwestern Gothic to achieve, finally, the lunar world of tragedy. This world is lit by the measured beauty of her prose, and the book's final line is worth the pain it takes to get there' *New Yorker*

'A modern-day *Little House on the Prairie* gone mad . . . Manette Ansay is a powerful storyteller with lyrical gifts, and a wry, observant eye' Amy Tan

978 0 7553 3548 0

headline
review

You can buy any of these other
Headline Review titles from your bookshop
or *direct from the publisher*.

FREE P&P AND UK DELIVERY
(Overseas and Ireland £3.50 per book)

The Vanishing Act of Esme Lennox	Maggie O'Farrell	£7.99
Wives of the East Wind	Liu Hong	£7.99
Villa Serena	Domenica de Rosa	£7.99
Midnight Champagne	Manette Ansay	£7.99
Vinegar Hill	Manette Ansay	£7.99
Reading In Bed	Sue Gee	£7.99
Markham Thorpe	Giles Waterfield	£7.99
Symphony	Jude Morgan	£7.99

TO ORDER SIMPLY CALL THIS NUMBER

01235 400 414

or visit our website: www.headline.co.uk

Prices and availability subject to change without notice.